The Queen of Swords

Books by R. S. Belcher

The Six-Gun Tarot

The Shotgun Arcana

Nightwise

The Brotherhood of the Wheel

The Queen of Swords

The Night Dahlia (forthcoming)

The Queen of Swords

R. S. BELCHER

TOR

A TOM DOHERTY ASSOCIATES BOOK

NEW YORK

THE QUEEN OF SWORDS

Copyright © 2017 by Rod Belcher

A Tor Book
Published by Tom Doherty Associates
175 Fifth Avenue
New York, NY 10010

www.tor-forge.com

The Library of Congress Cataloging-in-Publication Data is available upon request.

ISBN 978-0-7653-9009-7 (hardcover)
ISBN 978-0-7653-9011-0 (ebook)

Our books may be purchased in bulk for promotional, educational, or business use. Please contact your local bookseller or the Macmillan Corporate and Premium Sales Department at 1-800-221-7945, extension 5442, or by email at MacmillanSpecialMarkets@macmillan.com.

First Edition: June 2017

Printed in the United States of America

0 9 8 7 6 5 4 3 2 1

For my daughter Emily, the fiercest warrior I know. Keep fighting, you're worth the fight. Learn and grow stronger from every battle, every loss, every victory.

To the memory of Leslie Phillips Barger.

"If a thing loves, it is infinite."

—William Blake

The Queen of Swords

1

The Devil (Reversed)

Port Royal, Isle of Jamaica
June 11, 1721

She swore an oath that the child would be born in freedom. The baby's first breath would not be in the stinking air of the Marshalsea Prison, even if it took her last breath to see to it. The English guard had been true to his bargain, and that made it worth the pain. His price for the secret of escape, for looking the other way, was the gold in her mouth. She had ripped the back tooth out with her bare hands. After months of starvation, and, before that, a bout of scurvy on Jack's ship, it was easy, and that pain was nothing compared to the contractions.

The trapdoor was where the guard had said it would be. It led to a small tunnel—a simple storm drain, designed to slow the overflow of seawater if yet another hurricane hit the island. She crawled through the damp darkness, unable to drag herself on her belly anymore with the baby, so she did it on her side, pausing every few feet in the pitch blackness to gasp in pain, and curl up as best she could as another contraction wracked her body. They were coming closer together but her water had not yet broken.

After what seemed an eternity, she caught sight of moonlight beyond the grate at the end of the drain. She heard the sweetest sound she had ever known: the crash of the waves, the hiss of the sea foam. The ocean did what it always did: it promised freedom.

The storm drain's grate was loose in the crumbling mortar channel just as she had been told. If she were her old self, she could have kicked it free easily, but starvation, illness and the child in her belly had all conspired to sap her strength. She gripped the bars and pushed, then pulled, with all her might. She was so damned weak now. It made her angry.

As she gritted her teeth and struggled with the bars between her and the welcoming sea, that snotty bastard, Willie Goode, forced his way into her mind. He had thought he could have her, right there in that alleyway in Charleston. He was sixteen and she was twelve. He outweighed her by a good fifty pounds, the slobbering, full-gorged lout. He had pinned her and began to pull at her skirts. The pressure of him on her, the sour smell of his breath, and her heart was like a hare, thudding, kicking in her chest. He was so strong, so insistent, like his pego poking her stomach. She remembered London, what had happened there, and bit off Willie's ear. When he screamed and rose up she drove her knee into his bollocks and was satisfied when she felt a pop. It took two grown men to pull her off the sobbing little git.

She wouldn't let the bastards win then, and she had no intention of doing it now. With a final grunt and gasp, she tore the bars free. They fell with a dull thud to the ground, and her arms loose, like rubber, fell with them. Her water broke then and she knew she didn't have much time.

The pain was intensifying. She crawled out of the pipe and let the cool, damp air of the beach caress her like a lover. It took great effort, but she stood, resting her hands on her knees for support. A contraction knifed through her, taking her breath away, but she refused to fall. She staggered across the wet, packed sand toward the tumbling waves. She stood at the edge of what the sea had claimed for itself; the rushing foam tickled her dirty, scabbed feet. She looked up at the moon, as swollen as her own belly. She smiled at the pockmarked orb burning silently with ghost light, its scars and wounds making it even more beautiful. "Good to see you too, luv. Been too long," she whispered.

The water covered her feet now and grabbed greedily at her ankles as it sped past her. Tide was coming in, the sea's way of telling any sailor worth his salt it was time to move on. The pain came up sharp and sudden; it made her feel as if she had to void herself. She breathed through it. The wind and the surf were her midwives. She gulped in air when the birth pain passed. She tasted blood in her mouth where once there had been gold.

She wandered farther out into the water, up to her waist. For a moment she thought of the nasty saw-toothed sharks—the wee ones—that prowled the shallows, eager for a tasty leg to claim. But after the night she had endured to be here, she knew she could wrestle any fucking shark and win, and probably claim a bite out of it too, she was so hungry.

The pain came again, like her insides knotting and trying to spill out of her hat. She gave a little shriek but muffled herself; the water lapping against her belly was helping. She began to time her breaths to the rhythm of the tide. She had once acted as midwife, along with Mary, to a hostage off a Dutch sloop. Neither of them knew a fucking thing about delivering a kid, but Calico Jack figured since they were both women it was instinctual or some such shit. She recalled that breathing through the pains seemed to help, and pushing—pushing was good—but Mary had argued with her that the girl had to wait to push. "Wait for fucking what?" she had said. "A goddamned invitation?" In the end it hadn't mattered whether she pushed or not. The baby came on its own. It lived a few breaths longer than its mother.

There was a shiver down her spine as the pain stabbed her again, and then again, coming closer and stronger with each passing moment. The urge to push was maddening. The waves smashed against her and still she stood her ground; the cold water splashed across her face, the sea pulled at her trying to draw her deeper into its embrace, and still she stood.

She raised her head to scream; she forced her eyes wide open, looking up at the mute moon and the uncaring stars. In this moment she was the universe—her, a petty thief, a liar, pirate, adulteress, murderess. In this final effort of breath, she was a goddess, the creator, and all the cogs spun in the heavens just for her.

The baby arrived beneath the dark churning waters of Mother Ocean, and she did not fall; even as her knees buckled and her legs became like seaweed, she remained on her feet. The child arrived swimming, vibrant and hale. She gathered the infant up in her arms. As it broke the surface, the child snorted the saltwater from its tiny nose and let loose a scream, an angry howl of protest at life itself. She laughed as the baby spit, and cried.

"Ah, marriage music," she chuckled. "You go right ahead and get it out, wee one. This might be your first, but it sure as hell won't be your last cry."

She held the child up to examine and tsked when she saw the tiny penis. "So, it's a boy you are then. Well, lucky you, lad! This chamber pot just got a little rosier for you with that twig between your nethers." She laughed and pulled the baby to her bosom, spinning and trying to dance in the waves. She was dizzy and weak but she also felt high, like she had been smoking the poppy. She hummed a tune from her childhood in Cork, "Molly Brannigan."

The baby screamed then slowly calmed himself. "I know," she said, "as a singer, I'm a bloody fantastic dancer." He nuzzled into her small breasts and she helped him find a nipple. The child drank eagerly and she could feel him sigh and relax in contentment. "Not much of a meal, I'm afraid, wee lord," she said. "My milk's gone dry from my stay in the governor's digs, but take what you can."

She looked at the tiny squirming thing in her arms and for a long moment she considered forcing it back under the dark waters until it was still. It had no life worth living at her breast, that was sure and true. She thought back to all that had come before this in her life, and how often she had prayed to never have been, yet here she was. She recalled hearing Mary's screams a few cells down from her only a month ago, as her own baby arrived. After a time there were only the baby's screams and Mary was silent. Eventually guards came and took the child and Mary's body away.

She and Mary had both pled their bellies after the trial when they had been captured along with the other survivors of Calico Jack's crew. But Mary had found her way to Hell anyway, and she knew it likely that if she tried to flee with a baby at her hip, she would soon be at Mary's side again. So all reason, all her instincts, told her to drown the child and be on her way.

She glanced up at the moon again. The heavens were no help at all, as silent in their regard as they were beautiful. She sighed and looked down to the face of the baby boy. "You have any notions on this?" she asked. He grunted and released his first shit, dropping it in the ocean. "I couldn't agree more, lad," she said with a smile. "How could I drown anyone who already has such a perfect understanding of how all this works?"

She bit the birthing cord free as she walked slowly back to shore, the taste of the infant's blood mixing with her own, and the brine of the sea, in her mouth. She spat and tied the cord off with a reef knot, muttering as she did, "Right over left, left over right, make a knot both tidy and tight. There you go—your first sailor lesson, my wee lord."

She was exhausted, cold and starving. She needed to tend to those things and she needed to be off this accursed crown-kissing island by dawn. She tore at her filthy gown and used the fabric to clean and swaddle the baby. Off to her left, down the cove, she could see the silhouette of a town against the brilliant moonlight. There she would find roast pig, and bread and cheese and bitter grog and wine, sweet, sweet wine, and a proper bathtub, and loot, and sails to take her away from here. But first she would need to find steel, and with it gold, to make all the other things possible. She hefted her son, headed toward the sounds and smells of the port and plotted her first crime with her boy as an accomplice.

It was the devil's hour when she entered the common room of the Witches' Wrath. The Wrath was built on top of the corpses of the taverns Port Royal had once had in the golden days before piracy was outlawed on this island, and before the great earthquake had destroyed most of the city. The righteous claimed the quake was the anger of God Almighty, sweeping away the pirate nation and all their blood money had created. She knew well enough, though, that God annihilated saint as easily as sinner and didn't give a fuck where the tithe came from.

The stink of the place—pungent human smells, the fetor of old ale, all poorly hidden behind the sickly sweet vapors of burning clove—was familiar to her. To her surprise, she found she had missed it, missed the parrots squawking as they drank their fill of ale from discarded flagons, missed the chattering of the monkeys and the booming laughter of the sailors, the tittering of the wenches. A good tavern was all of life on display, a sweating, mumbling, drinking, fighting, fucking museum.

She had acquired clothing—warm breeches, decent, if somewhat-too-large boots, a tunic and a vest. Her greasy red hair fell well below her shoulders. She wore a cocked hat she had crimped off the same fine fellow who had donated the rest of her clothes—he wouldn't be needing them anymore. She wore the tricorne low, to allow the shadows to hide part of her face, but she made no attempts to pass for a man at present. Her sleeping son was strapped to her chest in a sling she had fashioned from her prison gown. She carried the dead man's steel, a heavy and well-worn machete, in one hand, and rested the palm of her other hand on the butt of the pistol hanging from the wide sash wrapped about her waist. There was a subtle change in the current of conversation when she entered. Eyes flicked to rest upon her, sizing her up as a victim, weak and ready to be culled, or as one of the hunters. When she felt the attention, sensed the menace, she smiled a little. She was home.

"Port," she said in the cant, the secret language of the old pirates. She dropped a few Spanish reales on the bar. The tavern keep frowned; then his face lit with surprise, and she knew he had recognized her. He slid the bottle to her. The tavern keep smiled. She saw most of his teeth were black or absent. He deftly pocketed the coins.

"Glad ta see you avoided gitting noozed," the keep replied in the cant. "Din't think they could git a rope about that pretty neck, Lady Calico. Too many brains in that skull of yours for the rope to fit about it. Sorry ta hear about your man's demise."

She took a long draw off the port. It was the sweetest thing she could recall after a year of stale water and maggoty bread. She wiped her mouth with the back of her hand. "Shit," she said. "I told Jack I was sorry to see him in the gallows with his lads, but if he'd fought like a man, he wouldn't have had to hang like a dog." The tavern keep had a laugh like a cannon going off. "Herodotus Markham? Where is he?" she asked. The tavern keep nodded toward the rear room. An old man with a mane of gray hair, and a tattered red velvet coat, sat on a bench, smoking a pipe.

"Makes his way here every few nights," the keep said. "He's dying, but it's a slow kind o' dying. Still the smartest man I ever knew—not that all skull music will keep him breathing one more day."

She slid more silver to him, "For your service, and your silence." The keep nodded and the coins vanished. She took the bottle and headed for the back of the tavern. A dirty hand shot out of the darkness as she walked past a table of men, grabbing her. "How much you selling the brat for, luv?" Her blade was at the man's throat before the utterance had finished leaving his lips.

"A damn sight more than I wager you're willing to pay," she said. The hand slipped back into the smoky darkness.

"I told you it was *her*, ya tosspot!" she heard one of the other sailors hiss as she walked on. "Yer damn lucky she didn't lop your sugar stick off."

Herodotus Markham looked as he had when she had last seen him just before she, Jack, and Mary had stolen the *William*. He resembled an old country squire—a gentleman of means who perhaps had fallen on hard times, or maybe had been laid upon by ruffians. His white wig was in disarray with faded ribbons of red still grasping on for dear life to the tail of it. His velvet coat was a deep burgundy marred by stains, faded by the sun and the salt of the sea. The coat had burnt patches and every cuff and collar was frayed. His face sagged like a half-empty sack of potatoes. His florid complexion was a combination of old rouge and too much drink. The only part of him that wasn't sad was the wicked steel glint in his dark eyes. It was the last place anyone would care to look and the only place that told you this broken-down old man was still very dangerous.

Markham's face lit up when he saw her. *"Rough with black winds and storms,"* he recited, *"unwanted shall admire."*

"Always charm with you, Dot," she said, sitting down next to the old man. He hugged her and she returned it. Markham gasped as the baby made a cooing sound from his hammock across her chest.

"A babe!" he exclaimed and she couldn't help but laugh at his surprise and delight. "Oh my sweet girl! Is it Jack's?"

"That's the prevailing theory," she said, adjusting the infant in his snug hammock. "Best I can figure he would have been conceived just before we took off with the *William,* or maybe on her."

"If it was on ship that makes him a true son of a gun," Markham said, "a sailor-born, just like his mother."

"I wasn't conceived on a ship," she said, taking a long pull off the bottle of port, "more likely the scullery maid's closet. Da gave Ma the goat's jig in between her changing linens, sometimes during."

Markham puffed his long churchwarden pipe and shook his head. "No," he said, a wreath of tobacco smoke preceding his words "if ever I met some-one born to the tides, it was you, Annie. You're more a sea dog than old Calico Jack, Charlie Vane, or any of their ilk."

She laughed. "One big difference," she said, "I'm still breathing."

"It's the end of the golden age of the freebooters, lass," Dot said. "The world will be less legendary, less wild, without them. We're replacing pirates with politicians."

"I always found pirates to be a damn sight more honest," she said. "They tell you up front what they're going to steal from you."

The old man chuckled. It turned into a dry, booming cough. "Come to say good-bye, have you, girl?" She knelt and took the old man's hands in her own.

"Yes, I have to be gone by first light. I need one last favor from you, Dot," she said. "That chest Jack left with you before we took the *William,* do you recall it?"

"Aye," Dot said. "The queer one, painted up with all those strange marks on it. Oh, yes, I recall it well. Sometimes . . . sometimes at night, I think I hear . . . singing coming out of it."

"Singing?"

"A strange language, one I've never heard," he said. "It sounds like a lot of voices, like women."

"I need it," she said.

"Of course, love, but are you sure? There's something damned in that box—it's the devil singing," Dot said. "It makes me dream of some steaming, scorching place—of unforgiving heat, of a city made out of . . . dead things. I think I dreamt of Hell."

"That box is this baby's birthright and the final share due me from Jack," she said. "It will lead me to a big enough score to lay down my sword. Can you fetch it for me, Dot?"

"Of course. Meet you here before dawn?" he asked. She stood and helped the old man to his feet as she did.

"No," she said. "The north docks, near Fort James and the custom houses."

"Done," he said and headed for the door without another word. She got the impression Herodotus was glad to be ridding himself of the box and wanted to waste no time doing so.

She sat back on the bench and took another long sip on the bottle of port. The box was not natural—she knew that—had known it since she and Jack had taken it from the cargo hold of that merchantman headed back to England from Africa. One of Jack's crew, a Spaniard named Thiago, had jumped from the crow's nest onto the deck below, screaming of a city of monsters that was eating the dreams out of his skull. He screamed a name as he took his fatal plunge—"Carcosa."

Both she and Jack had awoken from dreams of the necropolis squatting still and silent in the middle of some verdant, primal place. When they made it to port, they had consulted the smartest man either of them knew—Herodotus. He had no wisdom for them, but promised to keep the box safe.

She never told Jack but she, alone, had a final dream of the bone city. In it she stood in a sunbaked courtyard, vast like an arena. The floor of the place glittered with rubies, millions of them. She stood before a shining statue of a woman, flaring with the light of the bloated red sun. The statue was at the center of the arena, and was made of gold and ivory, diamonds and other precious stones, a king's fortune a hundred times over, or a queen's.

She was going to find that city and claim its treasures and its secrets, and she knew, she knew the first step on that path was the box, and then to head for Africa, from which it hailed. Now, sitting alone in the noise and life of the Witches' Wrath, she recalled the eyes of the statue in her dream. They were terrible, the immortal gaze of a goddess—regarding her, judging her with eyes darker than a murderer's soul, burning red at their core, hotter than any earthly forge.

She rubbed her eyes, and pushed the memory out of her mind. She realized then how much she wanted a pipe and some good tobacco.

"Now," she said to the baby slumbering at her breast, "what do I do with you, you little snapper?" She noticed a man sitting alone at a table writing with an inkwell and pen in a ledger, occasionally popping his head up to look about, or to drink from his tankard. He was a slender man, his hair and beard the color of wheat. She rose, and moved toward him.

"Nate?" she said. "Nate Mist? I'll be a fussock, it is you!" The man turned, frowning at first, but then broke into a wide smile once he recognized her.

"I heard your neck got stretched, Annie," Mist said. She raised the port in salute and Mist raised his tankard.

"Haven't found a rope clever enough," she said. "I'm surprised to see you here. I heard you were back in England—a writer they said."

"Publisher," Mist replied. "Oh, and down here I'm going by Charles Johnson these days—Captain Charles Johnson. Ran into a spot of trouble back home. Thought I'd travel a bit and see if I could finish my research on the history of pirates I'm writing."

"Well, 'Captain,'" she said, laughing and taking another drink, "I'm a walking, talking expert on that lot."

"That you are," Mist said. He flipped to a fresh page in his ledger and dipped his pen in the inkwell. "Let me ask you about . . ."

"You'll make a pretty bob off me and all my dead mates, won't you, Nate?" Mist began to answer, but she waved her free hand to dismiss his reply as she sat at his table. "I'll give it all to you, mate—you were always a good lad back then—always an honest sea dog. I'll tell you the tale of the last days of Calico Jack and his crew. How old Eddie Teach supped with the devil and stole some of his cursed gold for himself. I'll tell you the story of how we came across this great metal vessel the size of a hundred galleons! How it traveled under the waves and was captained by a mad genius."

Mist leaned forward, frantically scribbling in his ledger.

"I'll tell you the time I was stricken by the black mark—the one all pirates fear," she went on, knowing she had Mist now, her eyes locked on his, her voice weaving her stories tight about him, "and how I had to filch wine from Neptune himself to dodge that curse. You want to know about the island where immortal cannibal children are led by a ten-thousand-year-old boy who has no shadow? I'll give all the secrets of the pirates and the worlds they've been brave enough to sail through to you and you alone—enough for a hundred books—but first I want you to swear an oath to me, and do me a service, Nate. I want you to swear it on that god of yours that keeps getting you in so much trouble back home."

"What's the favor, Anne?" Mist asked.

She set the bottle on the table and slid her arms around and under the baby. "This," she said. "Take him to my da in Charles Town, Oyster Point."

"Carolina? The colonies?" Mist said. "I was thinking of sailing north in a few days. Why don't you just go yourself?"

"I have something to tend to first," she said. "You tell my father to keep him safe and I'll be along once I'm finished." She placed a bag of coins before Mist on the table. "For him and for you. Do you swear you'll keep him safe and deliver him to my kin?"

Mist looked at the baby's face, then to hers. "I swear it," he said. They spit in their palms and shook to seal the oath. "Now," she said, "let me start by telling you about the Secret Sea. . . ."

Night was unraveling in the East; threads of pink, orange and indigo frayed where the sky met sea. Herodotus hobbled along with the small chest. Sailors, eagerly preparing to leave with the morning tide, darted past the old man. There were shouts, curses, songs and orders in a dozen languages, all along the crowded row of docks and piers. Markham turned to look about and found himself facing a slender sailor, a man, his face shadowed with dirt that hinted at a beard. His long red hair was tied in a ponytail, the rest under a cocked hat. He wore a vest and tunic, a heavy blade and pistol held fast by a sash around his waist, breeches and boots. A ditty bag was hung over the man's shoulder. The sailor smiled and Dot finally recognized her.

"You're damned good at that, lass," he said, keeping his voice low. She laughed and even that had a rough, male sound to it.

"Lots of practice." She nodded to the box. "Thanks, Dot." He handed her the oddly painted wooden cask and she held it with both hands. "My ship is off in a few moments."

"You be careful with that twice-damned thing," Herodotus said. "Where's the boy?"

"Safe and on his way to my family in the colonies," she said. "Here," she said, handing him a purse full of coins. She had managed to increase her dwindling stolen stakes with a few games of bones on the docks while waiting for Dot. "There's a ship leaving later today for the Carolina colony," she said. "You remember Nate Mist? He's a passenger aboard, and I've secured you passage as well. Nate has my boy, taking him to my da. I'd consider it a kindness if you'd accompany them and see to my boy until I return."

"Nate's a good man," Markham said, nodding. He took the purse. "Very well, perhaps the change in climate will be good for what ails me."

"Thank you," she said. "And don't worry. I'm taking this thing home, scoring one last haul of loot, and then I'm quits with this freebooter life."

Herodotus laughed until he began coughing again. "I'll believe that when I bloody see it," he said. "You're born to this, Annie, moon and tide, steel and gold."

"Well, I'm retiring to be a proper lady," she said with a grin. "One of god-damned means, to boot. Good-bye, Dot. Take good care of yourself and my lad." They shook hands and she began to head for the gangplank of one of the ships.

"And good luck to you too, Lady . . ." Herodotus paused. "Anne, what the hell do I call you now? Lady Rackham? Cormac? What?"

She turned and gave the old pirate sage a wink. "I always liked my married name," she said, "liked it better than I liked the fucking marriage. I'll stick with that one, I think."

"Fair enough," Herodotus said. "Then good luck to you, Lady Bonny."

2

The Queen of Swords

Northern Utah

December 5, 1870

(One hundred and forty-nine years later)

The train rumbled through the badlands, the ancient, snow-silvered mountains indifferent to its blustering advance. The Transcontinental Railroad was the great artery, the road connecting civilization to the wilderness, to the frontier.

With the planting of a single golden spike, a flurry of speeches, pomp and circumstance, the track had been made whole, and the gateway to the mythical West swung open. Alter Cline, sitting in the mostly empty passenger car, foresaw the railroad's recent completion as a harbinger of death for that very myth.

Cline was twenty-four. His black hair fell to his shoulders in ringlets, parted on the side. He sported thick, stylish sideburns. Alter possessed a wiry, slender build with long legs. He stood a hair over six feet. His brown eyes were expressive and intelligent, and currently they were fixed on the striking woman sitting near the center of the passenger car.

The woman was traveling unchaperoned, which was queer. She was quite unaware of his notice, Alter was certain. Her hair was auburn, shot through with red-gold and silver strands. It was long, but she wore it up, away from her face, in a tight bun. Her skin was pale, her wrists small and delicate. Her figure was slight, and her overall appearance not the sort that would capture a man's second glance in a crowd or a busy street. However, there was something—something that hid in this woman beneath her surface appearance. Alter enjoyed the mystery, the parlor game of guessing who she was, why she was here, where she had come from.

The mental exercise helped Cline take his mind off his unease that this untamed place, this magnificent frontier, was living on borrowed time. He was happy to be headed back to New York, but there was a freedom, a spirit awake in these wild lands, something that slept in a lot of people back East. He'd miss that rawness, that primal feeling once he was home—not that there weren't a few neighborhoods in New York City that he was sure the toughest cow-puncher or gunslinger would find daunting.

It troubled him to think that when this frontier was gone perhaps that raw part of the human spirit would die with it. However, what he had witnessed out on the plains suggested that the same old human stains—greed, cruelty, callous indifference—traveled hand-in-hand with our primal selves wherever, whenever we go. It gave him grim reassurance that mankind was far from domesticated just yet. It made Cline wonder, too, that perhaps "civilized" people didn't respect the freedom and the splendor out here enough to deserve it, or keep it.

He had been sent out by his editor to cover the brisk expansion in the business of buffalo skinning, as a perfect example of man's knack for destroying wonder. It wasn't truly buffaloes that blackened the plains in their vast numbers, that made the ground shudder like thunder in their passing, but bison. Not that those killing them in the hundreds of thousands and leaving their skinned corpses to rot on the plains, leaving sun-bleached mountains of wide, horned skulls, cared a damn about the semantics of what they were killing.

Alter had ridden out with a skinning crew for several weeks, chronicling their lives and gory, lonely work. He had lived and worked as one of them, though they joked he had no stomach for it. The demands for the hides back East were bringing more and more men, mostly restless young soldiers from the war, out to the frontier.

Alter understood that gnawing restlessness all too well, an unseen wound of the war. It was like a metal spring—humming, made of bright, warm brass—wound too tight inside you. He had felt it after the war. Sitting in one place too long would wind the spring tighter, make it snap from the tension. A soft bed, a quiet meal, silence in the darkness could fill him with a tension that he could not voice or explain to anyone who had not seen the elephant, and men did not speak of such things to one another in polite conversation. Men didn't speak of it at all, if they could.

The pressure, the restlessness, was one of the reasons, perhaps the primary reason Alter had taken the position offered to him by *The Herald*. It afforded him the opportunity to travel—movement, the hint of action, those things seemed to unwind the bright coil within him. His parents, who had objected to him joining the Union Army, objected to him working for the newspaper too. They thought it unseemly, cheap and far beneath him. He didn't care; he loved it.

Alter had used the trip West for the buffalo piece as an excuse to work on a second story, one he thought even more indicative of the dark side of the great frontier. Chinese railroad workers for Union Pacific were making thirty-two dollars a month in wages compared to the fifty-two dollars their white peers earned, and this was causing a row among those whites seeking work, and a growing anti-Chinese sentiment that the immigrants were unfairly competing for jobs. Alter had seen this less as an insidious plot by immigrants and more of an underhanded act by the Rail Barons to exploit cheap labor from an alien people far from home and with no protection or advocates.

He hoped he could convince his editors to run both stories; however, *The Herald* had a reputation for leaning a bit to the nativist ideology of the Know-Nothing Party. Still, he was bringing back an adventure tale of roughing it on the incomprehensibly vast plains. He had even sketched a few decent drawings of the mighty bison to include in the tale. The public back home was eager for any stories of the Wild West. Alter thought he had a chance of getting the labor story out, before things got truly ugly for the Chinese, by piggybacking it on a ripping yarn about cowboys.

Alter opened his copy of *Around the Moon* and tried to read again, but his attention kept drifting back to the woman. There was . . . something, something about her—about her bearing—that fascinated him. Whatever it was, it made it very hard for Cline to focus on Monsieur Verne's prose. He used his skills as an investigator and professional observer to remain unobtrusive, and the lady's continued lack of notice seemed to indicate he was doing a fine job.

A few aisles away, the object of Alter Cline's attentions watched the Utah mountains drift pass her window. Maude Stapleton felt the young man's eyes moving over her. He was trying very hard to be discreet, behind his book, and to untrained eyes he was doing a fine job, but there were few upon the Earth with senses as keen as Maude's.

Maude's mind drifted to Constance, her daughter, and to Martin, her father, and to all that lay ahead of her. That made her think of Mutt, of Golgotha, and of what she was leaving behind. She was pulled from her thoughts by the young man's eyes, as insistent to her as if he had tapped her on the shoulder and cleared his throat.

The attention was pleasant and, if she allowed it, her blood would act of its own accord and produce a physiologic reaction, and she would blush. Maude decided it was best not to encourage the stranger, so she didn't blush. She had only allowed herself that freedom, that dizzy abandonment— out of control of her body and emotions—with one living man, and this train was taking her farther and farther away from him, possibly forever.

Maude did not consider herself a woman who attracted notice; in fact, she had been taught how to blend in, not even becoming a memory in the minds of others. However, the young man seemed rather focused in his attention on her. Her features might be called plain, handsome, or mannish by some men. Maude could give less than a damn what "some men" thought.

Besides herself and her admirer, a Chinese family—a husband, wife and their two small children—were the only occupants of the passenger car. When Maude had boarded the train at Hazen, the closest train station to Golgotha, the conductor, a corpulent man, sweating in his heavy, dark-blue coat with fancy brass buttons, had tried to roust the Chinese from the car.

"Don't you worry your pretty little head, ma'am," the conductor said, brandishing a wooden truncheon at the obviously terrified family, "I'll chase these coolies straight back to the nigger car. They won't give you a lick of trouble."

The father stood, about to interpose himself between this ugly little man and his family. Maude caught his eye and silently entreated him for patience. She turned to the conductor.

"I'm sure that will not be necessary," she said as she shifted her body language and vocal tone with the conductor, locking eyes with the odious creature. "You are a kind man, a merciful man, someone of great power and responsibilities. I can see that in your manner and bearing, sir. Obviously, such a menial chore is far beyond a man of your importance, isn't it?"

"Er, I mean to say . . . yes?" the conductor muttered. He found himself absently nodding with each subtle movement of this woman's head, her hands. Maude's voice was gently playing upon his nerves like she might pluck the strings of a harp.

"In fact, don't you think it's best they stay here with me, where they won't distress the other passengers?" In the end, the man had thought it his own idea, which was precisely what Maude had intended.

"Thank you," the father had said, in English, as the conductor lumbered away, very pleased with himself. "We are returning to New York to work in my uncle's business. My job on the railroad is complete. I did not know we were not allowed . . ."

"It's a foolish rule, created by foolish people," Maude replied in one of the Yue dialects of Chinese that Gran had taught her. "He won't trouble you again. I hope you and your family enjoy your trip." One of the children, the little boy, looked at her in amazement, having never heard the language of his parents coming out of a white person's mouth before. Maude smiled. The little boy waved and Maude waved back. The boy hid his face in his mother's lap and giggled.

The young man watching her had come aboard at one of the stations sometime later and began his furtive surveillance of Maude. In her own assessment of the young man, she noted that his clothing was of good quality. They spoke of some means but were not the clothes of the idle wealthy. He was obviously a working man in a field that left his hands smooth, but he had done a spot of rough work recently, and he had the blisters to show for it. She also saw in him the bearing of a man trained for war, but now looser, mostly relaxed or forgotten. He still carried the stress of combat in his lower spine, and that would catch up to him one day. He was handsome, though, she had to admit.

Gran entered Maude's mind unbidden, swaggering, as she usually did. Maude knew what Gran would say about her admirer, if she were still alive. She'd cackle like one of Macbeth's witches and say something like, *"Go on, lass, have a go at 'im! Get all hot cockles with the pretty boy. Life is too damn short for mooning about and playing it safe. Nobody gets out of this world alive, 'cept for me, of course!"*

The ghost she had summoned made her smile, and the young man almost dropped his book in response to it. Maude nearly laughed, but she lowered her eyes and held her composure.

The car's rear door opened with a bang, and a group of men entered the compartment. There were seven of them. They were dirty with trail dust, and they reeked of the sweat of their horses and their own bodies, of leather and gun oil. All of them were armed—six-guns and knives; some carried rifles and shotguns too. They slowly advanced down the car's center aisle. The leader, a burly man with a thick red beard and hooded eyes full of coiled violence, nodded to two of his men. They responded by dropping back from the pack and lingering near the rear door. The menace from them radiated like heat.

Maude silently prepared herself for what she knew was coming, had to come. She adjusted her posture subtly from one of avoiding notice to that intended to attract the eye, drawing the crew's attention toward her and away from the immigrant family and the young man.

She altered her breathing, preparing for a fight with a fast-fast rhythm of breath—drawing on her abdominal muscles—just as she had been taught. She had practiced different styles of breathing for different purposes over many years and under a harsh teacher. Again she heard Gran's cackle, saw the old woman beside the ocean with her *wadaiko*—her Japanese drum— on her lap, calling the tunes Maude's muscles and lungs learned to obey.

"There is no learning before you learn to breathe proper, girl," Gran had told her. *"Technique's called by many names in many lands. The Japanese call it* Ibuki, *and it's the first step in making you truly free. The air in your lungs is the fuel."*

Her blood was filled with oxygen, now. Maude was ready. The menacing men were armed and, now, so was she.

"Excuse me," the young man said, standing before her. "If I am not being too bold, may I join you?" He was pretty, to be sure. He was also the master of the worst possible timing imaginable.

"Of course," Maude said, directing him to a seat with a nod, "please."

"I'm not normally in the habit of being so forward," Alter said as he sat, "but I was concerned." He leaned closer and lowered his voice. "Those b'hoys coming in the car look like trouble, and a lady like yourself traveling alone . . ."

"That's very kind of you, Mr. . . ."

"Cline," he said, "Alter Cline."

The men walked past Maude and Alter. She saw their brutal intent radiating from the tension in how they moved, ready for trouble, to explode, with every step. Cline was turning to face them—the worst possible thing he could do. The men each gave her a rapacious glance as they passed and then saw the grim look on Alter's face. One of the men stopped before Cline and began to say something, his hand dropping to his six-gun. Maude placed a hand lightly on Cline's shoulder and Alter suddenly shifted back toward her, a surprised look on his face. For such a slip of a woman, she seemed quite strong.

"If you want to stay alive, Mr. Cline, be still," she said, whispering. Cline began to open his mouth. "And quiet," she added.

"Leave this dude be," one of the gunmen muttered to his kinsman whom Alter had riled, "We're on a schedule. 'Sides, Nick and Jed will see to 'em. Shake a leg."

The group of armed men opened the car's front door. They stepped through, man by man. The leader looked back at the two men waiting in Maude's car. He nodded to them and stepped through the door, shutting it behind him.

"Damn it," Maude muttered. Only Cline heard her. The younger of the two gunmen, close to Cline's age and with a lump of tobacco in his cheek, walked toward Maude and Cline. He paused, rested his hand on his holstered gun and looked Maude over like he was examining horseflesh to purchase.

"Well, ain't you a little stick of an adventuress," the boy said, laughing. The man by the rear door laughed, too, and turned toward the Chinese family. Maude's face remained emotionless.

"She's gotta be a whore, if'n she's ridin' in a car with these here yeller niggers, Nick," the gunman, obviously Jed, said. He cradled a Winchester rifle as he looked at the husband and his family.

Nick grinned. His teeth were brown and stained. He looked over to Cline, who was reddening in response to the coarse words. "I hope you didn't pay this scrawny little thing too much for her to upend her legs, boy. Or maybe you're her pimp?"

"You filthy . . ." Cline growled. The reporter began to rise, his fists clenched. Nick drew his six-gun—a fluid motion as natural to the man as breathing. Nick cocked the pistol aimed at the young man's face. Alter Cline was a dead man.

Alter and Nick were scarcely able to fully comprehend what happened next. The muscles in Nick's arm, wrist and hand fluttered in response to the command of his brain to pull the trigger, the quicksilver language of nerves and electrical impulses. Maude's eyes registered the movements; her body responded faster than thought allowed. Maude's arm flashed out and clutched Nick's wrist with a grip like iron. Her other hand chopped at his arm precisely above the elbow. Nick's gun arm folded, the gun turned upward toward his face as he pulled the trigger. The sound of the .44 was a hammer shattering the world. Alter jumped back, his eyes squeezing shut, anticipating a spray of hot blood. It didn't come. Nick crumpled to the floor. As he fell, Maude caught his still-smoking revolver. She flipped the gun in midair, clutching it by the hot barrel. She turned, using the strength of her pivoting hips as she hurled the gun at Jed like a tomahawk. Jed, just beginning to realize what was happening, raised his weapon. Nate's six-gun caught him square in the face. There was a gush of blood from his shattered nose, and he collapsed in a heap against the train car's rear door.

"How . . . how did you . . . do that?" Alter asked, looking down at Nick's motionless form. "Is he . . ."

"Dead?" Maude stepped out into the aisle over Nick's body. "No. The bullet grazed his chin, just knocked him out. The other one is alive too." She knelt by Nick, tore a strip from her dress, and began to bind his hands behind his back. Alter looked out the window, so as to not gawk at the flash of Maude's exposed leg. Nick groaned.

"Oh," Alter said. "I've never seen anyone move that fast before. How—"

"We really don't have time for that," Maude said, moving down the aisle toward the other gunman and the Chinese family. "If it makes you feel better, you can consider it a lucky accident—a hysterical woman's thrashing about that had a fortuitous outcome."

"I will do no such thing," Alter said. He knelt by Nick and examined the odd-looking but sturdy knot Maude had used to bind him. He did not recognize its make. "You are in complete control of your faculties, madame, and furthermore, your quick action saved my life. Thank you."

Maude paused in tying the other outlaw up to look back at Alter. She looked mildly surprised and smiled. "You're . . . quite welcome."

"That smile," Alter said, standing and adjusting his puff tie. "I imagine it gets you in a lot of trouble."

"Apparently so," Maude said as she stood. She handed Nick and Jed's bloody revolvers to the immigrant father. She said something to him in Chinese that Alter didn't understand. The father replied in his native tongue and took the guns. Maude knelt to retrieve the rifle. She spoke quietly to the little boy and ruffled his hair. His expression changed from fear to a smile. Maude stood and tossed the Winchester across the car to Alter. He caught it, and cocked the lever, chambering a round.

"You were in the army, and you know your way around a rifle, better than most," Maude said. She was putting on Jed's coat now and was tying his kerchief around her neck loosely. She walked past Cline, headed toward the door the rest of the outlaw crew had passed through.

"Yes," Alter said. "But how on Earth could you possibly know that? Wait, I know, 'no time.'"

"You're a quick study, good," Maude said.

She paused by the door and tore her dress in the front and back, giving herself enough freedom to run. Alter instinctively looked away again at the pale, bare skin. She tied the loose pieces of the brown dress together at each ankle—it now looked like she was wearing baggy ripped trousers. "Alter, I need you to backtrack, check the cars behind ours. See if they left any more men behind. If they did, I need you to deal with them, understand? Can you do that?"

"Yes," Alter said, looking back at the rear door. "Where are you going?"

Maude slid the kerchief over her mouth and nose and tightened it. She picked up Nick's floppy-brimmed felt hat from the floor and stuffed it on her head. Something in her posture, her way of walking, changed, and for an instant, Alter thought he was looking at a completely different person. "I'm going forward to do the same. Disarm these two completely before you head back."

"I thought you already did," he said.

"Nick has a knife in his left boot. This one has a parlor gun tucked in his vest pocket," she said. Even her voice sounded different now, deeper—more like a man's. "Be careful."

"How do you know th—" Alter began. The car's front door banged shut behind Maude. "The people you meet on the train, eh?" Alter said to the bewildered family as he pulled the blade from Nick's boot.

Outside the passenger car the winter wind was bitter as the train sped along at over forty miles an hour. Maude directed the blood within her body, willing it to act against the decrees of biology. Her skin warmed. The condensation of her breath that had trailed away from her mouth in silvered streams vanished.

She crossed the narrow gap between the train cars, hearing the coupler, which held the cars together, clatter beneath her. The window on the door to the next car was painted in frost, so she crouched by the door and placed her palms against it.

The vibrations of the train car, the rattling, shaking song of the distant engine, became part of her. She closed her eyes and breathed through the filter of the outlaw's filthy bandanna. Her senses began to reorder themselves—some growing still and silent, others opening wider . . . wider. She felt the pulse of the train, the hum of motion and vibration, the rhythm and pattern, and then she began to assign each pattern a distinctive identity.

One of the many games Gran had played with her when she was a young girl had involved three hard, thick, identical wooden boxes. She had to tell which box held the hornet's nest by touch alone, by letting her hands drink in the vibrations and motion. Then she was to open the two boxes that didn't hold the hornets. She had been stung so many times learning the game, but like all of Gran's games, it served a purpose. Now Maude was thankful for the painful lesson. *"Good!"* Gran had said, clapping, when Maude had mastered the game, *"Now, girl, tell me exactly how many hornets are in that nest . . ."*

The vibrations that were counter to the heartbeat of the train were people—one was five feet north of her, on the other side of the door, the other twenty feet farther away—two more gunmen, pacing. The other counter vibrations were lesser and ordered in their locations—seated passengers, about fifteen. She could afford no mistakes in this or people would die.

The outlaw by her door was facing away from her now. She had felt the wobble in his vibration, the subtle shift of his weight as he turned to face his comrade and the passengers. She stayed low and leaned in as she swung the door open violently. Maude's leg shot out like a snake striking and swept both of the outlaw's legs. The gunman fell hard on his face. Maude was up and moving, a blur. As she stepped over the fallen man, she drove a well-placed heel into a cluster of nerves at the base of his spine. The man moaned in pain but then was abruptly silent—he'd be powerless to move for at least thirty minutes.

His companion was twenty feet away and less than a second from firing his pistol at Maude's heart. The passengers were screaming and shouting, just beginning to comprehend the stimuli their brains were receiving. Maude launched herself off the paralyzed man, using his body like a ramp.

Her eyes read the language of the gunman's muscles as the pistol barked. In midair she twisted, tumbled, changing her trajectory using the canvas support straps mounted vertically above the seats along the length of the car. Angry, buzzing heat fluttered past her cheek as she came down feet-first on the outlaw's chest. Her legs folded and she followed him to the floor. With a single strike from the heel of her palm, she knocked him out.

"Thank the Almighty for you, stranger!" one of the passengers said as Maude stood.

"I've never seen a body move like that, fella," another man said, starting to rise. "You with the carnival or circus or something?"

Maude moved quickly past them toward the next door. Four down, three to go. She pointed toward the forward car door. "The other men who went this way," she asked, her voice still disguised as a man's. "Did they say anything, anything at all?"

"They said something about the mail car and then coming back to fleece us," a woman said, her children clinging to her. "The Lord be with you, brave sir."

"Disarm these men," Maude said. "Bind them. Stay here until you hear something from the conductor or the engineer. Any of the others come back, shoot them."

"Don't you need a gun?" one of the men called out, picking up one of the outlaw's pistols.

"What for?" Maude asked. She was through the next door and gone.

Connolly "Big Tooth" McGrath held the shotgun to the head of the postal clerk in the mail car. The boy had wet himself when they had shot through the door and now was on his hands and knees, shaking like a sick dog. "I know you got the damn key to the lock box," McGrath told the clerk. He gestured with the still-hot scattergun toward the mostly headless body of the other clerk that lay beside the locked and chained heavy metal chest. "He thought he'd play at hero, too, and you see what that got him."

"They didn't give me a key in case something like this happened!" the clerk screamed, looking down at the blood-soaked floor. "I'm no hero!"

McGrath stroked his heavy red beard and sniffed the air, catching the stench of gun smoke and piss. Even with the cold December air whistling through the car, it still reeked of fear. "Clearly," he said. "Well, then," Mc-Grath said, addressing his two men—one gathering up the canvas sacks of postage, the other standing watch by the now-destroyed rear door. "I guess we blast the chains off the chest and carry it, then. That means we don't need you, hero, so say so-long to your hat rest."

McGrath glanced up at his men. The one by the door had vanished. There was a rapidly diminishing scream, then a sound like meat hitting the tracks at forty miles an hour. The scream stopped.

"What the hell?" McGrath snapped his head toward his other conspira-tor. The outlaw's motionless body was slumped on a mattress of scattered mail sacks. A masked man stood beside the body, a postage envelope in the stranger's hand. "Who the fuck are you?" McGrath asked.

"Postmaster General," Maude said in her counterfeit male voice. "You're in a great deal of trouble."

"I don't care if you're General fuckin' Forrest!" McGrath shouted. "You picked the wrong desperado to mess with, stranger." He brought up the shotgun, leveling it at the masked man. Maude flicked her wrist, and the letter whizzed across the room accompanied by a snapping sound. McGrath felt a sharp sting at his wrist, and his trigger finger no longer worked. He strained, but the finger drooped in the trigger guard. He struggled to shift the gun to his other hand, now seeing a slender line of his blood trailing from the wrist of his gun hand. He never had a chance to complete the task before Maude crossed the room, grabbed the shotgun barrel, and jerked downward on it. The butt of the gun caught McGrath in the face, and he col-lapsed in a heap.

"There any more?" Maude asked the terrified clerk.

"N . . . no," the clerk said. "Whoever you are, thank you. I was sure I was dead, like . . . like Henry over there."

"He'll never shoot anyone with that hand ever again," Maude said, pick-ing up the letter from the floor and dropping it back into the pile of mail.

"Are you a passenger?" the clerk asked. There was no reply. The masked stranger was gone.

The train halted on the tracks near Promontory. The robbers were bound and gathered together by the train's crew, then forced into one of the pas-senger cars and guarded at gunpoint. The passengers were all taken off the train while it was searched to make sure no additional members of Mc-Grath's crew had escaped notice. Alter, rifle still in hand, was talking with the conductor and the engineer.

"We were damned lucky you were on the train, Mr. Cline," said the engineer, a balding man in greasy coveralls. "You have any clue who that masked fella was? He seems to have vanished just as quickly as he showed up."

"And we didn't even get a chance to thank him," added the burly conductor, still managing to sweat in the numbing cold.

Cline glanced over his shoulder toward the throng of passengers milling about, cussing and complaining about the cold. He spotted Maude standing in the cluster of Negro and Chinese passengers. She had removed Jed's coat and wrapped it around the two shivering Chinese kids. Somehow, she had managed to replace her skirt with an undamaged one, and she looked like she was shivering, just like the other passengers, but Cline noted no line of visible breath trailing from her lips. Maude's eyes found Cline's, and she nodded to him. He nodded back, and that hint of a smile returned to her face. Cline looked back to the engineer and conductor.

"Not even a notion, I'm afraid, gentlemen," Cline said. "I suppose I'll chalk it up to another mystery of the West."

"At least you'll get a hell of a story out of it," the conductor said. Cline looked back toward Maude. She had vanished.

"Yes," Cline said, "that I shall."

3

The High Priestess

London, England
December 21, 1870

Amadia Ibori moved through the tangled evening street traffic as silently as the falling snow. She loved snow, and London was in the grip of a major storm. Even with the weather, people hurried by her, balancing stacks of Christmas parcels tied with string. A cluster of children laughed and hurled snowballs at one another as their mother called for them to come along. A large man in a bloody butcher's apron carried a Christmas goose, wrapped in paper, on his shoulder for an elderly man with a walking stick. Amadia smelled the roasted chestnuts two blocks away before she heard the vendor hocking the treats. If anything, the storm was putting the city in even more of a Christmas mood.

If any of the people on the street were to focus on Amadia, they would be startled at her appearance; she was African—slender and tall. Her black hair was shaved close to her skull, with sideburns that ended in points. Tonight, she was wearing a man's overcoat, unbuttoned in spite of the storm. Under it was a man's white-collared shirt, open at her throat, a buttoned brown vest and men's pinstriped trousers with a pair of ankle boots. Her boots left no mark in the thick white powder, and she seemed impervious to the cold.

None of the hundreds of pedestrians she passed as she advanced up Duke Street glanced at her for more than a second. They saw her skin color, looked away and hurried on. She was a lone black face in a sea of white as she headed south toward Grosvenor Square. While there were parts of London where she would blend in, this was not one of them. She had the ability to be unseen, to move and leave no trace of her passing in the physical world or in the minds of men, but she didn't need any of her abilities in this place—her skin was enough.

Amadia took another puff on the cigar she had purchased from the tobacconist on St. James. She knew it was a dreadful habit. Even as efficiently as her lungs cleaned themselves, she could feel the damage it did, but it was a vice that she afforded herself whenever she traveled away from home. She knew her *iya* would chide her when she returned home, smelling the sweet tobacco on her no matter how hard she tried to hide its presence. As powerful as Amadia's senses were, *Iya*'s were far more acute.

She paused when she felt the child's notice—a little girl about six years old with brown curls and brilliant blue eyes. The parents were busy taking in a window display. Amadia nodded to the girl and smiled. "Very good," Amadia whispered. She directed the sound waves from her throat so that only the child heard her. Her English was as fluent as a native's—better than many natives', in fact, and she spoke with a slight British accent. "Aren't you a perceptive little one?"

The girl walked up to her, smiling. "Are you a lady?" the child asked, her voice soft and unafraid. "What happened to your hair, and why are you dressed like a man?"

Amadia laughed.

"I am a woman," Amadia said, now for all to hear. She knelt to look eye-to-eye with the child. "I don't like the word 'lady.' It's a word used to control what you should do and not do, or be, and I don't like being controlled. You don't either, do you?" The little girl laughed and shook her head.

"Good, don't change," Amadia said with a wink, the cigar clenched at the corner of her mouth.

"Sally!" It was the child's father, the parents rushing to the girl's side. The father grabbed Sally by the arm and jerked her violently away from Amadia. Sally squeaked in pain and was suddenly clutched tight in her father's arms. Both parents were red-faced.

"How dare you approach my child," the mother said. "You . . . teapot!"

Amadia rose, her face placid, as if she hadn't heard the racial slur. "I'm sorry, I was just saying hello to your daughter. You are very fortunate. She is a very intelligent, independent and precocious child. You should not grab her in such a forceful manner, sir."

"You presume to tell me how to treat my child?" the father said, his face flushed. "I shall handle my daughter in any way I see fit!"

"Come away, Sally," the mother said, her eyes narrowing at Amadia. The family turned and began to walk briskly in the direction they had come from. "Bloody fuzzies!" the father bellowed. "Allowed to walk the streets with decent people! What's this country coming to!" Sally peeked over her father's shoulder and waved good-bye to Amadia, who waved back and continued on her way, puffing on her cigar.

The townhouse at the corner of Duke and Brooks was a three-story fortress of thick stone walls and high iron fences. It had no house number. It was the most secure and impregnable structure in London, but only a handful of souls knew that.

Amadia walked through the gate, crushing out her cigar on the gatepost, and climbed the stairs to the stoop. She clutched the doorknob of the steel-reinforced front door. To open, the knob required the person using it to simultaneously apply precise, and differing, amounts of pressure to each of a hundred small points hidden across the circumference of the seemingly normal-looking knob. Amadia turned it effortlessly with a click and entered.

The house was quiet except for the muted hiss of the gas lamps that lit the foyer. She shook the snow off her coat and hung it on the wooden and brass coat stand in the corner behind the front door. She took the grand staircase to the parlor on the second floor, and found the others assembled there.

"Ah, Amadia, dear," Alexandria Poole said. Amadia noted that Alexandria said her name as if she had conjured Amadia into being, a typical British attitude. The world and all its people were just sitting around waiting for the white folk to find them and "help" them. Alexandria was tall, almost as tall as Amadia's own six feet. Her features were regal, pale and perfect, like a porcelain doll. Her eyes were blue, her long blond hair straight and she appeared to be in her late twenties.

Alexandria's appearance always created faint repulsion in Amadia. She knew the secret of what hid behind the mask of that innocent young face. It was the same reason Alexandria and generations of her family hated Amadia and her *iya*.

The crackling fire in the parlor's fireplace chased away the chill of the storm. The floor was covered by a Tabriz rug, and the walls were adorned with paintings—Raphael, Titian, Caravaggio. An ancient, crumbling stone tablet with an ankh featured prominently on its face rested in a wooden cradle, under glass, on a display table near a bookcase. There were also numerous medieval woodcuts on display, depicting the Lady of the Lake giving Arthur and Merlin Excalibur. Other cuts depicted Percival returning the blade to the woman of the waters. A large, round table of dark cherrywood sat at the center of room, and Alexandria and the others sat about it.

To Alexandria's left was Inna Barkov. Amadia had met Inna several times over the years, and she liked the Russian a great deal. Inna was a muscular woman with a great lion's mane of hair so blond as to appear white. She dressed like a peasant from her native land—a simple tunic, loose comfortable pants and fur-trimmed boots—even though back home Inna had been granted titles by the czar and riches beyond imagining for her service in defense of her homeland. Inna offered Amadia the empty chair to her left.

"Where's your daughter?" Amadia said in Russian as she sat. Her Russian was not as good as her English, but it was serviceable.

"At our estate outside London," Inna replied in her native tongue. "I saw no reason to bring her into this until I know what this is all about."

Amadia knew Inna and her daughter, Lesya, from several encounters they had shared over the years. Inna was as passionate in life as she was fierce in battle, and Amadia and the Russian had struck up a fast friendship that they maintained through correspondence. Lesya should be a teenager now, and far along in her training under her mother.

On Alexandria's right was Leng Ya. Ya's black hair was tied back into a ponytail away from her narrow face. She wore a simple and loosely fitting blouse and pants of black cotton. Her blouse had beautifully embroidered braided buttons of white. It was hard to determine Ya's age by her appearance, but a best guess would put her between forty and sixty years. Ya made no gestures of greeting to Amadia. Not a single muscle in her face reacted in the slightest to her arrival or joining them at the table. Amadia, for her part, gave her the curtest of bows, one that she knew would most likely be taken as an insult, before taking her seat.

On Ya's left was the final member of the circle present, Itzel. Itzel, seeming no more than a child in her teens, with her long, straight black hair falling past her shoulders and bangs that hooded her large, observant brown eyes. She was native to the Spanish colony of Guatemala, and was dressed like she was about to attend her first day of parochial school. Itzel wore a modest buttoned blouse of white and a conservative black skirt that ended just below her ankles, revealing only her plain, sensible work shoes. The only things about Itzel that broke the illusion of the pious schoolgirl were the jagged shards of obsidian jewelry she wore on her neck and wrist and the jar filled with beautiful blue-winged, fluttering butterflies that sat on the table before her.

Amadia had not met Itzel before, and knew her only by reputation. Itzel nodded as a greeting, and Amadia returned the nod.

"Good. Now that we're all here," Alexandria continued, "we can—"

"All here?" Amadia interrupted. "Where's Kavita? Where's the American woman and her daughter?"

"Kavita is dead," Alexandria said bluntly, obviously annoyed at being interrupted. "She was attacked in Kolkata by the Sons. They killed her whole family and left her dead on a rooftop."

"The Sons?" Amadia said. "*The* Sons, after all this time? You're sure?"

"Yes," Alexandria said. "My family and I possess information sources throughout the empire and the world. I'm quite sure. If I wasn't, I wouldn't have called out to all of you. They've been active for several months now; all the old nests have been reactivating. They are recruiting again, everywhere, aggressively. We all know what their renewed activity most likely means. We must prepare for war, sisters."

"The American and her daughter?" Itzel asked. "Did the Sons get them as well?"

"Ah, the American," Alexandria said the word as if it were infectious. "She is the cause of this problem, her and her child. We've all had the dreams, yes? The mine, the chamber with a silver floor that crawls with alien script, the American spilling the last of the Mother's blood from the Grail to save her child and quiet the beast curled at the heart of the world. The American has become our undoing. Her child will be the last of the Daughters."

"No!" Inna exclaimed, rising from her chair. "My Lesya is ready! She has endured years of training, overcome every challenge. She is ready to be initiated, to drink the Mother's blood!"

Alexandria's eyes lit up at the Russian's agitation. "I'm sure she is. However, thanks to the Americans, the flasks have all run dry."

The women reached for chains about their necks, and all of them withdrew the small flasks that hung from the chains. The flasks were of ancient iron, flecked with the green oxidized stains of time. Each flask was wrapped in a fine filigree of silver mesh. The cap of each flask was tipped with a small gemstone, each woman's flask having a different capstone—alexandrite for Inna's, jade for Ya's, onyx for Itzel's; Amadia's flask was capped with an amethyst. Alexandria had no flask.

"We who sit at this table are the last," Alexandria said, looking from face to face, "the last of the Daughters of Lilith to exist."

"How can that be?" Itzel said softly, placing her hand on the jar of swarming butterflies. The creatures stilled and came to rest on the leafy twig that was propped within the jar. "Ix Chel, the Mother, her blood is eternal. It has resisted the ravages of time for eons within the Grail. How did this American, Stapleton, deplete what is supposed to be infinite?"

"For that matter, how did this woman we know so little about come into the possession of the Grail at all?" Ya asked.

"Apparently, the pirate queen had one final student, Maude Stapleton," Alexandria said. "Her mind must have been more addled than we already knew it to be. She entrusted the Grail to this . . . washer woman. If the Grail had remained in the possession of my family," Alexandria looked across the table to Amadia, "this would not have happened."

"Raashida took the Grail from your family for good reason," Amadia said. "Your family was . . . abusing its gifts and power."

"And the former Oya's choice of caretaker has led us here," Alexandria said. "Led us to the edge of oblivion, to the destruction of all mankind. Do you honestly think there is any other power in this world that can stop the Sons, and their father?"

"I think you . . . exaggerate," Amadia said. "The dreams have been upsetting, but I see no reason to—"

"It's prophecy," Alexandria said, interrupting. "Written upon the tablet. *'When the blood fails, the Father of Monsters rises again to devour all.'* I've read it myself. We are facing fate, sisters."

"You'll forgive me if I give pause to your interpretation of fate," Amadia said. "You visited the bone city once, over sixty years ago, and whatever you encountered there, you have been . . . reluctant to return to it. You, Lady Alexandria, are the only one to have read this 'prophecy,' and as I have said you have a penchant for . . . exaggeration."

Alexandria managed to control the physical signs of her anger; however, Amadia noted a slight contraction of the pupils in the blue eyes that were now becoming storm gray. "Are you accusing me of lying?" Alexandria said.

"No," Amadia said. "I'm accusing you of cowardice *and* lying."

"What would I possibly gain by lying about this?" Alexandria asked.

"What you and your family have always wanted," Amadia said. "Power, control."

Alexandria smiled, and Amadia suddenly had the feeling that she had somehow fallen into a trap. "Of course I seek those things, Amadia," Alexandria said. "While your *iya*, your mother, sits in her hut in the middle of the wilds of Africa, as she has for uncounted centuries, the world has moved on. There are channels, conduits of power, here, in England, Europe, even in the wilderness that is America. Commerce, war, politics. We are to act as guardians, as counsel, to humanity. We are architects of the future. We can no longer sit passively by and attempt to change the world a single person at a time.

"The blood of the Mother no longer flows and the Sons are on the move against us once again, which can only mean their father has returned. These are facts, Amadia. If we are to stop our enemies, we must use all the weapons at our disposal. Power is not to be feared or eschewed. If there is anyone on the planet capable of using it wisely, it is us."

The others agreed. Amadia steepled her hands in front of her but said nothing.

"Alexandria is correct," Ya said in English. "Our ancient enemy has already slain one of our number, and without the Blood of Lilith from the Grail, we cannot continue our line."

"My Lesya is ready to take Kavita's place," Inna said. "We cannot allow the Daughters to die. We are all that stands between the Sons and humanity."

"If we are to survive this, we must act quickly," Alexandria said. "The prophecy offers us a means of salvation for the Daughters of Lilith, but it will require great will and great sacrifice."

"What must we do?" Itzel asked.

"First," Alexandria said, "we must find the American's daughter, Constance Stapleton, and bring her here."

"The American will not willingly give up her daughter," Inna said. "I wouldn't."

"No," Alexandria said, "she will not. As I said, great sacrifices will be required."

4

The Three of Cups

Charleston, South Carolina
December 24, 1870

There was no snow to greet Maude at the train depot on Line Street, only fog, thick, milky and swirling, clinging to everything. Over the hiss of the locomotive, she heard the church bells and imagined Constance and her grandfather riding in his fine carriage to Christmas Eve service at St. John's, just as they had done so many times when Maude was a child. Maude considered for a moment confronting him there, at the church, getting her daughter back tonight. The heat of the thought was cooled, stilled and put away. She would stick to her plan.

The air was cold and damp. Passengers streamed past her, greeted by family and friends on the platform. She thought about the port here in Charleston for an instant, imagined all the sailors from across the world huddled in taverns tonight, celebrating the holiday with drink and song. She wondered how many were alone, peering through the fog, trying to see their families, their faraway homes.

"Shall I fetch someone to get that for you, miss?" the porter asked as the baggage was unloaded. Maude shook her head.

"No thank you," she said. "I'll manage."

Maude picked up her single bag and walked through the crowd. She had managed to avoid Alter Cline and his attempts to locate her during the rest of the journey. He was persistent and quite skilled, she had to admit. He had the instincts of a natural-born hunter. It had given her abilities a thorough testing to misdirect him, but the game had made the trip seem shorter. Mr. Cline was very determined to continue their conversation, and that was something Maude didn't need.

A row of hansom cabs was waiting on the street outside the depot to collect passengers. The gas streetlights were ghostly orbs, will-o'-the-wisps, hovering in the mist. A cabbie, a thin man with a scrub of peppered beard across his face, dressed in a threadbare coat, hopped from his spring seat at the rear of the cab, removing his battered derby as he approached her.

"Could you take me out to Folly Beach, if you please?" Maude asked.

"Of course, miss," the cabbie replied, opening the wooden doors to the cab's interior. "Trip will take a bit, Miss," he added as he took Maude's gloved hand and helped her up the two small metal steps into the cab. "I trust that won't be too much of an inconvenience on your constitution."

"No," Maude said, "that will be fine." She paused before entering the cab, looking over her shoulder. She was being watched.

"Miss?" the cabbie asked.

The sensation was vague and as elusive as the fog. "It's nothing," she said to the driver.

Maude entered the cab, and the cabbie closed the doors. In a moment, the cab lurched, and they were underway. The cab headed west on Line and then turned left onto King Street.

Maude looked out the cab's window as they headed south into the heart of Charleston, passing row upon row of fine homes, many under construction. This part of town was well-to-do neighborhoods for the numerous families that were coming to Charleston to make their fortunes in some form of commerce or trade. It had been the same when she'd lived here— in fact, Arthur had bought them a beautiful home in the Radcliffes shortly after they were married. There were far more homes now than she recalled when she, Constance and Arthur had left Charleston almost a decade ago.

It had been a terrible day when they were forced to leave that house on Warren Street near the pond. Constance had been three? Four? And had cried as the bank's men carried out the contents of their home into the street, while Arthur stood mute, red-faced, shaking with anger and humiliation. Arthur looked to Maude, holding their sobbing daughter. The look on his face was one of accusation. In that moment, he had hated both of them for being a burden he could not cleanly and quickly detach himself of. That was the moment she knew she had made a terrible mistake.

As much as Maude tried to bury most of the memories of her marriage to Arthur Stapleton, they would occasionally bubble to the surface. She found most of them to be a bewildering mixture of sublime joy, soul-cutting pain and always, half-measured regret. For all of Arthur's faults, his abuses and his carelessness, Maude couldn't fully dismiss her marriage to him as a disaster because she had gained Constance from the union, and Constance had brought so much to her life.

The cab was turning right onto Spring Street, toward the ferry, when Maude's hearing caught an echo of clopping hooves behind them. She had been distracted, but her mind had still been tracking the sounds without her even being aware of it since leaving the train depot. She waited for a few blocks to confirm the distance and speed of their pursuer. Maude knocked on the roof of the cab.

"Miss?" the driver called out.

"If you please, speed up and then double back to this spot in about ten minutes," she said as she opened the wooden doors of the cab. The driver looked confused. His confusion changed to horror as Maude dropped from the moving cab into the darkness and the fog. Maude rolled and felt several of her garments rip as they were strained in ways they had never been designed to endure. She ended her tumble in the treeline at the corner of Perey and Spring Street, beside the large Methodist church. Her driver cursed but did as he was told, accelerating the hansom into the next block.

Maude was up and moving as quickly as her clothing would allow. With a flick of her wrist, the small derringer was in her hand from its concealed sleeve holster. There was a row of private carriages and a few cabs parked along the street before the church. Inside Maude heard voices raised in hymn—"O Holy Night." She moved between the carriages as if she were made out of the fog. The drivers and cabbies waiting for their patrons never saw her, never heard her. The hansom following her cab clattered by, the driver spurring the horse on as his quarry raced from view. Maude waited, measured her breath, and jumped as the cab raced by. She landed behind the driver, who was standing in his seat. She pressed a cluster of nerves in his neck, and he slumped. Maude gently guided the unconscious cabbie down into his spring saddle and tugged on the reins to slow the horse. The cab stopped about halfway up the following block. The doors to the cab crashed open as it rolled to a stop. "What the infernal blazes are you doing, man? She's getting away!" Alter Cline shouted as he popped up from behind the doors. The reporter found himself staring into the barrel of Maude's gun.

"Yes," Maude said, "she is."

"Miss. Stapleton," Cline said, "I assure you, I mean you no ill intent, I merely wanted to—"

"How did you find me again, Mr. Cline?" Maude asked, the gun not wavering. "I was certain I eluded you."

"You did," Alter said. "Quite completely. Your skills at the art of camouflage border on the preternatural, to be sure. I have, however, made a career of seeking out people who do not wish to be found. If you can't locate your quarry, then you look at those things they cannot fully control or hide, like their methods of egress from the environment."

"The cabs," Maude said, smiling a bit in spite of herself. "You watched the cabs."

"When I saw a cab departing that I had not noticed a fare entering, I assumed it contained you. I was correct," he said, pointing at the derringer, "obviously."

"You have to stop this, Mr. Cline," Maude said, "before you get hurt."

"Do you intend to murder me to keep your secrets, madame?" Cline asked. "If so, I assure you I have preparations in place. My editor in New York will shortly be in receipt of correspondence that details your exploits on the train, as well as what I do know of your identity—Maude Stapleton, formerly of Charleston, but having resided in the frontier mining town of Golgotha, Nevada, for the last decade. You are the daughter and only child of Martin Anderton, the shipping magnate and captain of commerce, and the late Claire Cormac-Anderton, governess and leader in the women's suffrage movement. You have one child, a daughter named Constance, and were widowed almost two years ago when your husband was murdered in Golgotha. You also possess extraordinary abilities of an as-yet-unknown origin."

The gun seemed to disappear into thin air with a flick of Maude's wrist. "You know all that about me after just a few days?" Maude said. Alter smiled.

"And you like your coffee black and your tea with honey. If anything untoward happens to me, madame, I assure you all of my lurid assumptions and conjectures, along with your identity, will find their way to print. Neither of us wants that. I much prefer the truth."

"The truth is you have sent no such correspondence. You're an excellent bluffer, Mr. Cline. Remind me not to play cards with you," Maude said, climbing down from the driver's seat. Her own cab was rapidly approaching from the other direction.

"Supper," Cline said.

"Pardon me?" Maude said. Her cabbie pulled the horse to a stop opposite Cline's cab on the street.

"Supper," Alter repeated. "Please allow me the pleasure of your company at supper. We can discuss all this further. I want to hear your story of how you came to possess these miraculous talents, and I give you my word nothing will go into print unless you allow it."

Maude narrowed her eyes and cocked her head. "You . . . you do realize I just had you at gunpoint a moment ago?"

"Yes."

"And now you're asking me to . . . supper."

"Yes," Cline said. "I'll be staying at the Mills House downtown. You can contact me there."

Cline climbed down from his coach and offered his hand to Maude, assisting her, as she climbed back into her own cab.

"You are the second strangest man I've ever met," Maude said.

"I'd hate to meet the strangest," Cline said.

"Yes," Maude said, "you would. No more following. I'll be in touch. Good evening, Mr. Cline." She nodded to the driver and then closed the cab's double doors. The cab rolled away.

The trip across the river by ferry was uneventful. The roads out to Folly Beach were rougher, and the cab bumped along, but Maude didn't even notice the jostling. She could hear the waves, smell the sea. She felt her anticipation grow; she was almost home. They had passed several estates and plantations, but for the last twenty minutes, the trip had been through wilderness. The fog rolled in over the dunes, and Maude could almost picture it drifting across the ocean.

Maude had been nine when she had first traveled this road, when her

father's work took him out of town and he informed her she was to be staying with her great-great-great-great maternal grandmother.

"How many 'greats' is that, Father?"

Martin Anderton had laughed. "Apparently, she's older than Moses," her
father remarked. "I'll fetch you as soon as I return, Maude; it won't be so
bad, dear."

The coach banged along the rutted road, bringing Maude back to the here
and now. They cornered a hill, and through a line of palmetto trees, she got
her first glimpse of the estate in over a decade wreathed in fog and shimmering in the moonlight off the ocean. It was called Grande Folly, it had
belonged to Gran, and she had left it to Maude. As a child, arriving that first
time, Grande Folly looked to Maude like a magic castle. In some ways it was.

The road smoothed as they passed the gateposts, from ruts to cobble-
stones. Bald cypress trees tangled in Spanish moss lined the drive. Maude
could see the lights were on in the manor house; Christmas candles flickered in every window. The cab slowed and stopped before the large stairs to
the porch that ringed the house.

"Here you are, miss," the driver said, opening the cab's door for her, and
offering a hand to help her down. Maude stepped down, not entirely in the
present. Over thirty years ago, she had stood here, deposited by her father's
employee—Martin was far too busy to ride out with Maude. She had looked
up at the front doors and seen them swing open, just as they were now. A
black man in shirtsleeves and a vest, handsome and clean shaven, had smiled
at her and knelt on one knee to meet her gaze with wise, kind eyes.

"Hello Miss Anderton," he had said, "my name is Isaiah. Welcome to
Grande Folly . . ."

"Miss Maude?" It was the same voice, the same man standing at the open
doors, only he was in his sixties now. However, the eyes were as full of kindness
as they had been all those years ago when he had put a frightened girl at ease.

Maude rushed up the stairs and hugged Isaiah tightly. He laughed and
hugged her back. "Welcome home, little girl," Isaiah Gaines said. "You have
been away far too long."

Maude paid and dismissed the cabbie. She insisted on carrying her own
bag up the stairs, across the porch and into the grand foyer. The house didn't
smell exactly the same as it had when she had been a child. There was the
smell of well-cared-for age, wood oil, but the hint of peppermint and sweet

pipe tobacco were gone from the air. It occurred to Maude that she had always associated those scents with Gran without ever realizing it until now.

"I'm sorry for the timing of my arrival," Maude said to Isaiah as she looked around the room and absently touched old, familiar things, all exactly where they should be. "I hope I didn't disrupt any family plans for the holiday."

"Not at all," he said. "Winnie and Thomas arrived earlier this week. Ella, earlier today. We were sitting down to a bit of dinner in the kitchen."

"I'm so sorry to have disturbed that," Maude said to Isaiah. "Please get back to your meal. I know my way around." He silenced her with a simple gesture.

"It's the first time all the children have been able to make it home since their mother passed," Isaiah said. "You arriving now is perfect, Maude. Now, all the children are here. Please, join us."

Maude had often eaten in the kitchen during her college days. She had to disguise herself as a man to attend the College of Charleston. Her father thought she was off at an exclusive ladies' finishing school that Gran was paying for. Maude would come home from classes to her usual brutal training regimen under Gran's hawkish regard, and then sometime well after dark, she'd stagger into the kitchen to eat. Gran often joined her; Isaiah and his wife, Winnie, were always there, with enough food to feed a starving army. They would sit at the old wooden table and she would tell them about her professors and all the wondrous new books and ideas she was being exposed to. They would talk, argue, laugh. When Maude thought of family, of home, and the secure feeling those words were supposed to engender inside you, she always thought of that old kitchen table at Grande Folly.

Winnie, Isaiah's oldest, named for her mother, was the closest to Maude's age. She was married and lived in Charleston. She had brought her husband, a local crabber, and their children to dinner as well. Their older children helped corral the younger ones. Isaiah, the beaming grandfather, had one of Winnie's kids on each knee, bouncing them.

Thomas, Isaiah's only son, was attending Howard University and talked a great deal of his desire to go on to medical school.

"If they won't take me here, I'll go overseas," Thomas said. "There are schools in Europe and Britain that accept Negro students. I'll find one."

"Maybe you could find you a nice girl while you're looking, 'doctor,'" Thomas's sister Ella said. Everyone but Thomas laughed. "Physician, heal thyself!"

Ella was a few years younger than Thomas and had done well for herself in New Orleans, acting as a tutor at the McDonogh School and choir director for St. Augustine's Church.

"A good woman would straighten you out, Tommy," Winnie said, jabbing a fork in her brother's direction, "a few children . . . I'm sure Father would like someone to carry on the family name."

"Don't get me mixed up in all this," Isaiah said.

"There will be time enough for all that nonsense once I've completed medical school," Thomas said. "Right, Maude? Tell them. You've got a family and you own your own business back in Golgotha."

Maude glanced across the table to Isaiah, who was lifting one of his giggling grandbabies into the air. She arched an eyebrow.

"Family can be . . . wonderful," Maude said, gesturing to the playing, laughing, boisterous children, to everyone around the table. "I wouldn't trade having Constance for anything in this world, but there are things I want to accomplish for myself, just for me. If you have a dream, Thomas, you chase it, don't you dare let it escape. The family that matters, you'll find them on your way, and they'll help you get there. You'll be a great doctor, Thomas, and you have a wonderful family already around this table."

Thomas nodded. "So do you," he said to Maude.

Isaiah rested his grandson on his knee and hefted his glass to the assembled table. "To family, real family," he said, "here and far away. Never forgotten."

Everyone raised their glasses. "To family," they all said.

Later in the evening, the children were all finally wound down and asleep in the guest rooms, excited for the Christmas dawn. Isaiah's children, one by one, bid their leave of Maude and their father in front of the roaring fireplace in the manor's parlor.

"You met a fellow in that one-horse town in Nevada," Isaiah said when they were finally alone. "Written all over your face, young lady."

Maude laughed.

"Yes," she said, "I suppose it is. So much for self-discipline. You'd like him, I think. Gran would have loved him."

"He have a name?" Isaiah asked.

"Actually, no," Maude said. "He calls himself Mutt." Isaiah frowned.

"Shabby name," he said. "Sounds like trouble."

"He is," Maude said, "but he is one of the most noble souls I've ever met."

Isaiah sighed, "He best be if he intends to court you, young lady. You love him?"

"Yes, desperately," Maude said. "It's terrifying."

"That's the best kind," Isaiah said, sipping his brandy.

They were silent for a time. The fire filled the silence with snapping and popping.

"Why didn't you go tonight to fetch Constance from your father?" Isaiah finally asked.

"I wanted to," Maude said. "I wanted to get her back from him right now. But in the eyes of the law, I'd be a criminal."

"We both know what Lady Anne would have said about that," Isaiah said. Maude chuckled.

"'To hell with man's laws,'" Maude said. "Spoken like a true pirate."

"All the men and women who worked and lived here at Grande Folly, my father and his father before him, were all free men," Isaiah said. "They worked hard, got a good wage for that work and a share of the profits from their labor. Most of them came from the slave coast, like my granddad, no family left there, their whole lives stolen away. Lady Anne had freed them. She hated having to hide that for so long, but in these parts, if they had known we were free, they would have burnt the whole place to the ground and hung all of us if they could. Lady Anne could whip any man you care to name, but some ugly things are bigger than men and you can't lick them in a fair fight.

"She hated that it was a crime to teach us children to read and write; she did it anyway. There are plenty of laws that need to be thrown on that fire there, Maude. It would take the law here a long time to find you out on the frontier." Maude shook her head.

"The frontier is shrinking, ending, with that railroad," she said. "One day, the frontier will be like," she gestured about the elegant room, "all this."

"It's a sad notion," Isaiah said. "The world needs some wildness in it; people need it too."

"An outlaw life is no life for a fourteen-year-old girl," Maude said. "Besides, I'm tired of having to bargain for my life with people who have no damn business telling me what to do. I intend to get custody of my daughter back legally, in public court. I intend to gain my inheritance back, including this house. I'm going to war, Isaiah. I'm getting back the rest of my life."

Isaiah looked into the fire for a time. "I see my son so eager to become a doctor, so determined, and in the back of my head I worry about all the hatred, and anger, and disgust he's going to have to face. Even if he's the best and the brightest in his class, even if he deserves it more than any other fella, he still might never get to do what he loves. I understand wanting to get it all back, Maude, just for yourself, just to say, 'I own all of me, not you.' Just be careful. Even though things change, words change, it gets a little better, the people who run this world still see you and I as commodities, not persons. Hell, they may never see us as persons. You go to war with them, Maude, you go to war with their world."

"I have a strategy," Maude said. "I'm using all the skills, all the lessons Gran taught me. I'm scouting out the enemy, learning their strengths and weaknesses, marshaling my own forces and gathering my allies. I've chosen my general, and when the time comes to battle, it will be on my terms, not theirs."

They were silent again for several minutes.

"I certainly hope that once you own the estate, you keep the old caretaker on," Isaiah finally said. Maude reached over and took the old man's warm, leathery hand.

"It wouldn't be home without him," she said.

Dawn balanced on the crumbling ledge of night. Constance Stapleton awoke fully aware of a presence in her room. She reached instinctively for her throwing knife under her pillow, but it was gone.

"A few months of easy living and you've already started getting sloppy," the voice at the foot of her bed said.

"Mother!" Constance said, jumping up and embracing Maude, holding her tight. Maude kissed her daughter gently on the forehead and cheek. Constance resembled Maude strongly, with long, thick brown hair with a touch of red-gold that fell to her shoulders, a slight build and pale skin. Her mouth was small, with full lips, and her eyes were her father's—large, brown and full of mischief and intelligence.

"I missed you," Constance said, not letting go of Maude. "I dreamed you would come, I knew it."

Maude looked over her daughter's shoulder and saw the collection of tonic bottles and envelopes of medicinal powders beside the bed. Constance noticed her gaze.

"They are getting worse, the dreams. I . . . don't sleep very long, or well, anymore."

In the year prior to Maude's father taking Constance from Golgotha, the girl had begun to develop powerful and horrifying prophetic dreams. The dreams were always set in a vast ancient city made of bones upon a great grassy plain, buzzing with insects and sweltering with heat. Maude assumed that the dreams were a side effect of the drastic and supernatural action she had taken to save Constance's life two years ago.

"The only reason I left with Grandpa was because I dreamed that I had to," Constance said. "If I don't follow the dreams or if I try to change them, terrible things happen to the people in them. I'm sorry, Mother, I had to go."

"I understand, darling," Maude said softly, pulling Constance back to her. "It's all right, I'm not angry. I missed you."

"I missed you too," Constance said. "Are you here to take me home?"

"Yes," Maude said, "but not yet. I need you to keep it secret that you have seen me, that you know I'm here. Grandfather Anderton mustn't know yet."

Constance nodded.

"I will, Mother," Constance said. "He won't know, but the others know we're here."

"Others?" Maude asked.

"From my dreams," Constance said. A strange calm came over her face and her eyes seemed to lose focus for a moment. "They are coming for me, to take me back to the bone city, to Carcosa."

"No one is taking you away from me ever again," Maude said. Constance's eyes cleared, and she clutched her mother tightly. "I promise you that, my sweet girl."

"They will take you away from me, Mother," Constance said. "They intend to kill you if you get in their way."

"Let them try," Maude said. "Nothing in this world or any other will keep us apart. I swear it, Constance." Maude led her back to the bed and tucked her in. "Try to rest, darling," Maude said, kissing her daughter's forehead. She handed the throwing knife back to Constance, who stuck out her tongue as she took the blade and secured it under her pillow again. "And then four hours of mindfulness training to sharpen those senses, young lady." They hugged one more time, tightly, so tightly.

"I love you, Mother," Constance said.

"I love you, dear," Maude said. "I'll be back for you, remember that. Merry Christmas, darling."

"Merry Christmas, Mother."

Even the arriving dawn did not see Maude leave.

5

The Eight of Cups

The middle of the Atlantic Ocean
June 26, 1721

The main deck of the *Lough Sheelin* was quiet except for the sounds of the waves lapping against the hull, the snoring of the sleeping crew and the occasional coughs or hoarse whispers of the men who were awake, crewing the ship and manning the midwatch. The ocean sky was clear of clouds, and the stars were scattered from horizon to horizon. The voyage since leaving Jamaica had been uneventful.

The *Lough Sheelin* was a brig out of Ireland. She had been doing the run between the West Indies and the slave coast of Western Africa for several years now. She had been light on crew when she arrived at Port Royal but had gotten underway with a full complement of sixteen men—well, fifteen men and Anne Bonny.

Anne, still disguised and traveling under the name Andrew Cormac, rose from her sleeping spot on the deck as quietly as she could. Anne had deliberately chosen a spot closer to the rails and farther back toward the poop deck, because she knew what she had planned for tonight.

"Who's there? Cormac, that you?" one of the watchmen called.

"Aye," Anne replied, "takin' a piss." Anne moved toward the rail and back, out of view of the watch and still hidden from the helmsman as well. She feigned staggering a bit, cussed, and rapped on the side of the captain's cabin as she did. She made a show of pretending to piss, but what she really wanted to do was free her breasts from the tight cloth binding them. She was making milk to feed her absent boy, and her chest ached in protest at being pinned down. She tried to ignore the sensation and continued acting like she was relieving herself over the rail, in case someone was spying, but she was pretty sure no one was. On a ship, if you kept your tongue, did your job well and didn't stir the pot, everyone left you be.

On cue, she heard the door to the captain's cabin creak open, then the thud of boots on the deck. "You there," a voice with an Irish brogue said, "Cormac, isn't it?"

"Aye, Captain," Anne replied, fastening up her trousers and turning.

Captain Will Curran was slight of build, but he made up for it with fierce hazel eyes that could stare down a pirate twice his size. His hair was brown. His cheeks were covered in pox scars that he hid as best he could behind a scrub of beard. "You told me you've some knowledge of the merchants we'll be dealing with in Badagry, yes?"

"Aye, sir," Anne said.

"Step in here a moment," Curran said. "I want to discuss a few things with you."

"But, Captain, we've only got a few more hours of shut-eye, could it wait till . . ."

"It cannot, Mr. Cormac. Now, if you please," the captain said. He retreated into his cabin. Anne spat over the rail, cussed under her breath, followed him in and shut the door.

The cabin was lit by a small brass oil lamp of a fashion from the Holy Lands in the East that sat on the table in the room. The table was covered with charts, parchment, an inkwell and quills, the remains of the captain's dinner, a half-full bottle of wine and Curran's sextant.

"What the hell was all that?" Curran asked, dropping into his armchair. Anne snatched up the bottle of wine off the table.

"You know a single Jack Tar who wouldn't bitch a bit about the captain keeping him from forty winks, and I'll show you a lad soon to be marked as shark bait, and I don't need that, Willy." She pulled the cork out of the bottle with her teeth and drank deeply from the bottle. "As it is, they're liable to think you're giving poor old Andy a good runnin' through."

Curran leaned forward in his chair. "If the crew knows I brought a woman on board, Annie, I'm the one looking at trouble." Anne laughed and sat in the other chair.

"Hell, Willy, they find out who I am, they're gonna make me the sodding cap'n." She took another drink and continued. "I think a few of the old salts might suspect me but not enough to make a sound about it. Besides, we're less than two weeks from port. Then we part company until you get me home to Charleston."

Curran nodded. "As long as you bring me back enough of this fortune you're headed off after to justify me waiting about and not filling my hold up with slaves."

"Slaving is foul work, Willy," she said. "You ain't got the heart for it. Besides, have I ever broke my word?"

"Too often to count," Curran replied. Anne burped softly and handed him the empty bottle. "But you always show back up and make it good, so, I'm willing to stretch my neck out a bit for you, Annie." Curran's eyes brightened a bit. He focused a moment too long on her face, and then his gaze ran over her body.

"Don't go thinking about stretching anything else out but your neck, m'lad," Anne said. "This is business. I passed a soddin' baby outta my hat not too long ago, and it felt like a peggin' cannonball, so the last thing on my mind right now is basket-making."

"Aye," he said, sitting up in his chair. "Just business, Annie." He pointed to the odd box in the corner, next to his own chest. "Now what about this cursed thing you needed to get at that required this whole duplicity in the first place?"

Anne knelt by the chest. The box had frayed rope handles on either side, and the wood was old and worm-eaten in some places. The whole thing was painted in strange, simple symbols. There were spirals, a legion of monstrous silhouettes made up of different parts of animals and tiny stick-people with spears raised against the horrors. There were other symbols, too, a wide circle made of what looked like, perhaps, femur bones, and a silhouette of exaggerated femininity that seemed to be guardian of the circle and the warrior figures. An angry sky figure, fist raised and rays of light emanating from his featureless face, looked down on the pictograph. The imagery was thin in its lines, and Anne felt a faint but painful pressure behind her eyes if she concentrated on the images for too long.

"Why do you say cursed?" Anne asked as she examined the worn bronze clasps that held the box shut.

"Because," Curran said, "sometimes at night, I swear I hear . . . sounds coming from that box, voices speaking in some tongue that makes me ill to try to listen to. Growls, like great beasts, hissing like a serpent and . . . laughter, children's laughter."

Anne looked over to Curran. She had known this man through squall, mutiny and battle. He didn't scare easily. Curran swallowed. "What is this thing, Annie?"

"The map to our gold," she said, snapping the clasp on the box open and lifting the lid. The ancient hinges groaned like they were in pain as the chest gave up its secrets.

The interior of the box was also covered in strange pictographs. The box looked like it was about half full of sand. She carefully slid her hand into the powder. It was cool to the touch and it felt like it had larger particles in it, like fragments of shell.

"What's in there?" Curran asked, bringing the lamp closer to chase away the shadows. Anne could now see the substance was gray, as was her hand. The disturbed dust raised a small cloud that remained within the confines of the box. Anne carefully examined her covered hand and sniffed furtively at it, wrinkling up her nose.

"I think it's bone dust," she said. "A few chips, but mostly very fine."

"Bones!" Curran muttered and crossed himself. "What manner of necromancy have you brought onto my ship, woman?"

Anne ignored him. She slid her hand back into the box and began to root through the grisly material. Her hand caught the edge of something solid and vaguely cylindrical. The ship rose a bit, and the hull creaked. It felt like the *Lough Sheelin* was hitting a rough patch of water.

She lifted a bone from the dust; it looked to be a human femur. It was painted with the same odd symbols as appeared on the box. Curran uttered a curse to himself under his breath. She examined the bone more closely. It was old, chipped and yellow. A cut line ran around the circumference of one end of the bone, just below the flared and knobby ball-like head. Anne carefully took the head and pulled it away from the rest of the femur. There was a pop, and the end came off, like the seal on a message case. The lamp's flame flared then fluttered, almost going out. The large aft windows in the cabin began to shudder and hum as a great wind shook them. Curran frowned at the change in the weather. Anne pulled the tightly wrapped cloth within the bone case free. As she did something fell from the case. It dropped into Anne's palm. It was a ruby, roughly the size of a single pea.

The ship lifted then dropped with a loud crack as the waves slapped the hull. Anne clutched the ruby tight and steadied herself against the odd box. Curran stood, bracing himself on the bulkhead. "What the blazes! I think we've hit a blow," he said. There was insistent thudding on the cabin door.

"Cap'n, Cap'n, come quickly, sir!" the hoarse voice on the other side of the door shouted above the rising din of waves crashing. Curran snuffed out the lamp, grabbed his coat, and threw open the cabin door. Anne stuffed the cloth and the ruby into her shirt and followed him out.

The sound of the storm was everywhere. The crew was racing about, doing their jobs, battening down the hatches as massive cresting waves crashed onto the deck. Other men frantically prepared to furl the sails, in anticipation of the captain's orders to ahull, drop anchor and wait out the storm. The crewmen who had drawn the odious duty of being bilge rats hurried below deck to make sure the *Lough Sheelin* didn't take on too much water. A few men clutched the rails, praying or making hand gestures to ward off evil.

Curran reached the conn and grabbed the grim-faced helmsmen by the shoulder. "Where the hell did all this come from? Why didn't we get a warning? I swear, if Hennessy was drunk again on watch, I'll shoot him myse—"

"No sir!" the helmsman shouted as a massive wave spilled over the rails. One of the men who had been praying screamed. The wave, like a massive claw, ripped him from the deck. In an instant, he was gone. "There was no warning, sir. Hennessy is dead—a wave took him out of the crow. No clouds, no front. The sea was smooth as you please . . . then, it just rose up all about us, sir. Ain't natural, Captain, not one bit."

Anne had rushed to the main deck to see if she could spot any of the men overboard, but there was nothing but another black foaming wave rising above the deck, peaking, falling with a roar. She hugged the rail tightly, locking her arms as the ocean tried its damnedest to claim her. There were seconds she was under the cold, salty water, feeling it pull at her, trying to pry her loose. Then she was breathing air again. Her nose stung from the salty froth, but she was alive. She spit at the dark waves. "Not today, your majesty, not bloody today!"

There were screams and shouting behind her. She turned to see several more of the crew were gone, claimed by the storm. She looked skyward, expecting to see brooding storm clouds muscling the stars from the sky; instead what she saw didn't seem possible. There was a darkness blotting out many of the stars, but it wasn't clouds. It took her mind a moment to process what the shape looked like, what it was moving like. In that moment, she understood why the sailors had been frozen in fear, praying.

The dark shadow blocking the starry sky was the ocean itself, raised up, looming over the *Lough Sheelin,* and taking the form of a woman, a giant figure made of seawater.

"What sea devil is this?" Curran shouted. "Step lively! Gilfoy, man the swivel gun!"

"What's grapeshot gonna do against that giant, Cap'n?" the terrified crewman asked as he and his powder monkey on the gun crew staggered over to the small cannon and hefted it, its fork-like mount and a small cask of powder toward the starboard rail the creature was facing.

"Just do it!" the captain barked. A massive hand made of water slapped against the hull, and the whole ship tipped, almost capsizing onto its side. Anne saw the water giant's other hand greedily pulling shouting, begging, horrified men from the main deck.

"Mmuommiriiiiii!" the giant bellowed in a distorted voice made out of thunder and fury.

The *Lough Sheelin* righted herself, and Anne let go of the rail. She had seen water spirits before in her more bizarre travels, but never something like this. "Mmuommiriiiiii!" the thing called out again and raised a fist the size of the ship's main deck to bring down on the vessel. The cry the spirit let loose sounded oddly familiar to some part of Anne's mind, *Mmuommiri . . . what the hell? Where did you hear it? Think, think, damn you.*

"Dear Lord preserve us!" she heard one of Gilfoy's gun crew call out as a massive fist of seawater smashed into the hull at the waterline. The world became dark and muted as Anne went below the water again. The sea clawed at her throat and lungs; she felt the slippery wooden deck under her feet give way and she was floating in the black water, feeling the ocean steal her heat as it stole her breath. With all her will, all her fading strength, Anne flailed out for anything to hang onto. Her fingers found and clutched a halyard line. Her heart thudded in her ears, like drums.

The water receded grudgingly. Anne, on her knees, choked and coughed as she found the deck beneath her again. She looked up and saw the angry elemental preparing to strike the ship again. In her waterlogged ears she thought she heard Curran shouting orders. A horrible thought stabbed at her, and she reached into her wet shirt and felt where she had placed the cloth and the gem from the bone case. Both were still tucked snug against the now-soaked wrap she was forced to wear. Both were still there, and to her astonishment, the cloth was completely dry.

She touched the ancient cloth that was currently the only dry thing for probably a hundred miles. The name the giant was calling out, she had heard it before. From a Haitian woman, dressed in red and white, Anne had met in Cap-Francais. The woman said she was a witch, had said that name—Mmuommiri—was old, a name from the homeland, from Africa. *"A powerful spirit of the water,"* she had said. *"She is a guardian of prosperity, a healer, an avenger. She can be many things, as the sea can be many things to those who travel her. Sailors court her and curse her. Here, we call her Mami Wata, and as a sailor, you would do well not to anger her. . . ."*

"Hell!" Anne shouted as she scrambled across the tumbling deck toward Curran's cabin. "Damn it all to hell!" The watery fist came crashing down, water surging everywhere, as Anne tumbled into the dark cabin along with the rushing waters. The ship almost capsized again, tipping dangerously close to the water's surface. The ocean tore into the room as the aft windows exploded. It hurried across the floor, retreating some as the ship righted itself. Anne reached the symbol-covered box and put her hand on it. It was dry, untouched by the water.

There was a terrible creaking—the sound of wood straining to its limit—and Anne was certain that the *Lough Sheelin* couldn't take much more pounding. She pulled out the still-tightly-wrapped cloth and the flawless ruby and slid them back into their bone case. She heard shouting outside but ignored it and quickly sealed the bone tube. She laid it back into its bed of ancient dust.

"My most sincere apologies, Mami Wata," Anne said in French, as she slammed the box shut. There was a rumble outside, the spirit's eerie voice full of anger and frustration, fading as if it were being pulled apart by the very wind that carried it. Waves broke and ran over the deck, and the ship shuddered from the relatively mild impact, but the hull held, and she did not capsize. Some water streamed through the open door onto the cabin floor. Not a drop dared to come near the painted box.

Anne slumped onto the wet floor, coughing, sniffing and then, quite uncontrollably, giggling. Finally, she lay still and listened to the sound of voices out on the deck, the gentle rocking of calm waves lapping against wood and the sound of her own heart, still thudding away in her chest.

Curran, silhouetted in the door of his cabin by the now-returned star-light, spoke softly into the darkened room. "We just lost eight good men. I'll get you to the slave coast as we agreed, Annie," he said. "Then we're quits, you and I. I'll keep that abominable box in the middle passage hold, below, and you will not touch it again until you, and it, are far, far from my ship. Do you understand? I don't want any treasure, I don't want anything that comes from such dark sorcery, anything with such a high price."

Anne rolled onto her back with a splash, her eyes closed. She softly patted the side of the marked box. "If you say so, Willy" she said. "More for me."

6

The Moon

Charleston, South Carolina
March 10, 1871

The letter from Golgotha arrived at Grande Folly. Maude had been at the mansion for some time, planning her campaign to reclaim Constance and her fortune. Isaiah brought the letter to her as part of a packet of correspondence. Maude had been making numerous inquiries seeking information and potential allies in her upcoming action against her father and his rather formidable resources.

The letter was in a simple brown envelope, the handwriting partly obscured by the ink of the postal stamps. Her heart stopped listening to her brain; instead it hammered in her chest faster, like she was running for her life. It was a lovely feeling to just let your heart beat as it wished, just like everyone else.

She ignored the other mail and all her papers, all her tactics and goals. She held the letter in her hands. Sunshine filled her chest and her face, flushing her cheeks, as she read her name written with a careful but unpracticed hand. She knew who it was from before she even opened it. One of the most disciplined human beings on the planet found it hard to draw a breath as she slit the envelope open with her razor-sharp fingernail. She unfolded the pages. It was dated February fourteenth. It read:

Hey Maude,

It's me, Mutt, but then I figure you already ciphered that out, didn't you? If there are any mistakes in this here letter, blame it on Jim and Jonathan, cause they're the ones who helped me with the words and the spelling.

Maude laughed. Mutt had written "fuck ups" and then crossed it out and replaced it with "mistakes." She could hear Mutt's deep voice, moving between smooth and sarcastic, an occasional rumbling growl at times. She saw his crooked grin, yellowed teeth and sharp, straight incisors. Something older than the Devil danced in his dark eyes. Mutt wasn't what you would call a handsome man, but there was something in his appearance that made him striking. He had taken the worst life had to throw at him and never compromised himself along the way, never let the world beat him down. Maude thought he was beautiful.

. . . The town is pretty much back to normal, or what passes for normal in these parts. Malachi Bick hired up a bunch of those Chinese laborers who got cut from the railroad to work on repairing the mess from that little war we had with the cult of cannibals back in November. There was a spot of trouble during the clean-up and rebuild, of course there was, right? I'll tell you about that in a spell.

They did a bang-up job of getting the buildings that got wrecked fixed up and pretty as a picture. Bick's got them working on new construction projects now too, trying to build up the town even more. I don't like it, but I'm not sure if that's because it's more people here—more people that can end up dead or crazy—or if I don't like it because it's what Malachi wants.

Auggie Shultz is working for Bick now, if you can believe that. He's running both the store on Main Street and the mining company store and acting as Malachi's . . . what the hell did he call it, oh yeah, "business manager." Sounds pretty highfalutin, you ask me, but Auggie's still Auggie and he's actually managed to convince some people that Bick isn't a complete son of a bitch. I'm pretty damn sure that was why Bick hired him in the first place, son of a bitch. Sorry, Jim said not to cuss too much in a letter to a lady.

The Shultzes are expecting. Gillian Shultz told me to tell you hey. Auggie's so proud he bust a few of them buttons off his new fancy vest bragging. She's due in September, according to the doc.

Speaking of the doc, that would be Clay Turlough these days. Yeah, I know, it's hard for me to get my head around that notion, too, but Clay's done hung out a shingle and everything, and let's face it, anyone's a step up from the last sawbones we had in these parts. Clay's come up with some tonic that's been helping folks all over. He fixed up Emily Bick with it, got her out of that wheelchair, and it actually caused those scales on old Mrs. Whateley's neck to fade away, which has done wonders for her social life.

If that isn't rattle-snake crazy enough for you, Clay's got him a lady friend these days, and she's living and breathing to boot . . . at least I'm pretty sure she is. Her name is Shelly Wollstone, and she's been doing work as a seamstress around town the last few months. I get a queer feeling about her, Maude, but then I keep thinking, for a body to take up with Clay, she'd have to be a bit peculiar, anyway, right?

Golgotha's still booming. Hell, now we got people coming from all over just to see Clay and get some of his snake oil. Folks from as far away as Hazen, Nightvale and even Desert Bluffs have been showing up. Harry Pratt is making hay all about how fast Golgotha is growing. He's cooking up some kind of a scheme with the railroad to get a dog-leg off the main transcontinental line here. Harry's up for reelection soon for mayor, and he's got competition this time, Daaron Bevalier. That's that old stone-ass Rony's son. I figure Harry thinks getting the railroad here will be a nice feather in his cap and keep him in the mayor's job for a spell longer. Who knows? Crazy white people fighting over who gets to run the asylum.

All that boom is, of course, keeping Jonathan, Jim, Kate and me busy. You figure one sheriff and three deputies would have their hands full most places with this many people, but especially here in Golgotha. You, better than most, know it ain't just drunks having a go, or some cattle-puncher who decides to slap leather with a gent in the saloon. Nope, we got that special kind of trouble that only seems to pop up here.

Give you a for instance. Like I mentioned before, in late January, the construction and clean-up crews around Golgotha started having men disappear without a trace. Me and Jonathan looked into it and discovered something peculiar in the debris of all the busted-up buildings. They looked like some kind of nests. They were big enough to hold something larger than a man and made out of shredded wood chips—like something had chewed up the wooden beams and spit them out. The whole mess was held together by some kind of glue-like sludge. Whatever the hell that stuff is, it stinks worse than a carcass out in the sun, and it glows in the dark, to boot.

The nests we found had shredded clothing and personal belongings of the missing men and cracked and brittle bones. Clay said it looked like something had drilled into the bones and sucked every last bit of marrow out of them. In a few of the nests we found dried husks of skin, like when a snake sheds. To make a long, nasty story short, we found the thing. It was about the size of a bear but moved like it was made out of a greased cloud. Fastest, quietest damn thing I'd seen since that Xiuhcoatl thing slithered into town. It looked kinda like a porcupine mixed with a duck and a lizard. Its bill was real long, narrow and pointed, sharp as hell too. The thing had a second mouth under the bill that could open about as wide as a wagon wheel and was six rows deep in fangs dripping some kind of poison glue.

The only thing that would keep the ugly son of a bitch down was wood from a yucca tree—don't ask how the hell Clay sussed that one out. He said it had something to do with the oils from the woods that it used to make its nests compared to the ones it just nibbled on. So we were finally able to kill it. Clay said the thing was kin to some kind of critter called an "echidna," odd little S.O.B. that lives in Australia. Remind me to never go to Australia.

Me and Jon got out of the scrap with the duck-billed marrow-sucker about how we usually do, banged up but alive. Jim ran things for a spell while me and Jon healed up, and I have to say that boy is a hell of a lawman. Jon thinks so too. He's growing like a weed. He asks after Constance damn near every day, so watch out. If I ever had a pup of my own, I'd want him to be like Jim Negrey. He's a good person, all the way through. . . .

Maude noticed that Mutt had started the next paragraph numerous times and marked each attempt out with slashes of ink. Finally, he seemed to find the words he wanted.

> *. . . I guess you can tell by all the small talk, which you know how damned much I enjoy, I'm hemming and hawing about what I want to say. I asked Jonathan, and he said to just say it plain, like how I cuss out the mayor or Bick, but plain-speaking with you about some things is more frightening to me than facing down a whole gaggle of bear-sized, duck-billed marrow-suckers. Is gaggle right, there? Maybe passel?*

"You're stalling," Maude said to the paper, arching her eyebrow.

> *. . . Yeah, I'm stalling. Well, okay, here we go. Last week, we had a curse running around town that made everyone tell the truth. People were catching the damned thing like it was the sniffles. A place like Golgotha, secrets keep the peace as much as the law does, maybe more. We had sixteen brawls break out, five attempted murders, and two that got the job done. We also ended up with twelve new marriages out of it, and Jon and I have a bet going about how many babies we see show up.*
>
> *We managed to trace it back to a fella who came in on the coach a few weeks back. He was originally from Poland and had this trinket on him that his grandma had given him. It was this bottle with these lights floating around in it. He said the lights were something called a* vjeestica, *apparently some kind of witch, and his grandmother had given it to him to guard when she passed. We wrangled the* vjeestica *back into its bottle. Everyone got back to lying to one another like usual and peace and quiet was restored. I think that lasted about two days.*
>
> *During all the scraping, at one point, I caught the damn curse. I had some straight truth come out of my mouth, truths I keep to myself, for a lot of reasons. Some of them truths were about you, Maude.*
>
> *You know I grew up without a name, which never meant much never mind to me, really. A person is what they do, not some handle. My mother had a name that she called me, and I picked*

my own when I was older. My people hated me and my mother,
on account of who my dad was, and because they were a bunch
of hypocritical assholes. Sorry about the cussing, dammit. They
hated us so much, they eventually chased us away.

When you're alone all the time, you build up these calluses to
keep you safe, to make you and everyone else believe that you're
fine being by your lonesome. My mother never complained once
about being alone, never let me feel cut off or lonely when I was
with her. She died in part out of loneliness, I think. She loved her
family so much, they were such a big part of her, that when they
were all gone, it killed her some and it did it slow.

As a pup, I remember the older boys teasing me about having
no father, during games. I can still remember the first time they
beat the daylights out of me. I can scrap better than most, and
I know how to take an ass-whooping; it's in my blood. I took all
that pain gladly, turned it into rage and anger and used it for a
long time. Truth be told, I still use it, sometimes . . .

Maude closed her eyes for a moment. She saw all the times Mutt had
taken a beating to within an inch of his life, and come up laughing, grinning.
It was the opposite of what she had been taught. To be that dangerously out
of control, to let pure emotion drive you, was to let the enemy win. What
Mutt called a strength she had always thought was a fatal weakness. Gran
had tried to teach her balance between reserve and passion; Gran, herself,
leaning to passion. Gran told Maude several times how leaping without
looking had almost gotten her killed, time and again. It was hard to recon-
cile, because of all the people she had ever met in her life, the man called
Mutt was, without a doubt, the strongest person she had ever known. She
looked back to the page.

. . . Worse than the beatings was the silence, like I wasn't there at
all. Those pained looks and then the quick glance away. I knew,
I knew in my bones when I was young, I was going to walk by myself
all my days and I callused up good and quick. I got real good at it
too. Funny thing is I still see those looks, feel that silence. Don't
matter if I'm a boy in my village or a man in Golgotha, the world
sees someone who don't fit in, don't belong, and they do their best

to either break me down or erase me from their pretty world. Neither one seems to have taken.

I can honestly say I didn't give a damn what people thought of me. That worked out real well for me for a long time. Jonathan was the first—only white man, hell, only man, who I actually liked, actually respected—then Jim, and then you came along, Maude. You caught me completely off guard, turned me around like a weather vane in a storm. I didn't see you coming at all, and you sure as hell weren't expecting me.

Most of the truths I was spitting out under that hex can wait until you're done with all you have to do back East. I think truths should be told close up, share the same air. They can be fragile things sometimes. But the one truth I wanted to tell you, needed you to know now, when you're far away and walking into a world of trouble, is that you tear all my calluses away. You make me care about something.

In a world neither of us fits too good in—and that sure as hell wasn't made for folks like us—you make me feel . . . not alone. No, more than that. Damn, but words are hard, and clumsier than a three-legged mule.

If I could show you the desert at night, let you look up at the moon and feel the blood thunder in your ears and that silver light sing in your body. The night makes you feel like everything is secret, and sacred, burning with the purest life. If I could share that with you, then maybe you'd know how you make me feel. I just wanted you to know you're not alone, either; you're never alone.

You know as well as I do that sometimes, in a tough scrap, you have to use everything you have in you to stay alive, to keep fighting, to get back on your feet and put the other son of a bitch down. If the fight you're fighting takes you to that place, I hope you'll find me there. I always will be.

Git home quick. We miss you. I miss you.

Your friend,
Mutt

Maude held the letter for a long time. She read it again. She folded it carefully along the creases in the paper and slid it back into the envelope. Its

presence in her hand gave her comfort and made her feel connected to
him—the one man in this world who had never let her down, had never
doubted her. The last time she saw him, he had wanted to go with her, willing to step away from his whole life just to support her cause. Maude had
refused his help.

"You think the courts there give any more of a damn about what a woman
and an Indian think is right or wrong than the courts here do?" she had
said. "And I will not steal my own daughter away in the night like some
thief. No, Mutt. I'm going home, back to Charleston, and I'm going to get
my daughter back and my inheritance back, and I'm going to make this
right and make it fair."

Most men would have balked at this—Arthur or her father certainly
would have—but Mutt was silent for a moment, holding her hand, then he
said, "I trust you. I always have. Do what you have to do. If you need me,
call and I'll come running."

She thought again about how even if her plans succeeded, even if against
daunting odds, she won, she might never be able to go back to Golgotha again.

Maude walked to the windows of the study. A cold rain was coming off
the brooding winter sea. A few fat droplets lazily patted against the panes
of glass and streamed down, chasing each other to oblivion. The sky darkened and then rumbled as if in pain. The rain began to fall heavy and fast
now; the sky was bleeding.

"I miss you too," she said.

Her voice was lost in the suffering of the rain.

7

The Three of Pentacles

Charleston, South Carolina
April 3, 1871

Martin Anderton had never learned how to separate his business from his private life, a habit his late wife, Claire, had pointed out to him at every available opportunity. Most men would have never brooked such insolence from their spouse, but as much as Martin had seemed huffed by the interruptions by his beloved, he knew she was right. Sadly, after her passing, Martin had thrown himself fully into his labors. This relentless pursuit of his trade had made him one of the wealthiest men in America and across the sea. However, it had made him poor company, first for his daughter, Maude, and now for his granddaughter, Constance.

"Grandpa, you should really put that away at the dinner table," Constance said. Anderton sat at the far end of the long Chippendale dining table, and his fourteen-year-old granddaughter sat at the other. Anderton scowled a bit at being caught poring over correspondence from his business partners and ship captains at the table. He was suddenly struck by a sense of familiarity. Anderton put the papers down and smiled across the table to Constance.

"I'll have you know, young lady," Anderton began, "that you are the third in a line of beautiful women to tell me the exact same thing at this table. It would seem you share the Anderton women's gift for not being afraid to express yourself."

Constance laughed, and Anderton looked at his soup as if he was only now discovering it. "When did this get here?" he asked.

"About your third grumble and second mutter under your breath," Constance said. "I stopped counting grimaces."

"Yes, well, when you are in business, dear," Anderton said, "work doesn't close up shop at the tick of five. I need to keep making money so I can buy you that pony for your birthday, hmm?"

Constance smiled. "Grandpa, you don't have to do that. I have a horse back home in Golgotha. You do need to eat. You work too much and don't take very good care of yourself."

Martin was a tall man, still imposing even in his late sixties. His hair was gray and worn in a crest-like pompadour, thinning a bit on top. He wore short sideburns and was clean shaven.

Anderton ate some soup and dabbed his lips with a napkin. "Charleston is your home now, dear," he said. "You don't seriously still want to live in that dirty hole of a frontier town, do you?"

"It's where I grew up," Constance said. "It's my home."

Her grandfather snorted.

"It was a mistake on your late father's part to take you all out there chasing milk and honey when you were so small," Anderton said. "No disrespect to the dead, of course."

"Mother and I have friends there," Constance said. "Life can be hard there compared to here, but it's a good place full of good people, Grandpa."

Anderton rang a small silver bell. Black servants entered to remove the dishes of the soup course and began busily preparing the salad course. "It may very well be, Constance," he said. "However, it's no place for a defenseless woman and her child, alone and without a husband, to live. I hope your mother will return to her senses and come home soon, dear."

Constance knew better than to push the issue any further. They had already had this conversation numerous times over the last few months since she had returned to Charleston with Grandfather. Mother was far from defenseless, and so was Constance, having undertaken the same training as Mother since she was twelve. What exactly was her mother up to since her covert visit Christmas morning? She knew that whatever it was, she had to be prepared.

She had been trying to maintain her training regimen as best she could under Grandpa's roof. It was difficult, to say the least. Back home, in

Golgotha, she had favorite places out in the desert, near the town, to go and practice her skills. Here, it was almost impossible to get enough time and privacy to do so. If she departed Grandpa's house under everyone's noses—which she could do quite easily—her absence would be detected in short order.

Making it even worse, Grandpa had employed two full-time governesses, tasked with the job of "making a proper lady" out of Constance. Miss Anhorn was from New York City and had been a governess to some of the finest families there. She was tall, somewhat raw-boned, and always dressed formally, with her gray hair in a tight bun, and never a stray hair out of place. She was cold and formal with Constance, with pretty much everyone.

Miss Applewhite was a younger, and considerably prettier, lady of the south, with blond hair and honeyed brown eyes. She had taught some of Atlanta's wealthiest scions how to behave in a proper fashion, and she assured Grandpa she could "chase the wildcat" out of Constance. Constance liked Miss Applewhite in spite of her constant disparaging comments about Golgotha. ("Just because you were raised in a wilderness doesn't mean you have to live like an animal, dear. A lady always rises above her circumstances, no matter how dire they may be.") If Miss Applewhite was the carrot, there was little doubt that Miss Anhorn was the stick.

Grandpa was planning her proper introduction to Charleston society through a seemingly endless series of poise exercises, formal dance classes, cooking, needlepoint, speech, music and etiquette lessons, and mock social teas. It was all so silly and pointless. Constance missed doing her high balance work, her escape training, knife catching and of course, her favorite, an education in poisons. All the things Mother had taught her seemed infinitely of more practical use in the real world than the proper way to eat a piece of fruit without causing a scandal.

She loved her grandfather very much, and she knew he was a decent man, just ignorant of the truth that Constance and her mother were more than capable of taking care of themselves and any trouble that came their way. She wondered again why the things she and Mother could do had to remain secret. If Mother only confided in him, trusted him, then they could go home to Golgotha, and Grandpa wouldn't have to worry so much anymore. No, it wasn't that simple. Deep down she knew it. It wasn't just about ignorance; it was about fear.

Constance had enough training to sometimes read the unspoken language people projected with their eyes, their bodies. Each time Grandpa interacted with the servants, most of them former slaves, even if it was only them entering the room, his posture changed, his eyes shifted, he became more cautious. He feared these people who lived in his home and cared for him every day. The fear was so deep under his skin, Constance doubted he was even aware of it himself. That level of fear was instilled at a very early age, like muscle memory, and it was taught, she was certain of that.

That was why it was necessary to keep her gifts a secret. Fear was the most dangerous of all emotions. It made the wise act the fool, the pedantic become unpredictable, uncontrollable. Fear could overcome any training, any plan. Fear was the fire in the forest of the mind.

"These damnable pirates!" Martin growled as he and Constance finished their meal, shaking the letters in his hands. "I have to attend to some urgent business this evening. I am sorry I won't be able to enjoy you playing the piano in the parlor. I understand from Miss Applewhite that you are a very quick study at picking it up."

"I like the piano," Constance said. "I'd rather practice it than learn how to not seem too smart in a conversation with a man."

"Men here are civilized," he said. "They expect a certain . . . level . . . of discourse from the ladies in their presence."

"Yeah," Constance said. "Smile, nod and act fascinated by whatever jaw music comes out of their mouths."

Behind her there was a sound Constance had come to dread. The quiet clearing of a throat. She turned to see Miss Anhorn regarding her with cool aplomb.

"Jaw music, Miss Stapleton? Indeed. And do we use such vulgar colloquialisms in polite company?"

"No, ma'am," Constance said. Martin nodded approvingly as he gathered up his papers. He kissed his granddaughter on the forehead and strode toward the main hall without looking back.

"Very good, Miss Anhorn. Carry on."

Miss Anhorn narrowed her eyes at Constance, still sitting at the table. "Miss Stapleton, do we say 'ma'am'? Is 'ma'am' ever a word we utter from our lips while making 'jaw music,' Miss Stapleton?"

"No, ma . . . no, Miss Anhorn," Constance said.

"It shall take considerable effort, but we will scrub this horrid frontier vernacular from your speech, young lady. I assure you of that. Now go retrieve your slate and write twenty-five times 'I will not use ma'am.'"

"Yes, Miss Anhorn," Constance said, rising from the table. For the thousandth time she hoped her mother would come soon, and for the millionth time she considered putting her poison skills to use on Miss Anhorn's tea.

Alter Cline sat at a table in one of the private dining rooms of the Mills House Hotel. In the few months he had remained in Charleston, he had managed to dig up enough stories on the grand renewal of the downtown area and the newly built federal courthouse and post office to appease his editors back home. When he had told them he was working on a much grander story and needed more time in the field, they had grudgingly agreed.

"*It had best be a sensation, Mr. Cline,*" his editor had said in one of the last telegrams he had received from *The Herald*. "*Or you shall find yourself relegated to opening and sorting correspondence in the mailroom upon your return.*"

Alter sipped his mint julep and reflected on his future life as a postal clerk. The mystery of Maude Stapleton had seemed to be one to which he would never receive a satisfying answer. He had begun writing a romantic fiction over the last few months about a preternatural heroine possessed of all manner of martial and physical legerdemain due to her upbringing as an orphan in a European circus. If he was banished to the realm of unopened postage, perhaps he could sell the novel at least.

The sliding doors to the private dining room slid open. The maître d' gestured through them and Maude entered quietly, thanking the waiter. Cline stood, the napkin in his lap dropping to the floor. Maude wore a shortwaisted bodice and a ruffled and flounced skirt of black and violet. Her long hair was braided, tight, to the sides of her face and back, joining into a braided ponytail. A choker of black lace, with a large oval amethyst hanging from it, adorned her pale throat.

"Miss Stapleton, Mr. Cline," the maître d' announced. He smiled and closed the doors behind him, muting the sounds of the restaurant's public room. Alter pulled Maude's chair away from the table for her.

"You . . . you look lovely," he said. Maude took her seat.

"Thank you," she said, smiling. "It's been a long time since I went out for supper."

"That's a crime," Alter said, returning to his own chair and recovering his napkin. "I am very thankful you contacted me, Miss Stapleton . . ."

"Maude is fine," she said. "I told you that I would. I'm sorry it took some time to do that, but I had quite a bit of work to do first. I am surprised you didn't head back to New York."

"The thought had crossed my—and my editor's—minds," he said. "However, seeing you now, I know I made the right decision."

"I owe you something in the manner of an explanation," she said. "However, before I begin, I must have your word that none of what I tell you will ever see print. Can you do that, Mr. Cline?"

"Alter," he said. "And yes, I gave you my word, nothing sees print unless you allow it."

The doors slid open and a waiter took their order and departed quickly. Maude steepled her fingers and looked across the table to Alter. "So you want to know . . ."

"Everything," Alter said. "How do you perform all the amazing things I've seen you do? How did you come by these abilities, and why do you work so hard to keep them secret?"

"You mean do I spend all my time running around in a mask and thrashing villains," Maude said.

"Well, that's a good place to start," Alter said. "Do you?"

Maude thought for a moment. "Actually, quite a bit more than I thought I did, yes."

"How did you learn to do what you can do?" Alter asked.

"What, like was I orphaned in a circus, or some ridiculous thing like that?"

"No . . . no, of course not!" Alter said. Maude noted he was blushing a bit for some reason. "That would be silly. How did it happen?"

"Slowly," Maude said. "When I was nine, my father's business took him away," Maude said. "My mother died giving birth to me, and I was cared for by a long line of surrogates—nannies, maids, governesses, female relatives."

"That must have been difficult," Alter said, "never getting to know your mother at all. I'm sorry."

Maude shook her head slightly. "My father was very good about telling me about her, even the parts he didn't like, like her work with the women's movement."

"It still must have been lonely," Alter said.

"It was," Maude said. "There have been many times in my life when I've wondered what my mother would have thought of me, of my choices, times when I wished I could have asked her advice."

Maude took a sip of her water and continued. "So I was nine, and this time I was shipped off to my mother's great-great-great-grandmother, Bonnie Cormac. She had an estate on Folly Beach called Grande Folly. That's where I've been staying since I arrived back in Charleston."

"You did that very well," Cline said.

"Pardon me?" Maude asked.

"You changed the subject from how you felt about your mother back to what you thought I really wanted to hear. You don't like talking about yourself or your feelings very much."

Maude paused for a moment. "Our food's arrived," she said a second before the doors slid open and their waiter rolled a cart into the room. The meal was served, and the waiter poured wine to accompany the meal. Once he was gone, Maude continued her story.

"Gran was unlike anyone I have ever known. She treated me like I had a brain in my head. She owned more books than I had ever seen in all my life. I loved living at Grande Folly. I loved her.

"At dinner she would challenge me with questions about religion, about philosophy. She made me think about how women were treated in the world. Often my nine-year-old mind didn't have an answer to the things she'd ask me, and she'd expect me to learn more, to find my answer and defend it the next time the subject came up. She taught me how to think. She told me stories about all the places in the world she had traveled to, the adventures she had had."

"She sounds like she was a suffragette before there was such a word," Alter said. Maude nodded.

"She told me she was very proud of my mother and all she had accomplished in her life. If Gran had possessed the opportunity to, she would have chosen Mother to undertake what she began with me, but by that time, Mother was too old to begin the instruction."

"Instruction?" Alter asked.

"What I tell you from here on you cannot write down or tell another living soul. Do you understand, Alter? This is very serious," Maude said.

"You have my word," he said.

"One morning, before sunup, I was awakened and told to ride out to meet Gran Bonnie on the beach behind the estate. I did, and I found Gran there, watching the waves come crashing onto the sand, waiting for me. She told me a story, a very, very old story."

Maude still remembered that morning, that meeting on the beach, over the roar of the waves. She heard Gran's voice, strong, as she had recited the oath to Maude for the first time.

"*I carry within me the clock of the moon.*

"*The clock of nature, inviolate, unerring.*

"*I carry within me the secret of God.*

"*The power of a new life in a universe of darkness and death.*

"*I carry within me the most powerful of swords.*

"*For my will can overcome any steel forged by man.*

"*And my suffering can overcome any trial of pain or sadness.*

"*For my blood is that of the first woman, she who would not bow down to the tyrant of Heaven and was cast out, called the mother of beasts. She who would not be bride to either Heaven or Hell, but walked her own sharp, lonely path.*

"*It is my birthright, these gifts, this pain, this wisdom.*

"*It is my privilege to understand them and in so doing understand and love myself.*

"*It is my load to carry them, to protect them, to use them in the defense of the worthy and the weak.*

"*And to teach this to others of the blood who live in chains of shame and guilt and fear forged by men and their gods, shackled to them by their own limited comprehension of their divine nature.*

"*This is the secret. This is the load you must bear alone all your days upon this earth. This is the price of truly being free.*"

"I was entrusted with a great power and an awesome responsibility. We call it the Load. My great-great-great-great-grandmother passed these gifts along to me, as they were passed along to her, and as I am in the process of passing them along to my daughter."

"A secret society!" Cline said. "Made up exclusively of women of a single bloodline!"

"No," Maude said. "It's not just my kin. Any woman, anywhere, can be called upon to carry the Load, to become one of us. Mothers tend to pass the teachings to daughters and so on, but it's not something my family started. It began before time was reckoned as we do today, hinted at in myths and legends. It began with the first woman."

"Lilith," Alter said. "She's mentioned in the Talmud, and in the earlier incarnation, the Babylonian Talmud, but the name and the mythology date back to Mesopotamian religion." Maude looked at the journalist and cocked an eyebrow. "My older brother is a rabbi," Alter explained. "Our uncle as well, he's at Congregation Shearith Israel. I was exposed to a lot of religious schooling as a boy. I've always been fascinated by the mystical side of my faith. My uncle said I liked the *assur* a little too much. Guess that's how I ended up a journalist. You like poking about in evil works, this is the job for you. My understanding is that Lilith is described as either a demon or the first wife of Adam, who turned against God and her husband. She is supposed to be the mother of all monsters."

"Don't believe everything you read," Maude said. "I was taught Lilith refused to submit to the will of anyone—man or his gods—and for wanting to be free of the control of others, she was driven out into the world to make her own way. She used her mind and body to survive, honed them to a superhuman edge. We consider ourselves Daughters of Lilith, heirs to her power, freedom and responsibilities."

"A cult of Lilith worshipers," Alter said, rubbing his chin. "All women. And what you do, all the miraculous things you can do, that comes from these teachings of Lilith? You know, even if I did print any of this, which I swear I won't, no one would believe it."

"We don't worship Lilith," Maude said, shaking her head. "The whole point is to be truly free of anyone's and everyone's control of your destiny, save yourself. The teachings give you near-absolute mastery and understanding of your body. It's not magic, but Gran told me it can sometimes seem that way to someone on the outside. There are holy men in the East who can slow their heart, ignore the pain and injury of walking on red-hot coals, and even control their breathing so as to appear dead. There are monks in the Orient who have mastered martial combat that uses their bodies as very versatile and deadly weapons. Not magic, merely discipline, focus and will."

Maude decided Cline didn't need to hear about the Blood of Lilith, about how at the completion of her initial instruction, Maude had ritually drunk from an ancient flask that Gran told her contained the moon-blood of the first woman herself. That blood seemed to fortify and strengthen her body to allow Maude to endure some of the more rigorous aspects of the training. Cline was already swimming a bit from her revelations, and she was certain that talk of ancient mystical blood from a mythological figure would be too much for him right now. Not to mention sometimes it was hard for her to believe it, and she had lived through it.

Maude didn't fully understand what the blood was or how it did what it did. Gran had told her once that she had been given the old iron flask by an African witch, who had instructed Gran long ago. Gran also said the blood forged a link between all those who had drunk it, an unconscious "knowing" of information shared between all the Daughters of Lilith.

The origins of the blood may be a moot point now, Maude thought. Two years ago she had been forced to give Constance a draft of the Blood of Lilith before she was ready in her training to accept it. The desperate measure was to counteract the effects of a hideous venom that Constance had been exposed to—the supposed blood of an antediluvian creature coiled at the heart of the Earth itself, a thing called the Greate Olde Wurm by its nihilistic worshipers.

The Wurm's followers had come to Golgotha and discovered the secret chamber that acted as the seal for their god's prison. They had succeeded in awakening the slumbering monstrosity, which then began literally tearing the world apart as it thrashed itself free.

Maude had given Constance some of Lilith's blood to heal her and then drained the rest of the flask into the well that opened into the Wurm's prison in hopes of subduing the creature and healing the shuddering planet. Far more of the Mother's blood had poured out into the well than was possible for such a vessel, and yet the effort seemed to empty the flask. In the end, the Wurm returned to its eons-old imprisonment and slumber. The world was saved, but the flask Gran had entrusted her with for future generations of the Daughters was empty. The Blood of Lilith was gone forever, and with it the Daughters of Lilith would die out too.

"How many of you are there?" Alter asked, as if he had been reading her mind. Maude took a sip of wine.

"Not many," she said. "A handful in any generation, scattered across the world. I don't know exactly."

"Don't you have gatherings?" Alter asked. "Um, covens, whatever you call them?"

Maude couldn't help but laugh. "You are determined to make us some kind of nefarious cult, aren't you? No, no meetings, no eating babies on the night of the full moon . . ."

"I'm sorry," he said, "I'm trying to understand all this, it's just . . . outside my experience. You seem so, well . . . normal."

"I am," Maude said. "I work, I own a business of my own back in Golgotha. I love and care for my daughter." She held up her wineglass. "I enjoy a good wine, and this one is excellent, by the way. I'm a typical person."

"There is nothing typical about you," Alter said. Maude felt the tension pass between them, read Alter's body language as if he was holding up a sign. She smiled but made sure that she presented nothing that he might interpret as an invitation for more.

"I was told that the only reason all of the Daughters would ever gather together would be some kind of emergency. I've never seen another Daughter of Lilith in my life, besides my Gran."

"She sounds remarkable," Alter said.

"More than you know," Maude said. She had decided that Alter Cline also didn't need to know that on that beach, so long ago, Gran Bonnie Cormac had told nine-year-old Maude that she was in reality Anne Bonny, an ancient, mythic pirate queen.

"So, satisfied? Worth the wait?" Maude asked.

"You're holding back on me," Alter said, "which only leads to grander questions, I'm afraid, but thank you, for being good to your word, and for giving me the truth, even a bit of it."

"It's such a fantastic story," Maude said, "how do you know it's the truth? How do you know I'm not mad as a hatter?"

"I don't believe you'd do that," he said. "I don't have supernatural powers, but I am a damn good judge of character, comes with the job, and you are a very good person . . . and not crazy. I can tell."

"Thank you," Maude said.

"I got the impression you are here in Charleston for some personal reason and that it is causing you some distress," Cline said. "I don't want to pry, but I did make inquiries about your father and I learned that your daughter Constance has been residing at his townhouse here for the last several months. Is there anything I might be able to do to help you?"

"You don't appear to need supernatural powers to perceive things,"

Maude said. "Yes, actually there is a way you can help me, if you don't feel it conflicts with the integrity of your profession."

"A-ha," Alter said, raising his own wineglass, "so the real reason for this little dinner date becomes clear. Well done."

"It's not a date," Maude said, "and you're the one who asked if you could help. I can guarantee you a story, Alter, almost as sensational as 'a secret cult of Lilith worshipers,' and this one you can give to your editors."

"I'm all ears," Cline said, leaning forward across the table.

"Well," Maude said, "I have a few particulars to firm up first. Before I can give you all the details, I need to consult with my attorney."

It was finally starting to feel like spring in Charleston. The morning was warm when Maude took the carriage out from Grande Folly into the city. She had very much wanted to ride a horse in, but Maude decided it might attract undue attention, so she settled for the small, two-wheeled buggy.

She stopped at the same rail passenger depot on Line Street that she had disembarked from when she first arrived back in Charleston in December. Maude was dressed sensibly for the warm weather in a simple pale blue house dress. Her hair was up in its usual bun, and she had seen no reason to carry more than a half-dozen concealed weapons on her for the simple trip.

She paid a young man at the cab stand to mind her carriage and lead her horse to a water trough, while she entered the depot. Maude checked the schedule scrawled on the large slate board near the ticket window. Satisfied that she was on time, she took a seat on one of the long wooden benches that stretched along the backside of the platform wall, making sure to take one as far from a large brass spittoon as possible, and waited for the train.

Within twenty minutes, she heard a long blast on the train's whistle cry out; a few moments later, there was the magnificent rumble of the powerful engine, and then the train came into view. It slowed, and she watched the passenger cars flash by her vantage point. Finally, there was the groan of the brakes and the hiss of the steam engine as it came to rest. Maude stood as the passengers began to disembark and make their way to the platform. It only took a moment to find who she was waiting for.

The woman making her way down the platform was tall and blond. She wore her hair short, to the nape of her neck, and swept back in a very man-like style. Her attire was a conservative gray. She wore a short-waisted Basque bodice and a narrow skirt. Her cuffs and collar were noticeably plain, not trimmed in ruffled lace as was the current fashion. She wore no cosmetics—her ears were slightly elfin in their points, and her fair eyes held a formidable and almost radiant intelligence. Maude saw she carried herself with utmost confidence and authority. Even though she was stepping off the train in a new city, this woman walked without a hint of hesitation or trepidation. The woman noticed Maude, gave a slight smile and approached.

"Miss Stapleton," the woman said, offering her hand in a handshake, "I'm Arabella Mansfield. It's a pleasure to meet you in person at last."

"No, the pleasure is mine, Mrs. Mansfield," Maude said, shaking her hand. "I hope the trip from Iowa was pleasant. Thank you so much for agreeing to come."

"Well," Mansfield said, "it isn't every day you get offered an opportunity to make history."

"You've already made history," Maude said.

"I suppose I did, didn't I?" Mansfield said. "Well then, an opportunity to make history twice, and give some pompous old gasbags a good fright while we're at it. I must admit I'm intrigued by your proposal, Miss Stapleton."

"Maude."

"You can call me Bella," Mansfield said. "I've actually come to prefer Arabella, but it's always hard to shake a childhood name. My brother says 'Arabella' is too 'putting on of airs,'" she said with a laugh. Arabella had very small, white, even teeth. "I must tell you, I have thoroughly enjoyed our correspondence, Maude."

"As have I, Bella. I have a carriage waiting, and I can have someone attend to your luggage."

"Thank you," Mansfield said. "Could you recommend lodgings to me?"

"You are more than welcome to stay at Grande Folly, my family's estate," Maude said, gesturing for a porter.

"You are very kind to offer, Maude," Bella said, "but I think I will need to be as close to the courthouse and city hall as I can possibly be. I have a lot of South Carolina law to review, and some key documents that need a proper examination."

"Of course," Maude said. "I'll make arrangements for you at the Mills House. A friend of mine is already staying there, and I think you will find it to your liking. The dining is excellent."

"Good," Mansfield said, walking toward the exit from the depot. "Well, Maude, this will not be easy, but I already have a few notions on how to proceed. We have quite a bit to do, you and I, quite a few feathers to ruffle. Let's get to it, shall we?"

8

The Magician

Badagry, West Africa
July 8, 1721

If there were a place upon the earth where Hell had pierced the skin of this world and festered, it was the slave market in Badagry. Anne walked through the wide, crowded streets of the three-hundred-year-old town nestled in a lagoon. Badagry was part of the great Oyo Empire of the Yoruba people. While it was part of an ancient, sprawling African civilization, European gold and guns gained more power here with each passing day.

There were a dozen different languages from across the world buzzing in the humid air. Rows of slaves, Africans, captured enemies of the Yoruba or tribute offerings from across the empire, shuffled by in heavy chains, linked collar to collar, with iron gags bolted across their jaws. Men, women and children were hustled to the auction blocks, then out across the Ajara River to the "point of no return," as it was known, where the slave ships were docked. There they would be packed in the holds one atop another, sealed in darkness, and bound for the West Indies and the Americas.

The flesh trade was big business, growing bigger by the day, and Badagry was one of the busiest ports for it on the Slave Coast. Anne had been here once before. She had hated it then. Now, after a year in prison, she was filled with a longing to draw her brace of pistols and shoot the slavers—

European and African both, who were leading this long chain of human misery.

Anne had ditched her disguise once she had taken her curt, and not terribly sentimental, leave of Captain Curran and the *Lough Sheelin*. She had let her hair down and finally freed her bosom from the accursed wraps. She carried the strange, painted box on one shoulder and had a ditty bag with all her worldly possessions over the other.

Anne's gaze caught that of one of the children in a line of slaves. The boy was no older than ten, perhaps, with a look of terror and confusion on his face. The boy walked along in a tiny iron collar, fashioned especially for child slaves. She knelt by the boy, setting her load down and stopping the procession in the process.

"*Akerele,*" Anne whispered to the boy in broken Yoruba. "You may be small, but you must be strong." The child tried to smile behind his iron gag, but the fear shone out of his eyes.

"Move along!" one of the white slavers called out. He sounded Portuguese by his accent. "You're holding up the line, you stupid bitch." The slaver reached for Anne's shoulder. She came up with one flintlock cocked and planted it under the slaver's chin. The other pistol flashed out to cover the Yoruba slaver who was unslinging his musket.

"Think how much your peggin' line will be held up if I take that meat pie you call a noggin off," she said. "You raise that musket, my lad, and I'll put a hole in you too," she called out to the Yoruba, who got the idea and lowered his weapon.

For a moment, Anne thought of ordering the men to unlock the slaves, starting with this little boy. Then she heard the shouting and the thick click of gun hammers being cocked and readied. This was only one link in the long train of slaves being led to the marketplace. There were dozens of slavers, dozens of guns being pointed at her. Even though it meant death, Anne still considered taking at least these two shit-eating carrion with her.

She stepped back, keeping her guns trained on the two slavers. The Portuguese spit at her, shouted out, and the procession began to move again. The boy kept looking at her with pleading eyes until he was swept away in the tide of lost lives. Anne stood there until the line passed her by. It was followed by another and another. It was not the first time in her life she had wished she had the power to fix broken things, and it sure as hell wouldn't be the last.

"Fuck," she said to no one at all.

One of the older inns in Badagry was the Broken Shackle. Anne and her mates had stayed there before, and she hoped that Titus was still the owner of the place. She walked in and heard his booming baritone before she even saw him through the throng.

The inn was packed with sailors and a good number of pirates, since Titus had been one of their number a long time ago. There were no slavers in here; none dared. Titus's reputation preceded him.

"Is that a ghost I'm seeing?" The voice rumbled across the tavern. "Anne Bonny, Queen of the Cutthroats herself, walking back through my door!"

The crowd shifted to make way for the former slave and pirate. Titus was close to seven feet in height, broad and thick with muscles. Ugly raised scars covered his dark skin. Titus shaved his head but maintained a thin beard. He had a gold hoop earring in his right ear, and his eyes were the color of glass. The legends said he sold his soul for revenge against his former owners and that his eyes lost their color because of it. Anne suspected that story might have some truth to it. She knew those eerie eyes could be warm and welcoming, as they were now, or cruel and merciless, as she had seen them in a scrap.

Titus hugged Anne firmly, lifting her up off the ground as she cackled and kissed his forehead. "Ah, get off me, you hulking leviathan," she said, "you'll snap me like a twig!"

He sat her down and shouted to one of the sailors at the bar, "Make way for the lady!" The patron scuttled off, tipping his hat to Anne as he did. "As I recall," Titus said, going back behind the bar, "the last time you and I crossed, you kicked my sorry ass, handily."

"True," Anne said, "but I think you might have grown a wee inch or two since then."

"Aye," Titus said, "in all kinds of places, love."

"You old charmer," Anne said. "Gimme a bottle of port, and is there any chance you have a room open for a weary old hoyden?"

Titus gestured over the bar. "For you, Annie, of course." A young black boy, about twelve, walked up to Titus. "Kalu, take the lady's things up to the third private room," Titus said to the boy in Yoruba.

"Mind the box, lad," Anne said to the boy as he hefted the strange chest and her ditty bag.

"What brings you back here?" Titus asked, handing Anne the wine bottle. "You swore you'd never set foot in Badagry again."

"Aye, and the place is still as big a pesthole as I remember it being," Anne replied. "I've never figured out why you stay here, Titus."

"This land is my home," he said, "and some days I can ease the misery in this place, so that makes enduring it worthwhile."

It was no secret Titus paid a handsome bounty to any pirates who attacked slaving ships and returned their cargo to Africa. Many of the powerful merchant companies that were behind the majority of the slave trade had made several attempts to bribe, then to kill Titus, but he was still here and still in business, lending even more credence to the legend that he was in league with supernatural powers.

"I'm undertaking a little expedition into the interior," Anne said.

"Whereabouts?" Titus asked.

"Not sure yet," Anne said. "Hopefully I'll know before I leave."

"Now that sounds like my Annie," Titus said. "You'll need provisions and bearers."

"Aye, and I think I may need a couple of strong sword-arms to watch my backside," Anne added. "You know anyone I can trust?"

Titus nodded. "I have a notion. He should be here tonight, once he sobers up enough to drink again. I'll introduce you two."

"Thanks," Anne said. "In the meantime—" She snagged up the bottle of port and dropped some Spanish silver on the bar—"I intend to have a bath and try to puzzle something out."

The afternoon sun fell in through the window to Anne's quarters on the second floor of the Broken Shackle. It filtered through the mosquito netting canopy that covered her bed and fluttered feebly in the tepid breeze. The room was small, but after a month at sea, the space and solitude was luxury. She had availed herself of the bath down the hall and paid extra for hot water. She had also paid Titus's boy to go out and collect a few things for her, including a pipe and some tobacco. Now clean, and in fresh, dry clothing, she smoked her pipe and opened the strange marked box once again. Inside, she found the large bone and the small, perfect ruby within, again buried in bone dust. Searching the rest of the box revealed they were the only two items that remained within. She sat at the small table and once again removed the end of the large bone scroll case. The cloth within slid out. Anne paused for a moment, waiting for ominous thunder or some other sting of cosmic displeasure at her actions. Her pistols, oiled and loaded, sat on the table next to her machete, just in case. There was only the hum of the busy town's traffic below and the chittering of life teeming within the jungle.

Anne carefully unfolded the cloth and laid it on the table. It was a map, hand-drawn on very old but well-preserved cloth. She recognized the coastline on the drawing as the western coast of Africa. The only landmark drawn on the cloth map was a crudely drawn circle of bones with a skull above it. It looked to be in the center of the map, the center of the mysterious continent. There were no directions, no distances, no indication of scale. Along the edges of the map were strange symbols, like those on the box. In the upper portion of the map there was a circle with a cross intersecting. It appeared to be a compass rose.

"Well, this is no sodding help at all," Anne muttered, setting the ruby back on the table and taking another drink from the nearly empty port bottle. "The place I'm looking for is somewhere in the middle of Africa. Grand."

She examined the interior of the bone tube case to see if something else was hidden. There was nothing. "Damn it to hell," she said, tossing the bone harshly onto the table. The bone skidded to a stop but knocked the ruby across the cloth. The ruby slid across the cloth, zigzagged of its own volition, and centered itself in the middle of the compass rose's circle. It then slowly moved to the northwest section of the circle and stopped.

Anne reached over to the stone. She picked up the ruby, and then dropped it on the opposite side of the cloth map. The ruby slowly slid across the cloth continent and once again centered itself in the middle of the compass circle. After a moment, it slid to the northwest section of the circle and stopped.

"I'll be damned," Anne said. She lifted up the cloth and held it perpendicular to the table. The ruby remained exactly where it was, as if pinned to the cloth map. She turned and walked toward the window. The ruby slid to the appropriate corner of the compass to compensate for the change in directions. "Witchcraft, then," Anne said. "That never ends very well, my girl, you know that."

She plucked the ruby from the hanging cloth, and it came free effortlessly. She gently placed it on the lower half of the cloth and the stone reattached and climbed the map to make its way to the compass rose once again. Anne celebrated with another drink of the rapidly diminishing port. "We have a map and a destination!" she said, laying the map back on the table. "Now all we need is provisions and a few good swords, and we can be on our way. Witchcraft be damned. I'm the craftiest witch that ever will be!" She finished off the port and collapsed onto her bed. It felt like a cloud in the heavens. She was snoring before the empty bottle thudded to the floor.

It was late into the hot night when Anne descended the stairs to the common room. The tavern was packed and somewhere a fiddler was playing and singing "A Messe of Good Fellows," and the common room was singing along to the best of its drunken ability. Titus and his maids were busy serving up food and drink as quick as they could. The giant owner of the tavern waved to Anne and pointed in the direction of a back table where a single white man sat, his flagon swaying in time to the song. Anne made her way through the crowd and sat on the bench across the table from the man.

The stranger looked to be in his late twenties. He had beautiful and well-groomed, rust-colored hair that fell to his shoulders and a goatee that was trimmed immaculately. His blue eyes were bleary from too much drink. He wore a filthy, torn and tattered blue-and-black tabard over a padded doublet and breeches. A dirk and a slender foil, both sheathed, on a narrow leather belt lay on the table. A wide-brimmed blue cavalier hat with an ostrich plume that had seen much better days lay on top of the sword belt. The man looked up with rheumy eyes at Anne and gave her a dismissive gesture. *"Non, non,"* the man mumbled in slurred French, *"je ne veux pas une pute, surtout si elle est laide. Verre de plus, s'il vous plaît."* He spoke with the accent of a native Frenchman.

"I'm no whore, and I'm no bar wench. You want more drink, then get it your peggin' self," Anne said, sitting down. "I hear you're good with a blade and willing to use it for coin?"

"My apologies," the man said in even more slurred English. He belched loudly and covered his mouth after the fact. "You are correct, *Madame laide.* You have the pleasure of making the acquaintance of *le Humingbird.*"

Anne arched her eyebrows as she grinned. "Hummingbird, eh? Looks more like a drowned goose to me."

She drew for one of her pistols, brought it up to aim at the Frenchman's chest. There was a crash, a blur and the Frenchman's blade was at her throat. He was still sitting. How he had reached the blade and drawn so fast was a wonder. "Now look what you made me do," the Hummingbird said. "I spilt my drink . . . and I believe I may have shit myself."

"You're fast enough," Anne said and slid the pistol back into her belt. The blade was sheathed, and the Hummingbird gestured for one of the bar maids.

"More drink, my lovely . . . and clean pants if you have them."

"Two reals a day, paid in full at the end of our little adventure," Anne said, "and if we come across any booty, you'll get a company share. I'll give you a week's pay up front before we leave Badagry, so you can settle any accounts. We have a deal?"

"*Oui,*" the Hummingbird said.

"Meet me here tomorrow afternoon to discuss particulars. Be sober and have clean pants," she said.

"Is it dangerous, this 'adventure'?" the Hummingbird asked.

"Very," Anne said.

The Frenchman laughed and clapped. "Good, good!" he said. "*Je cherchais quelque chose d'amusant de me tuer.*"

Anne tossed the Hummingbird a small bag of coins. She walked past Titus on her way out of the tavern.

"I like him," Anne said. "He's a crazy bastard, and he's French, the very best kind of crazy."

"They say he was in the King's Musketeers," Titus said. "Something bad happened."

"It usually does," Anne said.

The street outside the Broken Shackle was empty and quiet. The town was quiet except for the night sounds of the wilderness, the ocean and a few dogs barking. From this part of town, you couldn't hear the groans of human misery from the storey buildings and slave warehouses, worse than any prison. The air was thick and hot. Insects buzzed past her face. Anne sat on a wooden bench outside the tavern door and fished out her pipe and her tobacco pouch. She stuffed the pipe, lit it and leaned back against the stone wall of the building.

The stars fluttered in the void like guttering candles, legion across the sable sky, stretching to the edges of comprehension. The sight made Anne ask the question again. How could you have such a sight in the same universe, in the same city, where human beings were chattel, where men bartered in despair and suffering? She knew the answer, had known it since she was a child. It was explained to her clearly in a London alleyway. Some children were even fortunate enough to not see the true face of this world until they'd had a couple of years of peace and innocence, but only a few. She saw the little boy from the marketplace, standing there, naked, terrified, in a tiny iron collar.

By now, her son should be with his grandfather, Anne's father, in America, and he'd be cared for. Anne's father, William Cormac, was possessed of a very short list of laudable traits, but among them was a dogged and cold loyalty to his family. He'd keep the lad safe. He had always wanted a son anyway.

Anne remembered being six, her father's face close to her own, shouting. She was crying as her father cut her hair. William was red-faced as the locks tumbled to the floor. "Boys don't cry, damn you!" he bellowed. "Annie, if you cry, we'll be found out again! We'll have to move again. The fucking solicitor at the firm has kin in Cork! My fucking wife, that vindictive bitch! She has family everywhere, even here in London! They heard about me, about my bastard daughter. I had to borrow the devil's tongue to convince him that I wasn't who he thought I was. Told him of my little boy. You don't want us to have to run again, do you girl? Have your family live like bloody sea dogs, moving from place to place? You don't want to do that to your mother, do you? And to me?"

Anne had grown up on the run, hiding, lying. It was quite the scandal in County Cork when William McCormac had left his good lady wife for a housemaid with his bastard in her belly. Bastard, that was Anne. They'd had to leave the county to avoid the fuss made. But William's wife's family had a long reach and big mouths. The family eventually fled to England where they tried to hide, to live under the name Cormac and pretend that little Annie was little Andy.

Anne, age twenty, looked back and saw her child-self, saw the innocence drain from her eyes with the tears. They were the same eyes as the boy in the marketplace. "We are not McCormacs anymore," her father said, shaking the girl. "We're the Cormacs now, and you, you are our son, Andy. You must bury all those feelings, girl. They'll find us out and they'll hurt you and us, if you're weak. Your name is 'Andy' now, do you understand, 'Andy,' and you are strong and you do not cry. . . ."

And she never did again. Simple.

The truth was the stars were indifferent to the suffering, to the beauty, to people. If there was a god behind the celestial curtain, He didn't care either. In a just universe, all children would be spared the slaver's whip, the greed of men, the rage of sires. The only justice in this life was what you carved out yourself with mind, will and steel.

Anne shouldn't even be thinking about her whelp, shouldn't even think of her father. She had learned the lessons well that day. Well enough to endure the pain of her mother's death when Anne was twelve silently, stoically. Well enough to set fire to the Cormac plantation in South Carolina when Father disowned her for marrying Jim Bonny at fourteen.

Ah, fair Jimmy. She could still see him, skinny as a fickle promise, that crazy grin. He was the most alive person Anne had ever met, and she fell in love with him with every laugh, every dare he challenged her to and every dare he met. Jim Bonny showed her that there was joy in living, in savoring every single moment like it was wine—sometimes sweet, sometimes sour. His love had been a lie, but his lust was the most real thing Anne had ever known in her brief life.

There was no place in her now for tears, or regret, or especially for a child. She was about to undertake the greatest plunder of her career; she needed to focus on that, on the score, or she'd wind up dead.

"You're preoccupied," a voice said, close to her ear. She reacted, springing to her feet, her pipe falling, the brace of pistols out and sweeping the shadows.

"Show yourself," Anne said. A man stepped from the shadows to her right. He was black, a little over six feet tall. His hair was in the style of curled locks and he was clean-shaven. His brown eyes were calm and powerful in their serenity. He wore European clothing—a white linen tunic, dark blue vest, dark breeches and boots. At his belt was a sheathed *Ida*, an elongated, leaf-shaped sword, favored by the Yoruba. A leather bandolier, with three cross-holstered flintlock pistols of differing sizes, was draped across his broad chest. A pair of muskets were slung over the man's shoulder, along with a knapsack and several cured waterskins.

"You won't need the pistols," the man said in perfect English. "I'm here to help you." He paused and regarded her for a moment. "How old are you?"

"Well, aren't you a rude one. I'm old enough. I'm twenty-three," Anne said, lying. "Why?"

"You look closer to nineteen," the stranger said. "I understand from Titus you are setting off shortly for the interior. You need a guide, and no one knows this land better than I do, I assure you. I was born here. I speak all the local dialects fluently."

Anne stowed the pistols. "You don't talk like a local," she said, recovering her pipe from the ground. "You work with the slavers?" The man shook his head as he knelt to pick up her tobacco pouch. He handed it back to her.

"No," he said. "I've been a slave before, several times, actually. No, I picked up your language during my time in your part of the world. I enjoy traveling. Until a few days ago I was serving on the *Hopewell*."

"She's a good ship," Anne said. "Why are you coming ashore now?"

"We arrived two days ago," the man said. "This may sound a bit strange, but I heard about what you did in the marketplace today. Very brave. Very stupid, but very brave. A person who would do such a thing, she may be worth following to see what brave, stupid thing she does next."

"Titus will vouch for you?" Anne asked.

"Yes," the man said. Nothing else seemed to be very forthcoming. Anne took the man's measure for a long time, then thrust out a hand. He shook it.

"Then welcome to the expedition," she said. "Anne Bonny. What do you go by?"

"Around here they know me as Adu Ogyinae."

"We'll need bearers, Adu," Anne said, tossing him two bags of coins. "There's coin here to hire them as well as some funds for yourself. You say you know the region well; can you find us good folk to undertake the job for us?"

"Oh, yes," Adu said. "I know several people. Very trustworthy and loyal. Planning on carting off a bit of African gold, aren't you?"

"I am indeed," Anne said. "You have a problem with that?"

"Oh, no," Adu Ogyinae said. "It seems to be something you Europeans are very good at. I will tell you, however, you're going to need more than a quick draw and cockiness to make it through the interior."

Anne said nothing. She re-lit her pipe and took a deep inhalation of the Cavendish; a hint of the bourbon that flavored the tobacco leaves permeated the sweet smoke. "This is my last run," she said. "I've cheated the hangman's noose, I've raged, and roared, and adventured, and I intend to retire a very wealthy woman, a lady, even. Enough money will wash off the stink of being piss poor, hell, it even washes off blood."

"You cannot wash off who you truly are," Adu said as he turned and disappeared into the darkness of the street. His voice lingered a moment longer. "This land will help you discover that. All preparations shall be ready in two days' time, Anne Bonny. I bid you good night."

Anne took another puff on her pipe. This one was trouble. She had no idea why she had invited him along. She went back to admiring the stars, still frozen, still beautiful and pure. There was a crash off to her left, and a drunk tumbled out the door, landing in a disheveled heap a few feet from her. The man groaned, and he blinked a few times, his eyes finally focusing on her. "Well, well, the night's not a complete loss, is it, luv?" the drunk mumbled. "Aren't you a bit of a bushel bubby, then. Let's get you around back and have a go at the goat's jig, darlin'." The drunk was getting up; he drew a chivey, a thin, sharp dirk, from under his coat as he did. His eyes were unfocused, but what Anne saw there was clear enough.

Anne's hand dropped to the hilt of her machete. "Aye, darling," she said, "let's have a go."

So much for the stars.

9

The Five of Swords

Charleston, South Carolina
April 10, 1871

Martin Anderton waited by the carriage outside his Charleston townhouse for his granddaughter. They were going to be late. It was a warm night in Charleston and Owen and Amy Anderson were throwing an engagement party to announce the upcoming nuptials of Mr. Jestin Jeffries to Miss Faye Newsham at the Charleston Opera House. The cream of Charleston society was going to be there and it was an excellent opportunity to introduce Constance, formally. Now if only Constance would come along.

"Grandpa?" Constance asked from the top of the stairs. Martin looked up.

"We can't dawdle, Cons—" Martin stopped cold when he saw her.

Constance, her governesses, Miss Applewhite and Miss Anhorn, on either side of her, was wearing a rose-colored bustle dress with ruffled lace on the front lower skirt, as well as on the sleeves and collar. Her hair was fashioned high with ringlets tumbling down. The fourteen-year-old looked down to her grandfather.

"My dear," Martin said, "you look so much like your grandmother, and your mother. You're beautiful, Constance, truly."

Her whole face lit up when she smiled. "I look all right?" she asked.

Miss Anhorn cleared her throat. "A lady doesn't beg for compliments, child," Miss Anhorn said. Miss Applewhite, smiling as widely as Constance, reached out to the girl and touched her shoulder.

"You look lovely, honey," Miss Applewhite said. "Go have fun!"

"I am honored to escort you," Martin said. "Come, dear. Charleston eagerly awaits you."

They departed in the carriage headed down Elizabeth Street. They turned right onto Calhoun.

"Nervous, dear?" Martin asked. Constance was staring out the window, her pale face illuminated by the passing gas streetlights. She nodded.

"Grandpa," Constance said, "I'm sorry."

"Think nothing of it, dear," Martin said. "We shall be, as they say, 'fashionably late.'" He chuckled. "Besides, it's a lady's purview to make a man wait."

"No," Constance said. "For what's about to happen. I dreamed it, you see."

"What?" Martin said. "Dear girl, you're not making any sense."

"Mother would understand," she said. Martin looked at his beautiful granddaughter and saw such a terrible weight pressing down upon such young shoulders. Her eyes, so much like his dear departed wife's, were haunted.

Martin had heard the reports from the governesses that Constance ate sparingly, that she had great trouble getting to and staying asleep, even with medicinal aids. He had assumed it to be a normal melancholic condition that all women went through from time to time, especially teenage girls. He wished his daughter was here now. She should be. Maude needed to give up her silly notions of independence and tend to her daughter properly.

"I'm beginning to wonder if perhaps I make the terrible things I dream about happen," Constance said. "Perhaps if they succeed, then it will all stop."

Martin took Constance's pale hand. It was trembling. "If who succeeds in what, Constance?"

"Killing me," she said. "The monsters are here to kill me."

Two blocks up they turned left onto King. The opera house was farther up on the right. Martin rapped on the roof of the carriage and called out to his driver. "Freemont, we shall be returning to the residence at once. Miss Constance is not feeling well."

The cab jerked to a halt and Martin heard the horses neighing, bucking.

"Freemont, what on earth is happening?" Martin shouted, as he opened

one of the carriage doors to address the coachman. Martin twisted his body
to look up. Freemont's neck hung at a lazy, unnatural angle. His eyes were
vacuous in death, and the reins lay loosely in his palm.

"Dear Lord," Martin said.

He turned to see what was spooking the horses. Three men stood in the
center of King Street. They wore heavy dusters, derbies and bandannas covering the lower part of their faces. One of the men was hunched, and seemed
to have something jutting from his back. Another one of the trio appeared to
have large hideous, deformed hands, resembling giant lobster claws.

"Nothing personal, Marty," said a voice speaking in a clipped English
accent above and behind Martin, from the roof of the carriage. "Jist got no
use for you is all. Ta."

The fourth masked man swung his fist downward, toward Martin's defenseless skull. Constance's palm flashed out to block the punch, angling her
wrist just as Mother had taught her to redirect most of the force behind the
punch and stop it. Palm met fist. That should have been the end of it, but
the sheer strength of the masked man's strike was unnaturally powerful;
it carried through and knocked Martin to the street. Constance saw her
grandfather lying very still and for an instant she thought the masked man
had succeeded in slaying him. Then she saw Martin's chest rise and fall, and
she knew she had saved him, barely.

Constance switched the palm block to a grip on the attacker's wrist and
executed a sacrifice throw that sent the masked man and herself flying off
the carriage and tumbling to the street, several feet away from the coach and
from Martin's unconscious body. Constance rolled and came up on her feet
immediately. She almost tripped on her skirts, but hours of training let her
keep her balance. The masked man with the English accent was flat on his
face. He began to laugh.

"Oh, that's a nice trick, pet," the masked man said. "I see the Daughters
have given you a bit of the witchery, yeah?" The masked man grunted and
the fingers of his left hand sunk into the cobblestone of the street, down to
the first knuckle, with a thick crunch. "Let me show you a bit of mine."

He climbed back to his feet, ripping a large section of the stone free with
one hand as he stood. The bandanna had dropped and Constance could see
his face. The man had a blandly handsome face, pleasant enough but forgotten quickly. He bared his teeth like an animal might and she could see
the decay and rot eating them.

He grunted and hurled the chunk of street at the girl. Constance slipped out of the way, but her beautiful yet cumbersome dress caused her some drag and it nearly clipped her. The stonework exploded against a shop front about twenty yards behind her, demolishing part of the store's wall. Fragments from the collision threw debris everywhere, like pellets from a shotgun.

Constance found herself moving without thinking, her body remembering the endless drills her mother had forced her to endure. She spun, tumbled through the rain of rock. She felt a sharp sting in her arm and another at her shoulder. This damnable dress! It was slowing her down, breaking the rhythm of her breathing and her balance. Thinking about it slowed her even more as her muscles were forced to wait for her brain. She landed and found herself face-to-face with another of the masked men. The killer had cleared the distance to her swiftly and now his arcing, clumsy punch was headed straight for Constance's face. She stilled her mind, calmed the rising panic and fear in her, like Mother had taught her, and trusted her body and her training. She folded into the punch and felt it flutter by her. Without a wasted motion, her hand darted out and pulled the bandanna up over the man's eyes, blinding him. That was when she saw the wide, ugly scar on his right cheek. The scar opened wide to reveal a pupil with a sickly yellow-green iris the color of bile. The third eye glared at Constance with alien hatred.

Constance gasped at the eye's revelation. She was completely flat-footed when the man backhanded her. Instinct came to her rescue once again and she rolled with the hit at the last instant. It saved her life. Constance had never been struck so hard before. She saw a brilliant strobe of white light behind her eyes, and then she felt the rolling impact of the ground, again and again, felt herself sliding along it. Her hands, of their own accord, were slapping the ground with open palms to slow the impact and dissipate the kinetic energy.

She came to rest facedown. Her first awareness was of the poor horses whinnying, mad with fear. Her head felt like it was full of thick molasses; it was hard to think, harder still to get up, but she knew she had to, knew her life depended on getting up, so she did. The pain in doing so helped clear her head.

The four assassins circled her. The carriage was veering wildly down King Street, poor dead Freemont jerking about in his seat like some grisly marionette. Grandfather lay in the road, still unconscious, but thankfully none of the killers seemed to pay him any mind.

The man with the eye on his cheek had pulled his bandanna back over his nose and mouth. The assassin with the huge claws snapped them as he eyed Constance, and she noticed the claws secreted a viscous fluid that sprayed each time the claws clamped shut with a loud clack. The one she had thought was a hunchback at first had bone spines jutting out from his back. The two-foot-long bone spears were yellowed and sharp. The man with the bad teeth didn't bother to hide his face anymore. He seemed to be savoring every bit of this struggle, clapping and dancing as he and his companions closed the circle around Constance.

"Oh, I truly wish we could play with you a bit, luv. You've a cokum bit o' jam, ain't you?"

Constance felt the fear that was eating her brain drown in something else, something that seemed older, more powerful.

"I am not your love," she said in a voice not entirely her own. "I am not your pet." She filled herself with clean air and felt her whole body burn with a power she did not fully understand. "I am a Daughter of Lilith; I am the Mother's sword. If you're so eager, come play, come play with death."

Three of the assassins paused, even took a few steps back from Constance. Only the smiling man held his ground. "Oh, I know who you are," he said. "You are the last Daughter of Lilith; you are the Grail of the Mother. That is why you are going to die."

The four killers came at Constance as one, a pack of jackals spurred to action by the faux courage of their numbers. Constance readied for the onslaught. She blocked one's punch and then used his shoulder and back as an acrobatic horse to tumble out of the ring of death and get behind them, move them out of position. Like the smiling man's punch, the force of the blow was inhuman and it jarred her; she spun a wheel kick at her attacker that should have shattered his hip and completely disabled him, but it didn't seem to faze him very much.

The other three moved to regroup, with two of them attacking in unison, one with a roundhouse, the other with a low snap kick. She managed to slow down the punch but not stop it. The kick felt like it was from an angry mule. Constance staggered back and fell to the ground. The four moved in to finish her.

A storm tore through the assassins, a blur of motion and force, raging around the girl. The killers careened through the air, tumbling to the ground before the living whirlwind.

Maude stood beside her daughter, in an hourglass stance, legs apart, arms raised in fists. She was dressed in the men's clothing she used as a disguise, with a bandanna of her own hiding part of her face. Maude shifted into a defensive posture and helped Constance to her feet. "You cover my back and left," Maude said. "Defensive only. Don't go on the attack until we know what they are, and don't let them goad you into moving out of position."

"Yes, Mother," Constance said.

The smiling man was back on his feet, too, and he wasn't smiling anymore. "You have no need for a disguise with us, Maude Stapleton. We know you, we know all the Daughters of Lilith. We can smell your kind on the wind, bitch."

"Then you know what I'm going to do to you if you try to hurt this girl. Go now. Only mercy you'll receive."

"Mercy is for the weak," the smiling man said. "Kill them both for the glory of the Father!" The smiling man charged Maude and the others followed.

Maude was trying to understand what these men were and why they wanted to kill her daughter. Isaiah had given Maude Constance's cryptic letter that had been delivered that evening by one of Martin's servants. The note simply said, "I love you, Mother, good-bye." Maude had arrived at her father's residence shortly after Martin and Constance had departed for the opera house, and had tracked the carriage here, jumping rooftop to rooftop across Charleston.

Maude had tried to finish this quickly; Father most likely needed a doctor. However, the hurricane kata that she had executed as she jumped from the rooftop to save her daughter had been less effective than it should have been. Her attack was intended to cripple all four men; it should have, but it had hardly stunned them.

The strange assassins were up and upon them again. Maude sidestepped the man with the claw-hands, catching his follow-up assault with a forearm counter. The force of the impact almost broke her arm. Maude stumbled back from the impact and straight into the man with the extra eye. She pivoted to check his assault but again the strength behind the punch was superhuman and her defense began to crumble. Constance was suddenly there, adding her own strength to Maude's effort. It worked, and the two women held their ground.

"I told you not to break formation!" Maude shouted as they turned in unison to deflect, side step and jointly hit the spine-backed assassin.

"If I hadn't you'd be dead now!" Constance shouted back. The mother and daughter bashed Spine-back on opposite shoulders, simultaneously, as he lumbered by. It should have shattered his bones into powder; instead it felt to Maude like hitting a stone mountain. Spine-back grunted and toppled to the ground but then was already struggling to get back up.

Maude knew how to identify and adapt to virtually every known style of combat. Gran had told her many times over the years that martial arts from all the corners of the Earth were derived from the teachings of the Daughters of Lilith. With a few minutes of study, a Daughter could figure out the secret of any style and a counter to it.

The way these "men" fought was different, alien. To an untrained eye it appeared as no style at all, merely brutish brawling like you'd find in any back alley or tavern, but it was a system, a very subtle and specific one at that. When Maude began to see the edges of the design in their style it chilled her blood.

All combat has a rhythm, a music to it. The way these assassins had been trained was specifically without a rhythm; it was counterintuitive, it relied on raw power and chaos rather than pattern and technique. It was a fighting style specifically designed to bypass much of a Daughter's combat skills.

Constance swung a high kick at the smiling man as she drove a directed finger strike into the cheek eye of the three-eyed man. The smiling man took her most powerful kick square in the face; there was a shower of blood and rotted teeth as his head snapped to the side, the kick stunning him instead of breaking his neck as it should have done. The smiling man grabbed Constance's still extended leg and swung her off the ground by it like a rag doll, smashing her to the cobblestone street.

"Constance!" Maude called out.

Constance's eye gouge had proven very effective, and the three-eyed man clutched his vulnerable, blinded orb, hissing and doubled over in pain. Maude, seeing Spine-back was still struggling to rise, grabbed the three-eyed man's wrist in a reaping throw that completely ignored his superior strength and bulk, and hurled him with all the power she could conjure. The three-eyed man landed hard on Spine-back, impaling himself twice through the chest on the rising assassin's sharp bone protrusions. Spine-back crashed back to the ground, momentarily dazed by the force of the impact. The three-eyed man was silent and still, dead and pinned to his ally's back.

"You bitch!" the smiling man screamed, red-faced. He smashed Constance to the ground again. The girl no longer struggled and looked to be unconscious, or worse. "I'll flay you alive after I turn your brat into jelly!" With a seemingly effortless jerk of his arm, the smiling man lifted Constance's limp form into the air again, to crack her like a whip. He smashed her again and again, a look of almost ecstasy on his face as he did.

Maude closed the distance between herself and the smiling man. Something massive and sharp grabbed both her arms from behind before she could. It was the claw-handed assassin, and she hadn't even sensed his approach. His pincers had her. Maude heard the hiss of the liquid his monstrous appendages secreted as it burned the sleeves of her coat and shirt and began to sear the skin of her arm. Maude felt a wave of dizziness and nausea follow the searing pain, and she realized the ooze wasn't just acidic, it was also venomous.

Her vision was starting to blur and smear. She willed her blood to isolate, slow and direct the toxin to her stomach. She'd need to get it out of her body, to purge it. The pain in her arms was getting worse and she heard the claw-man growl in her ear, "Jackie there was my friend, whore of Lilith." He had a heavy German accent. "Let's see how tough you are when I burn both your fucking arms off."

The claw-man was lifting Maude off the ground by her pinned arms. It was like being squeezed in a red-hot vice. Maude struggled, but she lacked leverage. She saw the smiling man swinging Constance down to smash her into the street again. In her melting vision, Constance looked so young to Maude, too young for all this.

A butterfly with iridescent wings of metallic blue fluttered before Maude's face. "Hermana," a soft voice whispered in Maude's mind, in her blood. A living, billowing mass of blue swarmed over her, around her, and filled Clawman's face, his mouth, his nostrils. His shout of protest was muffled as he choked on thousands of tiny, beating wings. The claws released her and Maude dropped to the ground, lurching toward her daughter. The shifting, churning wall of coruscating blue opened to let her pass unmolested. Maude was already sweating out the venom, her heart hammering as she saw Constance rushing toward the ground again.

A black woman dressed in a man's suit and a large, fluttering topcoat dropped into view, driving both of her legs into the smiling man's lower spine. He yelped in pain and released Constance's leg sooner than he expected. Constance sailed through the air and Maude's muscles screamed in protest as she hurled herself toward her daughter. She caught Constance midair and used her own body to cushion their impact near where Martin lay.

Constance was still breathing raggedly. Her body was covered in black bruises. Maude sat her next to Martin and struggled back to her feet. She stepped away and retched up the toxin. Immediately, she felt her head clearing.

The woman in the suit was not giving the smiling man time to regroup, pounding him with one powerful punch after another, hopping and bobbing in between blows and snapping tight, lightning-fast kicks to his face. She landed another hit but they weren't having much effect.

"Get over here and help me!" the woman called to Maude. "Before we both end up dead, and your daughter too!"

Maude glanced over to where the claw-handed assassin had been, and all she could see now was an endless undulating wall of blue. There was a girl standing at the edges of the cloud, one hand raised as if she were conducting an orchestra. At first glance she didn't look much older than Constance. She was dressed in a simple, plain skirt and blouse. Her raven hair was in a conservative bun and her eyes were black mirrors reflecting flickers of blue. Spine-back charged into view again, the limp corpse of his comrade still pinned to his back. The killer barreled toward the girl, but she gestured with the hand that wasn't conducting the butterflies, and Spine-back drunkenly sidestepped a few feet. She easily dodged his attack. Maude recognized the fighting styles both women used all too well; they were Daughters of Lilith. However, whatever the young girl was doing with the butterflies and what she had just done to Spine-back was a mystery.

Maude flanked the smiling man, lashing him with alternating knife-hand and ridge-hand attacks at every vulnerable nerve cluster he should have. The effects should have been devastating pain, and paralysis, and crippling injury, but it seemed to just be annoying him. He swung at Maude and it almost connected but she folded before it and it missed. In the instant he reacted to Maude and counterattacked, the woman in the suit flashed out with a precise and powerful overhead casting punch to just behind his ear at a cluster of nerves. He roared in anger and tried to bash the mysterious

Daughter. Maude took the opening and swept his legs out from under him. It felt like she was trying to uproot a redwood, but she pushed with all her might. The smiling man fell to the ground with a crash, the wind seemingly knocked out of him. The woman in the suit nodded to Maude. They locked gazes and Maude returned the nod.

"The only nerves on them that still work like normal people's are related to their senses," the woman said to Maude. "Except their sense of touch— it's been severely diminished as part of their training."

"Good to know," Maude said.

"You've never faced them before, have you?"

"No."

"Never? I don't see how that's possible."

"I don't get out much," Maude said.

"Amadia," the woman in the suit said.

"Maude," she replied. "Thank you."

"Don't thank me," Amadia said.

There were shouts down the street, calls for aid. Charleston was becoming aware of the war being waged upon the street. Maude risked a glance to check on Constance, only to discover that Spine-back was right above her body, reaching for her. He had snapped one of his own spines off and was brandishing it like a knife. "For the glory of Father Typhon!" Spine-back shouted. "Death to the Daughters of Lilith! Death to the Grail!"

There was a loud boom with a second one following right on top of the first. Most of the back of Spine-back's skull exploded in red mist and shattered bone. The assassin dropped to the street, dead. Martin Anderton was propped up on one elbow, barely conscious, a smoking, double-barrel parlor gun in his steady hand.

"Get your hands off my granddaughter, you grotesque," he mumbled and then fell unconscious. Even with most of his head missing, Spine-back's body attempted to rise again; it tried a few more times and then stopped. The storm of butterflies lifted with a gesture from the raven-haired girl, revealing the body of the claw-handed assassin, lifeless on the street, his head and face a shroud of dead blue insects.

"That was for Kavita," the black-haired girl whispered to the corpse.

The smiling man had taken advantage of the distraction Martin inadvertently provided. He was gone.

"At least I recognize the vanishing trick," Maude said. She ran to Constance and gently touched her throat. Her daughter's pulse was steady and strong. She checked Martin; his pulse was thready, but still there.

"Three dead Sons," Amadia said, walking toward Maude and her fallen family. "Now I call that a good day."

"Sons?" Maude asked. "Who were those men? Who are you?" Maude said. "My teacher told me Daughters don't usually meet one another unless things are terribly dire."

"True," Amadia agreed. "They are. I wish that they weren't."

Shadows moved at the edges of the street, and scattered voices could be heard. The shrill shriek of watch whistles coming closer punctuated the voices of the onlookers.

"Amadia!" the dark-haired girl called out. "We must go or be discovered! Get the girl!"

Maude looked up from Constance's face to narrow her gaze at the Daughter. "What?"

"We must take her," Amadia said. "You do not understand what is at stake—the future of the Daughters, the fate of the world."

"Over my dead body," Maude said, rising to her feet. "The Daughters be damned, the world be damned." Amadia regarded her for a moment. The African Daughter looked to her companion and shook her head. The raven-haired girl's eyes darkened with anger and she made a sweeping gesture. Maude's world became flashes of metallic blue and the roar of thousands of tiny wings. Then it was all gone. She was alone on the street; the two mysterious Daughters had vanished. Maude hurriedly gathered Constance and Martin and was away.

10

The Ace of Wands

Kingdom of Dahomey, Africa
July 20, 1721

They were ten days out of Badagry, deep in the belly of the emerald beast, and three men were already dead. If Anne was to be honest, which she tried to be whenever it had no serious repercussions, she didn't feel bad for their passing in the least. They had been bearers that Adu Ogyinae had selected for the expedition, hopefully to carry back the gold and jewels of the bone city once they found it.

All three of the dead men had been useless in this initial part of the trip. They were lazy, ill-tempered and stirred up trouble with the other members of the expedition. Two days into the bush, one had died from the bite of a black mamba when he blundered into it, almost stepping on it. The snake had been a good four yards long, and it rose up to the height of the man as it struck him. After Anne killed the thing with a quick flash of her blade, Adu tried some local cure he had prepared, but the man had taken too much venom in the bite and died within the hour.

The other two died equally incompetent deaths. They ate some ackee fruit that other bearers in the company—the few that seemed competent and professional—said any local who'd ever been out of their village should know better than to eat when it was not ripe. By the time the expedition had made camp that night, both men were in agony with stomach cramps and violent vomiting. They were dead before sunup the next day.

Today, Anne noticed that several of the bearers had been looking at her with obvious lewd intent on their minds. Out in the jungle it was too damn hot and too damn uncomfortable to bother disguising herself, especially when she was paying these men to ogle her. Her hair was tied back and she wore a headscarf as she had often done on board a ship. She wore a long-sleeved tunic and made no attempt to wrap or tie down her breasts. Her breeches and boots were sensible but the gawking, snickering bearers were obviously titillated by seeing a woman in pants.

The jungle was endless, twisting in every direction. The morning fog had mostly burned away, but it would return with the next tepid downpour. Some of the more competent and well-mannered bearers were at the front hacking away at the bush, creating a barely navigable path through land that seemed as if it had never been seen by human eyes.

"What exactly did I pay you for?" Anne asked Adu. Without missing a step, Adu reached to his leather belt pouch and handed her back the coins she had given him in town the night they met.

"You paid me for nothing," Adu said. "Is there a problem?" Anne pocketed her coins and continued to keep pace with the large man.

"Aye," she said. "You've hired a mess of thatch-gallows for bearers!"

" 'Thatch-gallows'?" Adu asked, frowning. "I'm sorry, I only speak English."

"You know exactly what I'm saying," Anne said. "These men are rotten. I'm pretty sure most of them are plotting to kill you, have their way with me and leave us out here to rot."

"Quite possible," Adu said. "They are criminals, and worse. They may have their way with me too. I'm told I can be quite fetching."

"Have you completely gone mad?" Anne said, glancing back over her shoulder at the surly pack of men admiring her backside.

"No, of course not," Adu said. "The last time I went mad was . . . was it that awful business with that Phoenician king, what was his name? At any rate, it was quite a while ago. Not to worry. A good quarter of the men are true and loyal; I'll vouch for them."

"Why in hell did you hire a bunch of cutthroats?" Anne asked. "Are you trying to undermine the expedition?"

"No," Adu said. He and Anne stepped to the side and allowed the rest of the party to proceed on. The other members of the expedition, including the French mercenary who was known as the Hummingbird, moved past them and continued trudging forward. The former Musketeer had told Anne his real name, Renee Belrose, once he had sobered up. Belrose gave the two a glance as he passed but said nothing.

Adu looked up into the level upon level of branches, vines and dense foliage, scanning for any threat. The relentless African sun gleamed down, its golden late-morning light mostly devoured by the tangled canopy. "They are not here for you. They are here for me. They are here because of their crimes, because of the things they have done to their own people, their own families."

"What?" Anne asked. "I don't follow you."

"In a place like Badagry, these men were safe, even successful," Adu said. "They were scavengers, feeding on the weak and the unsuspecting. They have murdered and raped, they have sold their own families into slavery. They were protected by other scavengers, the whole parasitic system laughingly called civilization. Only out here, in the purity of the wilderness, can such men be brought face-to-face with their crimes and a fitting punishment be meted out."

"You hired them because they are evil," Anne said, "so you could bring them out here and let them die one by one."

"It is a public service I have performed from time to time," Adu said. "One of the names I am known by around here is Ogbunabali; it's a sort of title, I suppose."

"What the hell gives you the right to judge who's evil and who's not? Who's a fucking criminal and who's a good man? Plenty of times my hungry belly told me what was right and what was wrong. Leading these people out here to get slaughtered, how does that give you any standing to judge anyone?"

Adu looked slightly amused. "You are young, aren't you? I'm a traveler, Lady Bonny. I have seen enough, in enough places, gained a thimbleful of wisdom from my copious errors, to know what I know. I once had the same questions, the same doubts you voice. I do no longer. I know right and I know wrong when I see it. I choose to act upon it when I deem it appropriate, when my sensibilities can stomach it being ignored no longer. That is all the answer I feel you need, or could understand at this point in your life. I look forward to the day we can have this discussion again."

"So you're the Lord Almighty," Anne said. "You smite whoever you think deserves smiting."

"Yes," Adu said. "And I stand by the consequences of my actions. Surely one such as you has killed in righteous indignation before. If you had the power to lay all those slavers low in the marketplace when you first came to Badagry, you would have. I saw it on your face."

Anne nodded. "Yeah," she finally said. "I wanted to, but I wanted to live more."

"I have the luxury of having reached a point in my life where breathing is not as important to me as principle. It is a rare gift to receive, and not for everyone. You, I think it may suit . . . one day."

"I have to admit, it's a novel notion," Anne said. "And I'd be lying if I said I'd weep for any of these bastards, but how can I be sure you don't plan the same fate for me? Lead me out here with a load of shit and promises, just to kill me off with the other jackals."

Adu began walking again. "Oh, you're no scavenger," Adu replied. "You're a predator."

That night, after camp had been made and sentries posted, Anne sat by the fire with Adu and Belrose. The Frenchman sipped from a bottle of absinthe and lounged back. The mercenary offered the bottle to the others. Adu shook his head.

"There are plenty of green poisons all about us, my friend," Adu said. "No thank you."

"Ah," Belrose said, tipping the bottle toward Anne, "but it's always better to meet death on your terms, is it not?"

Anne took the bottle and took a long drink.

"I wouldn't know," Adu said.

"Where's your fancy little spoon and the sugar lump and the warm water, all that nonsense?" Anne asked, passing the bottle back and wiping her mouth with her sleeve.

"I am roughing it," Belrose said, and took another drink. "Where are we headed exactly?"

"Abomey," Anne said. The strange map in the box had been drawing them northwest and when she consulted the French and British maps she had acquired in Badagry, it looked as if the jewel was guiding them on a direct course to the city.

"Ah, charming place," Belrose said, offering her the bottle again. "Have you been?"

Anne shook her head as she took the bottle, and another drink.

"Nor have I, but I have heard some grand tales." The mercenary smiled. He had abandoned his heavy doublet for a simple cotton tunic and under-shirt, and a well-worn, comfortable looking pair of fall-front breeches, but he was still wearing his cavalier hat with its drooping peacock feather. Belrose's belt, blade, a Charleville musket and his powder horn and bullet bag were on the log next to him.

Belrose was an odd one, Anne thought. He was obviously well-versed in surviving the African wilderness, and he hadn't uttered a complaint. Yet he still insisted on maintaining his grooming, neatly trimming and waxing his goatee and mustache each morning. He drank like . . . well, like she did, but he never seemed to suffer a hangover, or if he did, he kept his bitching to himself. Anne liked that in a tippler. You're going to pull that trigger, you best be able to handle where the bullet goes.

"Abomey is the capital city of the Kingdom of Dahomey," Belrose said. "We're headed past the edges of the Yoruba's empire."

"This is the territory of the Fon?" Anne asked.

"Depends on who you ask," Belrose replied with a chuckle.

"'The Fon' is a rather sizable conglomeration of peoples from the inland territories," Adu said. "They banded together to resist the demands for trib-ute and slaves from the Yoruba, who consider them subjects. It's ironic, since the Fon now trade captives and political dissidents as slaves to the French and Spanish for guns to continue their war against the Yoruba."

"Guns, rum, flesh, gold," Belrose said. "It's what makes the world go round, my friends. Doesn't matter where you are or when."

"Sadly, Monsieur, you are more right than you know," Adu said.

"The Fon are great warriors," Belrose said to Anne. "They prize martial prowess above all other virtues. They've had to in order to unite and keep fighting the Yoruba. I heard tales that King Agaja employs Amazons in war and as his personal bodyguard."

"Amazons?" Anne asked. She looked to Adu, who was quietly staring into the flames of the fire. He looked up.

"You shall see," Adu said.

That night, Anne was awakened in the dead darkness. She couldn't quite recall what had stirred her from sleep, but she knew it made her reach for her blade. She pushed the netting aside and exited the tent as quietly as she could. A thick, humid fog clutched the ground like a desperate lover. The fog swirled and obscured everything more than a few feet away. It seemed to glow in the vine-choked moonlight.

There was no sound from the sentries, no sound from the other tents, no sounds from the jungle at all. The fog was eating all the noise, devouring it. Anne turned slowly, her machete ready, her palms and throat were dry.

Chirk, the sound came from behind her. Anne spun. There was a bird, a kite, crouched on a branch. The bird's body was marked with dark brown feathers, slowly shifting to tan on the lower edges of the feathers. Its sharp, prominent beak was bright yellow. Its blazing yellow eyes looked into Anne's and a voice spoke inside of her thoughts. It was a woman's voice.

"*Odu Ifa,*" the voice inside her said. "*Aje.*

"*You trample upon the brush. I trample upon the brush. We trample the brush down together. Ifa was consulted for Odu by these Awos. They said, 'Odu is going from Heaven to Earth. Whenever she arrives on earth.' They said, 'Thee Odu, this is your beginning.'*"

The bird's glowing gaze shifted to the floor of the jungle. Anne looked down and saw a panther with a hide as black as a starless night upon the sea. The big cat seemed to grow up out of the shadows of the jungle floor, partly hidden by the fog.

It snarled at Anne and she saw, for an instant, the force operating behind, through, the panther. A presence that permeated the icy cold between the stars, and the whispering poetry within every living body that made it unwind, unravel and, eventually, cease. The gulf between the lights in the sky, the inevitable failure of all breathing, bleeding flesh machines, the panther, all the same.

The panther was close enough to strike Anne. She tried to raise her blade but her arms were like stone. Her eyes could still move and they flickered to the kite's. The bird met her gaze.

"*Olodumare gave her a bird,*" the voice continued in Anne's mind. "*She took this bird with her to Earth. Aragamago is the name that Olodumare gave this bird. Aragamago is the name that Odu's bird carried. He said, 'You Odu, any undertaking upon which you send this bird, it will do.' He said, 'Any place that it pleases you to send this bird, it will go.' He said, 'If it is to do bad or good.' He said, 'Anything that it pleases you to tell it to do, it will do.' Odu brought this bird to Earth.*"

The bird's eyes flickered away from Anne's and it shot from the branch, making no sound, its talons raised, and it flashed past the panther, tearing at its head with its talons as it passed and turned to pass again. The panther's fierce growls were swallowed up by the swirling fog. The voice in Anne's head spoke again and this time, Anne recognized something in it, a familiarity that she could not fully grasp.

"Odu has said that no other person will be able to look upon it. She said that it must not be looked upon. If any enemy of Odu looks upon it, she will shatter his eyes. With the power of this bird, she will blind the eyes. If another of her enemies peers into the calabash of this bird. This bird, Aragamago, will shatter their eyes."

The kite flashed by silently, striking again and again, ripping at the cat's eyes, blinding it, ripping away its face, darting past and around its knife-like claws. The cat was blinded, maimed, lashing out, rising up on two legs to paw at nothing but air, missing the silent, gliding kite. Again and again. The kite dived, drifting past the big cat's throat, opening the veins in its neck, killing it. The panther's massive body heaved and it fell, passing through Anne's own body as if it were no more substantial than the fog.

As it moved through her, Anne saw herself as an old woman, her body dying under the creaking, burning celestial cogs, the constellations of a warm Carolina night, resplendent with the echoes of ancient, heavenly fires. She was walking into the sea, being pulled under black waters, accepting them, welcoming them. She saw her end. The panther's shadowy form vanished before it hit the ground. Anne touched her chest, her hair. She could move again. Her skin was damp and still young, her hair was wet, she tasted salt on her lips; was it sweat, or sea spray?

The raptor flew toward her. Anne held out her forearm and the bird lighted on it. She felt hot razors burn her skin, but there was only joy in the pain. The raptor locked eyes with her once again, as she felt the hot blood drip down her arm and mingle with the fog and the damp earth.

"She used this bird thusly," the voice said. Anne awoke in her tent. She was unsure if it had been a dream or not. She was clutching her machete tightly and she was slick with sweat. She looked down at her forearm. The fresh wounds of the talons were there.

11

The Two of Cups (Reversed)

Charleston, South Carolina
April 12, 1871

Martin's eyes opened and he blinked at the bright afternoon sunlight streaming in through his bedroom window. He struggled to sit up. He remembered firing on the assassin who had attacked them.

"Constance!" Martin shouted as he pushed the bedclothes away and swung his legs over the side of the bed. A wave of dizziness and nausea arose within him. A strong, warm hand restrained him.

"No, Daddy." Maude eased her father back onto the bed. "You need to rest. You have a concussion. Your physician said it could have been much worse."

"Maude?" Martin said. "You're . . . you're here. So good to see you, my dear. Constance?"

"Some very bad bruises, pulled muscles and a few hairline breaks along her ribs, but nothing life-threatening," Maude said, pulling the covers back over her father. "She was lucky too. Doctor Galbraith says she will be sore but up and about in a few days."

Maude had tended to both of them with some of the healing mixtures she had learned how to concoct, and a judicious application of acupuncture. The Blood of Lilith that Constance had drunk a few years back gave all the Daughters a resistance to injury and accelerated healing; that had allowed Constance to endure the punishment she had received at the hands of the would-be assassins. Her father had no such faculties. If Constance hadn't slowed the smiling man's attack, Father would be as dead as his driver.

"I'm . . . so glad you're home, dear," Martin said. "I knew you'd come to your senses."

Maude felt a twinge of anger, but put it aside. She had lots of practice at that. "We'll talk after you've rested," she said. "Try to get some more sleep."

Martin was asleep again within a few moments. He dreamed of dark hallways that reminded him of his childhood home. As he wandered them aimlessly, seeking something but constantly forgetting what it was, he discovered his dead wife, Claire, as beautiful and brilliant and kind as she had ever been in life. He spent a long time holding her hand and talking. When he awoke, he couldn't recall any of what they had spoken of and he longed to return to that dream, to that place.

Two days had passed since he had spoken with Maude. This time when he climbed out of bed, there was no crippling dizziness, only a dull headache deep behind his blackened eyes. He slipped a robe on over his bedclothes and made his way downstairs.

"You should still be in bed, Mr. Anderton," Greene the butler said as he saw him descending the stairs.

"Nonsense," Martin said. "I've slept too damn long as it is. Is my daughter here?"

"Here," Maude said, coming to the edge of the stairs. Miss Anhorn and Miss Applewhite followed her. "We're all here."

"Is Constance . . . is she . . . ?"

"I'm here, Grandpa," Constance said, stepping into view. The girl was smiling. Some fading bruises marked her face but she seemed in good health and good spirits. "I'm so glad you're up."

Martin made his way, somewhat wobbly, to the foot of the stairs. Maude and Greene tried to assist him, but Martin shrugged them off. "I can manage, thank you," he said as he walked the few feet to an armchair and sat. He closed his eyes for a moment and sighed.

"Tea, Mr. Anderton?" Greene asked. Martin nodded, keeping his eyes closed. The butler headed off to the kitchen and Maude, Constance and the governesses all sat in the other armchairs or the sofa near Martin, who finally opened his eyes and focused on Maude.

"I thought I dreamed you," he said. "Do the constabulary have any idea who our attackers were?"

"Kidnappers, they suspect," Miss Applewhite said. "Wanting to abscond with Constance for a ransom from you, Mr. Anderton. The sheriff wishes to speak with you when you are feeling up to it. They've been by a few times now. Greene has their card."

"I've been dealing with pirates harassing several of my shipping concerns for months now," Martin said. "Perhaps they have something to do with it as well. I shall have Greene notify the constables to call on me now that I'm up and about once again."

"Just please don't push too hard, Father," Maude said. "You still need your rest."

Martin smiled at his daughter. "I'm so glad you're here, Maude," he said. "I'm so glad you gave up all that foolishness and came home."

"I'm just glad you are all right," Maude said. "I've been catching up with Constance and getting to know her governesses. I approve wholeheartedly with their instruction."

"You do?" Constance said.

"I do," Maude said. "It never hurts to learn how best to navigate an unfamiliar environment. Knowledge of how to comport yourself like a lady in this society could prove invaluable at some unseen future date, dear."

Constance shook her head and sighed. "Yes, Mother."

"I'm so glad you approve, Miss Stapleton," Miss Applewhite said. "So I assume Constance moving back to Grande Folly with you will not interfere with her lessons here at Mr. Anderton's home?"

"What?" Martin said, sitting up in the chair. Maude ignored her father and continued.

"Not at all," Maude said. "In fact, I hope that I can work with my father to jointly compensate you for your services and make rooms available out at the mansion for you both. That way, Constance's education—"

"What the blazes are you going on about, Maude!" her father said. Constance reached over to touch his shoulder.

"Grandpa, please calm down," Constance said. "You're still not well."

"Constance, quiet!" Miss Anhorn said, her tone as sharp as a whip. "Adults are talking. This is no time for silly female hysterics, young lady." Maude turned to the governess.

"Never tell my daughter that again, Miss Anhorn," Maude said. "Ever." Miss Anhorn darkened visibly at the admonishment but remained silent. Greene returned with the tea service. "Mr. Greene, if you please, Constance and her teachers will have their tea out on the patio. My father and I need to speak privately," Maude said.

"Yes," Martin said, "that we do."

Once Constance and the others were gone, Martin took a sip of his tea, his eyes never leaving his daughter. He lowered the cup. "So, you've not recovered from your madness at all, have you?" he said.

"Why do you always ask me questions when your tone sounds like you've already decided the answer?" Maude asked. "Constance is my daughter. She should be with me."

"You have taken up residence at the estate without my permission," Martin said, "and now you presume to take my granddaughter out of her home here without consulting with me, to dictate the terms of her upbringing to my employees, again without considering my wishes in that regard."

"Doesn't feel very good, does it?" Maude said. "And her home is with me, in Nevada."

"I took Constance away from that pesthole you were too prideful, too stubborn and too . . . distracted to see was not the best place for her to grow up," Martin said. "I see nothing has changed. You have my permission to remain at Grande Folly and use it as you wish as long as you are here in Charleston."

"Your permission?" Maude said, some anger beginning to creep into her voice. She knew she should control it, could control it, but her father had a terrible way of making her not care if she kept her emotions in check. She had not wanted this exchange here and now, but her father's pigheadedness and his condescension was forcing her hand. "I own that estate, Father. It was left to me, not you. I own the resources associated with that estate, again left to me, not to you. And I have the final say in where my daughter lives, and how she is raised, not you!"

Martin quickly calmed. "I see there is no reasoning with you," he said. It was one of the tactics that absolutely drove Maude mad, every time he pulled it. "You are too hysterical and too emotional to be rational. It's the very reason we drew up the agreement between you, Arthur and myself. Women simply can't maintain the decorum and the cool head necessary for such weighty decisions."

Maude held her tongue. She used the same will that helped her to control her anger in battle to pull back all the fury this man who claimed to love her brought out in her so easily. This was a campaign, she was at war with her father, and this was merely the first shot across the bow. Maude stood, walked calmly to the coatrack near the front door, and withdrew some folded papers from the pocket of her coat. She walked back to Martin and handed him the papers.

"What is this?" he asked.

"It's me maintaining decorum and a cool head," she said. "These documents were filed with the courts the day before you and Constance were accosted. They make my intentions very clear."

Martin opened the papers and scanned them. "This is ridiculous," he said. "You're contesting the contract regarding your Gran Bonnie's estate and suing for custody of Constance? What idiot lawyer did you find to follow you on this fool's errand? A. B. Mansfield? Never heard of him! You have absolutely no standing! You're being a featherbrain . . ."

Maude swept the tea service off the table with a mighty crash. "Never, ever . . . call me that again, do you understand? If Mother were alive, she'd never have brooked you saying such a thing to your own flesh and blood, and she'd detest you for doing it."

Martin visibly paled at the summoning of Claire's presence into this fight. Maude had never done that before, and it was as powerful as if she had slapped his face.

Maude saw how summoning her mother had Martin on the ropes. If he was an enemy on the battlefield, now would be the time to break him, send him down so hard he never got back up. She could tell him that is was her and Constance who had saved him from the attackers, that a feeble old man like him could offer no protection to either of them, and it was laughable to think otherwise.

She'd be doing it to be cruel, and it would leave her vulnerable by revealing so many of the secrets her father could never understand or accept. It was poor strategy. She pulled back, but the final barb she planted for Constance's sake. No, that was a lie, she was doing it to hurt him, because he had hurt her.

"I'm taking Constance back to Grande Folly with me," she said. "It's out of the city and she will be safer there if these kidnappers or pirates try to take her again."

"Are you implying I can't keep her safe?" Martin growled. "I forbid it, Maude! I forbid it! You don't have some half-breed sheriff's deputy here to warm your bed and keep you out of trouble!" It was Maude's turn to feel as if she had been physically struck by her father's words.

Martin went on, struggling to rise from his chair as he did. "Oh yes, I heard all the tales about you and this . . . savage, how you two were going on! I heard how you rubbed elbows with whores and criminals, oh yes! You think the court will give you custody of Constance when they hear how you cavorted in that flea bag of a frontier camp?"

To hell with strategy, to hell with the campaign. Pulling Mutt into this filled her mind with rage, burning like wildfire. "I'm taking her. You try to stop me and I'll knock you down, old man," Maude said. "That 'half-breed,' that 'savage' has shown me more kindness and respect than you ever have in your whole miserable life. He's more of a man than you'll ever be."

"First that glib grifter, Arthur, and now some godless heathen barbarian. You think that man is going to be a father to Constance? Will he still be alive in a year, in two? You drag our family name through the mud constantly with your shabby . . . associations," Martin said. He put his hand to his head and slumped back in the chair.

Maude recognized all the physiological signs; he was pushing himself too far, and in this moment she didn't care. "We're going to court, and I'm claiming what's rightfully mine. You need to talk, we will talk through our counsels. Good-bye, Father."

Maude walked out of the parlor and slammed the front door. Constance was outside, leaning against a wall, her arms crossed.

"You didn't have to be that way with him, Mother," Constance said. "He's sick, and he has no idea what we can do. You were out of control in there."

"He has that effect on me," Maude said. "But you and I both know he will be safer if you're with me."

"Unless they come here looking for me first," Constance said. "They'll kill him, Mother. I need to stay here to make sure he's safe."

"Constance, you can't stop these people yourself, we already know that."

Something set behind Constance's eyes and Maude knew she had said the wrong thing.

"I saved him, and I saved you," Constance said.

"And I saved you too," Maude said. "Come with me, we're leaving."

"No," Constance said. "It would just be to let you win and to hurt him. I won't do that. As I said, you're angry and out of control, Mother," Constance continued. "What do you always tell me? Center yourself."

"You're right, I am angry," Maude said. "I'm also right. It took us working together to put any of those . . . whatever they are, down. You are technically a Daughter now, you've taken the blood, but your studies are far from complete. You know that's true."

"Yes," Constance said, "but there was something that happened back there for a moment, before you arrived, where I felt . . . connected . . . to something greater. I felt all this power and knowledge settle over me. It was strange. I didn't feel like . . . me."

"You did very well in the fight," Maude said. "I'm proud of you. I just don't like the thought of you being a target of these 'Sons' or the Daughters of Lilith."

"'Sons,' 'Daughters,'" Constance said. "Do you think there is a connection?"

"They fought in a manner specifically designed to undermine our style of combat," Maude said. "They've undertaken some form of body hardening exercises and nerve deadening; it renders a number of our techniques considerably less effective against them. They were trained specifically to oppose us. There's no doubt there's a connection, but I've never heard of them and Gran never mentioned them to me. That other Daughter, Amadia, she seemed surprised we hadn't fought them before."

Mother and daughter leaned against the wall. The azalea bushes that lined the edge of Martin's townhouse drive were in bloom. The sun was warm on their faces and for a moment they both enjoyed the simple act of being alive and in the presence of the world renewing itself.

"I'm sorry," Maude said. "I was out of control and you were right to call me on it. It's just that your grandfather has always been able to do that to me. Even after I was studying with Gran, even after I took the blood, he could still strip all my discipline away and leave me raw."

"You love him," Constance said. "What he thinks matters to you. I felt the same way about Father. I hated him sometimes, especially how he treated you those last few years; I hated him so much for that. Even with all that, I still loved him, still wanted him to approve of me."

"Did you hate me for letting Arthur do that to me?" Maude asked.

"Sometimes," Constance said. "You were telling me to be so strong and to not let anyone control me but me, and then you'd let him hit you, speak to you worse than a dog. I did hate you sometimes for not standing up to him. I never understood why you put up with it."

"I never want you to understand that," Maude said. They were both quiet for a time.

"Please Mother," Constance finally said, "you and I would both feel terrible if anything happened to Grandfather, you know that. I had the dream about the ambush, that's why I sent you the letter. I can't directly try to stop the dreams or change them. Somehow I just know that will only make it all worse. People will die if I try to change it, directly. That was why I left Golgotha with Grandpa in the first place—I dreamed that I did.

"But I could send you a letter close to when the ambush was going to happen, to say good-bye and hope you'd figure it out, and you did."

"I don't like or trust these dreams," Maude said. "They are making you sick, and I know they are getting worse, aren't they?" Constance nodded.

"Since last year, yes," she said. "Now there are always two people in the city made out of bone with me . . . not people, forces, ideas . . . I'm not sure what they are exactly but they look like people in the dream, a man and a woman. They love and hate one another. It's what they are made of, partly, love and hate."

Maude brushed the hair from her daughter's eyes. She'd be fifteen in a few months and she still was a child in so many ways. She was terrified of the powers behind these dreams, and she was trying so hard to be brave, to be grown up. It made Maude's heart ache, and for a moment she wondered if her father perhaps still saw her the same way, still his child.

"Please, trust me now," Constance said. "I need to keep Grandpa safe. At least long enough for you two to stop shouting at each other. I'll figure out some way to let you know if I dream about anything else happening."

"All right," Maude said. "Promise me you'll get him and yourself out of here if there is even a hint of trouble, and please, please, be careful. Be mindful of everything; this is no exercise, this is as real as it gets. I'm going to find out all I can about who these 'Sons' are, and why they are after you."

"They said I was the Grail of Lilith," Constance said. "And the last of the Daughters."

"It's a place to start, at least," Maude said. "I don't care who they are or why they want you, no one's going to hurt you. I promise."

Constance smiled, but inside herself she felt the strange otherness return, gnawing at her mind. She loved and trusted her mother, but a horrible feeling of inescapable inevitability was settling over her, a sense that no matter what course of action she took, in the end, the result was going to be the same.

Maude saw the worry, the weariness in her daughter's eyes and wished she knew the words to comfort her, to chase all the awful dreams away.

Beneath the earth, in the cold room of Stuhr-Burning Cabinet Makers and Undertakers, Alter Cline followed a young assistant undertaker, Glen, past rows of wooden tables laden with corpses. Glen's lantern illuminated their way. Their footsteps echoed on the sawdust-covered floor of the dark, cold room. The smell of formaldehyde and decay was everywhere with just a peaty hint of rich dirt.

Cline had learned in battle and in journalism that one had to trust one's instincts or else one ended up in a room like this. When he had gotten the tip from one of his newly cultivated contacts here in Charleston about strange bodies being discovered on the street near the opera house, he'd had an itch in the back of his mind that it was connected to Maude Stapleton and her Lilith cult.

Three cloth-shrouded bodies lay side by side on tables in the back of the room, as if even in the equality of death, these three were not welcome. Glen raised the lantern to give the reporter a better look.

"There they are, Mr. Cline," Glen said, "jist like I promised yew. The police brought 'em in, said they weren't to be fiddled with. I hear tell some big bugs all the way from Washington are coming to look at 'em. Pinkerton men, they say."

"May I, Glen?" Alter asked, his breath swirling in the chill, damp air of the stone cellar. He nodded toward the sheets.

"Sure," Glen said. "Yew paid for the full tour, so go ahead, but I hope you didn't eat supper yet."

Alter flipped the cover off the first corpse. It was a man. There was a strange blue residue around his nose and mouth, but otherwise he looked normal until you reached his wrists. He had large, crab-like claws that seemed to be made of a flesh-colored, callus-like tissue.

"Remarkable," Alter said. "Some freakish aberration, perhaps?"

"The coppers seemed to think they were from a circus sideshow maybe," Glen offered. Alter slid the cloth down on the other two—one with an odd-looking wound on his cheek; the other lay on his belly, massive bone spurs jutting up from his spine. Alter circled the tables from different angles.

"There is chicanery to most sideshow anomalies," Cline said. "I see none here. This looks real."

"That ain't the queerest part," Glen said. "They ain't got no blood in them, least not like people blood."

"What do you mean?" Alter asked. In way of a response, Glen moved the lantern to illuminate a long table set against the far wall. The lantern's light briefly revealed all manner of dirty medical tools and a long catheter connected to a jar full of a viscous dark fluid, like oil.

"They pumped it out of all of 'em," Glen said. "Smells . . . weird. It ain't like any blood I ever saw come out of a corpse before." Alter walked over to the work table. He knelt close to the jar.

"Glen, may I have a sample of this substance?"

"Sure," the young man said. "As far as the usual requests I get from folks wantin' into the cold room, that one's pretty gentle."

"Alexandria will not be pleased," Itzel said.

"Alexandria is an *alailopolo*," Amadia said. "Neither of us work for her. I say this whole prophecy business is a sham."

They were in the salon of the grand suite at the Pavilion Hotel, their residence since arriving a few days ago in Charleston. Itzel sat nude in one of the armchairs. She preferred to wear very few clothes, only dressing when it was necessary to avoid detection or drawing undue attention. She had several tiny hummingbirds currently enthralled. The birds hovered near her head. Amadia was in a robe and pacing the lavishly adorned room.

"*Alailopolo?*" Itzel asked, arching an eyebrow. "I'm sorry, I know very little of the African tongues."

"A fool," Amadia said, "a fool with no sense."

"Isn't that a bit redundant?" Itzel said. "I suppose most curses are. Amadia, I thought we had all agreed. None of us like this course of action, but Alexandria seems to be the only one who has a plan to keep the Daughters going. The Sons being here and trying to kill the girl does seem to lend some credence to the prophecy's validity, don't you think?"

"I think there are very few of us in this world as there is and we don't need to be killing our own."

Amadia held up a copy of *The Charleston Daily News*. On the front page was a story about the attempted abduction of Martin Anderton's granddaughter by unknown parties. "We've already attracted more notice here than we should have."

"And we'd be gone by now, with the girl, if you had followed through," Itzel said. "I do understand how you feel, my friend. The girl distinguished herself admirably in combat with the Sons, as did her mother, but the fact remains that unless we at least attempt this ritual, the Sons will pick us off one by one until there is no one to stop them. The Daughters must be able to endure into the future. This is bigger than the life of a single child."

Amadia tossed down the newspaper and walked to the window overlooking Hasel Street. "That sounds like Alexandria talking out of your mouth, Itzel."

"You may detest her," Itzel replied, "but that does not mean she is wrong. Why do you two hate each other so much?"

Amadia turned from the window. "How much do you know about the Grail of Lilith?" she asked. Itzel furrowed her brow and the hummingbirds lighted on her outstretched index finger.

"I know what I was taught by the Nagul," she said. "The goddess, Ix Chel—who is also known as Lilith—shed her moon-blood into the flask that came to be known as the Grail. It was the first container to hold the essence of her power and wisdom. In time, as the Daughters grew in number and spread across the world to battle the monstrous Sons of Tezcatlipoca, certain Daughters were given lesser flasks that were connected to the first Grail and the great endless river of the Mother's blood, stored within it."

"Guardianship of the Grail is a great responsibility and a privilege," Amadia said. "Over nine hundred years ago, Alexandria Poole's ancestors were given that privilege, the first whites to ever be so honored. Three centuries ago, my *iya*, my mother, took the Grail away from Alexandria's family for abusing its power."

"Abusing it? How?" Itzel asked, dismissing the charmed hummingbirds from her thrall. They flew across the room and lighted in a small birdcage. She leaned forward intently

"The Pooles were drinking from the Grail more than just the one time prescribed by the initiation ritual. Lilith's blood was . . . influencing them, affecting their children . . . changing them in unnatural ways."

Itzel winced a little. "More than once? I can't imagine. It felt like starlight and acid was burning through me when I took the blood at seven."

"Seven?" Amadia said. "So young."

"It's the way of the Nagul," Itzel said. "In order to develop the nonphysical powers the blood grants us, we must begin the training a bit younger than most traditions do. The blood alters the brain as it grows and develops in your childhood." Itzel noted the look on Amadia's face. "You don't consider me 'unnatural,' do you, Amadia?"

"I must admit, I find what you do a bit . . . unnerving," Amadia said. Itzel smiled slightly at the admission. "But, no," Amadia continued, "if anything it seems your training has given you well-balanced mental faculties."

"We are taught to respect this gift from Ix Chel," Itzel said. "To use it to better understand all living things and to harness it to better defend the world from wickedness. If one were to take the blood that young without proper instruction, it would be very dangerous, very bad."

"The Pooles, including Alexandria, are unstable, often dangerously so," Amadia said. "They used the Grail in their own attempt to gain control of the British Isles shortly after the fall of the Roman's empire. They . . . it's better not to discuss it. Needless to say, they proved they could not be trusted with the Grail, and it was recovered by my *iya*, Raashida. The Pooles hate Raashida, and since she trained me, they hate me as well."

"If she took the Grail away from Alexandria's family," Itzel asked, "why did she give it to the pirate queen to trust?"

"A very good question," Amadia said. "Whenever she'd tell me the story all she would say on the matter was that her faith was restored and she knew she had found a good guardian for the Grail."

Itzel snorted. "Obviously not, or else we wouldn't be in this mess now."

"I trust my *iya*," Amadia said. "I'm sure she had her reasons."

"Well, that explains the sense I got between you and Alexandria," Itzel said. "Now why do you and Ya hate one another so much?"

Amadia laughed. "It was wise of the Mother to make it a rule that we Daughters do not come together unless it is a dire crisis. I once had to pursue a bit of business in her country about six years ago. China was in the middle of a bloody civil war, and I was there to stop a monstrous creature that fed off of war and hatred." Amadia's eyes dulled a bit. "It ate its fill. Tens of millions dead. I ended it, but Ya resented my intrusion into 'her' country, and she disagreed with my methods. We nearly came to blows several times and there was a . . . personal matter that I do confess I was in the wrong about."

Itzel was silent for a moment. "It is strange we can have so many things in common and yet be so divided."

"Everyone thinks their path is the proper one," Amadia said. "Especially the wicked." Amadia sat down on the sofa next to her fellow Daughter. "I know we agreed to take on this mission, but I think it wise to advise Alexandria and the others that the Sons are here and that they have targeted the girl. We could send a coded telegram and keep an eye on the girl to make sure she is safe."

"I suppose that seems reasonable given the change in circumstances. You're stalling," Itzel said.

"And you didn't even have to read my mind," Amadia said. "You . . . you can't do that, can you?"

Itzel said nothing. The ghost of a smile returned to her child-like face.

The *Leviathan* was docked in a slip near Boyce's Wharves, in the sprawling, vibrant and chaotic maze of Charleston's port. The ship was an old opium clipper, well past her prime. The figurehead on the bow of the ship was a grotesque mermaid, partly digested by time. It had blue-green scaled skin and a jagged, uneven crown sunk, painfully, into her brow. Most of the mermaid's features had been eroded away; she no longer had eyes or a nose, but her mouth was like a lamprey's, wreathed in gnarled tentacles. The ship's wooden, worm-eaten hull was stained dark against the black, lapping tongues of the sea. Her ship rig was furled, the spidery forest of masts and lines silhouetted in the meager moonlight like the skeletal remains of trees in a burned-out forest. The old salts all muttered about how queer the ship was. No crew seemed to occupy her in the accusing light of day, but shadows moved along her decks and nests once night fell. Some of the venerable sailors would spit and cross themselves, whispering the ship was cursed, crewed by devils and the undead. They were close to the truth, but it was far worse.

The smiling man, his given name Rory Danvers, entered the captain's cabin and fell to one knee. His usual sardonic tone abandoned him. He was in the presence of a god, his god, ancient and merciless. "Father," he said.

The interior of the cabin was sparse and poorly lit by a single oil lamp.

There was a bunk, desk and chair. On a wooden table in the corner were several pieces of broken ancient clay tablets marked with odd chicken-scratch-like print. An ankh figured prominently on the tablets' faces. There was also an ancient vase painted with figures. Rory thought it might be Grecian. It depicted a bearded man hurling lightning at a grinning winged being with the upper body of a man and a lower body made up of snakes.

Sitting in the chair was the master of the ship and Rory's master as well. The man in the chair was tall and lanky, a bit like a scarecrow. His hair was black and straight, worn in a short cut with a side part. He was clean shaven.

Most of his face fell in the shadows cast by the lamp, but Rory knew Father's false face well and had seen it many times. His eyes were bright green, almost luminous, and seemed to burn their way out of the shadow. Looking into those eyes was akin to looking into the eyes of a lizard, or snake; there was nothing of human empathy in them. The mouth was too wide, the nostrils flared and shaped oddly, the shape of the eyes just slightly wrong. Every detail was minutely asymmetrical, more than normal human variation might allow, and all the proportions were subtly off as well.

The whole of the man's face looked as though it had been crafted by an artist that had never seen a human being before. If you saw the man you wouldn't know immediately that something was wrong about him, but the parts of your brain that worked on instinct would know you were in the presence of something alien and would silently scream in the primordial chemical language of fear.

Father wore a dark suit with a vest, a few years out of fashion. He put down on the desk the book he had been reading, *The Coming Race,* by Edward Bulwer-Lytton, with a hand that had slightly-too-long fingers.

"Yes, Rory?" Father said.

"Forgive me for interrupting," Rory said, still kneeling. He kept his head down, looking at the floor. He noticed a rat's corpse curled up near the bulk-head. The creature was frozen in death, a grimace of pain on its tiny face. For a moment he wondered what had killed it, then his mind filled in the blanks for him when he glanced up and saw Father's wide, inhuman shadow on the wall, writhing and undulating. The shadow didn't match the veneer of the man sitting calmly in the chair.

"An interesting premise," Father said, gently tapping the book. "I foresee we can help some very disturbed minds get inspiration from it, which should be delightful to watch unfold. I take it your mission was not successful?"

"No, Father," Rory said, a tiny trickle of terror seeping into his broken mind. "I'm the only one to escape alive. Forgive me, it was those damn Daughters of the Whore-Mother. They are here in Charleston. They want the girl too."

"Of course they do," Father said. "They think they need her to survive." Father laughed and Rory nearly wet himself from the sound, even though he had heard it many times before. Father's laugh was akin to hearing a live skinned cat tossed into scalding water.

"You and the others did very well, Rory," Father said. "I didn't expect you to stop them, just convince them. I'm sure you were all very sincere in your efforts."

When the Sons of Typhon had found Rory, he was eleven years old and slitting the throats of alley bums in Leeds. He was semi-feral, constantly hungry, with the conscience and moral faculties of a sewer rat. All he had known since then was the brutal love and discipline of the Sons. When he had undergone his initiation and drunk Father's blood, his rebirth had involved only mental changes. His mind was now truly inhuman and cosmically obscene in its contemplation. All his genius departed him in the presence of Father, however, and he became dull with fear, like an animal. He was smart enough to know he was before a thing that saw all of humanity as bacteria. Father had demonstrated many times his capacity for casual, almost thoughtless murder since his return from his imprisonment. Rory feared very few things upon the Earth, but Father was not of the Earth.

"The beauty of it is," Father explained, "even for all their much-lauded moral superiority, in the end they are exactly like any other stupid animal; they will do anything to try to survive. Life, Rory, is the ultimate narcotic. Those who have had a taste of it drift vapidly through this illusory world, slapped together by an imperfect architect with delusions of divinity. His ham-handed design is a fusion of slaughterhouse and asylum, but the true jest is that the poor addled addicts will do anything for more. They beg for more time in this abattoir. The Daughters will have to cut the child open and drain her dry to complete the ritual. Then there's our little surprise. So your failure is our victory, my most loyal of sons. Rise. Tell me what happened. Use that beautifully altered ten-dimensional brain of yours to give me every salient detail."

Rory stood and did as he was told, providing as much detail as his incalculable memory could summon. As Rory told his tale, Father rose from his chair and walked to the table holding the various artifacts.

"My old love is beginning to awaken inside the girl. We can't have that. And it troubles me that Maude Stapleton has forgotten the kindness I did for her, not so long ago. Have I told you the story, Rory, since I returned? How I owe my freedom to Maude Stapleton and how she owes me her life?"

"No, Father," Rory said.

"Several months . . . is it months? It's so hard to keep track of how you little things follow time. Several months ago, Maude came to me in my dreary little prison under the town of Golgotha. Had I been imprisoned there for over a century? Yes, a century. It's so strange, Rory, that you people have so many words for time, for the thing that eats you alive. I think you do that to make you feel like you control it, and not the other way around.

"Maude had been in a fierce battle. She was bleeding out, dying. I talked with her. She had disturbed the *pharmakis* wards that had been holding me there when she stumbled, dying into my chamber. I wanted to try to under-stand what you finite things experience when you are ending; when you look back at your pathetic flutter of existence, what do you regret, what do you treasure? Maude's answer intrigued me, it amused me, and so I decided I'd keep her around for a bit. I saved her life, healed her. Once I discovered she was one of the Daughters, I warned her about interfering with me. And now she is in the middle of my gambit against the Daughters. Sweet little Con-stance is exactly what I need to be able to return to Carcosa and reclaim what is rightfully mine. Maude is the only variable not accounted for in my design. Her arrival is no coincidence. Still, Maude did accidentally free me. I should have gratitude for that, I suppose, shouldn't I, Rory? Isn't that what human beings do, show appreciation? Compassion? Understanding?"

"I . . . I wouldn't know, sir," Rory responded. Father ran a sinuous finger over the ancient Grecian urn. He seemed lost in his own thoughts as he traced the shape of the winged man-snake's face with the tip of his finger.

"No, of course you wouldn't, how could you? You were elevated above them, above the chattel you descended from. I fanned the feeble, dying flame of Maude's blink of a life and renewed it when she had fallen before her enemies, just as her thread was about to be snipped. A little gratitude would be nice, is that the word, *nice*? I did warn her to not interfere in my ascen-dancc back into the world. I sense my ex-wife's meddling will is behind Maude's interference."

Father turned away from his treasures.

"Rory, how many Sons do we have in this city? Adepts with full training."

"Including the ship's crew we brought with us, it was seven, Father," Rory replied. "After the other night, it's down to four."

"How many of the Unfeeling do we have here?"

"Ten we can mobilize, Father, but none have taken your blood. They are not true Sons yet."

"They will do for the task ahead," Father said. "It is time to teach Miss Stapleton a lesson in gratitude."

12

The Seven of Swords

Abomey, Kingdom of Dahomey, Africa
July 24, 1721

They arrived at the earthen-red walls of Abomey. The walls that circled the city, furrowed and streaked from the rains, began six miles out. The exterior of the walls were ringed by a wide trench, five feet deep, and filled with thorny acacia bushes, the traditional fortress fortification in this part of Africa.

The traffic on the roads into the city was funneled across bridges over the acacia trench. Each bridge led to a fortified gate. Adu told them that there were six gates around the city.

They were nearing one such gate, where a cluster of warriors, armed with French muskets as well as swords, stood and stopped each visitor before they passed through. A Fon woman, tall and officious in bearing, was interviewing each traveler before allowing them entrance into the city. A colorful headdress was perched on her head. She wore an ornate necklace of bronze and pearl that was perhaps a badge of office. Besides the necklace, she wore no top, and was dressed only in a dyed purple and white *kanga*.

"They put women in charge of the gate?" Belrose chuckled.

"There are counterparts of the opposite sex for many roles in the government," Adu said. "Vodun, the religion of the Fon and the Yoruba, believes in balance and equanimity in both the spirit and the flesh worlds, and in masculine and feminine forces. They respect the strengths and the weaknesses of both."

"Is it true their kings claim to be gods?" Belrose asked as they shuffled forward in the line.

"Not exactly," Adu said. "The Fon hold great reverence and respect for their ancestors and they worship the spirits of their dead kings. Each king of Dahomey has built a palace here in Abomey that is also something of a shrine. The royal bloodline is said to have descended from the union of Princess Aligbonon of Tado and a panther spirit."

"Panther?" Anne said.

"If you'd ever seen them fight," Adu said, "you'd believe it."

At the checkpoint, Adu stepped forward and began to address the woman in the Fon tongue. Anne knew less than a smattering of the tongue, but one word she thought she heard both of them use several times was *Purrah*.

After a rapid conversation that involved a great deal of pointing at Anne, and especially her red hair, Adu finally seemed to have made the woman happy. The official gestured the party toward the gateway arch. "Welcome to the city of kings," she said in broken French. "May your stay be peaceful and enjoyable. And may Mawu-Lisa and the Vodu walk with you here."

They passed through the gate into Abomey proper. The streets were narrow paved mazes, bustling with people dressed in colorful garb of oranges, reds, blues, greens and yellows. Every imaginable hue and pattern blurred by them. Anne saw bracelets and entire tunics meticulously made of smooth wooden beads, rainbow headdresses of feathers, shell and pearl, and complex jewelry made of bronze, gold and iron worn by people on the street that would put to shame the crude baubles of some European nobles.

The hot, humid air was full of all the familiar smells of a big city—food cooking, the musky smell of animals and human sweat, mixed with the aroma of clay baking in the blazing sun. There was the hum of voices, the cool splashing sounds of water under shaded groves of palms.

"Why were we given the royal ass-kissing at the door?" Anne asked. "And what pray tell is a Purrah?"

"It's a local association," Adu said, enjoying the feel of the great city settling around him. He waved his hand dismissively as if chasing away a fly. "Like a guild of sorts. The lovely lady at the gate is affiliated with an allied organization of the Purrah and the Sande, in this district. She smoothed things over for us a bit. We can arrange to resupply here, and be on our way in a few days' time."

"Maybe by then I'll have some clue why we're here," Anne said, "and where we're headed next."

This was a sprawling city teeming with people, mostly Fon, or one of the neighboring tribal groups. Occasionally, Anne glimpsed a white face—most likely a slaver or other merchant—in the crowds. The buildings were clustered together along the narrow streets. Farther up the road from the gate was the din of a massive open-air marketplace. Twisting bronze sculpture stood like guardians at the intersections of crossroads, delineating between fields of crops that fed this metropolis and the numerous villages, like neighborhoods, that existed within Abomey's expansive walls.

There was art everywhere and most of it was unlike anything Anne had ever seen. The interior of the massive city walls and the walls of most of the buildings within were covered with paintings of kings, gods, animals and spirits that were unions of man and beast. Many of the paintings and reliefs were devoted to the history and mythology of the Dahomey kings. Some newer pieces included images of muskets, European sailing vessels and white men interacting with the god-like king. A busy public square they walked through had at its center a heavy iron statue of a bipedal scaled creature that was a union of man and shark adorned with the trappings of a king.

"Hopefully your friend back there won't get too curious about us," Anne said as a group of male and female soldiers walked by, dressed in beaded vests and simple skirt-like wraps. The crowds parted for them as they passed. Anne noticed one of the female warriors give her a sidelong look, that suspicious age-old recognition between guard and criminal. Somehow seeing the same look on the Amazon's face that she had seen from the law her entire life made Anne feel a little more at home.

A few hours later, the company was in negotiations with a lodge keeper to secure quarters for the approaching night. A contingent of armed female warriors surrounded the expedition, muskets and blades at the ready. Belrose began to draw his rapier, but Anne motioned for him to hold.

"Have a care, Hummingbird," Adu said. "These are the Ahosi, those 'Amazons' you heard of. They are very good. They might just clip your wings."

The woman official who had been at the gate earlier in the day was with them, as was her male counterpart. The female official stepped forward.

"You and your companions are honored to be guests of his majesty, King Agaja," the official said in French. "The king further honors you. He has sent his personal bodyguard, the Ahosi—the King's Brides—to escort you to the royal palace, so that no harm may befall you."

"One could die from so much honor," Belrose muttered quietly to Anne.

"Lucky us," Anne said, glaring at Adu. "You sure I'm not on your list of community service projects?"

"Calm yourself. If they were going to kill us," Adu said, "we'd be dead . . . unless of course they intend to make us into a sacrificial offering. Is it sacrifice season again so soon?" Anne and Belrose looked at each other, then back to Adu.

"Don't worry," Adu said. "I'll speak for us to the king. It will be fine."

"That's worked out so well so far," Anne said as they were herded by the Ahosi toward the palace.

The royal palace of King Agaja was like a city within a city. The compound was made up of multiple long, low buildings, each with their own court-yards for different political, social and religious purposes. There were opu-lent bedchambers for the king, his numerous wives and children, as well as his inner council of advisers, visiting merchants from Europe, dignitaries from other villages within the kingdom and secluded dens for the king to take council from his array of oracles, priests and fortune-tellers. There was also considerable barracks space provided for the Ahosi, the king's elite female bodyguards.

Each building's walls were thick to keep the interior cool and comfort-able even in the oppressive heat of midday. The cool darkness of the Kpodoji courtyard, where the king received Anne, Adu and Belrose, was lit with large sconces. The firelight shadows danced across the walls of the courtyard, covered with more murals depicting this king's history and accomplishments. Benches filled with tributes of furs, gold, jewels, boxes of pearls, gilded ornate weapons and European guns were off to the side, clearly there to impress and show the king's power.

The man did make a big impression, Anne thought. King Agaja was easily twice Anne's age. He was a little shy of six feet. His broad, muscular body was crisscrossed with scars from battle and he wore those scars the way a general wears his medals. His chest was bare. His face was broad, but not fat; there was little of the king that might be considered soft. Agaja had a calm, but cautious, countenance. He sat on his throne, an ornately carved chair of wood, as one born to power and authority over countless lives.

Anne had experienced two types of leaders, those who expected to be obeyed and followed out of some ridiculous notions of entitlement or tradition, and those who had bled to lead; it didn't matter if it was a pirate prince, guild master, tavern cook or king, they all fell into one category or the other. You could smell undeserved title on someone like cow flop. Anne noted that the king of the Dahomey looked like he had earned his throne, and was wise enough to know it was never truly won.

Behind Agaja on the right stood one of the Ahosi. She was almost as tall as the king but her build was as sinewy as Agaja's was broad. She was not a beautiful woman, but she was striking, and she had beautiful eyes, hazel, flecked with pale green, that scanned and saw everything. She wore the same beaded vest as the other Ahosi, but she had a series of gold bands adorning her long, regal neck. Her hair was shaved. Claws, fashioned of iron and sharpened to a point, were on each of her long fingers. Those all-seeing eyes locked on Anne and Anne stared back, unblinking. They knew each other, though they had never met.

"All who attend now, fall in reverence to the earth before Agaja, son of Houegbadja, brother of King Akaba, and fifth king of Dahomey, lord of all these lands," one of the king's ministers called out in Fon, as Anne and the rest of her expedition were brought into the royal presence. A translator, an old Fon gentleman, repeated everything in French for the Europeans. Adu, Belrose, the bearers and all the royal court fell to the paved stone floor of the courtyard before the king. Anne saw something she recognized all too well pass behind the king's eyes. He, along with the whole court, seemed fascinated by her red hair. Anne held the king's gaze and slowly lowered herself to one knee, but no farther. No one else saw the shadow of smile pass on Agaja's face for an instant.

"You are going to get yourself killed," Belrose hissed, "and us, too, most likely."

"What happened to meeting death on your own terms?" Anne whispered. "Why don't you clean the floor up a bit with that wicked tongue of yours while you're down there."

The minister searched Agaja's face for guidance about how the king wished to deal with Anne's affront. Agaja gestured, raising his hand, palm up. "Rise," the minister said. "All who seek petition in accordance with the laws and rites of the kingdom, approach the royal presence."

The court and the expedition stood. Adu addressed the minister in Fon and stepped forward. Anne grabbed his sleeve as he passed her. "Tell him we want supplies, and protection through the kingdom," she whispered. "See if they have any information about a city of bone."

"Is that all?" Adu said quietly. "You presume much. He should have taken your head off for your disrespect."

"Yeah," Anne said, "you're right. I think he fancies me."

Adu rolled his eyes and approached the throne. He bowed again before the king and then began to speak in fluent Fon. He made a point of announcing his full name, Adu Ogyinae, which seemed to cause quite a stir in the court. Several agitated ministers shouted at Adu, shaking their heads violently as they pointed at him.

"Want to bet he owes someone money here," Belrose said, leaning over to Anne, "or got someone's sister with child?"

The clamor of the incredulous advisers grew louder and more strident. A murmur began among the various factions and hangers-on within Agaja's court. Anne noticed Agaja watching all the discord silently, thoughtfully, taking advantage of the unexpected outbursts to note true intent, learning from each angry word, each whispered comment.

Adu raised his voice as he brought his hands over his head. His voice echoed far more than the acoustics of the chamber could explain, as if thunder had rumbled out of him. The sconces in the courtyard flared and the flames shivered as they changed to a bright blue color for an instant, then back to normal. The room fell silent.

Adu spoke slowly, with power and menace in each word. He repeated his name several times, striking his fist to his chest each time he said it. He pointed to the king and then to the murals on the walls depicting Agaja's father and his fathers before him, all the kings of Dahomey, as his voice softened slightly but maintained its forceful authority.

Adu gestured broadly, as if he were trying to encompass all the world in his arms. He lowered his voice to a growl and asked Agaja a question, pointing to a tapestry of yellow and blue dyed cloth, adorned with strips of gold and pearl, that hung in a shadowy corner of the room. The king nodded toward the cloth and quietly gave a command. A servant, trembling, pulled the tapestry aside to reveal another mural painted on the wall.

It was drawn in a very primitive, simplistic style, like cave paintings. The style immediately reminded Anne of the pictures on the box with the map. The first picture depicted an array of creatures—giant, angry, and alien—looming over tiny huddled figures of men. Beneath the puny men was a circle and curled within that ring was a thing that looked like a coiled snake.

The second picture had small figures, women, with spears and fire, arms raised in defiance of the cyclopean monsters. One figure that stood alone was that of a man with seeming lightning bolts coming from him, slaying monsters. Several of the creatures were on fire, others flailed, spears piercing their flesh and some of the giants lay slain, the women standing victorious atop them.

The serpent in the circle remained unchanged in the second mural, coiled and unmoving.

Adu pointed to the murals and raised his voice again. He gestured to the assembled Ahosi and then to Anne, pointing markedly at her and proclaiming something in a booming voice.

"Merde," Bellrose muttered.

"Aye," Anne said.

Agaja stood and spoke. The king's voice, a deep bass, filled all the empty spaces in the chamber and was easily the equal of Adu's. He turned to the woman at his side, nodded to her and then looked across the room to Anne.

"We shall see," the king said, in English. He clapped his hands once and called out a command in Fon. The court musicians began to play. The fiddle-like instruments, called *soku,* each played a single note, the musicians working in perfect union to create a driving rhythm. Several types of drums, the goblet-shaped *djembe,* and the *akuba,* thudded out an insistent tattoo. The *shekere,* bead-covered gourds, hissed like the hot afternoon rain, and the royal singers slid their voices up and down the range, warbling a single note in melisma, as they brought the whole court to sing, sway and clap to the music.

"What did you do now?" Anne growled at Adu as he walked over, a grim look on his face.

"It's a war song," Adu said. "You're going to war."

"War? The fuck I am," Anne said. "With who?" Adu pointed to the Amazon the king was now quietly addressing, the bald woman with the iron claws.

"Her," he said. "Her name is Nourbese Edenausegboye Sosi Ayawa."

"Nor-beec-e, Eden, what?" Anne said.

"She's the supreme commander and war chief of the Ahosi," Adu stated. "If you win, you get her job."

"Her what? I don't want her bloody job!" Anne said. Belrose had removed a small flask from his pocket and handed it to Anne.

The music was building in tempo now, the clapping and singing growing louder, faster, more frenzied, as if the music itself were a living entity, demanding action.

"I asked you to get us supplies, directions and an escort," Anne said to Adu, "and you pick a bloody row for me with the queen of the fucking Amazons!"

"You're grasping it perfectly," Adu said. "Things . . . moved quickly. Negotiations are always fluid, you know."

"You leasing bastard," Anne said, taking a sip on the flask. "What happens if she wins?"

"She keeps her job," Adu said. "And you'll be dead, also. It's to the death. You die."

Anne drained the flask and handed it back to Belrose, whispering something to him as she did. "You're bad as a bitch's back leg," she said to Adu as she tightened her headscarf to hold back her hair and removed any excess gear. "When this is over, you and I are going to have words, thundery voice and that trick you did with the fire notwithstanding, and you are going to give me some straight peggin' answers as to who the hell you are and what the hell you're trying to do to me."

"Fair enough," Adu said, taking Anne's burdens. He placed them on a bench. "You make it through this and you deserve those answers."

"So what are the rules to this daft game?" Anne asked. Across the room, Nourbese Edenausegboye Sosi Ayawa had strapped a nasty-looking short blade to her belt, and was twirling two long, heavy sticks of wood in her iron-clawed hands. Her gaze was cutting into Anne.

"No formal rules," Adu said. "This is ritual combat to the death. The Fon don't consider war a game, so anything goes."

"Good," Anne said as her pistol came up. She fired the flintlock at Nourbese, whose eyes widened in comprehension. A shower of sparks sprayed from the frizzen, accompanied by a thunderous explosion from the wide barrel. A section of the back of the king's throne shattered as the ball struck it. Nourbese, unwounded and hurtling toward Anne, let loose a warbling shriek as she swung one of the heavy wooden sticks at Anne's head. Anne brought up the still-smoking pistol and parried the first stick. Her second flintlock came up to gut-shoot the Amazon, but when Anne pulled the trigger, nothing happened.

"Shit," Anne had time to utter. The other fighting stick came down on the flintlock, setting off the faulty primer and the pistol boomed as it blasted the floor of the courtyard, scattering debris. Anne head-butted Nourbese and there was a crunch as Nourbese's nose broke, driving the Fon warrior back a few steps. Anne advanced, swinging the two heavy pistols as she did. Nourbese parried with her fighting sticks and the two women circled, trading blows and parries at a blinding pace.

Nourbese spit bright red blood into Anne's eyes and pressed her attack with the sticks. One caught the pirate firmly in the forearm. Anne felt something pop and the arm dropped, the pistol thudding to the floor. Blinded, she swung wildly with the other gun and felt it connect with Nourbese's jaw. The war chief stumbled back and skidded to the ground. The court was roaring with cheers and boos. The music continued at its breakneck tempo, voices raised in song, almost feverish.

Anne wiped the blood from her eyes with her throbbing injured arm. It still worked, but not well. Nourbese was getting to her feet. Anne howled and charged her, launching herself at the Amazon and tackling her just as she was about to stand. Nourbese managed to drive a foot into Anne's stomach as the pirate crashed down onto her, driving a fist into Nourbese's already broken nose. The force of the kick knocked Anne off and she rolled across the floor a few feet away.

Both women struggled to recover enough to get up. Nourbese made it up first and drew her blade. She crouched low and circled Anne, who was just recovering her breath. Anne rolled forward, tucking her head as Nourbese lunged with the sword, missing. Anne came up on her feet and spun, putting all her weight into a wild roundhouse punch. Nourbese side-stepped it and slashed again with her weapon, opening an ugly wound across Anne's upper stomach. Anne gasped at the sharp pain and lashed out, landing a weak uppercut on Nourbese's bruised chin with her injured arm.

It bought Anne a few seconds, enough time to get some distance between her and the sword. She glanced at Adu, who was sitting on a bench. He was looking at her with an expression of stone. Anne drew her cutlass, and went to en garde position. The expression on Adu's face slipped for a moment and Anne saw the disappointment peek out. Nourbese advanced, smiling now, as best she could with a swollen jaw. She said something in Fon.

"I don't speak your damn language," Anne said in very poor French as they circled. She dropped her weak arm, keeping it close to her chest and the gushing wound. Anne pulled up her sash in a feeble attempt to use it to help hold her guts in. Both women were looking for an opening; their blades were close to the same length, so neither had that advantage.

"I said, I've fought old, incontinent Yoruba women that gave me more of a challenge," Nourbese replied in French. "Some champion you are. You're not worthy of Oya's treasure."

"Okay, I don't exactly speak a lot of French either," Anne managed to say. "I don't know who the blazes Oya is, but you can peggin' have her!"

Anne lunged with her blade. Nourbese handily parried it, and flashed out with her iron finger-claws. Anne felt burning pain rip through the upper shoulder of her already badly injured arm. She hissed and that was enough distraction for Nourbese to disarm her with a forceful downward sword break across the blade of her machete. Anne's blade clattered to the floor. Nourbese's claws flashed out again as the pirate tried to stagger back. Anne swept her head back, and that saved her throat from being opened by the iron claws. A few strands of her long, red hair floated to the slippery, blood-soaked floor.

Anne slipped and fell back onto her ass. Her whole left arm was burning and soaked in blood. Her belly wound gushed and the shadows in the chamber seemed to lengthen and distort at the fraying edges of her vision. The music, the voices, the singing and the shouting echoed and distorted. Nourbese tossed aside her bloody blade and moved toward Anne, crouching low, her claws at the ready.

Belrose began to draw his sword, but Adu placed a cautioning hand on the former Musketeer's shoulder. "No," Adu said.

"She's lost too much blood," Belrose said. "I've seen this before, we have to help her."

"I've seen it too," Adu said. "If you act, Agaja will kill all of us."

"Just know this," Belrose said leaning in close to whisper in Adu's ear. "She told me if she dies, you die, and she's already paid me more than enough gold to do her that honor."

"I would expect nothing less," Adu said.

The music was sounding strangely familiar to Anne now, as she sat stuporous, bleeding out on the floor. All the pieces were there . . . the fiddles, the drums . . . yes! It was a port, a jig. A little strange in some parts but in others exactly the same. A peggin' bloody jig.

The flickering fires of the audience chamber became the familiar shadowy corners of a hearth-lit tavern. The voices raised in song and shouting in anger. She was eight, and she had run away again, to hide in the crowded harbors and ports of London. This was before . . . no, keep that away. You don't need it now; you never need it. All the people from every part of the world, all the sounds and smells, and the ships—those beautiful, tall, glorious ships—promising adventure, and distant worlds, promising a new life, a new Anne.

The inns and taverns were where she'd hide until her ma or da found her and dragged her home. Da usually beat her for running, for hanging out in those places. It was worth the beatings, just for the music. She used to love to watch the dances, the jigs, so full of wild abandon, wild lust for life. The music was like it was singing the song inside herself, wild, vital, pure, free. The memory was warm and safe, just as it had been when she was a little girl, and she was beginning to pull it up about herself, like a favorite quilt, when she saw the kite, perched on the bar, looking at her with golden eyes brimming with secrets.

"*Get up, girl,*" the kite said. It was a woman's voice, she almost knew it, an old woman. "*Get your narrow little hindquarters up, or you die here. What do you want more, to be living or to be dying? Make your choice, stick to it. In or out?*"

The dancers on the tavern floor drifted about, spinning and twirling in time to the mad music. The panther moved through them like hungry smoke, like the cool mist crawling along the hot jungle floor. It was coming closer, closer. It was a woman, Nourbese, now, her claw already wet with Anne's blood. Closer still. The kite perched on the king's broken throne.

"*Time's up,*" the kite said, "*piss or get off the pot.*"

Anne groaned and clutched tighter at her belly wound; her eyes fluttered, then closed as Nourbese struck. Anne tossed the contents of the torn paper cartridge of black powder, tucked into her sash, into the Amazon's eyes. Nourbese shouted in pain and reached instinctively for her eyes. Anne kicked up as hard as a pissed mule, driving Nourbese's clawed hands back into her own face. The warrior fell back, pulling her claws free from her bleeding, swollen face. Nourbese's one good eye, red and tearing, squinted open.

Anne managed to stand while Nourbese was recovering. Her awareness swam away for a moment, but she stayed on her feet. She heard the jig thrumming in her ears and she shuffled toward Nourbese, sliding to her blind side. She jabbed hard with her remaining good arm and connected with the warrior's face, with the eye that was swollen closed. Anne followed up with another punch low, then a low kick, and then another strike to the chin, all in time to the music.

"What the hell is she doing?" Adu asked.

"Dancing?" Belrose said. "It like's she trying to dance a jig."

Nourbese pivoted to try to see, but Anne was already driving her fist into Nourbese's open eye. Nourbese lashed out and the claws sank into Anne's stomach again. Blood spilled from Anne's mouth as she gurgled, but she refused to give ground, refused to drop. Anne screamed in pain and smashed her forearm into Nourbese's throat. The Amazon made a choking sound and fell back onto the floor, and lay still. A roar went up from the court. Anne tried to bow, but almost fell over; blood splashed out of her, and she looked up at King Agaja and laughed, crimson spilling from her split lips and mouth as she did.

Anne dropped on top of Nourbese, grabbed one of her limp hands and pulled off a bladed finger cap. She placed the small blade next to Nourbese's throat. She looked up at the king. His face said nothing, which in itself said something. She looked to Adu; his face was as the king's. She looked down at Nourbese's swollen, bloody face. She knew what both men, what the blood-drunk crowd, wanted her to do, almost willed her to do.

"Ream scrap, luv," Anne slurred through swollen lips. "Real flash, but I'd rather hold a candle to the devil than have your job." Anne dropped the finger blade. She looked up at the king, spit a fat glob of blood at his feet and collapsed. As her awareness drained away with her blood into deep darkness, Anne's last thought was, *Where had that damn bird gotten to?*

13

The Seven of Wands

Charleston, South Carolina
May 20, 1871

The stentorian voice of the bailiff silenced the murmur of the courtroom. "All rise, the Court of Common Pleas for the County of Charleston is now in session! The Honorable Judge O. E. Davenkirk presiding! All who would make petition before the court approach!"

Judge Davenkirk was a jowly man in his seventies, with gray hair swept back from a wide face, with uneven, florid patches. His eyes were brown and a little watery. He wore the traditional black robe, with a bit of shirt collar peeking out from under it. He sat down with a bit of a wheeze and a groan. The sharp crack of Davenkirk's gavel stilled the last whispers in the room.

"Y'all be seated," the judge said, glancing at Maude and smiling slightly.

The courtroom was already uncomfortably warm and humid and it was only nine A.M. An early morning May shower had turned mostly to steam, making the Charleston air heavy, hot and damp. Maude sat at one table with Arabella Mansfield. Bella was dressed in conservative attire. At the other counsel table was her father and his attorney, Andrew Rutledge.

Rutledge was a slender whip of a man, with dark hair that was rapidly graying, slicked back and parted sharply down the middle. His eyes were blue, bright and sharp. He whispered something to Martin and Martin chuckled and glanced at Maude and Arabella.

Martin looked as if he had recovered from his injuries and looked as healthy and formidable as ever. However, Maude noticed the slight stiffness in his movements and knew her father was far from recovered but had no intent of showing any weakness.

For her part, Maude was wearing an expensive, but subdued, dress of dark green with white silken ruffles at the collar and sleeves. Her hair was styled in a tight and proper chignon. Arabella had urged her to dress feminine and attractive but to make sure she looked business-like as well.

"I want you to get the judge's attention," she said, "but not hold it, if you get my meaning."

"Why?" Maude had asked.

"Men are drawn to attractive women," Arabella said. "They pay attention to them initially, but if the woman comes off as too attractive they diminish in the man's estimation, they become an objet d'art, not a person to be heard." Maude realized the strategy was very similar to the rules of camouflage and seduction Gran had taught her. Maude shook her head. "It's a balancing act," Arabella continued.

"Isn't it always," Maude said.

"All right, let's see if we can't clear the docket quickly today," Judge Davenkirk said. " 'Fore it gets too blessed hot!" He glanced to his bailiff, "First on the docket, Cooley?"

"Stapleton v. Anderton," Cooley announced loud enough for the principals and those in the gallery to hear. "All those involved in this matter present in the courtroom?"

"Andrew Rutledge for the defendant, your honor," Martin's lawyer said, standing and bowing slightly at the waist.

"Good to see you again, Andy," Judge Davenkirk said, nodding and smiling to the lawyer.

"Arabella Babb Mansfield for the plaintiff, your honor," Bella said, standing. Judge Davenkirk's face dropped from the smile.

"I thought you were her sister or somethin'," the judge said. "Up there to give her some comfort and such. You trying to tell me you're a lawyer, young lady, 'cause this here is a court of law and I don't take too kindly to pranks in my courtroom. Did Judge Horn put you up to this? Neil's always been a mischievous fella."

Bella didn't miss a beat, she didn't even blink. She picked up a packet of documents from the table. "Permission to approach, your honor?" Davenkirk nodded, gesturing for the documents.

"I submit these for the court's approval," Arabella said. "This is verification of my admission to the state bar of Iowa . . ."

"Your honor!" Rutledge interrupted, standing. "This is absolute nonsense! This woman could be the plaintiff's scullery maid for all we know . . ."

Bella continued to look at the judge. She waited for Rutledge to take a breath and then continued as if he had said nothing. ". . . and this packet of documents includes affidavits from several of the clerks of the Iowa District Court attesting to my successful passing of the bar examination, and my swearing in as an officer of the court, as well as letters of recommendation from numerous judges, sitting and retired, at both the state and federal jurisdictions. You will also find numerous letters of commendation from . . ."

"Your honor!" Rutledge raised his voice higher than before. "I must strongly object to this preposterous mockery of our sacred legal process! The plaintiff has access to competent legal counsel certified by this state's bar! She could pick any of dozens of reputable male attorneys here in Charleston that would pass muster to practice law in this court, instead . . ."

". . . letters of commendation from numerous attorneys and academics, for your honor's examination," Bella concluded, again calm and even-tempered. Maude was impressed by how unruffled Bella was; her body language, her respiration and pupil constriction all reflected that she was as still as a mountain lake. She presented the papers to Cooley, the bailiff, and Cooley looked to Davenkirk for guidance. The judge took the papers from the bailiff.

"What about that, Miss Stapleton?" Davenkirk asked as he leafed through the papers. "You could have picked a local attorney, why Miss Mansfield here?"

Maude stood. She nervously cleared her throat and looked toward the table for a moment. She was neither nervous, nor needed to clear her throat. They had anticipated this question being asked and they were ready for it. After an interval of a second or two, Maude looked up and matched Davenkirk's gaze. "Your honor, my father is a very wealthy and influential man in Charleston," she began. "I didn't feel that I could find representation locally that he didn't personally know or that he couldn't influence to not take my case."

Martin reddened at the accusation. Rutledge grunted in indignation. "Your honor, that is a bald-faced lie! My client . . ."

"Mr. Rutledge," Judge Davenkirk cut off the attorney. "That is enough! I expect you to comport yourself in my courtroom with some gentlemanly decorum." He looked over again to Maude. "Miss Stapleton, my apologies for such behavior in my court. It goes beyond the pale of the normal adversarial process demanded of the legal system, and is just plain rude behavior to a lady, and I will not brook it here. I knew your mother, a most gracious and intelligent woman, in spite of her radical politics, and I met you a few times when you were very young, Miss Maude. I see her in you."

"Thank you, your honor," Maude said, and she meant it.

"Please be seated," Davenkirk said, "and thank you for your candid answer."

Maude made herself blush a little and sat down as demurely as she had stood. The judge regarded the opposing counsels before him, and mopped his already sweaty forehead with a handkerchief. "Andy, I'm gonna review these documents and take Miss Mansfield's . . ."

"Mrs., your honor," Arabella said. "I was recently married. Mrs."

"Congratulations on the nuptials, Mrs. Mansfield, then," the judge said. "I'm gonna take her application under consideration. You have to admit, Martin knows everyone in this town. It might be a factor in her being able to acquire competent and unbiased council."

"There's no proof that this woman is competent to practice law," Rutledge said.

"The plaintiff is prepared to proceed at the court's pleasure, your honor, with no further delays," Arabella said in the same professional voice for the court, but her gaze was on Rutledge and a slight crease of a smile curved her lips, all for Rutledge to see, and not the judge, who was examining the papers before him. "We have no desire to waste the court's time with frivolity." Rutledge grew redder and turned to address Davenkirk.

"Your honor," he said, choking back the desire to raise his voice again, "the defense is prepared to stipulate to this . . . woman's credentials and proceed. My client is eager to put this unpleasantness behind him as soon as possible." *And as quietly as possible, too,* Maude thought. Maude glanced back in the gallery to see Alter Cline sitting, writing notes into a small book. He gave her a slight nod and Maude turned back to face the court. "As such," Rutledge added, "we request the plaintiff sign an agreement proclaiming that no appeal will be forthcoming from the judgment of this court based upon the grounds of incompetent representation."

Arabella waited a moment to pause as if she were weighing the option, but her mind was already racing far ahead. She fought with all her considerable

self-control to hide her intent. She turned to Maude, arching an eyebrow—
it was the first sign of excitement Maude had seen in her lawyer since they
entered the courtroom.

"We agree to the defense's request, your honor," Bella said. "Shall Mr. Rutledge draw up the agreement, or would he prefer I do it?" Rutledge almost
chuckled.

"I'll be happy to oblige the lady, your honor," Rutledge said. "I can draft
something this afternoon."

"Plaintiff will of course want to review the document prior to agreeing to
it," Bella said, "and we'd like the court to review it and sign off on it as well.
Unless the defendant objects?"

"Not in the slightest, madame," Rutledge said, obviously quite pleased
with himself.

"Very well then," Davenkirk said, raising his gavel. "I will review these
documents Mrs. Mansfield has provided me with, and we will adjourn until
tomorrow, say at 10 A.M." He banged the gavel. "Next on the docket, Cooley?"

Outside the courthouse, it was hot and bright. There wasn't even a gentle
wind off the ocean to move the thick air. The traffic of people, wagons and
horse-drawn trolley cars moved busily along Meeting Street this Saturday
morning. Arabella and Maude exited by the arches at the corner of Broad
and Meeting.

"That went splendidly," Arabella said. "Better than I expected, in fact."

"Did it?" Maude replied. They crossed Broad and a man driving a carriage stopped for them and doffed his hat. "I have to say, you certainly were
right about the judge, but Arabella, is it really going to help our cause pretending to be something I'm not? I did what you told me to do, I was as sweet
as pie, and I put on the demure act, but I'm here to claim what's mine, legally,
and I don't see how behaving like that does anything but support their view
of women. It doesn't help us."

"We're here to win this, Maude," Arabella said. "You told me this was a
war for you, one that you had planned. I was part of that plan. I'm your general, and you're going to have to trust your general or fire me."

"Well, since you won't let me pay you, that might be a bit difficult,"
Maude said. "Okay, general, explain what happened in there and how it
helped us."

"Tea and food first," Arabella said, nodding to a small cafe across from city hall. "Even mock court with my brother used to cause me to be famished. This was so much better!"

"And I'll pay, if you please," Maude said. "No army fights well on an empty stomach."

They were seated and their orders taken. It was dark and cool in the restaurant. The belts of the mechanical ceiling fans squeaked overhead as their paddles rushed about.

"So," Arabella began, "tell me your impressions of the judge."

"He knew my mother," Maude said. "He genuinely liked her but disapproved of her involvement in the women's movement. He's an old southern gentleman."

"That he is," Bella said, sipping her mint iced tea. She paused for a moment and admired the chilled, ice-filled glass. "I really need to take this back home with me, it's wonderful. You have excellent judgment when it comes to people, Maude. You pegged him, spot on. Yes, he's an old southern gentleman, an antebellum knight. His honor doesn't care for uppity Negros or mannish women. We need him sympathetic to your plight. I'm unsure how long that will last but I'm thankful for any advantage it gives us, even short term. If we went in there, bustling all shoulder-to-shoulder with poor Rutledge, he would have shut us down in five minutes."

"Poor Rutledge?" Maude said. "That man is a wolf on two legs. He plans to demolish us, Bella, and he's going to enjoy it."

"I do believe he is already hoisted on his own petard," Bella said. "It couldn't have worked out any better if I had planned for it." She took a bite of a small cucumber finger sandwich, made an approving sound and popped the rest of the sandwich in her mouth.

"I still don't understand," Maude said. "He's trying to get you kicked off the case before it evens begins."

"And he's already failed," Arabella said, wiping her lips with a linen napkin. "Because the mean old man called you a bald-faced liar in front of our host, Judge Davenkirk . . ."

". . . and no proper southern gentleman could allow that sort of behavior in his presence," Maude said, nodding her approval. Arabella lifted her iced tea and Maude joined her. They clinked the glasses together, quietly. They each took a sip.

"He came to your rescue, Maude, just like I suspected he would, and you played your part perfectly. We've cast Rutledge as the cad and villain of the piece, and severely diminished his ability to bluster and bully, which I intuit is a considerable amount of his courtroom acumen. He's got the weakness I've seen in a lot of successful attorneys—he's not hungry anymore."

"Masterfully played, general," Maude said. "'All warfare is based upon deception. When we are able to attack, we must seem unable.' It's from a Chinese philosopher my Gran had me study when I was a child."

"Sounds like my kind of lawyer," Bella said. "I'd love to read him."

"Only if you can read very old Chinese," Maude said, with a smile. "Besides, I do believe that you could have shown him a thing or two." Bella laughed. "The first shot in the war," Maude said.

Maude returned to Grande Folly that evening. Isaiah gave her a note from Cline that he had something of great import to discuss with her at her earliest convenience. Maude prepared a reply for the reporter and then went back to combing through Gran's extensive library to see if she could find any mention of the Sons or the Grail of Lilith. The archives were even more extensive than she recalled from her years living here. There were books, parchments of vellum, papyrus, animal hides, scrolls and even ancient artifacts, like the stone tablet resting on the reading table among the towers of books, with its stick figures and ankh. The tablet was the first thing Maude had ever touched in this room, so many years ago. She thought of her first time stepping into this room, into Gran's fantastic world, as she ran her fingers across its smooth surface, worn by the caress of time. Maude searched through the night fruitlessly, but she found nothing with any references to the Daughters, the Sons, or the Grail.

The following morning, Rutledge and Martin approached Maude and Arabella in the great well inside the courthouse. Rutledge brandished a copy of *The Charleston Courier* newspaper. "Take a look at what this foolishness has cost your family, Miss Stapleton!"

The headline on the morning paper proclaimed "Shipping Baron Anderton and daughter clash in court over inheritance rights."

"They say there's no such thing as bad publicity," Arabella said, scanning the article.

"This Alter Cline is no local newsman, either," Rutledge said, snatching the paper away from Bella's gaze. "He's a damn Jew carpetbagger from some northern newspaper! He said this story was going to run in papers in Baltimore, Philadelphia and New York! Perhaps as far away as St. Louis and San Francisco!"

"I'd curb that kind of language if I were you, Mr. Rutledge," Arabella said. "Quite a few Jewish folks here in Charleston. Your sheet is showing."

"Maude, do you have any idea what this kind of scandal will do to my business?" Martin said. "They shamelessly mention your mother in here as well, and her connection to the suffrage movement!"

"You were embarrassed by Mother, too, Father, I know," Maude said. "I'm sure her 'featherbrained hobbies' were bad for business as well."

"You have no call to talk to me like that," Martin said. "I loved your mother, and I supported her in everything she did, even the things that never fully made sense to me."

"How magnanimous of you," Maude said. "You tolerated her being a public humiliation to you, how you must have suffered."

"You know absolutely nothing about your mother and me," Martin said. "How could you, she died bringing your ungrateful self into this world! How dare you to presume to know my heart when it comes to Claire! You should be ashamed of yourself!"

Maude tensed; it felt as if she had been punched. Arabella took her by the arm and led her toward the courtroom. "All right, enough of this. Come along, Maude."

"Martin," Rutledge said, "lower your voice. Your health! And let's not give the damn press any more material for their scandal rags."

Alter Cline was just entering the well. Martin turned to the reporter and strode toward him. "You libelous son of a bitch!" Martin shouted across the well, his voice echoing everywhere. "You wrote this garbage, how dare you!"

"Every word of that story is accurate and true, Mr. Anderton," Alter said. "You may not like it but don't impugn my honor, sir. I stand by my work."

"Honor? Sir, you know nothing of that word! I should challenge you to a duel for such unworthy use of the English language!" Martin shouted.

"A duel?" Alter said. "That's barbaric, Mr. Anderton! This nation has seen more than its share of needless bloodshed in the past years! Surely, sir, you are not suggesting to gun down an agent of the press for doing his job, and reporting the facts!"

Rutledge pulled Martin back from Cline with the assistance of one of the court bailiffs.

"He means nothing of the sort," Rutledge said. "We are seriously considering action against that fishwrap that employs you, Mr. Cline! Good day, sir!" Rutledge hurried his client to a quiet meeting room to calm him down. Alter found Maude, pale and silent, on a bench outside the courtroom.

"Maude, are you all right?" Cline asked, sitting next to her.

"He blames me for killing my mother," Maude said softly. "No wonder he never wanted to be home with me, kept me at arm's length all those years. I took the love of his life away from him."

"People say things in anger," Cline said. "Terrible things. He didn't mean it. He's your father, he loves you."

"I am very adept at telling lie from truth, Alter," Maude said. "Sometimes it's a curse. He does love me, the largest part of him loves me very much, but a part of him hates me, and hates me true. I pushed that part out into the light."

"Maude," Alter said. "What you're doing is right. You deserve to be able to live your life as you please, and Constance belongs with you. What I'm doing is my job. Your father . . ."

"This is ugly," Maude said. "It's all so ugly. Damn him for being so stubborn, so sure he's right and I'm wrong. Damn him for making me do this."

The tears were hot and wet on her cheeks, and they surprised her. She controlled her body; she only cried if she willed it so. She touched them to make sure they were real, then looked at her wet fingertips as if they belonged to someone else.

"Maude," Alter said, softly.

Maude closed her eyes and focused her breathing, stilled her heart, controlled all the things she had learned how to control, but the hurt was strong and sharp and it refused to bow to reason, to control. How do you stop pain that has no physical source, no threshold of severity?

Not here, not now. No, you can't.

She made the tears stop. It felt wrong to do that, to force her emotions to hide inside. It felt like dying. Alter's handkerchief was in his hand. He offered it to her. She took it and wiped her eyes.

"Thank you," she said.

"You can't control everything," he said. "It's not the way humans work."

Maude said nothing. She clutched the wet handkerchief tight, and sighed.

"You ready?" Alter asked.

"Yes," Maude said, her voice even and strong again.

14

The High Priestess (Reversed)

Abomey, Kingdom of Dahomey, Africa
August 15, 1721

Existence, for a time, was pain. At first it was sharp and unbearable, twisting, then over time it lessened to dull but constant, married to fever dreams and nightmares, near madness, sweating, and restless, plodding agony. The pain was relieved by the cool darkness of not being, a desert of awareness, deeper and emptier than sleep.

As Anne felt the clammy, sticky, misery-soaked walls of living settle back about her, she heard voices near her body—a man and a woman—she thought the man's voice was Adu's. The woman's voice was older, dry, almost a rattle, but with an energy hidden in it. They spoke a language she didn't know, or recall if she knew, but she seemed to understand them.

"It's still close," Adu said. "We could lose her if we don't give it to her."

"Then we lose her," the raspy woman's voice said. "She is neither ready, nor worthy of it. I doubt she ever will be."

"Because she's white?" Adu asked.

"Because it's in their nature to think they deserve everything," the woman said. Anne tried to laugh at that but slipped on the knife edge of awareness back into the abyss of nothing. Awareness again, an inching ache in her belly. It hurt to breathe, it hurt not to. The same voices again, sounding like they were in a different spot, but close, like before.

"Why are you so convinced that she's worth all this?" the old-sounding woman asked. "She's a thief and pirate. She's here to plunder Carcosa, pick it clean, like any good white."

"And do you recall the circumstances of our first meeting?" Adu said. "I was a thief, trying to steal one of your chickens as I remember. You wanted to skin me alive."

"I still do," she replied. "That was my favorite chicken. What's your point?"

"I know Nimue disappointed your mother so terribly," Adu said.

"She stole her very last secret, and then she murdered her, cast her as the villain, and her stupid white dupes were more than willing to accept all of it," the old woman said, the poison dripping in every word. "Look what they are doing to our lands even now."

"I remember what Nimue Poole did," Adu said. "I was there if you'll recall. It took me a long time to let go of that anger, that betrayal; we cannot control those things outside us, we can only control how we let them change us.

"You have to try to let go of your hatred. It's unhealthy and it blinds your wisdom. Besides, you must see something you like, or you wouldn't have traveled all this way just to look at her and ask me about her. She's got your interest. She's more than a thief. She's passed the first trials already."

"Perhaps she got lucky," the old woman said.

"You call this pegging lucky, you bracket-faced old bat," Anne muttered and then drowned back into the emptiness, into cool limbo.

Another voice, close to her, breath pungent from strong drink. This one she recognized; it was Belrose. "Just a dab to wet your lips," he said in a soft voice, near her ear, "you have a wound of the gut, so no drinking, yes?" The wine was bittersweet, and wet, and wonderful on her lips, and she couldn't stop licking them.

"Get stronger," he said, "and there's more where that came from. Hell, we'll drink a whole vineyard dry." A coarse, hushed chuckle was his laugh. "You fought too well to perish now," the mercenary said. "You need to live so you can brag about it. Get better, *beaute*." Awareness darted away again, just ahead of the raking pain that came from drawing breath.

Adu's voice, near her ear, some liquid in a cup, hot and bitter, tasting of green, earthy jungles, at her lips, in her dry mouth, slowly drinking it, feeling it move down her throat and into her aching, shrunken belly. "Not too quickly," he said. "This will speed your recovery. You want your answers, you've earned them. I'm convinced you can be exactly what she needs, but you have to live first, Anne Bonny. Even more important, you have to want to live. You have no idea what you are truly capable of, only an inkling of what a treasure this world can be. I will point you to her, I can give you answers, but you have to come back first, come back from the dark."

She was in the emptiness, then she was in a room full of stars, drifting, floating about the velvet silence. A woman was there with her, older than her but not yet old. She had auburn hair, with a few silver and red-gold strands. She seemed familiar. The woman said something to Anne, her lips moved, but it was like she was out of sync. Anne tried to talk to her as well but nothing came out of her moving lips. It was like a glass wall separated them. Anne felt like she knew her from somewhere. The darkness swallowed them both and thought ended.

The intervals between pain and oblivion became shorter. The pain recessed, more into dullness that could be endured and overcome, not just survived.

Anne awoke. The light hurt. She had a headache and the acrid taste of some herb clung to her sticky, coated mouth and lips. Her throat was raw, but the pain lessened with each swallow. Her arm was wrapped in bloodstained cloth soaked in some solution. Her stomach was wrapped as well. Everything was sore, stiff and achy. Sharp pain met her first attempt to move her injured arm, nothing she couldn't handle. She gingerly touched her nose, and felt the slight shift in it. Third time broken in roughly twenty years of living and scraping. She wiggled it and it didn't hurt. She smiled; that didn't hurt too much either.

"You still have all your teeth, too, if you were curious," Adu said, stepping out of the beams of sunlight into the shade before her bed.

"Where am I?" she asked.

"The royal palace," Adu said. You are a guest of King Agaja. We all are."

Anne pushed her greasy, sweaty hair back. She smelled like a bilge rat. Her head was resting on a rattan headrest, a kind of wooden pillow. The sleeping mat she was lying on, made of woven *ncema* grass, was stiff with her dried blood. Adu crouched on his haunches next to her.

"'Throw them in irons guest' or 'guest' guest?" she asked.

"'Guest' guest," Adu said.

"I won?" she said, struggling to sit up. Adu nodded, a pleased look coming over his face.

"You did," he said. "In a most unorthodox way, I might add. You nearly danced her to death."

"Nearly?" Anne said, then added, "Wine, grog?"

"Yes, you spared her life at the last moment. Very surprising, I must admit," Adu said, handing her a gourd cup. "Water for now." Anne made a face and then drained the cup, making a little sound of approval as she did, then drank three more. Adu filled the cup each time. Anne belched and then clutched her stomach. "Easy," Adu said. "You were nearly dead. You had a nasty infection from the stomach wound, but you fought through it."

"Gut wound," Anne said. "I hate gut wounds. They usually kill you."

"King Agaja has some excellent healers," Adu said. "And I know a few tricks I picked up in Egypt and Greece."

"Thanks," Anne said, leaning back with a groan. "So what happens now?"

"You keep resting, keep healing. You drink every foul concoction they bring you without grousing about it. You sleep. When you are whole again, we will discuss the next leg of the journey and complete our business with the king."

Anne felt the weariness of her slight exertion from sitting up and drinking catching up to her. She adjusted herself on the headrest and mat, wincing as she did. "Who was that you were talking to while I was out?" she asked, yawning.

"She is known as Oya," he said.

Anne's eyes fluttered. "Oya," she said. "Is that any relation to Odu?"

" 'Odu' is a Yoruba word, it means 'container,' literally," Adu said. " 'Oya' is a title of sorts. Her birth name is Raashida."

"Odu Ifa," Anne muttered, almost asleep. She touched the claw scars on her forearm, gently. "The kite . . . The bird . . ." Her breathing deepened and she slept.

Adu covered her with a blanket, and stood. ". . . and the witch," he said. "Yes, soon."

"I kept my bargain, now keep yours," Anne said, pouring herself another cup of wine. Two more weeks had passed and she had grown stronger every day. For the past few days she had been eating solid food instead of the damn broth she had been subsisting on, and having herself a few drinks, thanks to the generosity of Belrose.

"What are you about, and who are you?" she asked. "What kind of man culls the scum from a city's streets for no personal gain, or talks in such bold words before the throne of kings? You made your voice like thunder and the torch flame change. You are no guide, Adu, and no mere sailor. I nearly died, and you promised me answers."

Anne and Adu sat outside alone on one of the patios of the palace beside a roaring fire pit. It was late summer and tonight the air was cool and damp. Gray, brooding clouds hid most of the stars. Adu wore his normal garb, but had added a brown leather frock coat. Anne was wrapped in a heavy blanket, her legs tucked up near her chest. She insisted on wearing no shoes outside. Old pirate ship habits died hard.

Adu tended the fire for a moment. He nodded, thoughtfully. "Yes. I did, and I will. You may not choose to believe what I tell you; you most certainly won't like most of it, but it is the truth.

"To begin, in answer to your question, the kind of man who does such things is a man who has lived long enough to see too much ugliness to bear it any longer, too much injustice to allow it to stand. I have known enough kings to know they are not divine agencies; they are men and they deserve to be spoken to as such, just as how you treated Agaja. As you get older, Anne, the value of life becomes more about quality than quantity."

"You're not all that much older than me," Anne said.

"Look in my eyes," he said. "Tell me true, what do you see there?" Anne leaned forward. They were very close. Her eyes, wide and quizzical, bored into his. Less than an inch separated them.

"An old soul," she said, "sad, wise." For an instant, she thought of kissing him but there was something in his eyes that made the notion feel like she would be kissing a mountain or the sky. Adu pulled away.

"There was a great worm," Adu began, "long ago. It bored deep into the earth, and made a great hole, a cave. From that cave, I and my brothers and sisters walked out much later. I do not know what I was before I emerged from that cave for the first time, I have no memory of an existence before that moment, I have no knowledge of a creator, or a childhood. I walked out exactly as I am now, standing before you, unchanged after all these long eons.

"The same was true for the other six men and five women who also emerged. I knew we were brothers and sisters, and I knew their names, and they knew mine—Adu Ogyinae—but nothing more. To the best of my knowledge, we were the first humans on Earth."

"That would make you pretty damn old," Anne said. "You bunkmates with Methuselah by any chance?"

Adu smiled. "You are at least open to the possibility I am telling you the truth," he said. "Good. I am old. As I told you, I've traveled quite a bit in my time. Like you, I had my young, foolhardy days and I hope I've learned a bit from my mistakes, my madnesses, my loves. I've been many men in my time— Gangleri, Enkimdu, Ziusudra, Markandeya, Barabbas, Merlin, a few others, here and there."

"If you're so old and mighty, mind telling me what you're doing muckin' up my life right here, right now?" Anne asked. "I'm nobody in the grand peggin' scheme of things. Seems to me one of the first men on Earth would have a few better things to be doing."

"Not really," Adu said. "It's been a dull millennium."

"If I shot you, what would happen?" Anne asked leaning forward, grinning.

"I would yell at you, and curse you, I'd bleed a lot, fall over and depending on how badly you shot me, seem dead. Eventually I'd get up and ask you not to do that anymore, and I'd have to pry the ball out of me. Not an enjoyable way to spend an evening, I can tell you."

"So you can't die," Anne said. "Bollocks."

"Oh, no, I can most certainly die," Adu said. "And I have an intuitive understanding of the one thing that can kill me. But if you think I'm telling you, you're more of a bobolyne than I thought you were."

"So why me?" Anne asked again. "Bored? Do you wander around and see if you can get random non-immortals killed for a good rib-tickler?"

"No," Adu said. "Well, not usually, anyway. This is about a city, a city made from the dead. It's called Carcosa, and you will find the greatest treasure of your life there, Anne Bonny, if you survive to claim it."

"How do you know about that?" Anne asked. "Did I say something while I was burning up? You go through my ditty?"

"No," Adu said. "Secrets are currency of trust and power. Your secrets are safe with me, and they are my secrets too. I know about the city of bone because I helped to build it. I am also the one who crafted the map fetish you found in the box. In my travels I learned many types of *Bo*. What the Yoruba call juju, and your people call witchcraft or sorcery."

"So you're not only one of the first men, you are also a hexer," Anne said. "You get around."

"I dabbled at first," Adu said, "seeking answers about my origins, but then I discovered I had the time to master these practices and I undertook to learn as much as I could, from whoever could teach me."

"So what did you learn?" Anne asked.

"That there is no such thing as a master in these spheres," Adu said. "The more you learn the clearer your choices become. Either you get more humble, more divorced of self, or the craft eats you alive. As to my origins, I discovered only that the world is a mosaic of beliefs, perceptions and powers. Where you stand in this world defines which realms of power you inhabit. There are thousands of different stories about the origins of man, the creation of the world, and they are all real, and they are all myth. Their power, their reality, lies in the strength of belief."

"Sounds pretty useless," Anne said. "I know I'm real, and I know I'm real all over! I know what I can do. Why put your trust in a gowpenful o' anything—gods, spirits, magic—that you can't rely on to be there when you need 'em?"

The cold wind diminished. "That is exactly why I'm with you now, Anne. You may be exactly what we're looking for, what is needed. You asked me when we first came here about the Purrah, remember?"

"Aye," she said.

"What I am about to tell you is forbidden knowledge to any who have not been initiated," Adu said. "I'd argue that you are on the initiation path now, so I will tell you a little. The Purrah is a secret society of men across Africa that directs many things. There is a companion society, called the Sande, which has women exclusively as its members.

"Africa holds the deepest secrets of the human soul, Anne, and more: secrets of the first humans and the countless civilizations that came before them. Some powers, some beliefs, live on long after their memory has faded due to the sheer magnitude of their impact on the worlds. They cast echoes, powerful echoes, across realms, across myths, as the stars we see are the influences of long-dead memories. Africa is home to many of these ancient, undying powers.

"Deep in wilderness never touched by human foot is the Den of the Animal Kings—beasts with minds and voices like men. This land is home to the last of the Serpent Men of long-fallen Valusia, who worship alien gods locked away in vaults of gold and star-metal, hiding from the justice of time. So many lost cities, lost civilizations here—Houssa, M'bwa, Kor, Bolgoni,

Opar, and the place you seek, the great city of bone, mankind's first city, the monsters' graveyard, a memorial to the first terrestrial war . . . Carcosa."

When Adu whispered the city's name, a cold, sharp wind stirred on the patio, making the fronds of the palms shudder and hiss.

"So many secrets here, Anne Bonny," Adu said. "So many treasures beyond imagining. It is the sacred duty of the Purrah to protect those secrets, that treasured knowledge, to hide it from all who would use it to enslave or destroy."

"So you were sent out by this Purrah of yours to stop me from reaching the city?" Anne asked. Adu shook his head.

"No, not exactly," Adu said. "I was alerted to your intent when you opened the box at sea and incurred the wrath of Mami Wata. One power dislikes the incursion of another unbidden into its realm. When you survived against the water spirit and arrived in Badagry, I had already been in contact with the High Purrah, the great council of elders, as to your possession of the box and the map. Once I saw how you behaved witnessing the plight of the slaves, I had confidence that you may have been exactly who she had been looking for for a very long time, to heal her and restore her faith."

"Who's this 'she'?" Anne asked. "This 'Oya'?"

"Yes," Adu said.

"Well, what if I don't want to be a part of her whatever-the-hell-it-is," Anne said. "I'm going to bring a spring upon her cable, thank you! I've got my own plunder to be about!"

"Yes," Adu said, "the city, its gold. If you fail the tests on the way there, I'm supposed to make sure that you die and that the secrets of Carcosa remain undiscovered. The Purrah will it."

"Not a ringing endorsement to trust you," she said.

"I didn't have to share any of this," he said. "I kept my word to you and I felt you deserved to know, especially after your success at the trial of combat."

"Well, ain't I a lucky little wagtail," Anne said. "So you talked me up to the king and said I called out his personal war chief. Thanks."

"Yes," Adu said. "It's my obligation to see you guided to each trial. But I sincerely believe that you will succeed at all of them. I want to help you as much as I can."

"Then why didn't you magic me up all better," Anne asked. "Instead of letting me nearly bleed out or die from fever?"

"Pain is highly instructive," Adu said, "you know that. It teaches you lessons nothing else can. And I did aid you, more than you know. My broths and elixirs helped pull you through a few rough spots."

"So what next?" Anne asked. "Drop me into a viper pit?"

"In a manner of speaking," Adu said. "You conclude your business with Agaja and Nourbese, and then we go where the map leads us."

"But you already know where we're going," Anne said. "Why not just lead me to the city?"

"Actually, the terrain has changed quite a bit since I was last there," he said. "The map knows the true way. We follow it."

"We?" Anne said. "So you can get me into more trouble?"

"Most likely," Adu said, "but I'll be there to help you too."

Anne rubbed her face and expelled air with a weary whoosh from her lips. She regarded Adu and the ancient man knew she was judging him, weighing the risk of trusting him against the gain. Finally she spit into her palm and thrust her hand out to Adu.

"All right," Anne said. "I'm game, you old bastard. I'll beat your trials. I'll beat your city of the dead, I'll show up your peggin' Purrah, and whoever this Oya thinks she is. I'll steal the dosh, and I'll look fucking brilliant while I do it. And from here on out it's on my terms, we understand each other? No more setting me up. If I'm walking into something dodgy, you tell me true. This is gonna be on my terms, my way, or you can fuck right the hell off. Do we understand each other?"

"Perfectly," Adu said. "Agreed." He spit into his own palm and they shook hands. "Tell me, do you know any other way for things to be, than on your own terms?"

"Not that it matters a piss," Anne said.

15

The Seven of Pentacles (Reversed)

Charleston, South Carolina

May 20, 1871

The gavel banged a few minutes after ten and the assembled gallery and participants all sat down at Judge Davenkirk's command. There were considerably more observers in the gallery today; it was almost full, and mostly men. Several other reporters besides Cline now sat among the Charleston participants who had heard about the trial and were eager to amuse themselves with the airing of the wealthy Anderton's dirty laundry and the novelty of a woman practicing law. Martin and Maude were both composed, now. If you had not seen the earlier outburst in the well, you'd have never known anything had transpired.

"I have reviewed the agreement between the parties," Davenkirk said. "It looks acceptable to me if everyone is on board with it."

"We are, your honor," Rutledge said.

"As is the plaintiff, your honor," Arabella said.

"Mrs. Mansfield, are you ready to proceed with your arguments?" the judge asked.

"We are, your honor," Arabella said.

"Proceed," the judge said. Arabella looked at Rutledge and then the gallery for a moment; she glanced to Maude and smiled, and then turned to face the judge.

"The plaintiff's maternal great-great-great-great-grandmother, Bonnie

Cormac, left the entirety of her estate, to wit, the plantation, manor house and all the contents thereof, as well as the grounds and surrounding property, to my client, as well as considerable funds, the exact amount disclosed in the papers filed with this court.

"Prior to marriage, an agreement was drafted between my client's deceased husband, Arthur Stapleton, and her father, the defendant. This agreement gave my client's husband control of the property and the funds as long as Martin Anderton agreed to the use of the property and the dispensation of the funds. My client agreed to this contract and signed it, with the understanding that her father was acting as her guardian, since the late Mr. Stapleton was not experienced in the governance of such a vast estate."

Maude kept her face set as Arabella recounted the lie. Bella didn't know it was a lie, of course, only Maude and Martin knew, now that Arthur was dead. Arthur had a reputation for losing money almost as quickly as he made it. Father had been suspicious that he was after Maude's inheritance, and had convinced her that to protect herself and her future, he should oversee everything.

She trusted her father, and it turned out he was right. Arthur had mismanaged and lost part of the money that Father had given him access to. In the end, they had been forced to leave Charleston because of the ensuing scandal and the angry investors who had lost their own money as well. It wasn't that Arthur was a swindler or a confidence man; he simply had poor instincts when it came to investing other people's money, including his wife's.

Arthur did learn a lesson from his failure. In the years they had lived in Golgotha, Arthur had become president of the Golgotha Bank and Trust. He performed his professional duties exceptionally well, but the first seed of doubt had been planted in her about his motives toward her, and therein began the rot that ate at the heart of their union.

"Mr. Stapleton died over two years ago," Arabella continued. "However the defendant has continued to manage and control the property and monies that are rightfully my client's inheritance. He also abducted my client's only child, a minor, just recently fifteen years of age . . ."

"I did no such thing!" Martin stood, shouting. "I didn't abduct anyone. My granddaughter returned home with me of her own volition from a godforsaken mining camp in Nevada!" Davenkirk cracked the gavel on the bench.

"Sit down and be quiet, Martin," the judge said. "You'll get a say in a moment. Mrs. Mansfield, continue, please."

"My client is imploring the court to find this agreement null and void," Bella continued, "and order Martin Anderton to release his control of my client's resources, as well as surrender custody of the child back to her mother, my client, Miss Stapleton, as he had no standing to remove her from her sole surviving parent."

Arabella sat back down. Rutledge stood, straightened his suit and walked out to address the judge. "Your honor, this agreement we are discussing is basic, ironclad contract law. Miss Stapleton trusted her husband and father to handle the complex fiscal burdens of such a vast estate. Martin Anderton has a lifetime of experience in such matters.

"His daughter and her family moved out to the western frontier over a decade ago and when his son-in-law, Arthur Stapleton, was murdered in Golgotha, the small mining community they had settled in, he corresponded with his daughter and provided her with sufficient funds to adequately and comfortably maintain her household. My client implored her to return to Charleston with his granddaughter. When his offers fell upon deaf ears, he made the arduous trek to Golgotha, Nevada, himself.

"My client was denied access to the town initially due to some issue of community hygiene, to wit, a plague. When he did make it to Golgotha with United States soldiers from Camp Bidwell, a nearby fort, he discovered there had been a lawless riot, a literal war between the locals and an army of marauding bandits. Dead bodies littered the blood-soaked streets! Mr. Anderton's granddaughter and the plaintiff were both injured in the hulla-baloo. Miss Stapleton had sent her then-fourteen-year-old daughter alone on horseback across the Nevada wasteland to seek aid at Camp Bidwell."

Maude felt the anger burn in her as this pompous man, who knew nothing of her, her daughter or their life, recounted the events of last year in Golgotha. She could kill him with little more volition than a thought required. Arabella gave her a light look that told her that her mask of control was slipping. She pulled the anger deep inside and calmed the fire with reason and discipline, but it was hard, harder than it should be for her. Rutledge droned on.

"My client pleaded with his only child, his daughter, that such a brutal environment was no place for a helpless widow to eke out an existence among lawless criminals, characters of ill repute and godless savages."

Whispered mutterings of disapproval drifted through the gallery. Rutledge fed on the energy he had tapped in the spectators. He raised his voice, sounding more like a stump politician or a revival preacher now than a lawyer.

"This vast, golden land that God Almighty has seen fit to bless the American people with is truly a treasure, and the West promises to be a glorious land of prosperity for the Lord's chosen people. I think I speak for every red-blooded man when I say that it is our duty, as Americans, and as Christians, to conquer these wild regions, to make them safe for habitation by all Americans, and to shepherd and educate the violent, child-like souls of the unsaved savages who infest these golden lands."

Maude had a momentary flash of what one of the "poor, unsaved savages" would have to say to Rutledge if he were here. Even when Mutt wasn't physically present, his memory was a comfort to her, and she felt a small amount of her anger diminish. She saw a brief flash in Bella's body language and realized her attorney was worried. She glanced casually at some of the faces in the gallery and saw all the silent indicators of approval of what Rutledge was saying, and a few unconscious nods of agreement with his hateful words.

"While it is a man's duty to tame this wilderness," Rutledge continued, now addressing the crowd, as well as the judge, "it is certainly no place for a *feme sole* to raise a young lady, especially when my client has ample resources here in Charleston to secure a safe and enriching life for both ladies, and to foster a proper Christian education for his granddaughter in a civilized bastion of culture."

Another wave of whispers and muttering from the gallery, this time of approval. Maude anticipated the judge would bang his gavel for silence, but he didn't. Rutledge let the gallery have a moment to feel they were part of the trial, then he spoke again.

"The plaintiff refused to leave her dangerous little camp on the edge of the desert. She had undertaken employment on her own since her husband's demise. This alleged 'business' put her, and her daughter, in contact with all manner of unsavory characters, including women of low morals." More disapproving gasps. "My client, who I remind the court is a well-liked, well-respected man in this community, a god-fearing man who risked his own life to travel out west to intercede and protect his family, respectfully requests the court grant him sole custody of the child, Constance Claire Stapleton, as her mother has demonstrated a flagrant disregard for her child's physical, moral and spiritual safety."

"Your honor," Bella said, rising, "I must object to this disgraceful characterization of my client and her character." She kept her voice controlled and respectful, free of emotion, but Maude's ear caught the tremor of stress in her words. Bella was trying to slow down the juggernaut that Rutledge was unleashing. She was hoping that Davenkirk's chivalry could still be invoked.

"Your honor, we have sent out subpoenas to numerous individuals in Golgotha to collaborate our charges against the plaintiff," Rutledge interjected.

"I object," Arabella said. "We have been given no prior notification of these witnesses appearing."

"We intended to notify the court and opposing counsel as soon as we received notification of which witness had been served and responded, your honor," Rutledge said. "The wheels of justice turn a bit less smoothly out in the frontier. We are having some trouble receiving verification of receipt of the subpoenas from the Golgotha sheriff's office. Numerous telegrams have remained unanswered. I've been led to understand that disruption of communication with Golgotha through various agencies, both natural and man-made, is not uncommon. My client, at his own expense, has dispatched Pinkerton agents to hand-deliver the subpoenas. I assure you no chicanery was intended."

Davenkirk nodded and rubbed his eyes. "Well then, we will table those allegations until such time as those witnesses can be confirmed, Mr. Rutledge." Maude felt the uncertainty in the judge's voice and unspoken communication. He was being swayed by Rutledge's arguments and inflammatory rhetoric.

Everyone had biases, and Rutledge was playing to them masterfully. Maude knew techniques, subtle postures, to minimize the impact of Rutledge's accusations. But her mind and her body were in chaos; she was hurting and this onslaught had come too soon after her confrontation with her father. She tried again to center herself, to focus. She had faced death, unspeakable violence and horror too many times to recall, always with a calm mind and steady heart, but this, this was killing her.

"Proceed, Andy," the judge said. Rutledge, like a predator smelling blood, walked toward Maude's table.

"In conclusion, your honor," he began, nodding at Maude. "The plaintiff has demonstrated the very reason for the binding legal agreement between herself and her father. Despite the widely radical politics of our age, it is still common sense, and common law, that the fairer sex does not have the rational mind and steady habits necessary for many of the complex challenges of life. It is the duty of the husband to care for and manage the property and resources outside the home. It is the god-given responsibility of Christian men to support and guide women. The Good Book says 'the head of every man is Christ, and the head of every woman, man.' Miss Stapleton has shown an emotional disregard for the best interests of herself and her child, and we implore the court to uphold the contract that she, her late husband and her father entered into, for her own sake and the sake of her daughter.

"It is our contention that Miss Stapleton is bound to the terms of this agreement which was made by her husband while she was *feme covert,* a married woman. Mr. Stapleton's right to manage his wife's affairs and to entrust an executor, in this case her father, to oversee the estate and protect her best interests is black-letter law under coverture, your honor, and extends beyond his lifetime. We merely ask the court to uphold what has been the law of the land for ages, and dismiss this frivolous petition."

Rutledge resumed his seat. There were a few claps from the gallery over the crowd's muted hum of approval. This time Davenkirk did crack his gavel for order and then addressed Bella.

"Mrs. Mansfield, please call your first witness."

"We call Professor Nathaniel Tully to the stand, your honor," Bella said. She quickly patted Maude's hand and gave a curt smile. "Here we go," she whispered. "Don't worry, he said the magic word. We're ready."

Tully was a distinguished, well-dressed, middle-aged gentleman. He still had a full head of graying hair, which he wore short in the back and combed forward in ringlets over his brow, in the style of the Roman emperors of old. The style was a bit dated, but it fit him and his patrician features well. Tully was sworn in on the Bible and took the witness chair.

"Professor Tully," Bella said, "please tell the court your position."

"I am a professor at the Columbia Law School in New York City," Tully said.

"Professor, the counsel for the defense mentioned a term in his remarks to the court a moment ago. Could you please explain what the concept of coverture is?"

Tully nodded. "Certainly," he said. "Coverture dates back to feudal times, back to English common law, from which most of our American legal tradition comes. Simply put, it is a doctrine that a woman, once married, loses her legal identity, merging it with that of her husband."

"So they become one legal entity," Bella said, "indistinguishable and equal in the eyes of the law?"

"No," Tully said. "Husband and wife do become one persona for legal purposes, but the persona they become is the husband."

"What does that mean for the woman?" Bella asked.

"The husband can constrain her liberty to keep her from leaving," Tully said. "He may have her returned to him, as if property, if in the company of others. He may forbid activities he does not approve of, and he may take legal actions in her name, including filing suits, signing contracts and executing deeds."

"Can a married woman do any of those actions of her own volition?" Arabella asked.

"Under the doctrine of coverture, no," Tully said.

"So under the shadow of coverture, a woman loses the power of her own independence," Bella said, turning as she spoke to address the gallery of spectators, "and any independent identity in legal matters."

"That is correct," Tully replied.

"It sounds a great deal like slavery to me," Arabella said.

"Objection, your honor!" Rutledge shouted, as he rose.

"Mrs. Mansfield, if you please," Judge Davenkirk said. Bella turned back to her witness.

"Professor, could you elaborate on the moral and ethical underpinnings that explain the development of coverture in the common law and the laws here in America?"

"Certainly," Tully said, and cleared his throat. "It considers women as being predisposed to a leadership role in the domestic issues of the union of marriage—being a wife and mother—while being too emotional, frail and erratic, as a sex, in their thoughts and actions, to deal with the complexities and burdens of life outside the home. The assumption is that women are like children, or slaves, incapable of the reasoning and judgment to make sound decisions about their own life and resources. It is a concept reinforced in the teachings of most of the major religions of the world, including Christianity."

Arabella walked toward Martin's table as she continued to speak. Maude noted that the gallery was still and quiet. She felt an undercurrent of discomfort and disapproval from the audience. "Professor, have there been any changes in the development of law in the United States in regards to coverture?"

"Oh, yes," Tully said, nodding. "Since the turn of this century many states have begun to rethink the entire coverture ethos. Mississippi passed legislation dealing with property rights for married women over thirty years ago. Arkansas and Maryland passed similar legislation a few years later, as did Michigan, Iowa, Ohio and Indiana. Texas crafted legislation almost forty years ago, while they were still an independent republic, to grant married women numerous rights and liberties. My home state of New York has greatly expanded the rights of women over the past three decades. As of seven years ago twenty-nine states have passed some form of women's property rights legislation that expands the liberties due to a woman under the notion of coverture."

"If my client was in New York, or Texas, would she require the remedy of this court to dissolve this prior agreement between her late husband and father, and manage her own affairs as she saw fit?"

Tully stroked his chin. "I'd say no. While there might be a few legalities to address, overall she would have strong legal footing and precedent to stand on in the disposition of this issue."

"Thank you, professor," Arabella said. "Nothing further for this witness."

"Mr. Rutledge?" the judge asked. Rutledge stood at the table but did not approach the witness stand.

"Mr. Tully, have you ever practiced law in the great state of South Carolina, sir?" Rutledge asked.

"No," Tully replied.

"Well, thank you so much for coming all the way down here from up north to lecture this court on common law and how other jurisdictions have decided to govern themselves," Rutledge said. "Our proud state was one of many who just recently shed our dearest blood, so that each state could have the right to govern itself as its people saw fit. Tell me, sir, are you familiar with the parts of the so-called Women's Earnings Act your high and mighty state of New York saw fit in its grand wisdom to repeal over nine years ago, sir?"

"Yes," Tully said.

"Please enlighten the court, professor."

"The legislature repealed the parts of the law that allowed women to manage the estates of their late husbands," the professor said, "and the right of a married woman to guardianship of her children."

"It seems to me that both those issues are very relevant to the proceeding you are testifying in today, don't you, Mr. Tully?"

Tully reddened a bit. "Yes," he said.

"So perhaps overturning this legally binding agreement wouldn't be such an easy sell for the plaintiff, even if she were in a carpetbagger court in New York, would it?"

Tully looked at Bella. "No," he said, "perhaps it wouldn't."

"Rutledge is worth all that money of yours your father is paying him," Arabella said, taking a sip of whiskey from her glass. Dinner at Grande Folly was done, and the lawyer was sitting in a high-backed chair before the fire. She held up the glass and watched the fire dance through the amber liquid. Maude was at the reading table in the library, poring over another very old book, her untouched glass of bourbon beside her. "What you learned is most assuredly correct," Arabella continued, "he's looking to run for a higher office. He wants your father's backing in that endeavor, clearly. How did you find that out? That reporter friend of yours?"

Maude was running a finger down a column of text in the book, then quickly whipped to another page. She growled a little in frustration, closed the book and opened another one.

"But he's not ready for what we're going to throw at him," Arabella continued. "Given the mood of the courtroom after that tent revival of his today, it may not make any difference, Maude. You need to be ready for that. We are swimming against the tide here."

Maude said nothing. She turned the pages, her brow furrowed in frustration. "Damn," she muttered.

"Have you heard anything I've said in the last ten minutes?" Bella asked. "Not that it's been any great revelation." Maude looked up from the book.

"I'm sorry," she said. "This is just damn frustrating. I'm looking for some very specific family information. I'm sure my Gran has it somewhere, but I'll be damned if I can find it. I know today didn't go as well as you had wanted it to go, but I have confidence in you, Arabella."

"Thank you." Bella sipped her whiskey. "I have confidence in me too. I can reason circles around this argument, but this isn't an argument, it's a litigation, and all litigation is political. You're not just challenging some contract, Maude, you're challenging these people's way of life, their concept of how the universe spins. They are going to fight back, try to crush you down."

"Yes," Maude said. "I felt it. We may win the battle but lose the war."

"Are you prepared for that?" Bella said, finishing off her drink. "Ready to implement our scorched earth option, if we fail to win this in the courtroom?"

"No," Maude said. "I refuse to believe that odious option is our only recourse. I was taught that the courts were where truth and justice resided in this nation, that people of good conscience and strong character could come to them and hew out the truth. I'm not ready to give up on that notion just yet. We have right on our side. I can't, Bella, I just . . . can't. To acquiescece to that is to agree with madness."

"If most of the good, god-fearin' people in that courtroom had their way," Bella said, imitating Rutledge's preacher voice for a moment, "Isaiah and his children would still be slaves, and you and I would never have a notion of being more than a wife or mother ever pop into our vapid little skulls. This world was born of madness, Maude, and when you're used to madness, you fear sanity."

16

The Sun

The meeting before the throne was between Anne, King Agaja and his de-
feated war chief and leader of the Ahosi, Nourbese. No members of the court
or even warriors or bodyguards were present. Nourbese, like Anne, had
healed from the worst of her injuries from the duel. Anne suspected that Adu
had been giving her some of his healing tonics as well. Nourbese looked at
Anne with sullen eyes, still smoldering with anger. Anne gave her a wink
and then returned to listening to Agaja.

"In accordance with the laws of my kingdom," Agaja said in English,
"you, Anne Bonny, seeker and champion of Oya, have won through trial by
combat the privilege and honor to lead my personal guard, the Ahosi. You
have further won the right to decide the fate of their former leader, Nourbese Edenausegboye Sosi Ayawa."

Anne sized up Nourbese. She was still dressed as one of the Amazon
warriors, however the ornate gold rings were no longer about her neck, nor
the iron blades at her fingertips.

"If you wish her dead," Agaja said, "you have but to say the word and she
will fall upon her blade."

"You fought like hell against me," Anne said to Nourbese. "Best scrap I've
ever been in. You'd do that? You'd die now, by your own hand?"

Nourbese didn't hesitate in her response. "I'd die to keep my word and honor my oath to my king," the Amazon said in English, her eyes still glistening with anger. "Life without those things is not life, it's breathing. It's something only a warrior could understand."

Anne looked to the king. "So you'll honor whatever I decide to do to this woman?" Agaja nodded. "Then I make her my second. She will follow me, and command the Ahosi in my name, and I'll command all of them in your name, your majesty."

Nourbese looked as if she just had fallen on her sword.

"You understand she may betray you," Agaja said. "Assassinate you, or give you poor advice in battle that leads to your downfall."

"I don't think so. She will give me her word," Anne said, "and she will give you her word as well." Anne was now facing Nourbese as close as they had been when the war chieftain had been stabbing steel into Anne's flesh. "If I think for one second that she isn't giving me her full loyalty, I'll take back the life I'm loaning her."

"I will kill you one day," Nourbese said. "Your kind befoul my country, my people. You are like a sickness that eats us away slowly. You are a thief and a whore. You have no code and believe in nothing past your own skin. One day I'll be free and I will kill you. I swear that too."

"Will you swear an oath to be loyal to this woman, to recognize her command of the Ahosi," Agaja asked, "and of you?"

"I will, my husband, my king," Nourbese said. "I swear it." Nourbese fell to the floor before the king upon his throne, her face nearly touching the stone. She stood and turned to Anne.

"Your orders?" she asked.

"How many Ahosi are there?" Anne asked.

"Three hundred," Nourbese said.

"Go tell them of what has happened here and that I am now your commander," Anne said. "Select two hundred of them to accompany us on our journey and have them prepared for the trip. The others will remain here and act as the king's guard until the rest of you return at our journey's end."

Nourbese swallowed hard, and Anne could tell the Amazon was fighting her instincts, her emotions, her urge to lash out at her. "It will be done," Nourbese said.

"And if possible, I'd like the ones to accompany us to have no family, no children," Anne said. Nourbese nearly snorted.

"You know nothing of us . . . war chieftain," she said. She bowed before the king and departed.

"All of the Ahosi are maidens," Agaja said after she had departed. "They are considered my wives, but it is purely ceremonial. They only take a husband and have children once I have released them from their duty to the throne."

"Good," Anne said. "Wise. No sense creating more orphans and widows if you don't have to. War does that just fine without any help."

"You fight like someone who has made your share of widows and orphans," the king said.

"I have," Anne said. "That's why I don't fancy making more. I've never killed anyone for pleasure, always business. 'Sides, it seems odd that a fellow so deep in the hole with slavers would be wobbly in the knees about killing."

"You do realize that disrespect to me is an offense punishable by death," Agaja said.

"Mmmhm," Anne said. "You already tried that. Sent your best warrior. I'm still here and now she works for me."

Agaja laughed heartily. "You have no fear in you," he said. "Good. You'll need that to face Oya."

"Who exactly is Oya?" Anne said. "I can't get a bloody straight answer to save my life . . . literally."

"Oya," the king said, with reverence and humility in his voice for the first time. "It means 'she tore.' Oya-Iyansan is mother of the nine, the goddess of the mighty Niger River. She is sister to the god of storms, and she is the Orisha of rebirth. She casts down the dead wood with her machete, and makes room for the green. She is the giver of truth and the bringer of justice."

"Oya is a goddess," Anne said. "No wonder the dodgy old bastard didn't want to say."

"On the path of Oya," Agaja said, "you either learn her wisdom or die trying."

"I've been through too much and I'm too close to retiring a landed lady," Anne said. "Dying is not in the cards here."

"You've seen enough of it to know," the king said, "death does as it will. There is no bargaining with it, no cheating it. King or slave, it will greet us all, in its time. If you seek the city of monsters, then you will find Oya, its guardian, and perhaps you will find death. I hope not, though. I fancy this world much more with you in it, I think."

"Why do you deal with the slavers?" Anne crossed her legs as she sat on the floor before the throne. "You don't seem the type. It doesn't suit you." To her surprise, Agaja joined her on the floor, sitting before his throne.

"Thank you for saying that," the king said. "Most believe it is for power. Wealth, guns, to make my kingdom stronger, larger. I have no love for selling slaves to the whites, but they are here now, and they must be dealt with. I choose to keep them close for now, and use them as they use us. But one day, I will rid my kingdom and all these lands of your people."

"Not my people," Anne said. "Fuck the lot of them, fucking scavengers. I've lived most of my life more slave, more criminal, than anything else. My sympathy is usually for the one in the shackles."

"You may have trouble believing it, but I do understand," Agaja said. "My people, the Fon, have known the yoke of the Oyo Empire, of the Yoruba. They have taken our people as slaves, demanded tribute in flesh, long before the whites arrived and showed us how to make a shameful tradition into a horrific industry."

"Everybody shits on everybody," Anne said. "We do it to ours, you do it to yours, we do it to each other. And the ones with the most money and the most power, with the right names, the right goddamn pedigree, the keys to the peggin' kingdom, they bugger us all as hard up the mine as they can." Agaja shook his head. "Oh, no offense, your majesty," she added. "I meant those *other* rich, powerful blighters." They both laughed.

"I've only a very few people in my life," the king said, "who've ever spoken to me without so much . . ."

"Shit?" Anne offered.

"Yes," the king replied. "Not the word I was thinking of, but yes, without so much shit. I like that."

"I'm an acquired taste," Anne said.

"Are you hungry?" Agaja asked. "Will you dine with me?"

"I'd be honored," Anne said.

They retired to one of the royal apartments in the palace, a room filled with silks and gold, more murals, ancient tapestries and thick lounging pillows of Egyptian cotton. Servants brought course after course of food while the court musicians played. Anne dug into every dish eagerly, much to the king's delight.

"You eat like a warrior, that's for sure," he said. "You eat like three warriors."

"Never pass up a meal," Anne said around a mouthful of food. "You can't be sure it won't be your last."

The dishes included *sosatie,* curried lamb on skewers, and *mesfouf,* a dish much like couscous. There were cakes of seasoned locust beans, and numerous mashed and spiced vegetables served on large platters covered in unleavened *kitcha* bread used to scoop up the mash. Anne particularly liked the *samosa*—fried pastries with a variety of fillings. She liked the spiced potato samosa very much. Dessert was an endless wave of sweets, fig rolls and a sweet bread called *himbasha* that Agaja said was normally only prepared for celebrations, and was being served in her honor. There was *kelewele,* fried sweet plantains, and braided syrup-covered pastries called *koeksister.* Of course there was much European wine and spirits. Anne drank her fill.

"That mural hidden by the tapestry in the throne room," Anne said, "what is that, why was it so important to Adu, to everyone?"

"It is a very old story," the king said, sipping his wine while reclining on cushions, "the story of the first war on Earth, the first war between men, monsters and gods. Adu was there, as was his family. Most fought for humanity and Earth; a few sided with the monsters and their father."

"Father?" Anne asked. She reclined back on the pillows, yawned and stretched. She felt Agaja's eyes roam across her body as she did. She decided she liked that.

"Yes," Agaja said. "Its true name is stricken from human speech, for it gives it strength to utter it. It is known that it is the son of Apophis, and groom to Echidna, the mother of all monsters. Adu helped the alliance of spirits, gods and people that Oya led against the monsters and their sire. The battle lasted one hundred hundred years, and it was fought on the great plain where the city you seek now resides."

"You know where I'm headed," Anne said. "Adu?"

"Yes," the king said. "He said you seek the wisdom of Oya, and if a mortal seeks Oya, it is said she may only be found in the shadow of the city made from the bones of the beasts she helped slay. I do wish you were not going there. It is a bad place, the earth is stained with much evil blood there. It's not a city for mortals to behold."

Anne let her head roll back on the cushions. "I'm not seeking fucking Oya, or any wisdom, luv; I'm seeking bloody treasure—gold, jewels, loot— enough to let me retire to a nice little palace of my own."

"I could give you palaces," Agaja said. "Gold, jewels, a dozen lifetimes worth." He reached over to Anne. His thick finger traced a surprisingly gentle path along her cheek, then slowly down her neck, toward her shoulder. The finger glided along her skin and sent a shudder, like soft lightning, through her body.

Anne's breath quickened and a flush, a dizzy thrill better than any liquor, spread across her, through her. She took his massive hand in her small pale one and stopped its descent effortlessly. He was touching her as if she were spun out of dreams and shadows and would evaporate if he were too forceful. The thought of such a large, powerful man—a king, a fighter, capable and used to getting exactly what he wanted—being so careful touching her made her flutter inside.

She kissed his knuckle while she looked into his eyes, dark and damp with a growing hunger. Hers were twinkling, mocking, a green devil dancing in them. Anne bit his finger playfully, grinning as she held it locked in her teeth.

"It's always better to take something than be given it," she said.

"Spoken like a true thief," Agaja said.

He pulled her toward him insistently. Anne met his embrace with one of her own, kissing him fiercely and with a muffled growl. The kiss devoured both of them, and they lost themselves in the unfettered need in it, the searing sweetness. Agaja's massive hands moved effortlessly to her waist as she slid over to straddle him, her hands on either side of his large neck, her nails faintly raking his skin as they moved down.

Agaja broke the kiss with a groan of frustration. He turned his head and addressed the musicians in a hoarse voice. "Leave us!" The music stopped, and the servants quickly departed. Anne chuckled and kissed, then nipped, at his neck.

"Poor king," she muttered into his warm flesh, "what you must go through."

"I could make you my queen," he said, and Anne saw he meant it. "I've never seen your like; you fight like a tiger, you drink and swear like a sailor, and you are more lovely than the dawn after a battle. Be my wife, in more than just name. Be mine."

Anne drank deeply of his lips again and she found sweet strength, comfort and solace in them, felt her body move of its own accord, like waves, against his, the land against the sea. A dark certainty, tempered of too many losses, too many lies, too many passions forged in flame and quenched in the cold water of time, whispered to her, and she heeded it, as she always did, putting the armor up again about her heart.

This was what it was, nothing more. To try to make it such only cheapened the glory, the joy, the magic inherent in it. When she broke the kiss, Agaja saw her eyes were full of devouring flame. It startled him more than any charging warrior ever had. He gasped at the intensity of her gaze.

"I've tried my hand at marriage," she said, flushed and breathless. "Didn't take." She sank her nails into the back of his neck and head as she pulled him to her for another kiss. Blood thudded in their ears, their bodies ached, arched and writhed. "What say we skip straight to the honeymoon?"

They consumed each other as the night is devoured by the day.

17

The Four of Cups

Charleston, South Carolina
May 20, 1871

Bella had taken the carriage back to Charleston and Maude had finally given up on another wasted night of searching for any mention of the Daughters, the mysterious Sons or how Constance was connected to the Grail of Lilith. She was supposed to meet Alter at the courthouse tomorrow to discuss his investigation into the dead Sons she and Constance had fought in Charleston, and what he had uncovered.

Isaiah entered the parlor with two mugs of tea. He gave one to Maude and then sat in the chair next to her before the fire. Maude sipped hers and then glanced up in surprise.

"This is Gran's Blood-Dragon Oolong," Maude exclaimed. "I haven't had this since I was little!" Isaiah nodded and sipped his own mug.

"The emperor himself gifted her a small cask of it after that whole godawful *Jiang Shi* affair," Isaiah said. "He said it was grown in the heart of Kunlun, harvested by the gods themselves. I don't know if you recall Ching Shih, she was a friend of your grandmother, a remarkable woman, one of the Daughters of Lilith, I believe. I met her a few times, when I was very young. Madame Ching used to bring a little of it to Lady Cormac whenever she visited. I managed to save a bit of it for you. I thought you might need it."

"Thank you," Maude said. "You always gave me this when she had been hard on me, when I was ready to give up."

"You never did," Isaiah said. "How are you, little girl? Still no luck with the research?"

"Nothing," Maude said. "You're certain she never mentioned any other archive, or a book she might have kept separate from all the others, papers, a lock box, a diary?"

"No," he said. "She mentioned a 'record' a few times, but never any specifics about it, and to my knowledge she never referenced it, at least not here at Grande Folly. There is a considerable amount of land connected to the estate, though; maybe it's hidden or buried somewhere on the property?"

"I can't start digging up miles of land at random," Maude said.

"No, she'd have left some kind of map, the old pirate," Isaiah said.

"I can't beat an enemy I don't understand," she said. "Gran told me the Daughters don't normally ever meet up, unless things are truly bad, like end-of-days bad. Something big is going on, it involves Constance, and I have only scraps of information to work with. The Daughter I spoke with briefly during the fight seemed surprised I hadn't encountered the Sons before, but Gran never mentioned them to me, and I can't help but wonder why. It's very frustrating."

Isaiah smiled, and sipped his tea. "She was always damn good at being frustrating," he said. "But she had so much faith in you, Maude. She struggled with whether she was too old to teach you or not, but she told me many times, and I quote, that you were going to do great things, and that she had prepared you with every tool, every resource you'd need. I believe her. I did then, and I do now. You will find a way. 'There's—'"

"'There's always a way,'" Maude finished. "Yeah, she was damn frustrating, wasn't she?"

"The greatest people usually are," Isaiah said.

Maude awoke in the darkness before dawn. She had been wrestling with something, some complex, tangled dream-thought, for what seemed most of the night, existing in that twilight place between slumber and conscious awareness. The struggle had finally driven her back to her waking mind. She sat up in her bed and rubbed her face. It was cool, but not cold. She had been sleeping nude, which she had always enjoyed, but seldom did back in Golgotha.

She got up and grabbed her robe, putting it on and belting it, and made her way down the stairs and out the kitchen door of the manor house. She wore no shoes, and had no need of them. The rocks, grass and twigs were all sensation, not pain. She welcomed them. Years of running in these woods, and along the scalding sands of the noon-day beach, had made her feet tough and strong.

She moved through the stand of trees, running her fingers over the tangles of Spanish moss that were drooping everywhere. She heard the waves crashing, smelled the salt foam and after a moment, she broke free of the foliage. The dark beach yawned before her. The sky was indigo; the stars had fled, sensing the impending dawn. The sky was lightening, but for now, it was dark and the only sound for miles was the defiant roar of the waves cresting, dying against the land, and the lapping, whispering of the water that heralded their rebirth.

Maude liked to believe she knew every grain of sand on this beach. She slid off her robe and welcomed the sea breeze on her skin. She walked out onto the cool, grasping sand. She left no footprints, out of instinct.

When Gran had taught her how to move and leave no trace or memory of her passing, she had expected Maude to maintain the practice, especially here, on their beach. Once, when Maude was still very young, she had been so excited to reach the water on a very hot July day she forgot and left big, ugly tracks in her wake. When she had emerged from the water, laughing and smiling, she had seen the prints and Gran standing beside them. The smile fell from Maude's face.

"Did you enjoy your swim, girl?" Anne had asked. Maude nodded slowly. "Good," she said. "Was it worth your life?"

Maude looked down at the sand and her footprints, partially exploded in the loose sand.

"That's no trick question, Maudie," Anne said. "Was it? You were laughing and enjoying the feel of the cool water, feeling life jumping and splashing all about you, just as you should. In that emotion, you left your training behind, and in the wrong circumstances it could mean you die for a mistake, for letting your emotions drive you."

"But it's hard to think cold all the time, Gran," Maude had replied. "I'm sorry, I messed up. I'll do better."

Gran walked across the beach, leaving tracks in her wake, looking up and laughing at the brilliant sun embracing her wrinkled face. "Ah, that feels so good. I swear the older I get the more I understand those damn lizards that sit on a rock all day and bake themselves. Feels glorious, it does.

"I don't want you to dry up inside and not feel, Maude. We all make mistakes, we all make a mess of it sometimes—hell, I've made more grand, glorious fuck-ups than I can even recall. We all have feelings, and to try to divorce ourselves from how we feel, what we feel, that's depriving ourselves of a mighty source of strength. It takes us away from the core of life itself and that is truly a crime and a shame."

"Father said that women are too emotional," Maude said. "That they let their hearts guide them too much to be able to do a lot of things men can do."

"Ah, Martin," Anne said, kneeling with a grunt beside the girl. "The 'things men can do,' like start a war, turn people into slaves, burn folk at the stake for their beliefs. Very unemotional bits of business, those.

"Your da is a good enough fella, Maude. He's like most of the folks in this world, though, men and women, walking around shuffling in their chains, no idea of the prison they were born into, the prison they help maintain every day of their lives, in their minds, in their hearts. Martin has his head filled up with a bunch of fool notions about what he can and can't do, what you can and can't do. It's silly and it's sad. Like a lot of prisons, there's no windows to look out and see past the darkness. Don't let some other fool's prison hold you too."

Anne pushed the strands of wet hair out of Maude's face. She squeezed Maude's nose and made a honking noise like a goose. Maude giggled. Anne laughed.

"You do whatever you please, lass," Anne said, "and you live with the consequences of that choice, good or bad, living or dying. Pay your debt. Just remember that at the end of it all—whatever it is—it should be worth the price you paid for it."

"So I didn't mess up when I tracked up the beach?" Maude said, a smile growing at the edges of her lips. Anne moved her open palm an inch or so above one of Maude's prints on the sand.

"Oh, no luv, you mucked up royally! Tracked up my pretty beach." Anne's hand glided over the print and in its wake the track was gone. The sand looked exactly as it would if Maude had never set foot upon it.

"How did you . . . what did you do?" Maude said, a look of amazement crossing over her face.

"You figure it out," Anne said. "Then you clean up all these tracks the same way. I don't want to be able to suss where there ever was a track on this ground, girl."

"Hey!" Maude said. "Some of these tracks belong to your big old boats! What about all that stuff about 'paying your own debts'?"

Anne feigned mock horror. "My dainty little feet, boats? Surely not! And trust me, teaching a hellcat handful like you is debt a'plenty! C'mere!"

Anne had chased her up and down the beach, both laughing hysterically, Maude made certain not to leave a trace she'd have to mend later. After a time, they chased the dipping seagulls, who glided and mocked them, and in due time, Maude learned how to catch them as well.

Maude stood alone on the sand in the portentous dawn. She filled herself completely with the clean, life-giving air, careful to not gulp it, to rush anything, only to sip, until each cell of her was full of potential.

It had been a very long time since she had meditated this way. Of all the gifts, all the education Gran had given her, she had never fully understood the benefit of these exercises. She had grasped and excelled at the healing meditations and the endless katas that maintained her muscle tone and muscle memory to keep her alive in combat. But these exercises were designed to quiet her mind and still it, and after a lifetime of being told to be still and quiet, Maude saw no value in ever voluntarily doing those things.

The idea had come to her while she grappled with sleep. In part of the knotted dream, Maude was eating dinner with Alter, but the hotel restaurant had been replaced by the two of them sitting on driftwood benches, a linen-covered table between them, on this very beach. Maude was telling him about how what she and the Daughters did was not magic, merely training.

As she talked, her words became someone else's. Alter melted, replaced by the black-haired Daughter who had commanded the butterflies in the battle with the Sons. The mysterious woman was now saying the same words that Maude was saying, "It's a property of the blood. We just 'know' things about the others who carry the Load, and them about us. It comes in dreams and in the secret parts of your mind that are always at work, always whispering, but which you are mostly unaware of . . ."

Maude closed her eyes, felt the sea wind caress her skin. She raised her hand above her head, palms out, as if holding cups of water, and then slowly brought them down toward her face, turning her palms, almost steepling her hands, but not quite. Maude exhaled, inhaled and began to move, to dance, with the world and within herself. Each motion flowing into the next one, each action fluid, and intuitive, as natural as breathing.

She began to feel the gentle suction of gravity on her, about her, felt the cool, wet sand anchoring her feet. Felt the spin of the Mother's body, solid and immutable, yet hurtling through the void, ever-moving, ever-changing. She was centered, anchored, flying, spinning free. The incongruity was sweet and perfect.

Time stretched out like taffy, then began to diffuse as it elongated further, and further. Time floated, drifted away on the wind, like the silky white hairs of a dandelion.

Her mind turned inward now, on itself. The ocean, the wind, her body, were all dim, recessing shadows. Maude went further away from the skin and deeper toward the piercing crystalline awareness, the clarifying light. Everything was washed out in the radiance, but she was not alone in it. Far away she saw a young woman with bright red hair looking into a mirror that hung in the air, unsupported. Her back was to Maude, but Maude felt a strong connection to the girl.

Maude turned away from the girl and her mirror to find herself facing the black-haired Daughter; she stood with her arms wrapped about herself, a polished piece of obsidian hovering before her face. Maude's own distorted image looked back at her as she stared into the polished stone.

"*Tonalpouhqui*," the woman with the black mirror for a face said, her voice like wet, slippery stone.

The red-headed woman turned and it was Gran, younger, bloody from a fight, almost panting, wild-eyed and beautiful, maybe twenty years old. "What the hell took you so long?" Anne said, then laughed. "We've got work to do. Find Hell's Belles, find the blood stone. They will help unlock the door to the Record. Find Hecate, find me. Hurry, girl, he's coming for you. You are all that stands between him and reentering the city of bone. It has been sealed to him since its founding, and he has circled its walls like a hungry beast, seeking a way in. He knows you mean to stop him. He is coming."

Maude's eyes slowly opened precisely as the dawn's eye opened across the sea. A sense of peace filled her that she had not felt in years, a feeling of connectedness to everything, to everyone. A gull squawked; it was Gran's laugh.

The sea moved gently, waves rising and falling in the silent embrace of the hidden moon.

In her bed at the Pavilion Hotel, Itzel awoke, a sheen of sweat covering her lithe, nude body. She hurried across the suite to Amadia's door, but the door came open before she even touched it.

"What is it, Itzel?" Amadia asked. "What woke us?

"It is the American," Itzel said, a genuine look of fear and amazement in her eyes. "Maude Stapleton has looked into Tezcatlipoca, into the Smoking Mirror!"

"I don't understand," Amadia said. "What are you talking about?"

"She has nearly mastered what it took years of my life to do, to open *tonalamatl,* to open the *Book of Fates*! We have to act before she does so again, Amadia!"

The door to the suite opened with a faint click.

"Then it is good that we have arrived when we have," Inna Barkov, the Russian Daughter of Lilith, said as she opened the door. Behind her was Leng Ya. "We're here to claim the girl," Inna said.

18

The Chariot

Ife, Oyo Empire, Africa
September 25, 1721

They were greeted at Ife with the groan of the kudu horn, the wail of the Nyanga pipes, and the voices of hundreds of masked, dancing revelers raised in song. The masks the crowd wore were all different, some elongated, some fashioned as a sun or moon, an animal, or grimacing skull, some in the shape of a human head and face with an almost eerie detail and realism. They were carved from dark wood, others from ivory, a few adorned with gold, shells and jewels.

Each mask, Adu said, was the face of one of the four hundred and one gods worshiped in this teeming city. There was celebration everywhere though the sun had not yet set when they reached the city's main gates.

"It's fortuitous that we arrived on the day of a festival," Belrose said, embracing a buxom woman who hugged him and handed him a gourd containing some unknown drink.

"That's most days here," Adu said, hugging a stranger. "This many gods, you have pretty good odds there's always going to be some kind of a party going on."

Belrose took a swig and grimaced at the taste and potency of the mysterious beverage. The woman retrieved her gourd and disappeared into the crowd. "I like this city," the mercenary said.

"What good can there be found in worshiping this many gods?" Nourbese said, waving away a well-wisher.

"Well, you've always got someone to blame," Anne said, taking a swig from another offered gourd.

Anne, Adu, Belrose and Nourbese were at the front of a column of fifty Ahosi Amazons and bearers. The city guard, also masked, stepped forward to halt their progress somewhat hesitantly.

The lead guard called out to the party in Yoruba as his fellow guards leveled flintlocks at the group. Adu raised a hand, smiling, and replied. There were several moments of exchange and then he walked back to Anne and the others.

"We can enter. I told him we are part of an escort for you and Belrose and we're here to resupply and be on our way. We won't be able to do any business for the next two days because of the festival. Only ten Ahosi may accompany us inside."

Anne looked at Nourbese. "You were right about that. It was worth a try."

"The Yoruba fear my warriors," Nourbese said.

"I want you with us inside," Anne said. "Pick nine of your people to accompany us. Make sure they are ready for anything. We still have no idea why the hell we're here."

"Ahosi are always ready for anything," Nourbese said, walking away from Anne and back toward her troops.

"She always makes things a little brighter when she's around," Belrose said, glancing back at Nourbese.

"She'll warm up," Anne said. "She knows her job and she does it very well."

Once they had seen that the map was leading them to Ife, it had been decided that the majority of the Amazon troops would remain camped outside the city. Anne had asked Adu numerous times about why they were coming to Ife.

"I can't discuss it," Adu had said. "It might influence the trial, how you handle it."

"Was it influencing the trial to go and pick a fight for me back in Abomey?"

"Stop your complaining, it's unbecoming of the leader of the Ahosi and future queen of Dahomey," Adu said. "Besides it all worked out for the best."

"'For the best'?" Anne said. "I had to practically sneak off with my knickers in my hand in the dead of night to keep from getting noozed, one way or another. It was a lovely time, a fine jig and all." Anne snorted. "But queen . . . no thank you."

Ife was laid out in rings, concentric circles of sacredness and cosmological power. The political and spiritual center of the city was the palace, which was called the Oke-Ile, the High House, and resided on a hill far off in the distance.

"This is where the world began," Adu said. "This city is built at the womb of creation. At least that's the Yoruba's version of things. They have employed their mysticism in their architecture. This whole city was constructed to gather and amplify spiritual power. Quite an accomplishment, and they didn't even ask for my help."

"Nice to know there's a few things you don't have a hand in," Anne said as they walked. "So if you won't tell me what I need to do here, how do I figure out what I should do?"

"Rest tonight," Adu said. "I know an excellent quarter where we can set up camp and we should be unmolested. Tomorrow we'll figure out the rest."

They were able to make camp in a grassy clearing with a few sparse stands of marula trees to provide shade. Several other groups of visiting merchants and pilgrims from as far away as Sao Salvador and Timbuktu shared the site with Anne's company. The early part of the night involved shared fires, food, song and tales. Eventually guards were posted and everyone slept.

Anne awoke to the sensation of eyes on her. She sat up in her tent, her flintlock at the ready. The kite was perched on her ditty bag, beside her bed mat. The bird made a sharp, disapproving *churk* sound, looked at her with what she assumed was bird-contempt, and flew out the now-open flaps of the tent into the darkness. Anne followed the bird. She pushed past the canvas curtain of her tent and found herself in a vast and brightly lit gallery. A woman's voice spoke to her and Anne was sure it came from the kite.

"*The Iyaami are the women who guide Olodumare, the supreme power of all creation, which sets all the forces in motion in the universe, even death,*" the voice said. "*Oduduwa is the mother, the womb, it is the power of omnipotence, the power to create and, by creation, to act and change this world and the other worlds. The Iyaami are the daughters of Oduduwa.*"

The gallery's walls were like glass with a warm, soft, milky light gently radiating from within. The walls were covered in masks, thousands of them, faces of bone, ivory, iron, silk, fur, feather, gem, silver and gold. Some were human, others alien, and each had dark, empty shadows for eyes. Anne walked along the gallery, her fingertips brushing the faces as she passed.

"Olodumare is man, Olodumare is not man," the voice said. *"Oduduwa is woman, Oduduwa is not woman. It simply is and all being is, by the simplicity of being. It has no master, is no master. It is, as the sun is burning, and the night freezing, it is."*

As she touched each mask a voice hissed out of their empty mouths.

"I bring you good fortune . . ."

"I bring you victory over your enemies . . ."

"I bring you those you desire . . ."

"I bring you joy in the afterlife, so that you never need end . . ."

"The Iyaami move in secret and they are often known as Aje, or witches, by those who do not understand, who blind themselves with limitations," the kite said.

"Me," the masks pleaded.

"Me . . ."

"No, me . . ."

"They are untrue . . . me!"

Anne saw a glimmer, a burst of brilliance, at the end of the hall and moved toward it; each mask she passed called out a promise, a threat, a feeble plea.

"Aje is the understanding of creation," the kite said. *"Aje is the force of justice and retribution. Aje is the balance that completes pairs. Aje requires understanding, compassion and morality, beyond most humans' limited understanding of such things. Aje maintains the harmony of society by enforcing earthly and cosmic laws and by ensuring humans respect and obey the unspoken truths, or else be punished for their transgressions. Aje is naturally passed down from mother to daughter, yet it can also be created through initiation. If the seeker has the will, and a heart that speaks loudly, they may become Aje, they may become Iyaami."*

Anne had reached the end of the gallery, the end of the long rows of begging, demanding masks. There was a final mask and it had no face, no features; it was made of clear glass and something beneath it was the source of the brilliant light. Anne reached out to the mask and found as she touched it that it had no voice, no promises, no threats.

"The Iyaami hear creation's silent voice in all things in this world and the others. The Iyaami sing to creation, and it respects their will, as they respect it."

Anne removed the glass mask from the gallery wall and as she did it shattered silently into a million shards. There was a sharp sting of pain in her hand as the glass cut her. Each piece of the mask, as it fell, evaporated into nothing. The pain diminished as Anne looked up from her bleeding hand and stared into her own face, reflected in a beautiful mirror.

"The Iyaami stand alone, among Olodumare, and Orisha, among beasts, and man. They are and must always be," the bird said. *"This is your initiation, your beginning and your end."*

Anne's hand bled and throbbed. The kite was before her now, no longer a bird but a woman, dressed in robes of brown and tan, matching the kite's markings. She wore a mask that was a huge bird's skull, the beak painted a brilliant yellow.

"Who are you?" Anne asked, clutching her bleeding hand.

"If you remove this mask," the woman said, and it was the same voice as the kite's, "if you removed any of these masks, tell me what face would you see beneath?"

Anne awoke. She was reaching out to remove the bird mask, but the dream had evaporated. It was still dark out, but she heard the gruff caw of a bird. Her extended hand was covered in dripping blood, but there was no mark upon it.

The company was finishing the morning meal when Yoruba warriors arrived at the camp. They spoke with Adu in an animated conversation that ended with many muskets being aimed. The Ahosi readied their own guns and blades. Anne jumped up.

"Stop! Nobody do anything, bloody hold!" she shouted. "What is it now?" she said to Adu. "What's going on?"

"We have been summoned before the Ooni, the king," Adu said, "his mystics and the city's priests. Apparently they are not happy with you."

"What a refreshing change," Anne said. "This your doing?" Adu shook his head.

"No, but I sense unseen forces moving to thwart you, and I can't determine who, or what. You need to be careful."

"'Unseen forces,' 'need to be careful,' you're a peggin' banquet of sagacity," she said.

"You get what you pay for," Adu said.

The Oke-Ile, the king's palace, was on a hilly rise overlooking the rest of Ife. The five city quarters all radiated out from the palace, literally the center of the Yoruba universe. The soldiers marched Anne, Belrose, Nourbese and Adu down one of the main streets of the city. Masked onlookers muttered and pointed at Anne and Belrose's red hair. Anne waved back and Belrose chuckled.

"It appears we are the devil's own," he said. "White and red-headed, positively diabolic."

The guards had insisted on Anne's party leaving their firearms behind. Nourbese had commanded the nine Amazons with her to get word to the others to prepare for the worst. They agreed on a signal.

"Nervous without your guns?" Nourbese said as they walked past the crowds milling on the street. The guards shouted and cleared the way for the group. "Most whites are." Anne shrugged.

"I didn't need them to lay your boat out, as I recall," she said. "I'll manage."

The closer they traveled to the center, the more sacred and revered the architecture became. They passed the sacred groves and gardens dedicated to Oduduwa, the mythical founder of the city, a shrine to the warrior god, Ogun, and the temple dedicated to Araba Agbaye, the chief diviner of the universe.

The palace was built to stand at the crossroads of the city's three major roads. Crossroads, Adu explained, were locations of great spiritual power in Yoruba Vodun. The crossroad before the palace that Anne, Belrose, Nourbese and Adu were marched along was known as "the king's mouth."

The gates to the palace were tall, brightly polished bronze doors. Past the gates were a series of mud-walled buildings stretching across the compound. These buildings included barracks and quarters, as well as the private sanctuaries of their royal oracles.

Their escort was joined by other warriors, most with guns, until they were outnumbered five to one. They were led into the throne room through an ancient door of dark wood. The door was carved with images of kings, gods and warriors as well as faces that reminded Anne of her dream.

Ojigidiri, the Ooni of Ife, was a middle-aged man in an old man's body, his face hidden behind a bronze mask that Anne suspected was actually fashioned to look like a younger version of his own features. He wore a long loin cloth and several heavy necklaces of gold and ivory. Adu had mentioned on the way to Ife that the Ooni was forbidden to leave the city and only appeared outside the palace during certain annual festivals and rites. It showed in the king's physique. His body was softer than Agaja's, with no scars or signs of battle, and he had a prodigious gut.

The room was full of men, dozens of them, all in masks, all talking. Their conversations hushed as the party was escorted into the room and brought before the throne. Besides the beautiful decorations of bronze and terracotta sculpture that adorned the room, there was a large wooden table that stood a few yards before the throne. The table was covered with cloth.

"My diviners tell me your presence here angers the Orishas," the Ooni said. His English was not bad, and his voice was higher pitched than his body would have suggested, and it sounded hollow and metallic behind his mask. "The priests say they have had dreams of your coming, woman, and they say the same. The gods are angry with you, and wish you to go no further in your journey."

"Nobody likes me these days," Anne said. "Well, your majesty, how exactly do we settle this, then?" She looked over her shoulder at the soldiers, with their guns loaded and ready for a word from their god-king to open fire. She saw Belrose figuring the odds and planning where he'd move. Nourbese was doing the same, occasionally giving her a bitter glance. Even Adu looked worried, but remained still as a column.

"I have consulted the oracles, the mouth of the Orishas," the king said. "You must show your loyalty, your respect, to the gods."

Two of the masked priests removed the cover off the table and revealed row upon row of masks, each representing a god. She could almost hear the echo of their voices whispering from their vacant mouths. Anne looked back at her people. Belrose and Nourbese both looked relieved. Adu looked . . . lost. Anne looked across the table, then turned to the Ooni.

"And what happens once I choose?" Anne asked.

"You join us in celebration and thanksgiving to the spirits that we serve," the king said. "You will be given all the supplies you need to continue your journey and protection through my empire and the realms of my kin."

"A moment to consult with my . . . diviner, your majesty?" The king reclined in his throne and immediately had a priest at either shoulder hissing words into his ears. Anne stepped back to her people and they huddled, whispering.

"Pick a damn god and let's be on our way," Belrose said. "I thought for sure they were going to shoot us and then eat us!"

"Spoken like a true European pig," Nourbese said. "You must choose carefully, Bonny. A callous choice will reflect poorly on you with all the Orishas and into the afterlife. Choose the one that speaks to your soul, your true self. This is a sacred thing."

"This would explain the energies gathering to oppose you that I sensed," Adu said. "The gods and spirits wish to know where you stand in the scheme of things. Truly, the universe itself is aligning against you."

"They're real," Anne said. "They're all real and they all are ganging up on me?"

"In this city, with these people, yes," Adu said. "They are as real as you or I. There are places upon this earth where the forces of other worlds, other rules, apply."

Anne looked over at the table, then back to Adu. She looked a little frightened. "What . . . what should I do?"

"I . . . cannot say," Adu said. Anne arched an eyebrow and stared at the mystic for a moment, and he stared back, then she nodded.

"Get ready," she said to her companions, and turned back to address the king.

"Ready?" Belrose whispered to Nourbese. "Ready for what?"

"Who can say with her," Nourbese replied. "She's mad, that's why the gods hate her."

"I'm ready to choose," Anne said to the king and the assemblage of soothsayers and holy men, who fell silent once again.

"Choose which god your soul is yoked to, girl," Ojigidiri said. Anne walked to the table, circled it. She looked across the masks to the assemblage of those who made their coin off the gods: a crowd of hungry false faces, all studying her intently, waiting, ready to claim her. Among the king's advisers, Anne now saw the old woman in the bird-skull mask, waiting as well. No one else seemed to notice her, and when Anne looked again, the bird-woman was gone.

"Do you wish to wait until I am a god myself?" the king asked. "Come along now, girl!" The men of the court chuckled at Anne's uncertainty and hesitation. Anne looked over the faces of the gods a final time.

"I'll have none of them," Anne said. "I've got no use for the lot!" There was an uproar from the oracles, the shamans, angry voices behind frozen visages. The king stood, his voice shaking behind his metal face.

"Execute them all!" he cried. "The gods demand blood for such arrogance!"

"The gods want blood," Anne snarled. "We'll give 'em blood." Anne flipped the table, and the masks flew everywhere, clattering, crashing to the stone floor.

There was a shimmer in the air, like the heat coming off the ground in stifling summer. Anne caught sight of a blur of bright yellow moving about the throne room. The blur was gone as quickly as it had appeared. The Yoruba warriors had raised their rifles to open fire on the company, but their guns crumbled before their eyes into broken pieces of wood and steel in their hands. Not a single shot was fired. Anne drew her machete as Belrose, Nourbese and Adu drew their own swords.

Anne dove toward a trio of stunned guards closest to her, each frantically fumbling for their *Ida* blades. "Nourbese, the signal!" Anne shouted as she crashed into the mass of warriors. Anne opened one man's throat before his blade had completely cleared his scabbard, drew and claimed the warrior's sword as her own with her free hand. Continuing the turn, out and away from the spray of blood, Anne slashed another warrior's mask with her machete and followed through by stabbing his companion's stolen sword deep into his chest. The second Yoruba warrior groaned, red bubbles foaming at his mask's lips, and died. Anne managed to parry the third warrior's blade, high, with her own, while she planted a foot on the second warrior and pulled her newly acquired blade free of the dead man's chest as he thudded to the ground.

Belrose gave a brief salute to the soldiers who closed upon him, a look of peace settling over the former Musketeer's face. Belrose's slender blade made the very air hum with its speed and the force with which the mercenary wielded it. He used the extra length of his rapier to excellent advantage, piercing the eye, then the brain of one and opening the artery in the throat of another before the remaining Yoruba could get within range with their shorter, heavier and wider *Ida*. The two men fell dead and the other two circled Belrose, looking for an opening in the Frenchman's whirring wall of defense; his foil seemed to be everywhere at once. If Anne's fighting style was a drunken tavern jig, then Belrose's was ballet.

Nourbese slipped a small ball out of her satchel as she maimed a charging warrior with a low slice to the leg that made the man fall, screaming. She used the second his fall gave her, blocking his companions, to fall back behind Belrose's guard. The iron sphere was roughly the size of a piece of marula fruit. Nourbese and Adu had painted various symbols for household guardian spirits and protector orishas on its uneven and pitted surface. The Yoruba had ignored it when Nourbese explained it was a Fon woman's tool for crushing grain into meal. She removed the plug in the ball and turned it to reveal a primer fitted into the other side. She popped the plug back into the ball's hole, which was filled with black powder.

Nourbese fell back more, and spent a moment dueling with two more Yoruba warriors. She allowed the two men to follow her back to the wall of the throne room. Once she felt the wall's cool smooth surface against her back, the Amazon drove the iron ball into one of the guards' faces. The warrior's teeth shattered like glass and his nose made a sound like a snapping twig as it broke, and he tumbled back clutching his face. The other guard pressed his attack at that moment. Nourbese parried his blade low and then reached up without taking her eyes off the warrior she was dueling and held the primer to the guttering torch in a sconce high on the wall. When she heard the hiss of fuse, she brought the armed grenadoe, a pirate bomb Bonny had given her to use if needed, down. She turned the Yoruba's blade aside and hacked a deep wound into his left shoulder, almost taking off his arm. She turned and tossed the bomb through one of the narrow windows that ran along the top of the throne room wall, and managed to pivot in time to narrowly avoid being run through by the warrior with the broken nose and teeth. They traded another round of lunges and parries before there was a tremendous, reverberating explosion from the grenadoe, and the whole palace seemed to shake.

The worst of the blast hit the other side of the wall, but the explosion still sent a strange, queasy ripple through the bellies of everyone in the throne room, and their ears felt as if they were filled with water from the fury of the blast. The wall behind Nourbese began to crack and crumble. The Amazon let fly a series of powerful attacks that drove her opponent backward so that now his back was to the spasming wall. Nourbese felt daylight warm her face and she broke off her onslaught and let the collapsing wall finish off her opponent. A huge section of wall struck the Yoruba on the head and then more debris buried him.

Anne had four warriors on her now, and she didn't have time to do more than give a quick glance in the direction of the crumbling wall. She saw Adu was surrounded by a half-dozen soldiers too. The ancient man had his blade lowered, and was standing still, his head down and his eyes closed. He said something to the men but she couldn't make it out over the ringing from the explosion in her ears and the low tone of his voice. The men raised their blades and closed on Adu. Anne had to concentrate on saving her own skin at that point. She parried with one blade and tried to force a line through the men circling her. It wasn't working. She felt an impact and then a sharp sting on her upper leg. The warrior to her left rear had scored a minor hit. Nothing too bad—a few stitches, at best—but it showed her defense was beginning to falter. She took advantage of the warrior's overextended line to hack at him, scoring a deep slash to his upper chest. The man cursed her and fell back, but one of his fellows took advantage of Anne's assault to swing a powerful overhead blow at her upper back and right arm; even her spine was vulnerable in that instant. The warrior's sword was parried at the last instant by Nourbese's blade. The Amazon drew two of the warriors off Anne and the two women circled each other in deadly orbits, swords swinging, spiraling, flashing.

"The signal has been sent," Nourbese said matter-of-factly.

"I noticed," Anne replied. "Thanks."

Anne spared a second to see how Adu was faring. All six warriors were dead, their blood on Adu's sword. The mystic was still standing, head bowed, eyes closed, arms open as if inviting his assassins to move closer as another group of Yoruba fighters took his bait.

Belrose was careening about the room gracefully, leaping from spot to spot, killing as he darted. He jumped onto the throne itself, and used its high back as a rearguard, tipping the heavy chair back so it and he were balancing on only two of the chair's legs as he parried and then dispatched two more guards. Belrose joyfully launched himself from the teetering throne to dive into a mob of Yoruba guards. The king, his holy advisers and seers were all shouting, cursing, praying and cowering in the section of the room behind the throne.

All Anne could see were masks and blades everywhere, crashing, shouting, steel biting steel. She had an ugly wound on her side now, to share with the one bleeding on her leg. Anne had got it saving Nourbese from a warrior's frantic advance. The two women were back to back now. They had killed dozens, but there were still too many to count.

She had known that, known that rejecting the gods, rejecting the king and the priests and the oracles' control would lead to this. They were going to die, they were all going to die, because of her and her . . . what, whatever the hell pushed her, filled her up with blinding, burning anger and made her do the things she did. Every choice she had made in her life was pushing its way into her mind, unbidden but unrelenting.

"Why?" her father was asking. "You fight against your schoolmaster, you fight against the priests, you openly defy me at every turn. Why do you do it, Annie?"

"Andy," she corrected. "Always Andy, remember, Da?" She was twelve, and living in Charleston. In months, her mother would be gone, and looming in her near future was beautiful, dangerous Jim Bonny and the beginning of the life she chose, a chaotic, bloody, joyful, miserable pageant. There were thin scars on her arms and legs, some of them crimson, others pale, faded ghosts of her secret war, her constant struggle to control the pain, the rage, her life.

The last fight her parents engaged in had given Anne herself back, thanks to her mother.

"She can be whatever she wants to be, William!" her mother had said as Anne stood before them with tears running down her small face. "It's a new land, a new beginning, and she won't pay for our sins any longer, do you hear me!"

Anne remembered her mother's kind eyes, still young, set in a face worn before its time from lies, from running, from bearing the brunt of William's rage and disappointment and his failures. Anne would remember that moment until the day she passed.

"It's your life, Annie, not ours, not theirs," Ma said. "You make whatever glorious mess of it you will. Just don't let anyone steal it away from you, my sweet girl."

Her mother won that day, and Da relented. For all the things she hated about William Cormac, Anne knew that he had loved her mother more than the breath in his lungs.

The memory made Anne fight harder, ignore the bright pain in her side, ignore her lungs burning, clawing for more air. She killed another masked assassin and another. Nourbese was no longer behind her—dead, or swept away in the red tide?

There were shouts from somewhere behind her, but Anne barely registered them. Stop the blade, hack another shoulder, parry and side-step, impale, spin the screaming dying man and use him as a shield. Kick him loose from her blade and have his body crash into his mates, use the momentary opening to advance. The chaos at her back was a shield, like she was an angel with wailing wings made of death.

A tiny part of Anne knew this was futile, that all it took was one second of poor luck, one misstep, a moment of fatigue, pausing too long to think, and she was dead. She felt concern for her wee lord, her tiny son, alone in the world without her, then buried it before it could get her killed even quicker right now. She could control this, this moment, this tiny universe of violence. She could control her sword, her body, her will to live more than the masked men, to spit in death's eye. Today, she would make them pay for her life. Today, their sacrifices would be dedicated to her.

There was gunfire behind her, around her. The whine of a shot hissing by, the dull-meat thud of bullets piercing men. The churning sea of flesh surged and receded and Anne saw the king directing his bodyguards. She charged with a snarl, and cut her way closer to the Ooni, closer.

There was a sharp, hot pain across her back; it would have severed her spine if she hadn't been so quick to move. She ignored it as best she could. The stone floor of the throne room in the holy city was inch-deep in blood and hacked flesh, but Anne had kept her footing on the decks of ships, slippery with sea-spray and life-blood, too many times to count. She moved closer to the masked king, and now Ojigidiri saw her as well, covered in the blood of his warriors, an almost rictus grin on her face.

Adu stepped in front of her. She almost struck him with one of her swords, but she recognized the mystic at the last moment.

"The Ahosi have arrived," he said. Anne noticed he was bleeding from multiple cuts and stab wounds, but he was not even sweating or panting. "Time to go!"

"I want that bastard's blood on my sword!" Anne screamed, and pointed to the Ooni. More cracks of gunfire, more screams of the dying. A Yoruba warrior charged at them. Adu's sword lashed out like lightning and the man was dead, almost before Anne had registered his approach.

"The trial is over," Adu said. "You succeeded. If we stay we will be overrun, outnumbered and outgunned. Is killing him really worth dying? We have to go!"

"Nourbese? The Hummingbird?"

"Outside already," Adu said.

Anne let the anger that had ridden her slip away, felt the tremors in her body that she always felt after a fight. She nodded to Adu. "Aye."

The flight from the palace was not easy and it took the better part of the day to withdraw back to the city gate. The king's bodyguard were as well trained and as well-armed as the Ahosi; however, the Amazons fought with a ferocity and focus that showed Anne they did truly live up to the name of the legendary warrior women.

Once Anne's forces had taken the main gate, they held there until nightfall and then retreated from Ife into the wilderness. They marched on through the night, finally stopping to camp north of the city, still deep in Oyo imperial territory. They had lost sixty-three of the Amazons in the fighting, and eight bearers. Belrose had, miraculously, managed to avoid getting wounded, but Nourbese, Adu and Anne all tended their wounds. They sat around the fire, stitching up deep cuts, passing around a jar of Adu's healing salve and a bottle of the Frenchman's beloved absinthe.

"That was wonderful," Belrose said, already a bit drunk.

"Says the luckiest bastard I have ever seen upon this earth," Adu said, wincing as Nourbese completed stitching up the sword wound on his side.

"I owe it all to clean living, my friend," Belrose said, "and never being entirely sober if I can help it."

"I don't see how you hurt, let alone kill, anyone with that thin little skewer you call a blade," Nourbese said. The Hummingbird shrugged.

"It is not the blade," he said, "but the swordsman."

"Says every man with a little skewer for a sword," Anne said.

"Jealousy ill becomes all of you," Belrose said with a chuckle. "I shall chalk it up to a disagreeable mood from the pain of your injuries. To our brave captain," he said and tipped the bottle toward Anne, who took it and drank. "She who pisses on gods and kings with equal contempt. Bravo!"

"We lost good warriors, good friends of mine, today." Nourbese rejected the bottle when Anne offered it to her. "I'd like to know why."

Anne took another drink of the absinthe and handed it to Adu, who actually drank some. "That's fair," Anne said. "I've been led about in the dark myself on this lark. I guess you and the Hummingbird deserve some idea of what's going on."

"For the record," Belrose said, burping slightly, "I'm really not interested in why, but I'll listen anyway."

Anne glanced at Adu. The ancient man shrugged and drank more from the bottle before handing it to Belrose.

"There's a lost city," Anne said. "Full of gold and treasures. I found a box with a map to it on a ship I plundered in the East Indies."

Nourbese sighed. "So I lost good women today so some white mercenary *bishi* can fill her coffers, go home to her own lands and tell tales of how she stole her fortune from us stupid savages. Thank you, I figured it was something like that." Nourbese looked to Adu. "You, Adu Ogyinae, you are a legend among our people, a hero, and you let this European *asiwere* lead you about like a slave? Helping her, speaking lies on her behalf before kings who trust your counsel. For some mythical gold?"

"The place is real!" Anne said. "It was written about on the wall of the palace in Agaja's throne room, that covered mural . . . it's very old and we're headed there, but first I have to satisfy some god or bird-woman . . . whatever it is, that's guardian of the place. And she's the one insisting on these silly tests, like whatever the hell that was back in Ife. So at the end of this is enough booty for us all to be rich and retire as proper ladies and gents."

"You 'retire' to some faraway place," Nourbese said. "For you, this land, its people, becomes an 'adventure,' an amusing memory. You'll blot out the parts with the suffering and injustice and the slavery of our people that your people foster here. I have seen it my whole life. You whites take and take and take, like locusts, and when there is nothing left to steal, no 'lost treasures' left to plunder, no one left to put in chains, you will sail home and lament the terrible condition we have let our lands fall into." Nourbese turned to Adu. "Don't you have something to add?"

"You are doing a fine job all on your own," he said.

"Your people, Agaja, your king, the Oyo, they all take slaves, sell them," Anne said. "He could refuse, you know? Take a stand, you all could. I'm not going to defend fucking slavers, but we didn't start any of this."

"My people are not without blame," Nourbese said, "but if we stand against your merchants, and the kings, the countries they secretly own, here and in your lands far away, we would be swept away in a heartbeat, crushed by our enemies and put into chains ourselves. Our choices are compromise or destruction. It is a very wicked game your people play, Anne Bonny, very wicked, and you're correct, you did not start this, but what have any of you done to stop it?"

Everyone became silent. Nourbese looked into the snapping, crackling fire.

"What is the name of this 'lost city'?" Nourbese asked.

"Carcosa," Anne said. The fire shivered and the wind picked up. Sparks, like wayward stars drifted away from the fire, darkened, and died.

"Carcosa," Nourbese said and looked to Adu. The mystic nodded. "It is the birthplace of all monsters, all evil, inhuman things that stalk across the world, that prey on the weak, and the innocent. They hail from Carcosa."

"That's the place," Anne said.

"Oya, the goddess, protects the world from the spawn of Carcosa, and any foolish enough to seek it," Nourbese said.

"Oya," Anne said, snapping her fingers, pointing to Nourbese, and taking another sip of the bottle. She was slurring a bit now. "That's the bird trying to kill me, yeah. Oya. Bitch."

"*Bishi*," Belrose corrected.

"Adu, you are a powerful Bokonon, one of the oldest men alive," Nourbese said. "How can you condone this, help this *mu yo* blunder into Carcosa? Do you have any idea the damage she might do?"

"Ahhh-ha!" Anne said, slumping to the side a bit, "so now you believe it's real!"

"It is Oya's will," Adu said, ". . . more or less."

"Carcosa." Nourbese rested her face in her hands.

"That's where we're headed, luv," Anne said. "Carcosa, city full o' peggin' gold . . . and monsters."

"Give me the bottle," Nourbese said.

19

The Four of Pentacles

Charleston, South Carolina
May 21, 1871

"Do you have any further witnesses you wish to call, Mrs. Mansfield?" Judge Davenkirk asked Arabella. Bella stood as she addressed the court.

"I do, your honor," Bella said. "I'd like to call Gibson Hall to the stand."

"Your honor, I object to this with the utmost vehemence!" Rutledge said, jumping to his feet. "Mr. Hall is a senior clerk at my legal firm! He's my clerk, your honor!"

"Mrs. Mansfield," the judge said with a weary tone, "I have endeavored to be as courteous to you as I can possibly be, and to humor your attempts here, but the courtroom is no place for silly theatrics, madame."

Arabella remained nonplussed. "I was merely seeking to insert into the court record a chain of actions, your honor. I was also planning to call you to the stand and Mr. Rutledge as well."

"And now you see, your honor, what comes of this mockery of a legal proceeding," Rutledge said, turning to address the gallery. "This woman has nothing left to present so she will waste the court's and my client's valuable time playing at the law like it was a parlor game!"

"A house is built a brick at a time, your honor," Arabella said calmly. "We can certainly forgo the questions I was going to ask you and Mr. Hall, but I will call Mr. Rutledge to the stand."

"Madame, this behavior is highly improper," Davenkirk said.

"Your honor, I'll be happy to take the stand," Rutledge said with a smile. He patted Martin on the shoulder. "Not to worry," he said to his client.

"Very well," Davenkirk said. "You're under no obligation to do this, Andy. You understand that, correct?"

"I do, your honor," Rutledge said. "If this gets us out of here by lunchtime, I'm delighted to play witness for the little lady. She needs the practice." The gallery laughed. Grinning, Rutledge walked past Arabella, growling just loud enough for her to hear, "Welcome to the first day of real law school, bitch." He took the witness stand and was sworn in on the Bible.

"Mr. Rutledge," Arabella said. "Would you please repeat for the court what you said to me just now as you passed me on your way to the stand?"

"I beg your pardon," Rutledge said. "I said nothing to you, madame. Perhaps you should see a physician about your hearing."

"Your honor," Arabella said, "may I assume that I am permitted the latitude to consider opposing council as an adverse witness?" Davenkirk nodded.

"Proceed," the judge said. Bella walked over to her table and plucked a sheet of paper off of it. She presented it to Rutledge.

"Mr. Rutledge, is this the contract that is in dispute in this matter?" Rutledge scanned the document.

"Yes," he said. "It is."

"And would you agree with me that the crux of this matter deals with my client's ability to alter or exit this agreement, which was brokered between her father and her late husband?"

". . . and to which she was a willing party to, and a signatory thereof," Rutledge said. "Yes, Mrs. Mansfield, your grasp of the obvious is astounding. How many farm animals have passed the bar in Iowa as well?" More laughter from the gallery. Davenkirk banged his gavel.

"Andy, no need for that kind of talk. Answer the question." He turned to the clerk. "Strike that last remark from the record, please," he said to the court's reporter.

"If it please the court," Arabella said, "I'd prefer it remain." Davenkirk sighed and shrugged.

"Mr. Rutledge, why was my client required to sign this document?" Bella asked.

"The property and inherited wealth were granted to her by the late Bonnie Cormac," Rutledge said. "So . . ."

"... So this land, these properties, this money, all belonged to my client; they were hers and hers alone," Bella said, interrupting Rutledge.

"Well, yes," Rutledge said, "Prior to her legal marriage to Mr. Arthur Stapleton. However, once they were wed, the property and inheritance became his to oversee and adjudicate, as he saw fit."

Arabella walked back to her table. Maude handed her another document. Bella returned and handed the document to Rutledge. "Will you attest to this document being a legally binding marriage certificate between Maude Claire Anderton and Arthur James Stapleton?"

"Yes, of course it is," Rutledge said. "This is growing tedious, Mrs. Mansfield."

"Well, perhaps this will liven it up a bit for you, Mr. Rutledge," Bella said, still calm and cool. "Would you be so kind as to look at the date of the marriage and the date on the contract?" As Rutledge did so, his face twitched just a little, just enough for Bella to see it. It was delicious.

"Mr. Rutledge, is something amiss?" Bella asked. "Read the date of the contract to the court, aloud, if you please."

Rutledge turned toward the judge. "Your honor, this must be a mistake, it is the silliest bit of fluff I have ever seen in a court of law . . ."

Arabella raised her voice, which was perfectly controlled, like a whip in the hands of a master. It was sharp and loud enough to carry across the courtroom. It echoed in the now dead-silent gallery. "The dates, Mr. Rutledge, if you please."

"They signed the agreement . . . on September 12 of 1855," Rutledge said. "They were married on October 15, 1855."

Arabella let the words fade and the silence sit in the courtroom for a moment. Even Davenkirk was slightly agape. She leaned in closer to the stand, her eyes locked on Rutledge when he looked up from the papers.

"Mr. Rutledge, at the expense of 'stating the obvious,' would you tell the court what significance that has for the contract between Arthur Stapleton and Martin Anderton in regards to my client's inheritance, if you please."

Rutledge was white with anger; his lips were pale, almost blue. He spoke each word as if it were being pulled out of him painfully, with pliers. "At the time the contract was signed by the parties, Mr. Stapleton was not yet married to your client."

Bella waited for Rutledge to finish. Maude looked over to her father and saw genuine confusion and concern growing on her father's face. "Come now, Mr. Rutledge, a jurist with as much experience as yourself must surely have come to the other obvious conclusion of this finding. Even a South Carolinian barn animal could fathom it, sir."

Rutledge clutched the rail of the stand, his hands trembling with rage, but he said nothing.

"Then allow me to educate you, sir," Arabella said. "This contract is null and void, because as it clearly states it is an agreement between the husband of my client and her father, and at the time it was signed, Mr. Stapleton could not enter into any agreement as to the disposition of my client's inheritance with her father, because he wasn't married to my client. Isn't that correct?"

"The contract is still binding!" Rutledge said, almost standing up in the witness chair, but managing to control himself. "It's still a binding agreement between a father and an unmarried daughter, a *feme sole!*"

"I see." Bella turned her back on Rutledge and walked toward the gallery. There were numerous shocked faces, some gasping like landed trout. Those same faces had been smugly laughing only a few moments ago. Bella froze the image in her mind, gilded it like a trophy.

"The wording of this agreement is very specific, Mr. Rutledge. It mentions nothing about my client being an unmarried woman, but there are pages of statute and law explaining why as a married woman she is legally entering into this agreement with her father and husband, not fiancée, Mr. Rutledge, not husband-to-be-in-a-month, but husband, present tense. Is that not correct? A few moments ago, you seemed quite certain of my client's legal status in regards to this agreement, so tell me, was she a married woman when she signed this agreement—a *feme covert*—or not? Since the status of her relationship to her late husband, as you so succinctly put it, seems to be the crux of the matter."

"I . . . I don't . . ." Rutledge stammered. Bella turned toward the judge, her demeanor sincere, a helpful agent of the court.

"I can produce affidavits from the minister who performed the ceremony. I can also produce the witness to the license, as well as the magistrate whose name and seal the marriage certificate bears, who can attest to the date it was issued, if you need them introduced into evidence, your honor?"

"No," both Rutledge and Davenkirk replied as one. Davenkirk followed it up with a dismissive wave. "No need for all that, Mrs. Mansfield."

"I have no further use for this witness," Bella said, walking away from

Rutledge and sitting back down at her table. Maude kept her face calm and clear, as did her counsel, but she gave Arabella's foot a quick tap under the table. Bella busied herself with her papers.

"Now we see what kind of judge the Honorable Odysseus Edward Davenkirk really is," Arabella whispered.

At first, Maude expected that to be the end of the proceedings for the day. Rutledge asked for a recess to confer with his client and confirm Bella's revelation. "Win or lose, we fight the last battle today," Arabella said. "I can feel it. It all hinges on the judge now." Bella had dashed off to deal with a few last-minute details of what she had told Maude would be the final gambit.

Maude sat alone in a conference room off from the main well, sipping from a tin cup of water a kindly bailiff had provided her. There was a gentle rap at the door and Alter peeked inside, smiled and entered. The reporter closed the door behind him.

"That," he said, sitting down across from Maude at the table, "was a sight to behold. I spoke to Arabella briefly on the record. She told me I'd find you in here. You've got a damn good lawyer, Maude."

"The best," Maude said. "Wait till you see round two. She's setting her sights higher."

"Why do you seem so worried, then?" Alter asked.

"You are too good at that," Maude said. "Because all of her legal legerdemain may mean nothing. If I was a man, this agreement would have been tossed out after Bella made Rutledge look like a fool today, but I'm not, and she's not, and in this time, and this place, being right and having the law on your side may not be enough."

"So what will you do if you lose?" Cline asked.

"What I have to," Maude said. "By any means necessary, get Constance back. I'm hoping the judge is a reasonable, fair man. If not . . . I have a contingency." Maude tried to summon a smile. "You said you had something for me on the dead Sons?"

"Yes," Cline said. He reached into his pocket. "I was able to get a sample of the goo that those poor devils had for blood." Alter held up a small glass vial with a rubber stopper. In it was a black, viscous liquid that resembled oil. He handed the vial to Maude. "I took it to a chemist," the reporter said.

"He said it had qualities akin to blood and venom, said he had never seen anything like it before."

Maude uncorked the stopper, closed her eyes and wafted the air over the open vial toward her nose. The fluid had a strong scent; it smelled like an open grave on a rainy day, a rotting, peaty musk mixed with something that didn't quite belong with the death smells, a sweet, cloying odor, like scorched clover honey. The faint whiff of the stuff sent an odd shiver down Maude's spine. She put the stopper back in place.

"I have," Maude said. "It's the Blood of the Wurm, a supernatural concoction that leaves death and madness in its wake. I assume you and your chemist friend didn't smell or touch it, Alter."

"Well, I did give it a whiff, and it had a . . . peculiar effect on me, for a moment."

"Arousal," Maude said, nodding. Alter blushed.

"Hell, yes," he blurted, slapping the table with his palm. "Tumescence, actually. Very odd, not that I don't get . . . I mean to say . . . I have . . . often, but not . . ."

"It's part of its lure," Maude said.

"Seemed to discombobulate the chemist as well," Alter said. "Not that we . . . discussed such matters . . . We didn't. He wanted a sample, but I thought it prudent to keep it and let you examine it."

"Good," Maude said. "There was nothing . . . moving in the bodies, in the blood, was there? Worm-like things?"

"God, no!" Alter said. Maude sighed, and put the vial away.

"Good. We'll need to burn those bodies, tonight," she said.

"That may be a problem," Cline said, then waved his hands, as if shooing gnats before his eyes. "Now wait a minute! You're not skimming over this, like everyone else just knows what the hell 'the Blood of the Wurm' is, Maude! I am not waiting months for you to get around to giving me a straight answer this time either! What is going on here?"

"The town I come from back West, Golgotha," Maude began, "a few years ago, there was a . . . plague—I suppose that is as good a word as any—people were infected with creatures that secreted this substance. Constance was one of the infected. It changed them into monsters. Constance was lucky, a lot of people weren't; they died because of this poison. You said the Sons had this as their blood?"

"Yes, and you can't just go burn the bodies now. My contact at the funeral home told me that some men from the Pinkerton Agency came and took the bodies away by wagon under Union military escort. They had a warrant from a federal judge to do it."

"Damn," Maude said. "They have no idea what they are mucking about with."

"Neither do I," Alter added.

"This substance is concocted, I'm led to understand," Maude said. "The cult that brought it to Golgotha was intent on ending the world. They came very close to accomplishing that."

"It's extremely unnerving to know things like that," Alter said. "You think these 'Sons' are another branch of this cult?"

"All I know is this just makes them even more dangerous," Maude said. "I don't have any more time to waste on my father's nonsense."

Cline saw something slide over Maude's eyes, a cold fury, a frustration that she no longer desired to keep in check. It frightened him. As beautiful and kind as this woman was, as demure-seeming she played at, as much as he desired her, loved her company, was fascinated by her, he saw for the first time that she belonged to a different world than he did. It was a world of monsters and madmen, cults and secrets that held the world's fate in their conspiratorial grasp, and unlike himself, she was at home in this violent, surreal landscape, she thrived in it, and she was done playing at the petty, foolish games of blind men.

There was a knock at the door just as it swung open. It was Bella. "Judge wants us in chambers, now," she said. "Endgame."

"Yes," Maude said, the anger in her eyes slipping back behind her mask as she stood. "Thank you, Alter, again. You're a good friend."

"I'll see if I can find out anything about where those bodies got to," Alter said, standing. "I've still got a few old army friends in uniform."

"Bodies?" Bella said, then waved dismissively. "I don't care to know. One disaster at a time."

"Thank you," Maude said to the reporter. "Be careful, Alter."

20

The Hermit

The verdant jade of the jungle gave way to browning veldts, and then finally, as the map led the expedition farther northeast, to the open desert they call the Sahara. The company had been traveling for over a month and more had died. Of their original bearers, only four remained, all of them the good men Adu had truly picked for the job. Some of the Ahosi had been chosen to replace them and carried the party's rapidly dwindling provisions, including life-sustaining water. They had lost another twenty-six of the Amazons to wounds from the battle at Ife that did not heal, and to skirmishes with Oyo troops, bandits and wild animals.

The heat worked on everyone like an oppressive lash, and as days turned to weeks even Belrose became silent and sullen. They trudged along through the emptiness, going somewhere, but no one knew where. At night, Anne and Adu would check the map, but the ruby remained still. By now, they had confided in Nourbese and Belrose as well about the supernatural talisman guiding them.

"We're close to whatever it is," Anne said.

"You've been saying that for days," Nourbese snapped. "Maybe the thing's broken, perhaps the heat, or the cold?"

Anne looked to Adu. "Are we close?" The ancient man said nothing. Belrose cursed under his breath.

"That is truly annoying," the mercenary said. "Do you intend to let us wander about aimlessly until all our water is gone and then let the sun bleach our bones?" Adu said nothing. "I could make you tell us," the Frenchman said.

"If you are that eager to end your suffering, you could certainly try," Adu said.

"Enough!" Anne said. "We got ourselves into this mess, we will get ourselves out."

"Truth be told," Nourbese said, "you got us into this mess."

"Fine," Anne said. "I'll get us out. We go three more days."

"Then what?" Nourbese said. "You said the same thing three days ago. Is your damn imaginary gold worth us all dying out here? Even if we find Carcosa, the Ahosi are in no shape to battle whatever horrors await us there."

"I heard you lot were the fiercest warriors in all of Africa," Anne said. "You telling me it ain't so?" Nourbese stood, angry.

"Care to try your luck with me again, you *ewure oshi*?" Nourbese said.

"Oh, darlin'," Anne said, rising, "I'll be more than happy to knock down your gnashgabbing ass one more time."

"We're all a bit worn." Adu stepped between the two. "Let's retire and get some rest."

As they scattered, Nourbese turned to Adu and spoke to him in Fon. "I'll give her a few more days, Adu Ogyinae, then I will decide how we proceed."

As frigid night bowed to oppressive day, Anne awoke. The kite had returned. The bird clicked at her, then screeched as it took off across the dunes. Anne stumbled to her feet and dashed out of her tent to follow, not even stopping to grab her boots. The kite was already soaring over the next dune as Anne ran after it. "Get your asses up!" she cried. "Follow the damn bird!"

She ran dangerously close to a startled horned viper, but avoided its strike out of sheer dumb luck. She crested the dune and tumbled down it. The kite was crossing the next one, giving a shriek as it glided on the warming air. Behind her she heard shouts as the camp rallied. She heard Nourbese calling for her to come back and Belrose cursing.

She topped another dune and then another. She was panting now but she could see the kite circling lazily ahead in the painful blue sky. Another few dunes, and she was staggering, no longer running. She wished she had her boots, her sword. The next dune was tall, and as she reached the summit a cool damp breeze kissed her. There was water, water as far as she could see, and the kite was circling it. A great lake resided here in the heart of the wasteland. Anne laughed and tumbled down the hill to the edge of the water, then she dove in and splashed and whooped with joy. Above her, the kite gave a sharp cry.

When the others caught up, Anne was soaking wet from head to toe and swimming on her back, laughing like a child. The others joined her, and even stern Nourbese laughed and sang a Fon song of thanksgiving as she splashed Belrose and Anne playfully. Adu stood at the edge of the great lake and nodded.

"Yes," he muttered to himself, "this is coming back to me."

They made camp near the water. Adu said this place was "Chad," a local word for "a great expanse of water." It gave life to much of this part of Africa, which had mostly been devoured by the Sahara.

"If we move along the shore and continue to head north," Adu said, "I think we will find what you are looking for in the next day or so."

"And what's that, exactly?" Anne asked. "The city?" Adu said nothing.

After two days of heading north, using the lake as a landmark, they came across a huge black pyramid, at least two hundred feet high and four hundred feet at its base, at the edge of an expansive forest of dead, gnarled trees. They approached it cautiously. The structure was made of black basalt, its surface unmarred with symbols, windows or doors. For days the company had experienced much wildlife flourishing along the edges of the Chad, but as they approached the pyramid the wilderness was silent. There was no sound of any animal, no indication of any life, save the party.

"Recognize this?" Anne asked Adu.

"Oh, yes," Adu said. "I was part of the Egyptian expedition that built it. This ended up becoming the first lodge for the Purrah, when it formed. It was abandoned thousands of years ago. This place marks a boundary."

"Between what?" Anne asked as she ran her hands over the warm stone of the structure's wall.

"On the other side of that forest is Carcosa," Adu said. "You've made it." Anne narrowed her eyes. "The only path to Carcosa is through those woods; they ring the city."

"What aren't you telling me . . . no, wait, I know, 'you can't say.'"

"Very astute," Adu said. "There should be rations and supplies within the pyramid, as well as the tombs of several high-ranking Egyptian commanders, distant members of the pharaoh's family. Enough treasure here to plunder to make you all very wealthy."

"Now I know there's a catch," Anne said.

"Everything you've faced, all that's yet to come," the mystic said, "remember to be true to yourself, Anne . . . that will be enough."

Anne walked away. "I'm gonna get drunk," she said.

"Hopefully . . . that will be enough," Adu amended himself.

There was a hidden compartment that opened the pyramid and Adu recalled where the lever was hidden. "This land has truly changed," the ancient man said as he slid open the small panel hidden in the cornerstone of the seemingly smooth stone wall. "This was once all grasslands, and now the desert has claimed it. No wonder this has all seemed so unfamiliar." Once the massive stone doors hissed open, the company cautiously entered and searched the structure. After hours of checking every passage, every chamber, they discovered enough supplies to maintain a small military garrison for months. It was more than enough provisions for the trek home.

The tombs in the pyramid, while nothing compared to the majesty of the pharaohs' resting places, were still impressive. Furniture covered in precious gems, plates and goblets, coffers and chests, weapons of solid gold, crates overflowing with bolts of the finest cotton, silks and priceless jewelry. It was enough money to make all the members of the company wealthy as kings several times over.

Anne found a necklace of solid gold in one of the tombs that she claimed as her own, a curving snake with rubies for eyes that rested between her slight breasts when she put the necklace on.

"Sutekh," Adu said, pointing at the necklace. "The god of the desert, of storms, disorder, destruction and ironically, foreigners. A good fit for you," he said. "Sutekh was a somewhat reluctant champion against the great serpent of chaos and darkness, Apep."

Anne shrugged as she ran her fingers over the coils of the golden snake, "Figured it would be worth a few quid," she said blandly.

The pregnant sun, boiling in oranges and umbers, crawled behind the dunes, and the stars began to come out like the animals at the watering hole once the lion departs. Anne stood alone, away from the camp and the fire, looking into the tangled maze of ancient leadwood tree skeletons that made up the forest. The interior of the forest became darker and darker as the sun sank. Adu joined her, and the two watched the forest until its interior faded to pitch.

"That's the same look you had when I first met you outside the Broken Shackle," Adu said. "You're somewhere else."

"Do you ever get frightened anymore?" she asked. "Or have you just done so much, been through so many things, that nothing moves you anymore? It seems that way with you."

"Oh, my child," Adu said softly, "I still fear. I wouldn't be human if I didn't."

"There's something in those woods, Adu," Anne said. "I can feel it."

"Yes," Adu said, "there is. That forest is all the defense the city of monsters needs. No one, save Oya, has returned from Carcosa since the city was abandoned, and the dead forest planted, back before recorded history. I find myself, against my better judgment, rather fond of you. I don't want the last time I see you to be when you enter that forest."

"Won't you come with me?" Anne asked. For a moment Adu saw again just how young she really was, past all the bluster. He shook his head.

"None of us can," he said. "It would be certain death for any but the chosen of Oya. I'm sorry, I wish I could."

"Chosen?" Anne said. "I'm going a'plundering, I'm not going to fill some fucking position, Adu! I thought you'd figured that out by now."

"And yet, you turn down treasure you have in hand for another risk, another chance to die. This was never about the gold for you, was it?"

"Of course it is," Anne said. "No, it isn't. It was at first. After a year in a prison cell thinking of a rope around my neck, money and a soft life sounded fine to me, just fine. Then you threw all this 'Carcosa' and 'Oya' shit in my way.

"All my life, the world's been telling me I was an inconvenience, a disappointment. You get fed that long enough and sooner or later you either take it as the truth of the world or you say *fuck you* to the world. You can pretty much guess which I chose. But even if you turn your back on the world, say you don't care, a piece of you does, a tiny sliver of you wants them to be wrong about you.

"I knew I was no damn good. The things I was always best at were fighting, fucking and running. Now you come along and tell me that for the first time in my life, I'm . . . special, I'm important. That I might be able to do something that no one else in the whole bloody world has been able to do. I got to see that one through, Adu. That's got more lure to it than any score, any treasure." She paused for a moment. "Not that I wouldn't mind a taste of gold, mind you. It makes everything easier."

"Have you ever done anything the easy way?" Adu asked. Anne chuckled.

"Not my nature," she said. "I blame my shabby upbringing, and my outcast lot."

Behind them there was singing and the evening meal and the welcoming fire, the companionship of others who'd shared hardship together. The two of them remained apart, unmoving.

"Not really for us, is it?" Anne asked.

"I'm afraid not," Adu said.

"You have any children?" she asked.

"Yes," he said. "Too many to count."

"I just became a mother not so long ago," Anne said. "I think I ran off on this bad business because, believe it or not, this is easier to me than dealing with all that, dealing with my father, and trying to pretend to know what the hell a mother is supposed to do."

"A mother loves," Adu said. "I have no doubt you have that in you, Anne, in abundance. All the other things come with necessity and time."

They stood a while longer. The singing and conversations died down around the fire as most of the camp, save the first watch, settled in for the night.

"Do you miss your child?" Adu asked.

"I should," Anne said. "I mean, I do, but it's like I think of him at the worst possible moments, right when I'm about to die, or I'm doing something daft. Then the rush comes over me and I don't have a care anymore and poof, he's gone."

"You're not afraid of dying," Adu said. "You're afraid of living."

"Dying is easy," Anne said. "I'm the worst person in the world to have a kid."

"You're just young," Adu said. "You're wiser than most I've met your age. You tell the truth, even to yourself, and that is a rare strength."

"I don't feel strong right now," Anne said. Her eyes were getting damp, and she fucking hated it. She remembered her vow and denied the tears a foothold. "I'm afraid because this little lark is going to end soon, one way or another, and either I'm going to be gone, and my lad will be on his own, stuck with my prat of a father, growing up without a proper ma to help him out with the tough bits, or I'll succeed and I'll have to go home and hope I don't fuck him up worse than if'n I had died."

"I sincerely doubt that," Adu said. "When you put your mind to something, you are quite a formidable force. You will be a good parent to your boy, Anne, and you don't have to go one step further. There's wealth here, more than enough to take home with you to your boy. Enough to raise him as you wish, without your father's interference. You have nothing to prove to anyone, Anne."

"Is there a better time for me to go in there?" Anne asked, nodding to the forest as she wiped her eyes and sniffed. "Daytime, night?"

"No," Adu said. "They are equally dangerous. You're not listening to me."

"Well, then," Anne said, "let's get this over with, right." She started to walk toward the forest. "If I fail, you get my share of that booty to my son. He's in the Carolina colony with my father. Give it to my boy when he's old enough, not my da. I know you can find them, Adu. You found me."

"You're running away again," Adu said, a little anger creeping into his voice. "Launching yourself into certain death because you're too scared to face up to your responsibilities."

"Responsibilities?" Anne said. "I'm a bloody pirate, a criminal! You're the one who set this whole thing up, and now you got cold cockles because I'm damned to see it through!" She drew one of her flintlocks and started toward the trees.

"Wait!" Adu shouted. "None of your weapons will help you against what's in there."

"What?" Anne said, stopping. "Seriously? That's fucking lovely. I can't even go down bloody swinging! What the fuck am I supposed to do in there, Adu?" She was shouting now. "Get so fucking in my cups that I taste bad and put the fucking beastie off its fucking food?!"

There was some commotion from the camp, and Belrose and Nourbese were rushing up to join them, both looking like they had just rolled out of bed. Belrose reeked of strong drink.

"Shut up and listen for a change," Adu said. "You have the potential to be so much more than you think you are! The creatures in there are bound by very powerful *Bo,* strong magic, to Oya's bidding. They will try to frighten you and then claim you for themselves if you fail. It is part of their compact with Oya."

"You two all right?" Nourbese said, slightly out of breath. "We heard shouting. What creatures?"

"The fucking creatures in the woods!" Anne said, still shouting, and pointing her pistol toward the dark tangled trees. "The fucking lead ball–proof, sword-proof, fucking monsters in the scary fucking wood beside the ominous fucking pyramid!"

"We thought you two were having a touching emotional moment," Belrose said. "You know, *un interlude d'appel d'offres*?" He looked to Nourbese. "You said they were having a touching emotional moment?"

"Do you know any word beside 'fuck,' girl?" Adu said, now shouting as well. "I swear to the Orishas! I was trying to impart some wisdom to you! You can be so maddening! Just go on in there, you can swear the Biloko to death with your incessant jabbering tongue!"

Belrose shook his head as he addressed Nourbese. "They're not having a touching emotional moment."

"You want some other words besides 'fuck,' old man!" Anne said. She let loose such a string of profanities that when she was finished everyone was silent and stunned.

"Oh," the ancient man said.

"Impressive," Belrose commented. The mercenary was blushing a bit.

"Wait, Biloko?" Nourbese said. "You said the Biloko are in there? No, no!" She grabbed Anne by the arm, pulling her back, away from the trees. "Bonny, you can't go in there! You mustn't!" Something in Nourbese's pleading tone sobered Anne. When some of the Amazons on watch responded to the outbursts, Nourbese waved them away.

"What's a Biloko?" Anne asked, quiet again.

"The spirits of dead men," Nourbese said, "evil dead men. It's an old story my mother told me and my brothers. The Biloko live inside trees. They can swallow a man whole. They hate the living, and they guard their forests very jealously."

Anne looked over to Adu. The mystic, calm now, nodded. "They are corrupted ancestral spirits," he said. "There is nothing alive for you to shoot or stab. I was trying to tell you," Adu said. "As I said, Anne, you don't have to go."

"You think I'll die if I go in there, don't you?" Anne said.

"No one has ever returned in uncounted centuries," Adu said. "Treasure hunters, pirates, conquerors and worse. They all now swell the ranks of the Biloko. You have found your gold. Go home, live."

"You said they will try to frighten me. What do they want to do, exactly?"

Adu sighed and shook his head. "They can only lay hands upon you if you do so first. So they will try to frighten you, unnerve you until you stumble, trip. Then they will fall upon you, rip you to pieces like the fiercest panther, and suck your soul out of your remains like a jackal sucking the marrow from a cracked bone. You will become one of them, full of hatred and spite and unending rage."

"So all I can do is try not to be scared," Anne said. She removed the sash she wore as a belt and laid her pistols and her machete on the sandy soil. Her hands were trembling.

"What are you doing?" Adu said.

"Trying to peggin' become more than I think I am," Anne said. "Besides, if you don't think I can do this, I have to show you up now, don't I?" Adu chuckled in spite of himself.

"I suppose you do," he said. "Focus on that amulet you're wearing; it has some power in it, it may help you if your will falters. Remember fear is human, it's all right. Just don't let it control you." Nourbese stepped up beside Anne.

"What are you doing?" Anne asked.

"I'm going with you," Nourbese said. "It is my duty to protect you."

"No," Anne said. "You stay. Take care of our Ahosi. Make sure the families of the dead all get a share of the money."

"My mother told me stories. They say all women faint at the mere sight of the Biloko," Nourbese said. "Please, let me go and help you. You may be many things that I dislike, but you have a good heart, which is rare in this world, and you treat the people around you fairly, no matter what they think of you, no matter their station. You spared my life when I would not have spared yours. You saved my life back in Ife. Let me try to save yours now." Anne was quiet and Nourbese was almost on the verge of tears. "You without a word to say!" Nourbese sniffed. "That's remarkable."

"Adu will tell King Agaja I insisted on going alone," Anne said, turning to face the jagged shadow of the forest. "I'm trusting you and him to carry out my wishes for my son. Protect him, and more important, teach him. Tell him about me, that I wasn't a complete fuck-up."

"I'm under no such obligations," Belrose said, stepping between her and the woods. The Frenchman was smiling. "You are entirely too sober to be making such decisions, *mon belle erreur.*"

"I am," Anne said. She pulled Belrose to her and kissed him deeply, soulfully, her tongue exploring his mouth. The swordsman moaned a little and returned the kiss. Anne pulled away, grinning. She waved to the three of them and then trotted toward the woods.

"Wait!" Belrose called, touching his lips. He had a strange, almost stunned look on his face. "What was that?"

"Don't put too much in it, luv," Anne called out. "I just wanted a last taste of liqueur on my lips!" She vanished, swallowed by the night.

"What do we do now?" Belrose asked Adu.

"The hardest thing to ever do," the first man said. "We wait."

21

The Emperor (Reversed)

Charleston, South Carolina
May 21, 1871

The judge's chamber held the afternoon's heat and sunlight at bay. There was a beautiful, ornate Johann Beha cuckoo clock on the wall near the door. The walls were paneled in dark oak and a thick Turkish rug, in muted shades of gray and green, blanketed the floor. Books on shelves were everywhere, although Maude noted there was dust on almost all of them.

Davenkirk sat behind a wide, stained-oak desk. His robe hung on a hat rack beside the single blinded window in the office, behind his desk. The judge wore a white broadcloth shirt, stained with sweat, and suspenders that held up his baggy trousers. The ruby in the judge's thick gold masonic ring caught a stray beam of sunlight and flashed in the darkness. The room smelled of sweet pipe tobacco, stale flatulence and gun oil.

"I thought it best we talk this out in here," Davenkirk said, stuffing a pipe. "Before we go back in my courtroom."

Bella and Maude sat in chairs to the left of the judge's desk, Rutledge and Martin sat to the right.

"Mrs. Mansfield, I have decided, after much deliberation and observation, that I am not going to accept your credentials to practice law in my jurisdiction," Davenkirk said. "I find your courtroom demeanor while examining the last witness to be unseemly, and unfitting a member of the fairer sex."

"You'll forgive me if I'm not shocked, your honor," Bella said. "Did you make your decision before or after I trounced Mr. Rutledge?"

"Now just a moment, madame!" Rutledge said, rising, "How dare you . . ."

"Sit down and shut up, Andy," Davenkirk said. "She did kick your ass, and you volunteered for the ass-kicking." He turned his attention to Bella. "And you, madame, you need to watch your mouth; it's going to get you into trouble, if you're not careful. You got no call to be talking to me that way. I gave you a damn sight more latitude in my courtroom than any of my colleagues would have."

"That is true," Arabella said, nodding. "You at least let me speak on behalf of my client for a time; you didn't just shut me down right out of the gate. Thank you for that. It was a pleasure to practice in your court. It's an experience I will treasure fondly all my life. I'm just sorry you didn't have the gumption to see this through, your honor."

Davenkirk laughed. "You're a ballsy one, ain't you?" he said. "I was curious to see how you'd do. You did too well, I'm sorry to say. Folks around here just aren't ready for lady lawyers, especially winning lady lawyers. Sorry, dear."

"So you're dismissing this nonsense," Rutledge said. "Good riddance." Davenkirk raised a hand and shook his head.

"Whoa, no, I'm not dismissing anything," the judge said, "and you should thank your lucky stars, Andy, you got caught with your britches down. Since I am not recognizing Mrs. Mansfield as qualified counsel, Miss Stapleton is gonna need to go find herself a lawyer and decide if she wants to start this mess all over again."

"Good luck finding one in a thousand miles willing to even talk to her," Rutledge said.

"Thus depriving her of her Sixth Amendment rights," Bella said, shaking her head.

Davenkirk looked at Maude, and his tone was soft. "Your father's people will have dug up all kinds of nasty witnesses from back in that frontier shithole by the time you find a real lawyer, Miss. If it's anything like most of those frontier towns, they can probably buy a witness against you for a cheap bottle of rye.

"Between us, your father has always been a decent, churchgoing man, honest businessman. Your mother, God rest her soul, was one of the kindest people I ever knew. She sat and cared for my mother when she was dying. I see a lot of her fire in you, but that fire caused her and your father a whole passel of trouble. Women and politics just don't mix, never have, never will.

"I hate to see all this dirt getting kicked on a good family name, not to mention dragging your poor little girl into it too. You sure we can't settle this without it going back into a courtroom? I'm sure your father would be willing to provide you a very generous allowance."

"This has never been about money, Maude," Martin said, looking to his daughter. "I just wanted you to be safe, to not get hurt, or allow Constance to be hurt. I'm willing to let you two live at Grande Folly; you can spend your inheritance as you see fit, within reason. You'll never have to work a day in your life, neither will Constance. She can attend the finest finishing schools in Europe, be permitted access to marry into the cream of the aristocracy. Please, Maude, be reasonable."

All three men and Bella looked at Maude. The afternoon shadows lengthened through the squinting blinds. The cuckoo clock ticked. Maude sighed and looked to her father.

"'To be safe,'" Maude began, "'not allow Constance to be hurt' . . . 'willing to let me live,' to 'spend my money as I see fit, within reason' . . . 'never have to work a day' . . . Constance would 'be permitted to marry.' That's reasonable, Daddy? Is this really how it all works, past the black robes, and the oaths sworn on Bibles? 'The whole truth and nothing but the truth'? This is my day in court? A backroom promise of a very comfortable slavery for me, for my daughter, as long as we are reasonable, as long as we don't ask for too much, get too uppity, make too much of a noise and a fuss?"

The compassion slid off Martin's face and he shook his head. "You don't understand, Maude, you've never understood."

"Did you ever make that offer to Mother?" Maude asked, standing. She nodded to Bella and Mansfield opened her battered leather case. "She must have gotten to hate those words so much—'reasonable,' 'emotional,' 'irrational,' 'settle down,' 'permitted,' 'allowed.'"

Arabella withdrew a packet of papers and handed them to each of the men.

"What is this?" Rutledge asked, scowling. "It's the agreement we signed about her not seeking to appeal based on incompetent counsel, so what?"

"And these are statements copied from my company ledgers," Martin said. "Where the devil did you get these?"

Bella removed another document from her case. She held it up for all to see. "The reason I wanted to depose Rutledge's clerk and you, your honor, was to establish all the parties had signed off on the agreement, get it into the court record. However, during the recess today I checked with the office of the clerk of the court and as of yesterday, this agreement, signed by all of us, is an official legal document of record. That should be good enough if we need it."

"I'm really getting tired of your mouth, woman!" Rutledge said. "Who cares?!" Bella turned to the other lawyer.

"The law of your land, Mr. Rutledge, is that a married woman has no rights once she is bound to her husband, correct?"

"Don't you ever get tired of hearing your own voice?" Rutledge growled. "Yes, you vapid cow, of course it is!"

"Andy," Maude said, modulating her voice to play specifically on the lawyer's nerves, to create unreasoning anxiety, almost fear, in him, "your left kneecap is already weakening from age, wear and from being eighteen-and-a-half pounds overweight. I couldn't help but notice you favor the right leg. You call either Mrs. Mansfield or myself another derogatory name and you will be on a cane the rest of your life. I assure it."

Rutledge visibly paled and shut up.

"The law says that the bond between husband and wife extends beyond the grave itself," Bella continued, "the great pervasive doctrine of coverture, the shade of the husband chaining the wife to him for all her days. A widow can't even sell her own home, sign a deed, buy a horse—simple business you do every day of your lives."

"If you have a point, please get to it, Mrs. Mansfield," the judge said. "I'd like to hear it before I have you and Miss Stapleton ejected from the courthouse."

Bella tapped a finger on the documents she had handed Davenkirk and the others. "You, your honor, and Mr. Rutledge both signed a legally binding agreement with a woman who, under your own asinine system of laws, is still considered the property of her dead husband."

Rutledge started to open his mouth, then closed it. Judge Davenkirk stood, the florid color of his face draining away. "Whatever you plan on doing with that, madame . . ."

"I'm planning on filing a complaint against you and Mr. Rutledge with the State Bar Association about your conduct during this case, your honor," Bella said. "In that complaint I will cite and attach this agreement as a demonstration of your incompetence in allowing a 'vapid cow,' not even qualified to practice law in your courtroom, to hornswoggle you both into a patently unenforceable and quite illegal agreement under the laws of your state.

"You, Mr. Rutledge, have your eye on several political positions, possibly beyond this state. This embarrassment will hurt you. And you, Judge, you have your appointment for life, but a man in your position lives or dies by his reputation. This will hurt and embarrass you, especially with your peers. How do you think this will influence your legacy, how you are thought of after you are gone?"

"I'm a well-respected member of this community," Rutledge said, "powerful, and influential. Judge Davenkirk, even more so. We personally know most of the Bar ethics committee. Hell, I get drunk with them every other Wednesday. This won't mean a damn thing. It will never see the light of day."

"You two are very well-respected," Bella said, nodding. "You could weather a quiet little scandal, the kind your type perpetuate—make the accuser look like a crazy, emotional lunatic, a hysterical female with delusions of equality. All the old boys circle the wagons—and that usually works . . . if it weren't for Mr. Cline and his newspaper stories."

Davenkirk and Rutledge looked at each other. Bella continued. "I assure you, gentlemen, I will have a doozy of a story to tell him on my way to the Bar Association committee. A story that I'm sure will receive as wide coverage as the last one he wrote, perhaps even further. The public loves to see influential, powerful people laid low. They have a positive bloodlust for it. Cloistered little clubs like you two are members of still have to explain themselves to the public when their actions are dragged into the light of day."

Bella took out another document and laid it on the desk in front of Davenkirk.

"This is an agreement I drafted," Arabella said, "to be signed by Mr. Anderton, relinquishing all control of Miss Stapleton's inheritance, including the Grande Folly estate, back to her, and conceding custody of Constance to her as well. It includes a promise of no further litigation on this matter."

"There's a clause in there that if anything happens to me," Maude added, "I do want my father to be her guardian until she is eighteen, then all my possessions, all my money, it all goes to her, free and clear, no strings."

"What on earth makes you think I will ever sign such a thing?" Martin said.

"Martin," Rutledge said, "please, be . . ."

"Reasonable?" Bella offered.

"Those ledger pages," Maude said. "They show that the piracy your ships have been plagued with has cut into your profits over fifteen percent this year. Isn't that correct, Father?"

"How did you know such things?" Martin asked.

"Because even if you thought I was too stupid to pay attention to your work growing up, I did pay attention and I did learn, because I had some vain hope that you'd want your only child to run your business one day, even if she was only a woman."

"Maude . . ." Martin began, but Maude continued.

"I also know that, to date, not a single man on your crews has been killed, have they?"

Martin looked up from the papers. He looked at Maude in a way she had never seen him do before. She always thought she'd enjoy this moment, but she felt ashamed. She buried that feeling; too much was at stake to give into it.

"I happen to know someone back in that Nevada camp who is on very good terms with those particular pirates," Maude said. "Apparently, one of the criminals or whores I was consorting with in Golgotha." That much of it was true. Black Rowan was no friend of Maude's, but the Barbary Coast pirate she had met in Golgotha last year had agreed to Maude's proposal, sent via correspondence, to interfere with Martin's shipping while assuring that no harm came to her father's sailors. "You sign that paper and your troubles with them cease. In fact, your ships will have unseen protection until such time as you've made up for the losses you've incurred. You refuse and the attacks grow more frequent. Who knows, the pirates might even start taking hostages, demanding ransom. None of that will set well with your business partners and the banks."

"I can't believe my own flesh and blood is behaving this way," Martin said. "How could you be capable of such duplicity, Maude?"

"How could I?" Maude said, the flint returning to her eyes. Her shame washed away in a flood of cold rage. "You raised me to believe in the law and the blindness, the fairness of it. This is all you have left me, Father. When you take away any hope of justice, of equity, you create criminals.

"You could have trusted me to take care of my girl, believed in me; you could have trusted that you raised me strong enough, and tough enough, to handle whatever life brings at me. You don't have an inkling of what I have been through to keep her alive, keep her safe, and what I would gladly endure all over again to make sure she stays that way. You have no idea who I am, what I can do and less than any desire to know. To you, I'm nothing but a weak, ineffectual 'featherbrain,' and you refuse to think that I could be anything more than that. You were mistaken, and now you've paid for it."

Martin's eyes became moist. Maude almost stopped, but an anger so long buried, so abused and ignored, is a hard beast to tame. "I am so much more than you know, Daddy, so much more than you've ever seen. You've tried my whole life to keep me from that realization; you murdered a little girl's dreams, and tried to steal a woman's life. How could I? How could *you*?"

Martin stood. He leaned over Davenkirk's desk, took a pen and signed the agreement. He handed the papers to Maude.

"You don't know me either," Martin said, almost croaking. "If that's what you think I see when I see you, you couldn't be more wrong. I'll have Constance and her things out to Grande Folly as soon as possible. Andrew," he said to Rutledge, "please see that the agreement is finalized and filed with the court as soon as possible." Martin regarded Rutledge, and the judge. "Gentlemen, good day to you both." He departed the office without looking back at Maude. The door clicked shut behind him.

Maude looked at the papers in her hands. They won, the war was won. Bella placed a hand on Maude's shoulder. "Maude," she said, softly. "I'll deal with the rest of this. You go on home, now. I'll meet you there later."

As the door was closing, Maude heard Judge Davenkirk say around the stem of his pipe, "It's a damn shame."

Outside the courthouse, Maude barely felt the heat, barely felt anything. Her body was conditioned to regulate her temperature, keep her cool when everyone else was sweating automatically. Automatic, like a machine.

She was walking, balancing, swimming against the invisible oppression of gravity. Her heart pumped blood and her lungs took in air. The bright, brutal sunlight felt like it was hitting her skin from some distant solar system. Everything was muted, everything except the ache in her. The tearing inside was sharp and immediate and unrelenting, unforgiving. She tried to stay outside of herself, to ignore the pain.

She'd won, she'd lost. Her righteous anger had abandoned her now, when she needed it more than ever. There was no true victory in a war, only half measures of suffering and regret, something gained, something compromised, something lost. The cold combatant in her had known this moment would have to come from the start of her campaign to reclaim what was hers; for her to see victory, her father would need to taste defeat. However, she had avoided the shape and the texture of that abstract, of what came after the endgame. It felt as if her father had died in that judge's chambers, and Maude felt his loss, an immeasurable ache in her. He was not taken from her, she had done this, planned it, executed it.

The cabbie opened the door for her and took her hand, helping Maude up into the coach. Her mouth said the words that would tell him where to take her. It felt as if someone else were saying them. The coach shuddered, and began to move, taking her to Grande Folly, to her home, her land. She recalled in perfect detail the last words her father had said to her, and her senses had told her, even as he said them, that they were the absolute truth. *"You don't know me either."*

She retained a vague memory of a dream she'd had when she was seven, maybe eight. It was of her mother: a blurred, indistinct imagining of the woman who had given birth to her and then died. The woman in her dream had sweat-tousled hair and kind, but weary, brown eyes. She smiled at Maude and it was like the sun warming her heart.

"Hello, my darling," Claire Anderton had said. "So strong to survive this, so brave and so beautiful."

The nightmare part began when Maude was taken away from her. She heard her mother screaming, calling Maude's name as the darkness swallowed them both. Maude awoke, weeping, screaming for her mother.

Her father had been there, had held her while she cried at the shadow play her brain had put on for her. Martin held her so tight, like she would fly away into a million pieces if he let her go, and in that moment, Maude had felt like she might, but his love held her together. She remembered her daddy's face, the warm tears rolling down from his eyes, the same eyes she had seen today.

"I got you, I know," Martin had said, his usually strong voice trembling, just as it had trembled today in the judge's chambers. "I know, I miss her too, all the time. It will be okay, Maude."

In the carriage, headed toward her newly won home, Maude knew the tears would come, and she would allow them this time, but she didn't think she deserved them.

22

The Heirophant

Charleston, South Carolina
May 22, 1871

It hadn't taken Maude long to find Hell's Belles. What Gran had mentioned in Maude's meditative vision was *Datura stramonium*, a plant known commonly as Jimsonweed, and sometimes called Hell's Belles. It was part of the nightshade family and Maude remembered Gran teaching her about it long ago during her training in poisons.

When Maude had cracked open the old, massive pharmacopoeia that Gran had insisted she memorize, she found a strip of yellowed paper marking the page relating to *Datura stramonium*. Gran had seldom used bookmarks, ever, saying a good well-trained memory was all the bookmark you needed. Maude ran her fingers along the old paper and discovered there was something irregularly, and invisibly, coating the surface of the page.

Sniffing the paper, Maude discovered that Gran had left her another clue in a very subtle code. Steganography was placing a secret message hidden or embedded in another commonplace item or location, so that to the unaware it would most likely be overlooked. The greatest danger in such messages is if they were discovered in their obvious hiding places, information might be compromised, so a steganograph was usually combined with another code or cipher. Gran had taught Maude a unique and cryptic code, based on discriminating between scents and smells, with each scent representing a letter or number. The scent code required a degree of sensitivity and discrimination of smell that only someone of the Blood of Lilith, or a certain deputy back in Golgotha, could possess, and only Maude had been taught how to crack Gran's code. She carefully wrote each symbol associated with the scent and then double checked it several times. The decoded message read:

> Back of the old clay tablet on the table in library, Hell's Belles in proper dilute dosage for non-lethal result. Swallow the blood stone as you drink solution. I told you meditation was useful. Glad you kept up on your poisons and ciphers. Gran.

Maude examined the large clay tablet on the library reading table, the one with the ankh—the looping cross—and the lines of cuneiform text. She ran her fingers over it, searching. Gran had made her learn to read print in a pitch-black room, blindfolded, with only her fingertips to guide her. It took the better part of an hour, but finally, she detected the spot where delicate, powerful fingers had gouged an opening in the back of the tablet and then repaired it, nearly flawlessly. Maude recalled Gran erasing her prints in the sand without even seeming to touch them; once again, only someone with Maude's degree of training, her sensitivity of touch, could possibly detect this obfuscation.

She directed her strength to her fingertips and carefully tore open the seal. A tiny bead, the size of a pea, was revealed in the powdery gray debris. Maude gingerly plucked it up. It was a ruby, a deep wine color, flawless and beautiful.

She retired with the ruby and some of the Jimsonweed she had harvested from the estate grounds to the all-but-abandoned infirmary and laboratory that Gran had constructed on the third floor of the manor. Maude remembered the room from her years toiling here to understand the secrets of chemicals and compounds, to understand how to use those agents to heal or harm, and Gran's numerous lessons on combat and field medicine. Maude had often thought she might have enjoyed using the powers granted her to save lives as a doctor.

The room had seemed so much larger back then than it did now. Maude removed the dust-covered cloths that covered the various tools and instruments of the chemist's craft. By that evening, Maude had cooked the dark seeds of the deadly poisonous plant and extracted the correct dosage of the chemical within it to create a substance that would induce hallucination, not death. Gran had taught that cultures across the globe used Jimson-weed extract for healing purposes as well as for mystical and religious rites.

She knew what Gran wanted her to do, but an uncertainty bordering on fear held Maude. She had been required, under Gran's care and supervision, to ingest every imaginable kind of poison, drug and hallucinogen, so that she could understand their effects, recognize them, even function under them to a certain degree.

Maude had hated that aspect of her training. She hated the feeling of loss of control, of helplessness that it gave her, and she despised having her innermost thoughts, insecurities and desires laid bare and held up to her waking mind to address. Alter was right, she didn't like to dwell inside herself, didn't like to look inward. Maude saw no use for it, believed no good could come from it. There were things in her that she was very glad she had the discipline to ignore and keep quiet. It was a mystery to her how anyone could enjoy those feelings, do that to themselves willingly. She had been drunk maybe three times in her entire life and had never had a desire to use any drug.

A contradiction hit her that evening as she sat at the kitchen table with Isaiah; she had enjoyed feeling out of control, those few times she had had to push herself hard to do some impossible thing, usually when she was three-fourths dead, or when she let herself feel fully, let the joy, the abandon, of life take her. She felt that same dizzy feeling of being out of control with Mutt, the only man who could match her, who could understand her, whose love felt so pure and so primal. The freedom she felt in those moments was exhilarating. Perhaps there was power in being out of control, and perhaps some part of her understood that better than she had assumed she did.

"Whatever you're thinking about, it's making you blush and smile stupid," Isaiah said as he rinsed the dishes in the sink. Maude shook the thoughts away, like brushing cobwebs from her face.

"Sorry," she said, "just a stray thought hit me. Isaiah, have I always been so . . . reserved?"

Isaiah chuckled. "Reserved? Oh, dear child, is that what you think?" he said. "You don't remember wrestling with the other farm kids, and they gave you as good as they got! You'd come in for supper covered in mud, dung and blood, a big grin on your face, your two front teeth missing! A few times I went to stop you from fighting, but Lady Cormac, she'd hold me back, said it was good for you, you needed to learn how to get scuffed up, 'take some of the paint off the china doll.'"

"I'd forgotten about all that," she said. "I loved it! I whooped Eli Wynn's boy damn good, and he was a horse compared to me!"

"You always been a scrapper," Isaish said. "I think that was what she saw in you that drew her to you at first. She saw how pushed down you'd been by your father, and you still fought to climb out and just be you. No, you learned how to be reserved, Maude; by nature, you're a tiger by the tail."

Maude smiled and sipped her iced tea. "I guess I am, aren't I?"

"And don't get me started on that time you were up in the barn loft with Eli's son, little girl," he added as he dried the glasses with a cloth.

"My first kiss," Maude said wistfully.

"He still asks after you, by the way," Isaiah said with a chuckle.

"He was a better kisser than a scrapper, that was for sure," Maude said.

It was close to midnight when she decided it was time. Isaiah insisted on sitting with her for the ordeal, but Maude was hesitant. "When I'm under the influence of the drug, I have no idea what I'll do."

"More reason you need someone around to look after you, keep you safe."

"What if I accidentally hurt you?" Maude said.

"You'd never do that," Isaiah said. "I trust you like I trust myself. Let's get this show on the road."

They cleared the section of the rugged floor in the study before the crackling fire in the fireplace. Maude dressed in the loose, comfortable dark men's clothing and boots that they had both come to call her "working clothes." Isaiah settled her down and put a barrier of thick pillows around her as she positioned herself cross-legged in the meditation stance.

"I never cared much for Lady Cormac's love affair with intoxicants," Isaiah said, "the wine, the whiskey, opium, hashish and then all those hallucinogens she'd come back with from some far-off place." He handed Maude the glass vial with the drug. "You sure about this?"

"Gran wanted me to do it," Maude said, "and it may be the only way I get the answers I need to keep Constance safe. You'd do it for your children, Isaiah."

"I'd do this for you if I could," he said and she leaned forward and hugged him tight.

Maude held up the small ruby between her thumb and forefinger. "This part is the true mystery," she said. "I have no idea why it was hidden and what it means. Gran called it a 'blood stone' in the message. I examined it microscopically, and examined its refractive index properties as well. It seems to be a normal small ruby. Beautiful, but ordinary."

Maude looked up and saw concern line the old man's face.

"I'll be okay," she said. She placed the ruby on her tongue as if it were a pill, uncorked the vial and drained it. The drug tasted bitter and left a metallic, burning sensation in her mouth. The ruby felt as though it were a bubble of liquid now, on her tongue. She swallowed all of it.

"There is a fine line with *Datura stramonium* between hallucination and delirium," Maude said. "I may start running a bit of a fever. Try to keep water in me, as best you can. If you think I've gone as far as I can go, administer this." She handed him another corked vial. "It should start neutralizing it pretty quickly. Otherwise I should return to my senses just before dawn."

Isaiah began to sit but Maude smiled and shook her head. "I'll be fine. You go. I'm going to meditate. I will call if I need anything."

"Good hunting," Isaiah said. "I'll check in on you in a quarter of an hour." He stepped out of the room, reluctantly.

Maude began her cleansing breathing as she stared into the flames in the fireplace, and began to feel herself slipping into a trance. Her breathing was deep and even her body was feeling lighter, and her mind began to feel less attached to her body. She felt herself becoming divorced from time as she felt an alien heat, churning, growing, like a furnace of potential and chaos, at the core of her, spreading out through her. White-hot starlight pierced every pore of her body.

She tasted bitter light on her tongue, and the illumination moved through all of her, pulling her sense of self apart like taffy. Maude's will was immutable cold stone, anchoring part of her mind back to her body, spiking it there. The wildfire running through her, through the crumbling playhouse of her thoughts and memories, left no walls, no polite partitions between present action and halcyon memory.

Maude felt like her body was made of warm wax. She felt cool, silver comfort dribble across her lips and down into her throat and change to steam in the crucible of the sun.

"Please, Miss Maude, drink some more, please, and sit down. It's been hours, and you're burning up." It was Isaiah's voice, her father's voice. She was staring into the conflagration at the center of her, scorching her every nerve, her every cell.

The realization came as the inferno roared out of her, a nova exploding, branding her soul, her mind, all that remained of her. Her wax body was melting, going, going, gone. Maude had felt something like this before, but not this intense, this pure, never this degree of sensation, of power. It was the blood, the Blood of Lilith. It was like the initiation ritual from so long ago . . . or maybe she was still in the initiation ritual, her twenty-one-year-old self looking through the burning light to regard her forty-year-old self.

A powerful feeling of déjà vu, of split perceptions filled Maude. She was her younger self in this moment of frozen, searing time, and she was her present self, and she was . . . her . . . hundred-and-fifty? Two-hundred? year-old self, looking back, waving her off.

Old Maude was inside some kind of horseless coach, *a car*? The word felt odd to her present self, her young self. A young man in a cowboy hat sat beside her, controlling the strange vehicle. It was cool inside the compartment. Music was playing in the air. They were driving through the painfully bright, hot Nevada desert, and she "remembered" they were headed back to Golgotha to stop the humming thing with killing eyes, a thing named Odom Sodd, the manufactured monster that had killed someone so dear to Maude . . .

"Too far, too soon," future Maude said, turning toward present Maude while sitting in the car, calling along the pulsing, thrumming line that connected them. "You always did try to overachieve too damn much!"

"I do no such thing, thank you!" present Maude said. "And a woman your age still having those kinds of lascivious feelings and desires is . . ."

". . . the best," old Maude finished, and reached over to caress the cheek of the handsome young cowboy with sand-colored hair. The cowboy looked over and smiled sweetly at her, and her, and her. It was Jim Negrey, Mutt's fellow deputy in Golgotha. Older, maybe in his late twenties, with a scruff of three-day beard, but it was Jim.

"Stop your gawking," future Maude said. "You're getting lost in your own damn skein. This might never be exactly this way anyway, you pull them too tight and they snap, and leave them too loose, they droop and tangle. Go back. Find the Record. God, was I always so thick?" There was a shout, echoing and muffled like down a tunnel behind her. It sounded like Gran.

"This way, you little wagtail! This way! Follow the blood, follow the line!"

Cool water on her lips, down her throat. A gentle hand brushing the hair out of her eyes and off her hot skin. She looked up and saw Isaiah putting a cool compress to her forehead. She tried to talk but her tongue was too thick.

There was a brilliant white afterimage when Maude closed her eyes. The radiance lessened and detail began to bleed into the light. She was in a library, was it Grande Folly's? A few yards from the fireplace? It seemed much, much farther away than that. All the books, all the scrolls and papers were connected by strands of milky white light, almost like cobwebs in moonlight. Maude ran her fingers along the threads; they were so soft, silky and fragile, but they did not break when she touched them, stronger than they seemed.

Each strand she touched held a voice, an idea, a thought, and by running her fingers over them, the knowledge and the stories sang to her. It was beautiful, all that history, all those concepts—feelings, failures, lives, loves, misunderstandings, joys, hatreds, unions, wars, triumphs, laughter, disappointments, tears, births—all of the human mosaic trembling in every subtle color of thought. Maude wept as she strummed the threads and listened to humanity sing their songs.

She was in the library just off from the study, she was hot and her body felt thick and odd. The tears on her face were drying on her fevered cheeks. Isaiah was trying to tell her something. He looked so worried, his skin was like crumbling dust before her eyes. He was offering her a glass of water and she drank it down, feeling it spill across her chin and hiss as it hit the cooking flesh of her breasts.

Isaiah offered her a small glass vial, but she looked away for a moment . . . a year . . . an eon . . . and she saw all the threads of the library tangled together, still running through her fingers. They led to a knotted strand of incalculable knowledge and subtle hues that drifted out of the library and down the hall to the front door.

Maude followed the strand. She pushed on the front door and the world broke in a rain of angry, shouting splinters. She held on to the thread and felt the cool grass of the lawn under her feet, damp with dew. The thread thinned, fluttered, and dissolved under her fingertips on the night wind.

She was on the lawn of Grande Folly. Somehow, she had lost her shoes, or had she ever had them? There were fireflies burning, drifting all across the lawn. The last gossamer threads from the library were sailing on the moonlight, falling into the tiny yellow suns that blazed and diminished like the heartbeat, the breath, of creation.

Maude walked into the cold darkness between the stars and stood at the core of the flitting, golden lights. She was walking on the cold black marble of space. She was at the core of the galaxy, the seat of self and other.

"This is the Record," Gran said. Her buccaneer boots echoing on the cold marble floor, she came into view out of the shadows cast by the chorus of tiny lights. This version of Gran looked to be Maude's age, not as young as she had been when she saw her staring before the mirror, nor as old as she had been when Maude met her as a child. "There are very few that can access it. They have different names for it—the Akasha, the Astral, the Smoking Mirror, the Collective Unconsciousness, the Race Memory . . . the Cloud." Anne paused. "That last one's a joke, but you won't get it for a very long time, lass. We are part of the few that can access the Record, Maude. It is something unique to our bloodline, I think, in part because we have tasted the purest blood of the Mother, far purer than the blood you drank from the Grail."

"The Blood of Lilith?" Maude said. Circling the room, moving between the pulsing lights.

"The blood gives us access," Anne said, "but it is dangerous to wander too far into the Record, or your own skein, your own time line. You can get lost here, and then you are lost to the physical world. Your body will wither and die without the mind and soul. The blood is your anchor as well as your passport; even now you can feel it tugging you back to your little island of self."

"Yes. How can this be, Gran?" Maude asked.

"This is the second initiation," Gran said. "Most Daughters never learn of it, let alone reach it. You will be able to tap into the Record while still in your skin, access knowledge, learn techniques instantly, not as well as someone who's mastered them, mind you, but this realm can be an invaluable asset, a treasure trove of discovery. It will take meditation and practice to reach it, remain connected to it. Sometimes, I was able to reach here in desperation, when my life was in danger, but don't count on that, don't make it a crutch, it's fickle. Some traditions of the Daughters focus more on the Record, the mystic, the powers of the mind that the blood can unlock, than others."

"This is how that Daughter was able to control the butterflies," Maude said, "and make that Son think she was somewhere else and miss her."

"Yes," Anne said. "Her name is Itzel, and her skein is here, as is mine, as is yours. Every Daughter of Lilith is connected here, bound by the blood inside us."

"This is how one Daughter just 'knows' what another one has learned how to do," Maude said, placing her hand close to one of the tiny glowing lights. "We're all connected here."

"It's a very dodgy connection," Anne said, "and most of the Daughters only access it without even being aware they are doing so. Just a feeling, an instinct, just knowing something."

Anne saw a look cross Maude's face. "Don't spend all your time trying to get in here, girl! This library is too big even for you, little bookworm." Anne smiled at Maude. "This place is a memorial, and a tool, but it's not a home, nor a place to dwell all the time with the dead. Remember, Maudie, life is for living."

"Is this what's been harming Constance?" Maude asked. "Do those dreams she's been having come from here?"

"In part," Anne said. "She's of our bloodline, so the connection is stronger for her, and she's been infected with its blood too. That's what's slowly driving the poor girl mad."

"Whose blood?" Maude asked. "The Great Wurm, that thing in the mines back in Golgotha?"

Maude was in the silver-floored well room in the Argent Mine now. Reliving the rumbling of the unfathomable beast shaking the world apart as it awoke, as it freed itself. Constance lying before her, with eyes of bleeding ink. Maude put the ancient iron flask to her daughter's lips and fed her the same burning, powerful, alien blood that Maude had drunk long ago, the moon blood of the first woman, the first rebel, Lilith.

"Focus." Gran's voice was almost like a slap. Maude was back in the Record, the floor of cold space, the drifting lights.

"You did the right thing, giving her a drink from the Grail," Anne said.

"It was the only thing that could save her. The two bloods are constantly at war inside of her, poor child. The only way she can have peace is to surrender to one of them, the Mother or the Wurm. Either one would mean she'd lose herself in the process, forever."

"I'm so sorry I destroyed the flask, the Grail, Gran," Maude said. "It seemed like the right thing to do."

"You trusted your gut and your gut did right by you," Anne said. "What you did, giving the last of the Mother's blood to seal the breach and heal the world of the Wurm's poison, it was meant to be—Lilith's will sent to you through the Record. You did good, lass. I always knew you would, Maude."

"Lilith?" Maude said. "The real Lilith is in here?"

"That's a simple question with a complicated answer," Anne said. "Is the ocean in every drop of water?" The tiny lights of the Record drifted, darkened and then pulsed back to life again. Something was wrong, somewhere. Maude felt something distracting her.

"Those men who tried to take Constance, the Sons," Maude said, "they said she was the Grail, now. What does that mean?"

Anne sighed. "That's . . . a bit more complicated, too, luv. Games within games, lies to hide other lies to reach a truth. Schemes and plots, traps and counter-traps. I wish it weren't this way, but it is. It's the Mother's will being worked in her own design. Constance's blood is . . . changing. In a way, she is becoming the Mother, just as the Wurm wants to use her body as its agency in the world. Those of the Blood of the Wurm cannot enter the city of monsters, they are held in check by powerful wards, old magic, first magic. There's more to it than that, and so much trickery. I'm truly sorry your girl is at the center of all of it, Maude. Constance is the king in this game of chess—the endgame—but you, you, Maudie, you're the queen, the spoiler, the one they won't see coming."

There was a strong tug in the center of Maude's being, along the cord of fire that led back to her mortal shell. Maude tried to ignore it.

"Who are the Sons, Gran?" Maude asked.

The tug was stronger, more insistent. Her body wanted something, needed something, desperately. Maude ignored it again.

"I told you that's not good for you, lass," Anne said. "You can't stay in here and lose yourself in the process."

"Who are they?" Maude said. "Why didn't you tell me about them, prepare me?" The sensations, the details of the Record, were beginning to wash out, into directionless light. She focused on Gran, even as the sound was being washed out in the radiance. She tasted coppery acid in her mouth, burning her throat. She was feeling her body again. It felt horrid.

"The Sons!" Maude screamed. "They want to hurt my girl. Please, Gran!"

"It was my fool pride, girl." Anne's fading voice said. "I thought I had dealt with the old bastard forever, that no one would ever have to fear him again. I was wrong. I'm sorry, luv. I failed you there. Remember your way back here," Anne shouted. It sounded like a whisper. "They are the Sons of Typhon, his children, as we are Lilith's."

"Typhon," Maude muttered.

"Typhon," Anne said. "Birthed of the Great Olde Wurm, nightmare given flesh . . ." Maude was feeling her face against something wet that was poking it, her body was a lead weight dragging her down, back to a much less simple place, a much less ordered place. ". . . Tulpa," Anne said, her fading voice drowned out by the thudding of blood in Maude's ears. ". . . Father of Monsters, enemy of all life, husband to Lilith . . ."

"What?" Maude said.

Her eyes fluttered open. She was on the lawn of Grande Folly. It was still dark. Her whole body felt as though it were made of liquid lead, especially her skull. There was a horrible, bitter taste in her mouth. All she wanted to do was drink a lake full of cold water and sleep in a soft bed for a week. Irregular flashbacks from the drug were still making time and space seem jerky and loose. Maude felt like she was not fully fitted back into the regular continuity of the universe. It was a disjointed, broken feeling. She hoped real sleep would dispel it.

She staggered up the front steps to the shattered oak front door. Had she done that? She vaguely recalled wanting outside, but she couldn't hang on to the memory; it was slippery. She stepped into the hall, and shuffled toward the study.

Isaiah was lying on the floor, his blood soaking into the expensive rug. There were men, many men standing in the shadows of the room; the drug's aftershocks made them seem like they were born of shadow themselves. A tall, lanky man in a threadbare and unstylish cut of suit stood before the hearth. The fire was out; only dying, orange embers remained.

The man turned. His face was . . . wrong. His green eyes, his mouth . . . just not right entirely. For a shuddering second, the drug tore away his veneer, his body, as if a magician were ripping a cloth off a covered box with a flourish. What Maude saw in that second was an endless thing, an ocean of writhing, twisting tentacles, a legion of hungry mouths, a hulking obscenity. Then the man façade was back, reality was back, but Maude knew that what she had seen was this thing's true face.

"The door was open," Typhon said. "I let myself in."

23

The Five of Wands

Charleston, South Carolina
May 23, 1871

Martin heard the shout from his bedroom. It was Greene, his butler, and then he heard Miss Applewhite screaming. He climbed out of bed, groaning a bit from the exertion, and retrieved his revolver out of his bedside table drawer. He made his way to the stairs and then down.

"Whoever you are, you won't get away with this!" Miss Applewhite said. She was being held by a masked man, who was actually a bit shorter than the governess, one of a group of five masked intruders in the parlor. Greene was on the floor, unmoving, a rolling pin in the butler's hand, obviously a hastily grabbed weapon. Miss Anhorn was still on the loveseat, breathing but unconscious. Constance was nowhere to be seen. Martin stepped into view and cocked the short barreled .32 revolver as he aimed at the tallest of the masked men.

"She's quite correct," Martin said. "You'll gain no benefit from this. Let her go, and I swear if you've hurt that man. . . . ."

"He's unconscious," the tall man said. His voice was deep, but sounded strange to Martin, perhaps an accent of some kind? "We're here for the girl. No harm has to come to anyone in this if you'll be reasonable."

"I've come to hate the word 'reasonable' in the last few days," Martin said. "Get the hell out of my house, now!" He fired the pistol. There was a sharp crack and the bullet grazed the jacket shoulder of the leader of the masked kidnappers. The masked man did not flinch.

"That was a warning shot," Martin said.

"Yes," the tall masked man said. "I know."

"I can shoot the fleas off a mongrel at a hundred yards," Martin said. "Now let her go and get out of my house!"

"Can I please take him, mama?" the shortest of the intruders asked the tall leader. He sounded younger too. "I want you to see!"

"We don't have time for this!" another of the masked men said. "We didn't need to wake anyone up to take her."

"As I recall, it was you who seemed to make an uncharacteristic amount of noise," another kidnapper opined.

"Take him, my сладкий соловей," the tall leader said.

"Don't hurt him!" the kidnapper accused of making a loud entrance shouted. The youngster in a mask was halfway up the stairwell before Martin even realized it. He fired the gun at the boy's feet. "Stay back, I'm warning you!" he said. "I have no desire to shoot a child, but I will if I have to."

"You can try, old man," the masked boy said. "Go on, try to shoot me."

"Lesya!" the tall leader called out. "No, you're not ready for that!"

"I am, Mother," the boy said. Martin was confused by the words, but as the youth took another step up toward him, Martin fired at the center body mass, as he had been trained to do. The boy pivoted on the balls of his feet and the bullet whined past him, splintering part of the banister rail as it passed. Horrified, Martin fired again and again at the approaching masked figure, who twisted closer and closer, miraculously dodging the bullets. "Lesya" mis-stepped on the narrow stair and one of Martin's shots was true, blasting a bloody hole in the youth's upper shoulder. There was a very feminine-sounding gasp of pain and the intruder stumbled, falling to one knee.

"Lesya!" the tall leader screamed. Martin looked down at the child on his knees, shuddering in pain and shock. When he looked up, the tall leader was on him, as if she had magically appeared. "грязное животное!" the masked leader snarled, his voice also slipping and sounding strangely feminine now. "How dare you hurt her, you filthy animal! She's a child!" The gun was plucked out of Martin's right hand and twisted as the weapon was pulled away. He felt the bones of his fingers and hand snap like dry twigs, felt terrible pressure and burning pain as the nerves caught up with the damage quickly. The next blow from the masked man snapped Anderton's ribs and drove them deep into his organs. Martin moaned in pain as he fell to his knees.

"Damn it, Inna," the noisy intruder shouted and raced up the stairs, as the others followed.

The small intruder holding Miss Applewhite touched her temple. "Sleep now, dream." The governess made a soft cooing sound and slid to the floor. The tall masked man had Martin by his night shirt and was about to strike him again.

"Let him be, or I swear I'll snap her neck!" Constance's voice came from behind Inna. To Martin's eyes his granddaughter had seemingly appeared out of thin air, but Inna and the other Daughters knew the Stapleton girl was making exceedingly good use of the stealth skills her mother had taught her. The Russian Daughter continued to hold Martin as she looked over her shoulder.

"Constance?" Martin groaned. He must be losing his faculties. His sweet, innocent granddaughter was holding the marauder he had shot in some kind of wrestling hold. Her eyes were steely and sure. Martin struggled to make any of this nightmare make sense, even as Inna understood only too well what was happening.

Constance had her daughter, Lesya, in a submission hold; it would take her only the slightest pressure to crack the girl's spinal column and kill her. Lesya struggled to stay awake, but blood was gushing from her shoulder wound.

"Let him go," Constance said through gritted teeth. She shifted to put the stairwell wall behind her. Amadia, Itzel and Leng Ya were below her on the staircase. Everything had a nauseating sense of familiarity to it. Constance had dreamed all the outcomes, and knew whatever she did it wouldn't matter, it all led her to the same singularity of fate. She felt damned, doomed.

Constance's dreams now contained the addition of a woman and a man, both in deep shadow, both struggling to grab her and pull her into their darkness. When they grabbed her, Constance felt her own personality draining away, drowning in the immense oceans of their power, their age and their will. She stood on a tiny island of self between them. She had seen her grandfather die, her mother die. She had to change that outcome, no matter the cost to her.

"If you tend to your daughter soon, she will live," Constance said, "but if you force us into a stalemate, she'll die."

Constance didn't get a chance to finish. Lesya slipped free of the hold, and using her one good arm, tossed Constance away. Constance crashed through the hard wood of the banister and fell toward the floor below. She managed to right herself and landed, crouched on her feet.

"Silly," Lesya said. "Your mother never taught you the counter to that hold? She is a poor teacher. My mother did."

Inna tossed Martin over the rail and he tumbled to the floor, head and neck first, near Constance. He was not moving. The Russian scooped up her daughter. "We will get this cared for at once, my darling nightingale. You did very well, but it was foolish what you did with the bullets. You are not ready for that yet."

"But I dodged three," Lesya said, and nodded into unconsciousness.

Constance was beside her grandfather. Martin's breathing was a gurgling wheeze. She moved her trembling fingers over his torso. Broken ribs, lacerated organs, internal bleeding and spinal injury from the fall. Her grandfather was dying. She looked up the four assembled Daughters of Lilith with tears in her eyes. "You can save him, please."

"Take the girl," Inna said. "We'll be on our way to the ship."

"No," Amadia said, stepping away from the Russian. "This is madness, my old friend. We are not like this, we are behaving like the Sons; we are kidnapping, murdering for no reason. This girl and her mother are not our enemies, they are like us. This man was defending his flesh and blood, as any of us would do. No more. I'm done doing Alexandria Poole's dirty work."

The Russian was silent.

"Amadia," Itzel said, "please, my friend, we have no choice."

"The very first thing we all learned," Amadia said, "is that you always have a choice. You live with the consequences of those choices. I'm choosing."

Amadia flipped down to stand beside Constance and Martin. "You want her, you will have to kill me first," Amadia said.

"Very well," Leng Ya said. "You stand alone, Amadia Ibori. If you try to stop us from fulfilling the mission, I have no desire to kill you . . ."

"Oh, Ya, you and I have wanted to kill each other since the day we met. You detest me," Amadia said, "and I have no love for you."

"True," Ya replied. "But I shall not, unless you give me cause by interfering in our duty. You seem to be incapable of understanding one must often do odious things for the collective good. You revel in your uniqueness, and that makes you a poor member of any group that you associate with. I find it most disgusting."

"Please." Constance looked up to Amadia. "I'll go with them, I won't fight. Just please save him, and my mother. She's in terrible danger. It's the Sons, and he's with them."

"These women, they mean to kill you, you know that?" Amadia said. Constance nodded.

"Please save them," the girl said again. "Tell them both I love them, and they were worth what comes next."

Amadia knelt by Martin. Constance gently helped her lay him on his back. His breathing was not regular, and he made a whistling groan. The other Daughters descended the staircase. Constance kissed Martin's forehead and then stood, her legs like water, and walked to join her kidnappers.

"I am ready to face my fate," Constance said.

"Last chance to change your mind, my dear friend," Inna said. Amadia said nothing and began to work on Martin. "Very well," the Russian said, "to the ship, and back to London."

"Thank you," Constance said to Amadia.

"Don't thank me for this, child."

The Daughters departed, and Amadia and Constance exchanged one final glance before the girl and her captors disappeared.

24

Death

"You don't remember me, Maude? How disappointing," Typhon said. "After all we went through together in that dreary oubliette beneath Golgotha? Promises were exchanged, I saved your life, and this is how you repay me." The thing disguised as a man tsked. He didn't do it very well.

"I . . . remember . . . being shot at by cultists," Maude said, groggily. "Madmen taking over the town. I fell into the old dry well. There was a voice, and pain."

"Yes," Typhon said, almost hissing. "You do remember, good. I was that voice. I am that pain."

It was so hard to think, to focus. Maude wanted to pass out. The drug that had introduced her to the Daughter's Record had put a terrible strain on her body and her mind. Her fever had broken, but it had done its damage. She knelt next to Isaiah and checked his pulse. He was alive, but badly beaten, and in need of medical care at once. His knuckles were raw and bloody; he had put up a hell of a fight.

"He tried to stop us," Typhon said. "It was a valiant struggle for an old man. He is dear to you?"

"Yes," Maude said, her hand cradling Isaiah's cold face.

"Well, he's dying," Typhon said, chuckling. It sounded like gravel crunching, and Maude looked up at him with seething hatred. "My condolences—is that the right term, condolences? I'm really out of practice at pretending to be human."

Rage filled her, and it was the only fuel Maude had left to burn. Calm discipline wouldn't get her up off the floor right now. She swept Typhon's legs. It felt like trying to trip the planet, but he tumbled down and back, crashing into the chairs before the fireplace.

The men, Typhon's agents, detached from the shadows and spilled forward. They were dressed in dark clothing, heavy coats, derby hats shielded part of their faces. None of them seemed to be deformed as the Sons in Charleston had been, but her perception was still twisting and spinning under the aftereffects of the hallucinogen. Everything strobed between real time and frozen, distorted instants.

They were coming at her from every possible direction, except for the fireplace at her back. Maude could no longer afford to restrain herself and she no longer wanted to. Everything that had happened with her father, the terrible emotional blood-letting of the trial, the nightmares eating her daughter alive, the forces trying to abduct and kill Constance, and now Isaiah dying on the floor while she had been wandering helplessly on some damn fool vision quest. Enough.

Maude drew the iron fireplace poker while still crouched next to Isaiah, and swung low with it, using *Kenjutsu* techniques Gran had helped her master decades ago. The poker tore the legs off the first of the men to close with her at the knees.

As his body was dropping, Maude stayed low in a *Suwari No Tori* stance and drove the poker upward, under the rib cage and into the chest of the next incoming attacker, burying it there. As he struggled with his last breath, she let the poker go and scooped up a handful of hot ash and a glowing coal from the fireplace. She willed the pain in her hand to a distant and unimportant place, and discovered that the anger helped her with that too. She arose fluidly, turning as she did, and tossed the fine soot into the eyes of three of the men coming at her from the right; she popped the hot coal in the gaping mouth of a fourth, and followed it up with a one-inch punch to his diaphragm that forced him to gulp and swallow the burning ingot even as it sent him flying backward, destroying an end table and then splintering the wooden wall with his impact before he slid to the floor, dead, smoke wafting from his mouth. Her hand, palm down, flashed in an arc in front of her three blinded attackers, and their throats slid open, slit by her razor sharp nails.

With her free hand, she retrieved the poker from the dying man's heart and took an *In No Kamae* position with it, the poker upright and close to her face, ready for the next attacker. In less than three seconds, six of Typhon's men were dead.

That was the moment when the world itself rose up and smashed into her. Her perceptions tumbled, melted away, as the remnants of the hallucinogen, her fever, her dehydration, and her exhaustion all crashed into her. Maude stepped back, trying to think, trying to clear her head.

Four more attackers fell on her, striking her jaw, her stomach, her head. Everywhere was a fist or a boot. Maude saw flashes of brilliant light behind her eyes. She tried to roll with the onslaught, but her mind was spinning. Her body remembered what to do but it was beyond exhaustion. The pain and weariness began to wash over her anger and extinguish it. What did she have left other than the anger to keep her on her feet? The iron poker clattered to the floor, free of her numb fingers.

She heard the man-monster, Typhon, speaking calmly over the sounds of his men beating her, again and again. "That was impressive. If you were in your prime right now, you would have taken them all, Maude."

She tasted blood, managed to counter another punch, deflect a kick, but Maude couldn't clear the weary buzzing out of her head, couldn't direct her body to obey. She was acting on pure muscle memory, with very little muscle left behind it.

"These are not my Sons, not like the ones you fought in Charleston," Typhon said. "These are the Unfeeling. They are acolytes, much like you and your sisters are until you take the Blood of Lilith. They have pledged themselves to my service. Most of them, when the Sons find them, are beaten down by this obscene joke called life. They are usually trained young. You'd be surprised how many cast-off children there are out there in the world."

Something ruptured in Maude's side from the kick of a steel-toed boot, popping like a balloon, and Maude gasped in pain. A powerful fist drove her head down, and she almost fell. Her palm shot upward and drove into someone's larynx with a crunch, another one dead. How many did that leave, three, four? The drugs were still twisting and bending her mind. Maude wanted to vomit so badly, to just close her eyes and give in to the pain, the fatigue, but she knew if she allowed herself to do so, she was done.

"They have suffered much, burned and damaged their nerves, undertaken brutal training, so that they no longer feel, to further divorce themselves from life. For as you know, dear Maude—quite intimately at the moment—to feel, to live, is to allow yourself to know pain."

Maude fell to one knee. If she just had a moment to focus, if the dull buzz in her head would just stop . . . if the constant pounding, kicking would pause. There was a way to get clear of this, she couldn't fall.

"Some Unfeeling undertake a ritual, much as your kind does," Typhon said. "They drink of my blood, the blood of my creator, and they become one with us, become stronger, harder to kill, and virtually immune to pain. The blood . . . changes each of them, alters them from the obscene creator's image of perfection and brings out their savage beauty, their true nature."

"What . . . are . . . you?" Maude muttered. Her blood sprayed everywhere as she tried to speak.

"An excellent question," Typhon said. "Are you still aware enough for the answer? I'll assume you are. If it helps your little meat-mind to understand, I am the monster at the heart of the world's nightmares made real. The closest approximation would be what the fakirs of the east would call a *tulpa*. I am a projection of the Great Olde Wurm's desire, its anger and lust to end the accursed noise of life, given life. I'm the Wurm's child; I, and my little brother, were created long ago to give birth to more monsters, more agents of death."

It was getting difficult for Maude to focus at all. For a second she felt she was slipping away from her body again, and was thankful for the retreat. She heard a million million voices speaking to her, calling out her name, and in her head, she saw a white light. *No,* she had to stay with her body, no matter the pain. She couldn't run away, she couldn't give up. Constance, Isaiah, she had to save them. There had to be a way. *There was always a way* . . . Gran's words, Gran's voice. *"Let us help you . . ."* the voices of the Record whispered, *"listen . . ."*

"Your accursed 'Mother' was once my mate," Typhon said. "She was magnificent in her primal fury at the Divine for her treatment. She felt betrayed, and rightly so. Our union was violent and brutal and perfect. The Great Dying . . . glorious. We were in love." The Unfeeling were snarling and laughing as they continued to beat Maude, the vicious circle blocking her view of Typhon. "Of course, she allowed her anger and her resolve to waiver," Typhon said, shaking his oddly shaped head. He tried adjusting his illusion of humanity, as a human might adjust his shirt collar if it were too tight. "She came to love this little shit ball, hurtling alone in defiance of the void. Came to love its people. So 'Lilith,' as you call her, turned on me, betrayed me and our children. The bitch."

Typhon tried to peer into the circle. "Are you still alive, Maude?" he asked. "Still sensate? I hope so, I promised my men they could do whatever they like with you once they had broken you. I'm disappointed. I figured you'd at least make it through the Unfeeling. I have my full Sons outside, waiting for a chance at you."

There was a loud crunch, like a tree branch breaking, and one of the Unfeeling actually screamed with long-forgotten pain as he smashed against the wall, went partly through it, and died. The other two attackers screamed as well as they were tossed back as if by a bomb blast; their bodies thudded around the wrecked study, dead.

The technique was called "The Iron Shirt," and it had been explained, somewhat rapidly and crudely, to Maude by Ng Mui Si Tai, a Buddhist nun, one of the greatest of the Daughters, and Leng Ya's teacher and mentor. At least in this instance, the aftereffects of the drug had been a boon, helping her connect with the great teacher inside the Record.

As she had experienced Ng's skein, Maude caught a brief glimpse of Amadia and Ya's lives tangled up in the ancient master's. The African Daughter had stolen Ya's lover, but in the end the woman had perished and they had both lost her. The story was washed away as Ng chided Maude for not focusing on the matter at hand. Maude was shown how to feel the energy of her life, her Chi, how to fan that fading ember until it was a raging inferno, a violent squall inside her, and then to turn all the force back on her attackers, exploding outward, using her own life energy to turn her attacker's destructive force against them.

Maude, bloody, cut, bruised, more than half-dead, stood. The Iron Shirt had splintered and cratered the very floor at her feet with its force. Panting, her eyes hooded with a cold power that gave even Typhon pause, Maude assumed a bow stance and looked into the green eyes of the Father of all Monsters.

"By all means," Maude said, "show them in."

"You do not disappoint," Typhon said. "You truly are the epitome of the Daughters. You clutch to life when all about you is death. Foolish, futile, but impressive. It's a pity you can't see how it all ends, or refuse to." Typhon clapped loudly and Maude sensed more than heard the Sons charging, approaching. She drew as deep and powerful a cleansing breath as she was able with her injuries, her precious Chi spent, and her head awash in the dregs of powerful drugs. She centered herself.

"You stand against life," Maude said. "We'll defeat you, just as the Daughters led humanity against you and your children and vanquished you all, long ago. I saw it in the Record."

"Ah, the Record," Typhon said. "That explains it. Very impressive. You have no idea how badly I want to slither in there and give my account of history, lay a few eggs perhaps. Maybe with your sweet daughter's help, I will."

The walls of the mansion shook and exploded, heralding the arrival of the Sons. There were four of them, and each bore a deformity. One of the Sons had an additional, stuporous-looking face growing out of his misshapen head. One had wicked, hooked, blood-soaked bone blades growing out of his wrists and elbows. The body of another of Typhon's sworn soldiers had no apparent skin, and was covered in a slick sheen of blood, dark lines of muscle tissue and nerves. The final Son was muscular and nearly eight feet tall. His skin bubbled, rose and fell like baking dough.

The smiling man that Maude and the others had faced on the streets of Charleston, the only Son to survive that encounter, walked in through the shattered front door, dusting off his coat as he did. The sky was lightening behind him.

"Hello, mate," Rory Danvers said to Maude, "remember me?"

"Last I saw of you was your backside as you ran away," Maude said, "'mate.'" Rory reddened, the smile still plastered on his face.

"No place to run for you, this time," Rory said. "No one to save you. You're all out of tricks."

"I don't think she is, though," Maude said.

Amadia materialized, flying in out of the graying dawn behind two of the Sons. She wrapped her legs around the head and upper body of the bloody one with no skin, and snapped his neck with a wrenching sacrifice move. She fell to the floor with the body but was in an awful defensive position as the one with the bone hooks began to strike at her again and again with frightening speed.

Maude used Amadia's appearance to buy her the seconds she needed to slip the dropped fireplace poker under her foot and flip it back to her hand. She hurled the iron poker like a javelin at the Son who was attacking Amadia. The stout metal spear exploded through his chest and the Son fell dead. Amadia rolled to her feet and vaulted over a partly demolished love seat to land beside Maude. The two Daughters closed ranks and stood side by side, ready. The two remaining Sons rushed to engage them.

"You look like hell," Amadia said. Maude grunted.

"Master, it's nearly dawn," Rory said, unnerved by the sudden death of his fellows. When he had imbibed the Blood of Typhon, Rory's mind had been expanded to, in his way of thinking, an almost-god-like degree, able to see near-infinite outcomes to each action he perceived in the moment. He could, with time and concentration, parse these outcomes to give him insight into the best possible outcome.

It was a blessing and a curse, because he could not do it instantly, and so it did not help greatly in things like combat. However, standing back, next to his master, Rory's inhuman brain had calculated all the possible permutations of the encounter with what was now two Daughters of Lilith. He saw failure arise more often than victory.

"You have a coach waiting outside," Rory said. "We should depart. We have a ship to catch."

"Ah, thank you, Rory, my good, dutiful boy. I lost track of time catching up with dear Maude here."

Maude felt her body beginning to shut down. She forced more adrenaline into her blood, but even that recourse was nearly depleted. The dregs of the drug were shredding her nervous system and the injuries were too many and too brutal to ignore.

"Running away again," Maude called out to Typhon and Rory, as she stopped the two-headed Son's superhuman punch using both arms. The block held, but she felt her arms quivering as though they were made of rubber. Maude used the momentum to pivot the Son into a position stalling the advance of his giant comrade with pulsating skin. The maneuver gave the Daughters a second to concentrate on the single berserk attacker. Maude managed to hold the block long enough for Amadia to get into position.

The African Daughter jumped high into the air, spinning like a top, completely horizontal, releasing a savage *kiai* shout as she drove a flying two-legged sacrifice kick into the double-faced monster's throat, crushing his windpipe with enough force to shatter steel plates. The Son gurgled, tried to keep fighting, but his second face's eyes widened in fear for a moment, then both countenances slacked.

Maude pushed as Amadia fell. The Son's body stumbled backward and thudded to the floor. Maude caught Amadia as a ballet dance partner might, cradling her, supporting her full weight with muscles that were beyond exhaustion, spinning her and then lowering her gently. They held each others' eyes for an instant, feeling a perfect harmonious bond, breathing, hearts beating perfectly as one, and then Maude set her back on the ground. They stood shoulder to shoulder, ready to face the last Son.

"I'm more of a night person," Typhon said, walking toward the shattered front door. "Just remember, Maude, even if you survive this little skirmish, even if you save your precious Constance, you doom the Daughters to extinction, and grant me victory."

The giant Son shrugged off Amadia's Eagle Strike, leaving the Daughter with a badly sprained wrist for her effort. Maude tried a skipping axe kick in unison with Amadia's blow but neither seemed to even slow the behemoth down. The berserker swept them with his powerful arms and knocked both Daughters across the room. Maude fell toward the hallway to the foyer and saw Typhon and Rory descending the steps outside.

"No!" Maude shouted, climbing to her feet, slipping and falling, then recovering herself. "They're getting away!"

"Who?" Amadia asked as she, too, got to her feet. The remaining giant Son was lifting the broken carcass of the love seat above his head, preparing to hurl it at one of them.

"Typhon," Maude said, running, stumbling as best she could toward the front door. "I have to stop him! Keep this one busy, I'll be back!"

"Wait, Stapleton!" Amadia cried, "Maude, if it's truly Typhon, you can't . . ."

Maude was already out the door and down the porch stairs toward the circular drive. She saw a black carriage with a great black mare tethered to it. The sky was slate; dawn was nearly here. Rory held the door for the Father as Typhon began to step inside the dark compartment of the coach.

"Typhon!" Maude shouted. The thing pretending to be a man turned and again, the misfiring synapses in Maude's brain gave her a single blink, just for an instant, of what Typhon truly was, as vast as human indifference, and endless as man's cruelty.

"Ah, Maude," Typhon said. "Look at you, ready to fight to the last." He turned back toward her and began to walk to her. "You understand, don't you, I am 'to the last.'"

Maude heaved herself at Typhon. Focusing her last fading energy into a focused *kiai* scream, she flew toward him, directing every last bit of her Chi into a targeted hit right between his glistening green eyes. Typhon's head snapped back and he dropped to the ground as Maude went tumbling and landed a few feet from him. She sat there in the grass, barely able to stay upright. Typhon's head lolled at an impossible angle. He began to climb back to his feet, chuckling as he did. "All these rules you people have to obey and live with: mass, energy, gravity, velocity. It's no wonder you're all so fragile. Sometimes, when I'm trying to fit in, I forget they don't apply to me. Live and learn, I suppose." He adjusted his head as he stood and reset his broken neck. He didn't get it quite right. "Another pass? Or are you ready to stop this nonsense now?"

Maude groaned and pulled herself to her feet. She stumbled toward Typhon. She raised her fists. She drove a hard right into his face, a knee into his groin. Typhon stood and took the blows. Maude's fist felt as though she had punched the ground. Typhon didn't blink, didn't budge.

"You see, Maude," Typhon said, as she continued to strike and kick furiously at him, "there is only so much a tiny, insignificant little human, even one with all the fabulous parlor tricks you possess, can do against the infinite. Do you begin to understand what it is you're up against?"

Maude refused to stop. She drove a stunning palm-heel into Typhon's chin, trying to get an opening to his throat, but he hardly seemed to even notice.

"Are you trying to get to this?" Typhon said, raising his head and exposing his throat. Maude slashed at his arteries with her sharpened fingernails. It did nothing.

"I am a dream," Typhon said. "An endless, deathless god's dream of a universe fed into a slaughterhouse, of an eternity of death and silence. Maude, you know deep inside you can't hurt me. All your kind know it, sense it. I am what terrifies you all in the darkness, and I never end until all of this ends. Until Constance ends, until Martin ends, until Isaiah ends, until even poor old Mutt is put out of his misery."

Maude had nothing left; her knuckles were bloody and in tatters. Her vision was dimming. She stood, barely on her feet, before the Father of Monsters.

"Maude, you're a mess," Typhon said. "You weren't even in this bad a shape when I met you, remember? You were suffering from multiple near-fatal gunshots wounds, as I recall."

Maude suddenly felt very cold. She was shaking, brilliant flowers of pain opening in her back, in her chest, her arms and legs. The old gunshot wounds Typhon had healed were reopening. Her blood was gushing everywhere.

"Like those," Typhon said. Maude looked down and touched one of the burning hollows of pain on her chest, near her heart. Her hand was covered in fresh blood, her blood. The world was tumbling drunkenly; her vision was narrowing, like a funnel.

"Always . . . a . . . way . . ." Maude mumbled.

"I told you back in Golgotha," Typhon said, "I admired your warrior spirit. You told me then you wanted to live, to have your death have some greater meaning. Here's the secret, Maude, my final parting gift to you: There is no meaning to life, to death. There are only the lies we tell each other and try to make ourselves believe."

Typhon's arm was rising, was coming at her, but Maude couldn't raise her arms to stop it, couldn't move out of its way. Everything was slowing down.

"I grant you your wish," Typhon said as he backhanded her, "a true warrior's death against the greatest monster of them all."

The force of the slap shattered Maude's world, fracturing it into jagged barbs of crimson and obsidian. She was flying backward, flying through the air. She felt herself crash through a wall of the mansion, her flesh breaking and twisting to make way, another impact, another wall, then falling and it all stopped. Everything was gone now. Her last thoughts, her last bit of will, drained out of her and spilled on the floor. She regretted not being able to tell Mutt . . . tell him . . . everything, to see him one last time. To kiss him good-bye, and say the magic words. She was so cold and everything was dark. There was a sound, like wings rushing, drumming in her ears. It was her own heart. The sound slowed, softened and ceased.

25

The Fool (Reversed)

Somewhere in Northern Africa
November 4, 1721

Anne walked through the tangled forest of dead trees, her lantern casting a feeble halo of light against the pall. The leadwood, as tough as its name implied, seemed to devour the sound of her boots crunching on the rocky soil. There was a clear path into the wood and through the jagged maze. Anne stuck to it. She wished she had taken at least her blade with her, even if Adu had said it would do her no good against what dwelled here.

The night was hot and heavy, like narcotic sleep. It felt odd to Anne, in such an open and expansive land as this, to be filled with a sensation of suffocation here in the wood. She was unsure how long she had been traveling, following the winding path.

Anne paused to look back at the way she had come. Her lantern revealed there was no longer a passage behind her, only a wall of rough, twisted branches. Ahead of her, in the darkness, something screamed, a warbling falsetto that lowered to a guttural bass. Her hand dropped instinctively to her sword. It wasn't there.

"Ah, lass," Anne whispered, "you are well and truly tupped." When she swung the lantern back in the direction of the unearthly sound, the direction she had been walking in, the path had narrowed considerably, seemingly while the lantern was off of it. Anne steadied herself and began walking again. The path tightened more and she began to have to turn slightly to the side to avoid the sharp branches of the trees. She tried to keep the lantern out in front of her as best she could. There was another howl, this one from behind her, in the dense forest.

She walked ahead, the gaps between the knotted trees narrowing with each step. She forced the lamp before her, and its circle of light caught a face opening in the dark bark of the dead tree's trunk. Burning orange eyes with black irises and an elongated mouth full of dirty needle-like teeth screeched at her as the thing pulled itself from the decayed heart of the leadwood tree's twisted trunk. Its sinewy arms reached for her. Anne was but inches from its taloned grasp.

"Annnnneeeeeee," the face hissed. *"Come here, come live in the trees with ussssss."* Another of the things grew out of the tree a few feet beside her, its clawed hands flailing at the air, the razor-sharp nails barely missing her face. She took another shaky step. More of the things called Biloko seeped out from inside the tree trunks, snarling and trying to grab at her. *"Sooooo much anger, so much pain . . . You belong with us, Annnnnneeeeeee . . . you areeee home . . . you are already one of usssssssss, just give us your flesh . . ."*

The fear vomited up in her, uncontrollably, beginning to fill her mind like filthy bilge water filling a hull. Her heart was a panicked horse. Images were pulled up out of her mind, out of the distant corners that she had banished them to. Anne learned long ago to not spend too much time inside her head; too many monsters waited there to gobble her up. The Biloko's voices, those glowing eyes, seemed to rip open all the things inside her, all her mindscars that she had worked so hard to bury, to hide from everyone, especially herself.

The first time she had boarded a ship with her howling pirate mates, disguised as a man, it had been exhilarating and terrifying, jumping into chaos, men screaming, dying, pistols blasting, blades flashing everywhere. Truth be told, the fear made it better, excited her. That night, though, she had trembled under the balmy Caribbean moon like a shivering child, had wept tears alone, in so much pain, and yet that pain had no name, no face for her. She began to get drunk every night to escape the faceless dread, the guilt and terror that visited her unbidden.

She forced her gaze away from the demonic eyes, tried to ignore the voices. She felt like passing out. Anne remembered Nourbese's warning and knew she would never awaken again if she did faint. A step . . . forward . . . another step . . . turn to the side, between the branches, and the slender grasping hands. Ignore the monsters in the trees, ignore their cries, their clawed hands, almost reaching her. The next step . . . Anne's eyes were locked on another of the monsters who tore at her mind as it struggled to tear at her flesh. The orange eyes bored into her mind, knocking over the carefully arranged barricades of denial and repression, pounding at her fortifications of will, dragging her back to one awful moment after another.

The face of the first man she ever had to kill was held up to her mind. His eyes began full of haughty anger, then the anger draining away like water escaping a barrel with a hole as her blade found his guts. The anger gone, meaningless now, sadness, regret, fear, awareness and then, finally, his life. It had been her or him and she was glad it was him. Why did her damn hands shake, why did she vomit like some sickly lubber? She'd forget that look, forget his face dumb in death, she'd forget taking a life. When the memory pounced on her, once again, the wine was there to dull it, kill it, at least for the night. If that wasn't enough for the growing mountain of memories, there was the opium, sweet blissful oblivion.

"God damn you little bastards," Anne growled. "Stay out of my memories. They're mine, mine! You have no business with them, with me."

"They belong to us now, Annnnnneeee. Seeeee how much weeeee share?" the Biloko said.

Anne's mind sought a safe place and retreated to the warmth and light of the old tavern she used to hide at, in the East End of London, in Spitalfields, when she was young and called herself Andy. It was the place she ran to when she couldn't stand her father anymore, couldn't bear another beating.

A sharp branch on one of the leadwood trees scratched her face, leaving a wet trail of blood behind. The Biloko howled at the scent of her blood. A dark stain, an old painful memory, grew like a tumor from the safe place her mind had been flailing for.

It was the night the fat old man, the man who smelled of rotten eggs, had come into the tavern. He had bought her bowl after bowl of hot soup and even some sweets and hot cider.

"No!" Anne screamed. "I won't remember! I can't! You vile cockchaffing sons of bitches! Leave it!" She almost said please, almost begged them to stop, but she didn't. The memory opened in her like a stinking flower planted on a grave.

Her memory of leaving the tavern with the fat man was less clear; she was sure now that he had been putting something dodgy in her food. The haze over her memory lifted when he tore down her breeches in a filthy alleyway. He had roared with anger at his discovery that she was actually a girl. The bad-egg man took her that night the way he would have taken her if she had been a boy, and then he beat her—the worst beating of her young life—and left her bloody on the garbage-strewn floor of the alley. Almost weeping, but boys didn't weep. Andy, always Andy. Tears were surrender. Never.

"We'reeeeee sooooo hungry, Annnneeeee," the Biloko called out all around her. Her fingers trembled to hang onto the lantern, she had to keep moving forward, one step, another . . . another. Her feet were barely moving, shuffling. The trees were so close now the branches scratched her skin; each cut was cold and it burned.

Years after that night with the rotten-egg man, Anne would wake shaking, wet from sweat, from the nightmare, his bloated face, florid and sweaty, the stink of rancid gas billowing off him. In her mind that smell was what evil smelled like.

The Biloko's claws were long like straight razors, and their burning orange eyes nibbled at her soul each time Anne looked into them. The jaws were unhinging like serpents', drool splattering her face from their howling maws, so close to her that she could smell their breath. . . . It smelled of rotten eggs. *"Feeeeed usssss,"* they moaned, *"give ussss your fleeeeessss-hhhh . . ."*

Anne fumbled and found the amulet, the gold snake, at her breast. She clutched it and focused on the warm gold shape of it in her mind, trying to push out the Biloko's voices, their words like cold syrup pouring into the folds of her brain, trying to wipe away her will to resist them, to let them to fall upon her and strip her flesh from her bones like piranha.

When she had staggered home from the alleyway, Anne endured a second beating at the hands of her father, who accused her of whoring herself. Anne took that beating with no tears, never a whimper. Never again would she give a man the satisfaction of making her cry. It was just flesh, and flesh was worth sacrificing to keep the fire inside you alive, untouched. When it was over, her mother took care of her. Anne never told anyone what happened that night, but her mother knew. Without a word, she understood, and that was enough.

This will not break me, Anne thought. *That did not break me . . . you will not break me!*

Anne pushed the unreasoning fear away. The Biloko had peeled back her memories, used them to try to destroy her. The realization made Anne angry, and she threw her fear into the pyre of that anger. Looking around her, the Biloko were everywhere, shrieking, spitting, frenzied for a taste of her flesh, of her soul. There was no more path forward, and there was no path back.

"*You belong to ussssss, Annnneeeee,*" the Biloko said. "*There is noooooo escape for youuuuuuu . . .*"

Anne reached into her coat pocket and retrieved the extra flask of lamp oil she was carrying. She uncorked it and splashed it on the Biloko's dead trees, all around her. She raised the lantern, her eyes flashing with cold fury.

"There's no escape for you bastards either!" she screamed, and smashed the lantern against the trees.

The lamp exploded, igniting with a loud *thump* as the oil caught and began to burn, jumping from tree to tree.

"*What!*" the Biloko wailed, a chorus of hatred and fear. "*What haveeeeee you done, womannnnnn?*"

"You picked the wrong bone-bucket to taff about in, fuckers!" Anne shouted over the greedy roar of the growing blaze. "Burn, you bastards! Burn!" The evil spirits wailed. In moments, the whole forest was ablaze, the ancient dead trees turning to ash, collapsing under their faltering, hollow weight. The fire spread farther, faster. There was no way out for Anne; everywhere was beautiful, bright, dancing death.

At the center of the firestorm, Anne Bonny cackled as she heard the Biloko beg for mercy, plead to the gods they had so long angrily defied. The monsters screamed in pain and loss, their foul spirits bleeding out of the disintegrating wood, in plumes of thick black smoke.

"I'll see you boys in Hell!" she said.

The pirate queen listened to the last of the unliving die. The burning forest was finally silent except for the snap and whine of the fire devouring the now-empty wood. They were the last sounds Anne heard before the smoke and fire claimed her, too—but only her flesh.

Hell smelled like boiling vegetables and cinnamon. Anne coughed and tried to move. Her chest felt like it was on fire; she coughed more, desperately trying to catch a breath between the hacking spasms. Her throat felt like a chimney that needed a good sweep.

She remembered a figure, masked and hooded, coming through the fire toward her as the evil ghosts howled and perished. Anne had thought it was Death, come to claim her. She recalled soft hands, like worn leather, picking her up as if she weighed nothing. Flying into the air, the figure seemed to climb the fires as if they were solid, leaping from one flickering spear of fatal flame to the next. Her rescuer's cloak smoldered, but it never caught. There had been a final leap into the cool darkness, and then nothing, until now.

Anne opened her eyes. That was a mistake; her head throbbed, almost dizzy with pain. She was on a sleeping mat in a small hut. There was a cook fire a few feet away from her, and an iron pot bubbled and steamed over the flame.

"Good," a strangely familiar woman's voice said behind her. "You're not dead, and you woke up just in time for the evening meal." Anne rolled over and found herself looking at the old woman who had been wearing the speckled cloak and bird skull mask in the royal court of Ife. The woman's voice was the voice from her strange dreams, the voice that Adu had been talking with when she had been recovering from the duel with Nourbese.

"Oya?" Anne said, struggling to her feet. She made it as far as her hands and knees before another coughing fit took her. She gasped and retched. "I'm ready to fight . . ." she said, gasping for breath.

"I see," the old woman said. She spoke very good English. Without the skull-mask, Oya's face was brown, wrinkled and cracked like a dry riverbed. Her eyes were the color of tiger eye stones, and had a positive gleam to them. Her hair was white and wiry in a loose halo around her head. "But humor me and have some water and a bit of stew before you pummel me, yes?"

Anne flopped back on the mat. "Well, if you insist."

The night sky was a deep indigo and stars spread across the firmament like scattered grains of sand. Oya's home was near the bank of the Chad. They ate outside near a small fire. The cool, fresh air felt good on Anne's red and blistered skin and soothed her raw throat. Anne was polishing off her second bowl of the vegetable stew Oya had served her on a bed of couscous.

"This is the best stew I've ever eaten," Anne said.

"Of course it is. Have you heard the story of the strawberry?" Oya asked. Anne shook her head as she sopped up a bit of her meal with a piece of unleavened bread. "A man was walking one day, when he was beset by a hungry tiger. He ran and the tiger gave chase. Seeing he had come to the edge of cliff, and the tiger was bearing down upon him, the man's only hope was to clutch a vine with both hands and swing over the side of the cliff, which is exactly what he did.

"Looking below, he saw two more hungry tigers pacing in the ravine beneath him. The first tiger was also waiting at the edge of the cliff above. Two rats, a white one and a black one, scuttled out of their holes in the side of the cliff and began to gnaw on the vine. The man tried to shoo them away, but to no avail.

"As the vine began to thin and weaken under the rats' attention, the man knew he was going to die. At that moment, he noticed a single wild strawberry growing in a fissure between two rocks on the cliff face. He hung onto the vine with only one hand and reached out to pluck the strawberry. When he ate it, it was exquisite."

Anne was silent on her side of the fire, Oya silent upon completing the story. Finally Anne began to giggle, then to laugh. She nodded as she wiped her eyes. Oya's face seemed to split as she grinned widely.

"Do they even grow bloody strawberries in Africa?" Anne asked, still laughing.

"A few," Oya said, "a few." She opened a small clay pot and with a wooden gourd ladle dipped a liquid out of the pot and into a wooden cup. She offered it to Anne, who wiped a few more tears of laughter from her eyes. "Tonto?" Oya said, referring to the drink. Anne took the cup.

"Thanks," she said, and took a sip. "Mmm," she said. "Got a little kick. What is it?"

"Banana beer," Oya said, as she poured herself a cup as well. "Often used in ceremonies."

"This a ceremony?" Anne asked. Oya nodded and raised her cup.

"A rite of passage," she said. Anne raised her cup, and both women drank.

"You know I'm not here to pass some daft tests, right?" Anne said.

"Life is a test," Oya said, "death too."

"Am I dead?" Anne asked. "Did I die in that fire?"

"That remains to be seen," Oya said. "We walk through the gates of life and death all the time; we're usually too preoccupied to notice."

"Can I ask you something," Anne said. Oya gave a shrug. "How did you talk to me in my dreams? How could you possibly save me from that fire? How did that bird show up there and in the real world, too, the kite . . ."

"The kite is her bird, the Mother's symbol, her servant," Oya said. "There is a way for Daughters of certain bloodlines to walk in the great lodges of their ancestors, to learn secrets and lost knowledge. But it is a jealously guarded craft that takes a lifetime to master. It is possible, given a long enough life, aptitude and patience, to learn to walk in the dreams of the living and the dead."

"The dead dream?" Anne asked. Oya nodded.

"Oh yes," she said. "That is how they talk to us."

"What do the dead dream about?"

"That is a secret for those initiated," Oya said. "Some think this world we live in is what the dead dream."

"More like a nightmare," Anne said, upending her cup. Oya refilled it.

"I was not entering your dreams," Oya said. "I thought you were somehow influencing and appearing in my dreams. I marveled how a relative child . . ."

"I am soddin' tired of you long-toothed bastards calling me a child!" Anne said. "Just because I haven't thrown fucking bones with King Solomon doesn't mean I'm a snapper!"

Oya grinned at the outburst. "My apologies, young woman. Very maturely stated, I might add. As I was saying, I couldn't figure out how you were doing that, so I approached Adu while you were healing in Agaja's court, and he told me how highly he thought of your prospects to succeed and reach me. I have to admit I was skeptical and somewhat bigoted. My encounters with whites have all ended . . . poorly, especially the last one I trusted with a responsibility."

Anne shrugged. "People in general tend to fuck you," she said, her eyes drooping, "don't give no matter to the shade of 'em." She took another sip of the beer. The sip turned into polishing off most of the cup of the sweet, bitter, potent drink. "So, if it wasn't you showing me all that, and it wasn't me showing you all that . . . then, who's been running a rig on us? Whose voice have I been hearing in my dreams, in these visions?"

"Someone old and powerful," Oya said. Anne yawned widely and then belched.

"As for rescuing you from the fire. You will learn how to do that as well in time."

"What? Not burn up?" Anne muttered. Her eyes were fighting to stay open. "Dance across flames like swinging in the rigging of a ship? It's impossible."

"Flame is energy," Oya said. "Everything is energy. Once you understand there is no difference in the thing, save the name we place upon it, you will begin to see that we can have power over the primal thing if we do not give its name power over us with words like 'impossible.'"

"What difference does a name make?" Anne asked.

"Exactly," Oya said. "Once you see past the name of a thing, its mask, and see its essence, it no longer has power over you. You have power over it."

"Sounds like bloody magic," Anne said.

"'Magic' is just a name as well," Oya said. "There is truth and there is falsehood, in all things. One gives you power, the other takes it away."

Anne started to reply but she yawned again instead. "Rest, strawberry," Oya said. "We'll talk more in the morning."

Anne drank the last of the beer and dropped the cup beside her. "Are you really a goddess?" she asked Oya as she rolled over onto her side on the pile of furs by the fire. Her belly was full and her eyes were heavy.

"As much as any of us are, child," Oya said. Anne slept.

Anne awoke to bright sunlight on her face. It was late morning and last night's fire was only a memory, the fire pit full of gray ash. Anne climbed to her feet with a groan and looked about. Oya's hut was about three hundred yards from the shore of the lake. Off to the southwest a thin ribbon of black smoke drifted higher in the iridescent blue sky. Anne checked the hut, but Oya was nowhere to be found. Anne started to walk in the direction of the trailing streamers of smoke and, in about twenty minutes, she found the old woman, sitting cross-legged in the barren sandy soil, looking at the charred remains of the Biloko's forest.

"Do you know how many have tried to cross those woods in the count-less eons since Carcosa was founded?" Oya said. "Kings, warlords, mystics, monks, seekers of glory, knowledge and riches. Most lost their minds within moments of the Biloko falling upon them, opening them; then they lost their lives, and finally their souls."

Anne sat down beside her. "I almost did," she said. "I almost lost every-thing in there. I wanted to just run, blindly. I've never been more scared of anything in my life."

"And you would have been lost if you had," Oya said.

"Those things . . . they tore me open," Anne said. "It made me just a little madder than I was scared." She chuckled.

"And you burned everything down," Oya said, "regardless of the consequence, regardless of what it did to you."

"Aye," Anne said. She stood, and dusted off the bottom of her breeches. "End of the dance, all you have is yourself. Those evil tossers tried to take all that away from me." Anne took a few steps back and raised her fists. "Okay, I'm ready."

Oya, still sitting, looked at her. "What are you doing, exactly?"

"I'm ready to scrap," Anne said.

"Scrap?" Oya said. "Fight?"

"Aye," Anne said. "Adu said you were the one putting all those tests in my way, that you were the last guardian of Carcosa. You saved me from that fire and you fed me and let me rest. You've been more than fair. I'm ready."

Oya stood. It was almost as if gravity didn't have a hold on her as she glided up to her feet. "There's no need for that anymore," she said. "I think I'm convinced. But if I know you, and I think I do, you won't be satisfied until we do this. So, begin."

Anne charged Oya with a snarl. She threw a wild right at the old woman's head. It was on target, except the old woman's head was no longer there; she was somehow a few feet to the left of where Anne swore she had been. Oya shoved Anne gently, little more than a push. It felt like Anne had struck a tree. The pirate queen flew back a good ten yards and landed with a thump on her butt, then skidded till she finally came to a stop. Anne scrambled back to her feet, and charged at Oya again.

"C'mon then! *Faire!*" Anne howled the old Irish battle cry as she hurled a series of punches and kicks at Oya. Oya stood rock still, but every swing, every kick, missed her. Oya brought her hands together in front of her in a clap, and there was thunder, deafening Anne. She felt the force of the shock wave over her whole body, like running straight into an invisible brick wall. She was airborne again, and fell to the rocky soil with a crunch.

"Had enough yet?" Anne said.

"You'd keep going, wouldn't you?" Oya said. "Until I had to actually incapacitate or kill you."

"I don't care what you are," Anne said, struggling to her feet, again. "Demon, orisha, goddess, I ain't backing down, and you will have to kill me to stop me."

"Very well," Oya said. Her arms windmilled and Anne actually felt the force of the breeze from ten feet away. The old woman shifted her body into a crouch, her left foot pointing forward and her left arm cocked, her right arm extended, palm out. She locked eyes with Anne, who was taking up a boxing stance. Oya slipped out of the posture, as effortlessly as she entered it, and stood placidly. "I surrender," she said. "You win."

"What?" Anne said. "You can do magic and you're just letting me win?"

"It's not magic," Oya said, then paused. "Well . . . maybe it's a little magic, but it's mostly just knowledge and practice and will; will is everything. A child can learn it. As to letting you win, there is only one thing that is valuable in Carcosa." Oya walked toward Anne. The pirate still had her arms raised to fight. "Trust me, you do not want it," Oya added. "The treasure of Carcosa is a legend, sent out into the world, into your parts of the world, like your map box, to draw those unafraid of monsters and gods, to see if any of them are worthy of the only true treasure to be found here."

Anne lowered her fists. "It's all a lie? Another test." Oya nodded, placing her hand on Anne's shoulder.

"Not a lie, not entirely. The treasure here is knowledge, and power. When Adu saw you in the slave market, do you recall what you wanted to do when you confronted the slavers?"

"Stop it," Anne said. "Make them stop."

"You wanted the power to do that," Oya said, "to defy their guns and shatter their chains."

"You could read my mind?" Anne asked.

"No," Oya replied. "Anyone with eyes and knowledge of a good heart could divine it."

Anne laughed. "I've no good heart, Oya. I've killed, lied, cheated and stolen, oh, so much stealing!"

"That you have," Oya said, guiding Anne back in the direction of the lake and the hut, "and every time a cause that pulls at your heart, at your true nature, has gotten in the way of all that, you've pursued it, fought for it, stood until the bitter end, and that's cost you time and time again. You put your full heart into whatever you believe in, whoever you believe in. That is rare, and a fragile thing, easy to break, easy to lose. You know the definition of a hero, Anne? It's someone who keeps their head about them for five minutes longer than everyone around them.

"You stood against the slavers, you bested a mighty enemy in the war chief of the Amazons, and with your mercy, made her into an ally. You had only to choose a god, any god, to pay lip service to, as most people do, and you would have had a much easier time of it in Ife, but you refused to bend a knee to any king or to any god that you didn't respect. Finally, you, and you alone, faced your darkest fears, and refused to let them devour you. Instead, you used them to make yourself stronger. You burned down the forest of fear, rather than become lost to it. I hate to break the news to you, Anne Bonny, but you have all the makings of a hero."

"In my experience, heroes usually end up with tosh," Anne said.

They walked toward the hut for a long time in silence. Finally, Oya spoke. "Long ago, when humans had only walked upon the land for a short time, Kauket, the primordial darkness, created creatures, torn from the void, to do its bidding in the world. The most powerful of these beings was Typhon. Typhon and his brother fell to Earth, and began to war upon all life, everywhere. They slaughtered and destroyed everything in their path."

"Just two of them," Anne said. "Didn't someone try to stop them?"

"Many took up arms," Oya said, "and were annihilated by the brothers. Then, the monsters were joined by a third; some call her the first woman, the first rebel against the will of the gods. She is known by many names in many lands: Echidna, Ayza, Ix Chel, Anuket, Pandora, Lilith. Her exile had made her bitter and angry, and she joined with Typhon to hurt those who still stood in the gods' favor. In time they became as husband and wife. They spawned an even greater army of inhuman banes to torment, tempt and exterminate the human race, to end all life, everywhere."

The hut was in sight now and it was near noon.

"I'll make us something to eat," Oya said. "Then we'll rest. It will be hot today. This evening, I'll tell you the rest of the story."

Anne was restless, and though the thought of a long nap appealed to her body, especially after the meal of something delicious and filling called *koshari,* her mind couldn't still itself. She sat on the banks of the lake, skipping stones and watching the clouds drift in the most flawless sky she had ever seen. She wondered about Adu and the others. Were they waiting for her, mourning her or had they marked her off as dead and just moved on? The sun began to dip toward the horizon and it gleamed gold and white off the lake water, casting sparkles of blinding light. She thought about her son. Perhaps it was cruel, even selfish, to bring an innocent soul into a world that was full of so much evil and injustice, so many monsters. She believed Oya's tale. She had seen enough in her young life already to be open to the possibilities, and in the last few months she had seen even more.

She wished she could blame all the sickness, all the wrongs in this world on the things chittering under the bed in the shadows, on some omnipresent bastion of evil, but she couldn't. There were plenty of grubby, petty, little evils that belonged to no one but humanity . . .

The world wasn't a fairy tale, or a tragedy, or a comedy, it wasn't even a ripping adventure tale. It was an unfinished work, she mused, that moved on relentlessly, seeking a good enough ending, killing characters, introducing new ones, and always finding itself lacking. The only resolution, Anne decided, sitting at the edge of the blue-green waters of the Chad, was the one you made for yourself.

She lay on her back and watched the cloud-castles drift like ethereal continents on oceans of sky. She heard the water kiss the earth, gently, relentlessly, and finally, she slept.

"It is unknown what changed within Lilith," Oya said, picking up the tale again. They were sitting by the evening fire crackling outside the hut again. The wasteland had become much colder at night, a partner to the sweltering day. "Some think she realized her anger was at the gods and not those who lived beneath them, who were created by them. I like to think that is the true tale." The old woman smiled and looked wistfully into the fire. "Whatever the reason, she parted ways violently with her husband, Typhon, his brother and the countless monsters they had brought into the world. Lilith went into the wilderness and wished no company for a long time. Finally, she sought out the people. At first they did not trust or believe Lilith, but in time they saw her change of heart to be true and they rallied to her. Lilith took the women of many tribes, many lands and taught them her secret ways, her magic, her power. They were the first of the Daughters of Lilith, sworn to counsel and protect all humanity. I am proudly one of these Daughters."

"So you're not a goddess?" Anne said, sipping more banana beer.

"'Oya' is a title," the old woman said. "I have carried that title and its responsibilities for over three hundred years, but I am but one voice in a chorus of women who have been Oya, who have guarded the secrets of Carcosa, dating all the way back to the first Oya, who fought alongside the first Daughters against Typhon and his armies of the night. The name I was born with is Raashida."

"Three hundred years . . ." Anne said, and whistled.

"You don't have to say it like that," Raashida said, running a preening hand through her tufts of gray hair. "I'm not that old, you know, and I am still very active. I . . . get about."

Anne touched Raashida on the shoulder, "No offense intended. I doubt I'll look any better at three hundred, rotting in a hole somewhere."

Raashida took a sip of her beer and continued. "The Daughters of Lilith, the Mother herself, all the human allies that could be brought to bear, and Adu, and many of his brothers and sisters—the first humans—stood together here, in these very lands. This desert was once a great grassy plain in those ancient days.

"Against them stood all the world's monsters, countless fiends, nightmares wrapped loosely in tattered flesh. They were led by Typhon, Father of Monsters, and his brother Carcosa, Father of Ill Dreams. The war lasted for time out of time, and the very fabric of space and thought was rent by the combatants. There are stories of the war between the gods, between the powers of light and darkness at the beginning of time all over the world, and in virtually every culture. They were all born here.

"When the war ended," Raashida said with a smile, "the human race endured. The night terrors and horrors scattered to the corners of the Earth, like whipped curs, leaderless, their army shattered. Carcosa—his hideous form the size of mountain ranges—lay dead on the field, slain by the Daughters of Lilith. With Carcosa's death, mankind won the freedom to dream as they wished, to dream of anything, to dream greater things than even gods.

"What became of Typhon is unknown; seeing his brother slain by mere mortals, he fled the field, vanished, swearing his vengeance on the Daughters and on all life, everywhere."

"What happened to Lilith?" Anne asked.

"Lilith was weary of war and hatred and strife," Raashida said. "She was sick with the burden of all the horrible things she had released into the world. She retreated from the world to rest her weary soul. Before she did, she gave the surviving Daughters a commission, entreated them to go forth into the world and fight evil wherever they found it, to counsel for wisdom and peace among all men, to gird the loins of those who must fight for their freedom. It has come to be known by the Daughters as Lilith's Load."

Raashida stood. She looked into the night sky and faced the moon. She began to speak, her hands raised to the cold, burning orb.

"I carry within me the clock of the moon,

"The clock of nature, inviolate, unerring.

"I carry within me the secret of God.

"The power of a new life in a universe of darkness and death.

"I carry within me the most powerful of swords.

"For my will can overcome any steel forged by a man.

"And my suffering can overcome any trial of pain or sadness.

"For my blood is that of the first woman, she who would not bow down to the tyrant of Heaven and was cast out, called the mother of beasts. She who would not be bride to either Heaven or Hell, but walked her own sharp, lonely path.

"It is my birthright, these gifts, this pain, this wisdom.

"It is my privilege to understand them and in doing so understand and love myself.

"It is my load to carry them, to protect them, to use them in the defense of the worthy and the weak.

"And to teach this to others of the blood who live in chains of shame and guilt and fear forged by men and their gods, shackled to them by their own limited comprehension of their divine nature.

"This is the secret. This is the load you must bear alone all your days upon this earth. This is the price of truly being free."

Raashida looked down at Anne. "Freedom, Anne, true freedom. Power to make a difference. What do you say?"

Anne stood. "You want me to be part of the Daughters of Lilith? What do I call you, Raashida or Oya?"

"Your choice," Raashida said, "and yes, but not a part of the Daughters, *a* Daughter. We each stand independent, to operate as we see fit, travel where we are needed. We only come together in the most dire of emergencies."

"I . . . I don't even know what to say?" Anne stammered. "It sounds like such a big responsibility, and I'm not the most responsible lass you will ever meet."

"You have everything it takes, Anne," Raashida said. "Life isn't about achieving perfection, life is about doing your best with whatever you have at hand. No one becomes a hero, or someone who will change the world out of *doing* or not doing something, they become it by *being*. They live, they stumble and they rise. Sound familiar?"

Anne looked across the fire to the old woman who carried the name of a goddess. She looked into the fire, and held this moment, this frightening, intoxicating moment, inside her for as long as she could. Something scratched at the back of her mind. It was a voice, calling to her. It was not Raashida's voice; it was someone else, talking to her, calling out to her. It didn't seem to belong there and she turned it over in her thoughts, and then smiled. She looked over to Raashida. "I'm in," she said. "Just remember, I warned you. You're going to teach me how to fight like you do?"

Raashida smiled. "I'm going to teach you how to live. Some parts won't be easy," she said. "Most Daughters begin learning when they are about half your age."

"I don't think my education is going to be typical, anyway," Anne said. "I'm actually sure of it. Tomorrow I need to head to Carcosa." Raashida frowned.

"Child, Carcosa is a week's journey north of here into the deep desert. Often the desert buries Carcosa whole, depending on its mood. I told you, there's no treasure there for you."

"I know," Anne said, "but *she* wants me there."

26

The Empress

Charleston, South Carolina
May 23, 1871

Maude saw herself on the wrecked floor of the mansion. She was looking down on her own body, covered in plaster, crumbling stone and blood. She felt very calm, though, and it didn't seem to bother her that her body was no longer breathing. An ever-widening pool of her blood spread out from her body.

There was a warm, brilliant light above her and then all around her as she floated higher and higher. She could only vaguely make out the details of the room anymore, could barely hear Amadia's voice calling to her as she knelt by Maude's body.

She was in the radiance outside the Record again. Another presence was there with her, but whoever it was stayed at a distance. Maude couldn't make out the other's features. A woman's voice spoke to her.

"Your heart is stopping, Maude," the woman said. "You are at the doorstep of death."

"Yes," Maude said. "Who are you?"

"I want to try to help you," the woman said. She sounded like she was Maude's age, her voice strong and clear. "Do you remember when Gran Bonnie buried you alive in that tiny cave with all the heavy rocks placed over the opening?

"No," Maude said. "I don't think so."

"I'm not surprised, it was horrible. You cried and had nightmares for months afterward. She said it was part of a Buddhist ritual to help you understand death. You were in there for forty-nine days. Try to remember, Maude, please, it's important."

There was something happening to Maude's mind. The memories of her life, her experiences were slipping loose from their emotional contexts. It was like being in a gallery of living sculptures, each memory an event that Maude could look at now, divorced of feeling.

"Yes," Maude said, and she tasted the cold, crumbly dirt on her lips. Her hands couldn't reach her mouth to brush it away. The bone-aching cold that turned to numb pain and eventually went beyond pain. She felt the bugs crawling over her skin, her eyes, in her nose, biting, feeding on her in tiny portions. "I was twelve."

Maude had a stray thought that she hadn't had in decades: perhaps she was still in that grave, and all these years of living had been a brief hallucination brought on by a starving mind, clawing for anything to keep it sane in the unfeeling darkness.

"No," the woman in the light said, "it's all been real."

"That's only true if you're real," Maude said. "I can't see you very well. Who are you?"

"Right now I need you to please trust me," the woman said. "We know each other, but there are no good memories of me to build an image for you. Maude, you have to begin using the exercises Gran taught you to survive in the grave; you have to slow your breathing, slow your heartbeat, slow your blood flow. If you don't, you will die. Please! You can do this!"

It was hard to feel the connection to her body anymore, and her mind, her memories were crystallizing as part of the Record, merging with all the other lives, other memories that touched upon her own, those who had already passed on. Gran's vast life crashed over her like a wave and she nearly drowned in it. She saw . . . things . . . understood things, if only she could hang on to them, like revelations born of dream and lost in a waking haze.

"Maude Claire!" the woman in the light said, her voice forceful, powerful, but not angry. "Focus on your body now! Slow it, Maude, slow it as you were taught. The cells, the nerves, they are still working, still alive. Lilith's blood is still trying to help you endure this. Fight, Maude, fight!"

She willed her body to slow to a metabolic crawl. It was easy this close to death; the trick was to keep all the systems working, moving, providing a sip of oxygen to her cells, to her brain, slow . . . slow . . . almost stopped . . . there. Her life balanced on the edge of a single ragged breath.

"Good, Maude, very good," the woman in the light said. "I know it was hard to get moving, to keep moving, but you have to, darling. You must. Now you're going to do a little trick that's in the Record, you can do it, it's easy. Your heart has stopped, and we need to get it going again. You are conserving oxygen and keeping your brain alive, but we must get the heart going again. Do you understand?"

"Yes," Maude said. "I can almost see you, can you come closer?"

"I can't, love," the woman said. "This is all you have of me to work through. I'm sorry, I dearly wish there was more. I'm thankful you have this bit, though, that some part of you hung onto a tiny piece of me.

"Maude, a Daughter named Khutuln perfected a technique to restart her heart when she was poisoned by an enemy. We're going to take the subtle fluid, the electricity in your brain cells and in your nerves and we're going to agitate it and use it to shock your heart back into beating. There is a tiny charge in every cell in your brain, Maude. I need you to direct the slow-moving blood to your brain and then concentrate on sending a bolt of lightning from your mind to your heart. You can do this."

"I've never, I don't understand how," Maude said.

"No," the woman said, "but Khutuln does. So find her in the Record, follow the trail of the Mother's blood like a burning red road. Find her, and talk to her, train with her. Time is nearly meaningless here. Find her . . . She can teach you how to wake up your heart."

Maude found the pulsing thread of the blood, glowing like a hot brand, twisting and turning all throughout the record of human life. She followed, and drifted past so many Daughters she never knew of—Tomoe Gozen, Pantea, Arteshbod, Onomaris, Boudica—until she found Khutuln, a warrior princess of the line of the great Khan, Genghis.

Maude, in some distant corner of her slowly starving brain, imagined an electrical storm building and summoned it; a storm made up of billions of tiny nerve cells, dark thunder heads growling, lightning dancing between them; the storm was building, growing.

"Who are you, please, tell me," Maude said. "You're not a Daughter. I don't know you, but you know me, you love me."

"I've always loved you, Maude," the woman in the light said. "I always will. I'm so proud of you. Now live and be happy, darling. Fight for your life, fight for it. Please tell Martin how much I love him still. He tries, Maude, he tries so hard. Your father balances all his love for you with all his fears, all his ridiculous expectations for himself. He wants to understand you, and you can trust him, my darling. We both love you so very much. I'll always love you both."

Maude saw the woman's face for the briefest of instants; she was weary, pale and exhausted. She had sweat-tousled brown hair with hints of red-gold and kind brown eyes. Tears of joy ran down her cheeks. She smiled at Maude with all the light in her being, all the light in this warm endless place. "I love you," she said.

The storm's fury was a sizzling blue-hot wall of numbing, convulsing pain. It washed away the image of the woman, it washed away everything. Darkness, then finally, there was a sound. It was far away, but it persisted; it was the beating of a distant, weary drum.

27

The Emperor

Charleston, South Carolina
June 15, 1871

Maude opened her eyes. She was in her bedroom at Grande Folly. Isaiah sat beside her, reading to her from *Little Women*. He paused when he saw her eyes were open and smiled. He had a large bandage covering most of his head and one of his eyes.

"How are you, little girl? I missed you," Isaiah said. "Would you like water?"

"Yes," she rasped, "please. I missed you too. I was very far away. Are you all right? They hurt you."

"They did," Isaiah said. "But Amadia was able to help once she worked on you, and Mr. Cline summoned doctors from town. I'm fit as a fiddle, but you, young lady, you gave us a good scare."

"You're holding something back," Maude said. "What is it, Isaiah?"

He handed her a glass of water and tried to help her drink it, but she struggled to sit and drink herself. Her whole body was stiff with old pain. There were compresses stained with yellowish fluids and brown blood all over her chest and she felt more on her back. The water was the best thing she had ever drunk. Isaiah refilled the glass several times for her, and the buzzing headache began to depart.

"More?" he asked, filling the glass again and offering it to her.

"You've tried to drown me, now please tell me," Maude said. "What's happened?"

"They took Constance," Isaiah said, "the Daughters of Lilith. Your father is very ill. He was injured trying to stop them. He may never walk again."

Maude swung her legs off the bed. Everything hurt, but she scarcely noticed.

"Maude, you have to be still," Isaiah said. "You lost so much blood. The doctors weren't sure if you'd ever wake up. You died twice while Amadia was ministering to you. Please!"

"Third time's the charm," Maude said.

She was on her feet, looking for clothes. She almost fell over as a wave of dizziness struck her, but she steadied herself on the dresser. "How much of a head start do they have?" she asked. "How long have I been lying like a damned rock in this bed?"

"A little over three weeks," Amadia said, standing in the open doorway. "They are most likely in England already."

Maude stopped. She stood still as the words sank in. "God . . . damn it!" she screamed and struck the dresser. The sturdy furniture exploded, shattered wood and clothing scattering everywhere. Maude's fists were shaking as she stood frozen, unable to suppress the anger and grief, the guilt. All the weakness, the dizziness didn't matter.

"Goddamn it," she muttered again. Isaiah came to her and began to hug her. "It's not your fault, child," he said, softly. Maude pushed him away, gently. "No," she said and looked up to Amadia. "It's yours, yours and that lot of bitches with you. You know where they took my baby, you know why?"

"I do," Amadia said, "and I am to blame. I'll do whatever I can to help you." Maude pushed her wild, tangled hair up and out of her face. It fell back. "Isaiah, will you please leave us for a moment," she said. As Isaiah walked to the door, Maude said, "I'm glad you're all right. Thank you. I love you."

"I love you, too, little girl," the old man said. "Don't go picking a fight now; we both owe her our lives." He nodded to Amadia and departed, closing the door behind him.

"You seem to have won him over," Maude said. She looked down at the tangle of splintered oak and tousled clothing. One of Gran's old poet blouses lay at her feet. She picked it up and clutched it to her.

"He is a very good, very kind man," Amadia said. "He loves you very much, like his own blood. He reminds me of my *iya*, my adopted mother."

"He's family. Explain yourself," Maude said. "Who exactly are you, and why are you helping me and mine now?

"My name is Amadia Ibori. I am a Daughter of Lilith, like you. I am the current Oya, given the responsibility of acting in defense of my native lands, and protector of my people."

"Oya?" Maude asked.

"It is a title from my homeland. There has been a long line of Daughters in Africa who act under the title of Oya. My *iya*, my mother, Raashida, passed the title on to me once I completed my initiation and took the Blood of the Mother."

"I assume you finished off that last Son we were fighting?" Maude asked.

"I tried," Amadia said, "but as you well know, they are quite formidable. I was trying to stay alive myself and figure out some way to drop the brute. I led him on a merry chase, I'm afraid. Most of the manor is in shambles."

"I'm pretty sure it's not the first time," Maude said. She found a pair of Gran's breeches and picked them up as well. "From some of the stories I've heard anyway. Gran implied it was a pretty routine happening."

"I've tried to clean up as best I can," Amadia said. "I didn't have much else to do around here, waiting to see if you'd live or not. I promised your daughter I'd protect you and your father."

"How did you stop him?"

"By then, it was after dawn and I drew him outside," Amadia said, sitting down in the chair Isaiah had been in. "I tried to drown him in the ocean. He returned the favor. I could hold my breath longer, just barely. They truly are frighteningly resilient creatures."

"They have blood in their veins from a creature that existed before death," Maude said. "Quite the tonic, apparently." Maude pulled her nightgown off over her head. Her entire body was a painting made of bruises that covered the spectrum of blue, green, purple, yellow and black. There were fresh stitches. Bandages covered all the wounds that Typhon had reopened with a gesture. Her pale scars were like routes on an atlas of old pain. Amadia looked at her. "What?" Maude asked, a little defensively.

"Nothing," Amadia said, and lowered her eyes. She fumbled in the pocket of her jacket. "Do you smoke?"

"No, of course not," Maude said, slipping on Gran's poet blouse and then sitting on the edge of the bed as she pulled up the beeches. Amadia withdrew a cigar, bit the end off, and spit it into a spittoon near the door. She held the cigar between her lips and then put her fingers near the tip. She moved the thumb and forefinger back and forth furiously. After a moment there was a flash at her fingers, and the tip began to glow from the flame.

"You should try it sometime," Amadia said. "It's a habit worth forming."

"They didn't hurt her taking her, did they?" Maude asked. "Constance?"

"No," Amadia said. "She surrendered, said she had foreseen this coming in a dream. Had me promise to help you and your father. She was very brave. You trained her well."

"She's always been brave," Maude said. "I did nothing."

"She told me to tell you, and your father, that she loved you, and that to save you two was worth her sacrifice."

Maude sat back on the bed, partly exhausted just from the simple effort of getting dressed, but more from the idea of her baby far across the world alone, and among dangerous people who wanted to do her harm. "Where are they taking her, and why?" she asked.

"London," Amadia said. "At least as a first stop. They are traveling on a merchant vessel, the *Caliburn*. There is a chapter house in the city, built for the Daughters of Lilith a few centuries ago, by the family of one of our own, a woman named Alexandria Poole. Alexandria fancies herself leader of the Daughters. She's very wealthy and well-connected politically. The *Caliburn* is one of her family's ships. She's the one who gathered us all together for the first time in this generation. She's the one who claims to understand the prophecy and sent us out to collect Constance."

"So she's the one I need to kill," Maude said.

"I argued with them that there are too few of us now to fight off Typhon and his Sons as it is," Amadia said. "I didn't agree with killing Constance and I won't help you kill Alexandria. She's a scheming witch, but we need her."

"This prophecy says my daughter is the Grail of Lilith, whatever that is," Maude interjected. Amadia nodded and blew a stream of sweet smoke into the air above them.

"Yes," she said. "Carcosa is usually only seen in dreams by most human beings, even by us Daughters. Very few have ever seen it with their physical eyes. Alexandria claims to have traveled there in the flesh and read a prophecy from a tablet about the last Daughter of the line of Lilith and how the line can be saved. By the way, when I was cleaning up the library, I came across that stone tablet you have with the ankh carved on it."

"On the reading table, yes," Maude said. "Gran told me it was African. I found an odd stone in it, like a ruby. I discovered it was crystallized blood, very potent, like the Blood we drink from the flask at our initiation, but far, far more powerful."

"That tablet looks exactly like the one Alexandria has in the chapter house in London," Amadia said. "The one she claims is from Carcosa. She keeps it locked away. I didn't have an opportunity to translate it, but yours looks like hers and it's supposed to contain this prophecy."

"That would mean Gran traveled to Carcosa at some point," Maude said. "What exactly does this Poole woman claim the prophecy says?"

"The prophecy says the last Daughter to drink of the Grail shall become closer to the Mother in understanding and power than any before her," Amadia said. "Her blood will be as Lilith's blood, she shall be as the Grail made flesh."

"I had to use up the last of the blood in Gran's flask to try to heal the Earth and put the Great Wurm back to sleep a few years ago," Maude said. "Constance was the last to drink from the flask before I did that; I was trying to save her. The cult had fed her some of the Wurm's blood too. The Mother's blood helped restore her to herself but then these horrible dreams began."

"I'm confident you did the right thing," Amadia said. "The pirate queen put her trust in you as her student, the way my *iya* put her confidence in Anne Bonny, and gave her the Grail. Besides, we're still all alive, so," she said with a tip of her cigar, "well done."

Maude gave her a grudging smile as she wrestled on a pair of buccaneer boots that had also belonged to Gran. "They are taking her to this Poole woman in London," Maude said. "We need to pursue, if there is any small chance that Constance is still alive."

"There's supposedly a ritual to shed the last Daughter's blood to renew the Grail," Amadia said. "Only Alexandria claims to know all of it from the tablet. So they'd need to consult her before they did anything with Constance. But they already have enough of a head start to be in England by now."

Maude, stood, a little shakily. Amadia stood also. "I'll take that chance," Maude said. "I have a few things to settle quickly, then we'll need to be off with the tide tonight. Can you be ready?"

"Yes, of course," Amadia said. "But it may be impossible to find a ship by tonight. Mr. Cline and Mrs. Mansfield have both been to see you often.

A Judge Davenkirk came by to pay his respects as well, brought flowers a few times."

"I'll be damned," Maude said.

"Thank you for trusting me," Amadia said. "I know I've given you many reasons not to."

"You've saved my life several times and you saved my father and a man who in many ways is also my father. Thank you."

"I didn't have an opportunity to examine your father's back," Amadia said. "His physicians shooed me away like I was infectious. People here seem to think 'black' is catching," she said with a puff on her cigar. "I'm not sure if anything can be done for him or not. I'm sorry."

"I'll take a look when I see him."

"Do you still have the old Grail, the iron flask?" Amadia asked. "We may need it."

"I do," Maude said. "I . . ." She started to speak, looked in the full mirror at her reflection. Why on earth had she chosen such a get-up as she was wearing? Amadia's cigar smoke rolled over the edges of the silvered glass. She looked like . . . Maude froze for a moment. Gran, a young Gran, stared back at her from the glass. An association shifted and locked in her brain. Gran's laughter, her voice in the Record. *"We've got work to do,"* she had said to Maude. *"Find the blood stone, unlock the door to the Record, find Hecate. Find me."*

"Hecate?" Maude said.

"What?" Amadia said. "Are you all right?"

"Isaiah!" she called. He arrived at the door.

"Yes?" he said, looking a bit surprised at how Maude was dressed.

"Did Gran ever mention a 'Hecate' to you?"

"Ah," Isaiah said, "I remember the *Hecate,* that was your gran's old ship, a beauty she was too. A fifty-five-foot corvette. The first ship I ever saw. She used to anchor off that beach she loved so much behind the manor. Lady Cormac said it was the fastest ship in the sea, blessed by Poseidon himself. She was very proud of it."

"What happened to it?" Maude asked.

"I think she sold it?" Isaiah said, closing his eyes, and jabbing the air with his forefinger, trying to summon memories. "My father may have said . . . it sank after a battle with . . . an empire of evil sea anemone creatures . . . was it? I'm really not sure. Your Gran was running about the world so much at that point, gone for months at a time, so many adventures, and so many strange and colorful guests at the mansion, and of course the manor getting wrecked every few months, usually because of those adventures or colorful guests. I'm sorry, Maude, I don't recall what became of it."

"It's all right," Maude said. "Thank you. I'm off to Charleston to see my father, and I think I know where to start looking for Gran's ship. Could you please let Arabella and Alter know I'd like to see them, tonight."

Greene opened the door to Martin's townhouse in Charleston. It was after dark, and the butler held a small revolver close to his chest. He smiled when he saw it was Maude and swung the door open. "Miss Maude! It's so good to see you up and about, madame," Greene said.

"How is he, Chester?" Maude asked, as she hugged him. Greene took her coat and shut the door.

"They've done all they can for him," Greene said. "The kidnappers tossed him off the stairs. It did something to his back. The doctors don't know if anything can be done for it. He's been very distressed, Miss Maude, between what happened to Miss Constance and to you. I've never seen him like this before. He will be so glad to see you."

"I hope so," Maude said.

Greene led Maude through the townhouse to the door of Martin's study. He rapped on it and then opened it to allow Maude to step inside.

"Mr. Anderton," Greene said, "Miss Maude is here to see you, sir."

Martin was in a high-backed wheelchair near the window overlooking the street. He was in bedclothes and had a blanket draped over his lap. Maude stepped inside and closed the door behind her.

"Hello, Daddy," she said softly. Martin turned the chair toward her. Maude had never seen her father look so frail, so old. Martin looked up and his eyes smiled in his sunken face.

"I'm glad you're all right," Martin said. His voice was cracked from lack of use. "I have some papers for you."

"Daddy," Maude said, afraid to cross the distance to him, but her heart ached to hold him. Ghosts of anger, of ugly words said and heard, held her in place. Truth be told, it was fear, fear of rejection, of somehow making it worse between them, if that was even possible. "None of that matters."

Martin turned the chair. He wrestled with it and Maude saw the anger, the frustration, in his every movement. Finally, the chair responded and he pivoted it to face his desk. He picked up a sheath of papers with hands that shook a little. "I think you'll find it all very self-explanatory," Martin said, "and it's all been run past Mr. Rutledge, much to his chagrin, I'm afraid. You just need to sign them and file them with the court."

He held out the papers. Maude crossed to him and took them. She glanced over them and then paused. "Daddy, you've signed control of your companies over to me, you've signed everything over to me? You don't want to do that, that business is your life."

"No," Martin said, "it never was supposed to be. I'm sorry, Maude, I tried to stop them from taking her. I did everything in my power." His voice was cracking in pain, and he was fighting to hold back the tears; he failed. "It just wasn't enough, I wasn't good enough to . . ." Maude knelt beside him and put her arm around him. "I couldn't save her, I couldn't save her. I . . ." Martin wept and Maude held him tight, so tight he couldn't fly away.

"It's all right, Daddy," Maude said. "It's all right, I got you." It all fell on her like a wall collapsing under too much weight, the trial, the Sons, Typhon, her father, her baby. Maude wept with her father, and he held her as tightly as his trembling arms would let him. Martin sniffled and fought back the tears long enough to speak.

"I never thought any of those things about you," he said. "I know how strong you are, how capable, how unafraid. You have her in you, and she was all those things. She was always stronger than me, Maude. She ignored my ignorance and my stubborn pride. She forgave me for all the times I hurt her, and I did hurt her, just like I hurt you." The wracking sobs came again, his soul pouring out of him, all the pain he could no longer hold in.

"It's okay," Maude whispered to him. "I hurt you too. I said such awful things to you, did such awful things. I love you, Daddy."

"I love you, Maude," Martin said. "When I came to after they had hurt me, I had this horrible notion that I was dying and that the last thing you'd ever remember of me was how terrible I was to you."

"No, no, Daddy," Maude said, her chest shuddering with each sob; she had no control over her body now, didn't want to. "You've always been good to me."

"No," Martin said. "I have not. I tried to hold you back, hold you down. I just wanted to have a chance to explain to you, but I was too damn proud, too angry and hurt. A man doesn't explain his feelings, he just acts; a man doesn't express his love, he does what his loved ones need. You're expected to act sure, confident, capable, even when you don't have a damned idea in your head what you're going to do, or how. To admit fear, to show it, or talk about it, makes you a weakling. I stumbled around so afraid of words, of seeming weak, that I almost lost the chance to ever explain it to you, to get the words out of me.

"I tried so hard to do what I thought was right by you, not what you wanted. When we lost your mother, when I lost Claire . . ." He fell into sobbing again, fighting to get the words out past all the withheld pain, decades of sealed-away sorrow. "All I had left of her was you, and part of me was so angry at you. I blamed you for her dying; that festered in me, an unreasoning hatred of this tiny, innocent little person. I didn't have anyone to talk to about it. I didn't have any one to counsel me. I prayed to God, but if He had wisdom for me, I was too dull to understand it."

Martin caught a good breath, and wiped his eyes and his nose. He looked into his daughter's eyes. "So I threw myself into the work, the damned work. I stayed away from you, because I didn't want to poison you with my anger, and because I didn't know what to do with it. I provided, whatever the hell that even means. I gave you security and wealth and a long line of women to give you love and attention, because I was too damn selfish in my grief to let it go."

"Daddy," Maude said, sniffing and wiping her own eyes now, "no, I always felt your love, I knew you loved me."

"But you felt the hate too," Martin said, "and that made the chasm between us grow. Parents and children . . . we can wound each other so much, in a million different ways, never meaning to."

Martin had exorcised the tears but his voice was still low, still croaking. He still held onto his daughter as tightly as he was able. "Every day I saw more of Claire in you, and I came to realize that she lived on, in you. But then I became so frightened of losing you, of losing the last, best part of her, of me, all over again. I let that fear drive me. Even when I knew, I saw that you were strong enough to make it on your own, that you were doing a fine job of raising Constance out in the middle of nowhere. You never needed Arthur, you never needed me. I just got afraid of losing you. I did the same thing to your mother, she was just strong enough, and she loved me good enough, to ignore it." The tears came again, a gentle rain now, instead of a shuddering storm. "Her love was always the best part of me, and I hurt her so many ways, so many stupid, prideful ways. I'm sorry, Maude, I'm so sorry."

"Daddy, it's all right," Maude said. "I should have known, but I let my own feelings, my own emotions, my own anger, cloud my vision. I can read a stranger on the street's intent, their history, just with a glance, but I was blind to you. I'm sorry too."

"If I had left you two alone," Martin said, "Constance would be safe now with you, back in Golgotha, instead of in the hands of those bastards." A sharpness came back into his voice.

"I know where they've taken her, Daddy," Maude said. "She's in London. I'm going after her tonight. I'm going to get her back."

"Maude, it's too . . ." Martin began to say, then stopped himself. "Very well. I'd come with you if I wouldn't just slow you down."

Maude shook her head, "Nonsense," she said. "Nothing will ever slow you down, Daddy. I know you. I think I might be able to help you with your injury." She ran her fingers along his spine, gingerly. "Please be still."

Maude found the problem; it was one of his lumbar vertebrae. It was cracked, badly out of alignment, and crushing the cord. She was unable to tell how badly the cord had been lacerated. "Daddy," Maude said, "I can try to fix what's keeping your legs from working."

"Maude?" Martin said. "How? You're no physician, dear." Maude took a deep breath before she spoke. She remembered her mother's words, her promise.

"Daddy, I can do things. I have skills and abilities that might seem . . . preternatural. I can know people's secrets, I can go anywhere, I can heal, I can harm, I can make a difference in this world, and so much more than that. Gran taught me. I'm the latest in a long line of Cormac women who have learned their secrets. I've been learning how to do these remarkable things since I was nine. I've kept them secret my whole life, because Gran said people would not understand, that they might turn on me, think me some kind of freak.

"I'm trusting you with my secret, with my heart, the same way you just trusted me with yours. I always wanted to show you, to tell you. I was just afraid of how you'd react, what you'd do and say. I was afraid I'd lose you, drive you away. I'm not afraid anymore."

Martin looked confused, but he nodded. "I thought I remembered seeing you brawling with those blackguards who attacked us in the coach. I thought I was delusional from the concussion." He looked at his daughter's beautiful face. Saw her waiting, holding her breath. "Gran Bonnie, eh? Your mother once said she had been given an opportunity to learn some old family traditions from Bonnie, but she had just found out she was going to have you, and had told her she couldn't. She said between me and her work with the suffragettes, when would she find the time?

"I always felt your mother regretted a little not taking your Gran up on the offer, but only a little. When she did mention it, she said that she was doing her part of the family tradition through her work, and that she wanted to spend every possible second she could ensuring a better future." Martin smiled at Maude, and took her hand, squeezing it. "She would be so happy, and so proud of you, following in Gran's footsteps, and in hers. I don't have to understand what you do, or how, or even why, Maude. I know you, and I do trust you. You're strong like her, Maude, fearless like her."

"I'm so proud to be your daughter," Maude said. "Most men, most people, couldn't face the things inside and let them out after so long." Martin shook his head.

"I swore if I got the chance," he said, "I'd try to make it right."

Maude adjusted her fingers slightly and moved to a position with better leverage. "Let me try to help you now. This may make things worse, Daddy," Maude said.

"I trust you," Martin said. "I truly do, Maude, with my life. Do it, I'm ready."

Maude slid her finger to the proper spot as she felt the blood move about in her body, strengthening her arm, wrist and finger greatly. She increased the sensitivity of her sense of touch dramatically, so that she could feel the ridges and the hairline cracks on the vertebrae through Martin's clothing and skin. She located the exact spot she needed.

"Here we go," she whispered. "I love you, Daddy," and pushed the vertebrae in and up with a soft crunch.

Martin gasped in pain and his eyes rolled back in his head. "I love you, too, darling," he muttered as he slipped into unconsciousness. Maude examined her father's spinal cord and found it felt as though it were still intact. Only time would tell how much of a difference her ministrations would make. She kissed him on the forehead and lifted Martin, carrying him to his bed.

When Martin awoke, the light in the room was dimmer. Maude was on the floor, to the side of the bed, cross-legged and facing the open windows;

the white translucent curtains billowed around her and she was bathed in the diminishing light. "What time is it?" he asked. Maude seemed not to hear him for a moment and then she opened her eyes and fluidly rose off the floor.

"It's almost five," she said. "How do you feel?"

"Better," he said. He looked down at his legs and feet. They didn't move.

"It may take time and work," Maude said, "but what I did was successful."

"You need to be away soon on the evening tide," Martin said. "I can arrange for one of my ships to take you to London right away."

"Thank you," Maude said, "but I've discovered a faster route. Daddy, there is one thing you can do that would help a great deal."

"Name it," Martin said.

"Telegraph your people in London, have them make inquiries about an Alexandria Poole and any business she may be undertaking. There's a ship called the *Caliburn,* she's the owner . . ."

"Yes," Martin said, "I know. Her father was the late Sir Dewyin Poole, a very powerful man in trade all over the globe. I've been in business with the Pooles since you were a baby, Maude. Are you saying that Dewyin's daughter is the one who has Constance?"

Maude nodded. "We need to know everything we can about the Pooles," she said. "Maybe we can find out where they are holding Constance or if they've moved her out of London, get an idea of where."

"I'll telegraph my people and have them put their best men on her trail," Martin said.

"Tell them to be very careful," Maude said. "This woman is very dangerous, and she will most likely pick up that she is being watched and followed."

"I will," Martin said. "I wish I was going with you, dear. I should be."

"You have a better chance for your spine to heal properly if you rest," Maude said. "You are going with me, in all the ways that matter. I love you."

"I love you too," Martin said. "I meant what I said in those papers. I want you to have everything, dear. You are more than capable of handling our family business, obviously even more than I already suspected."

"I'm beginning to think the Anderton family business might actually be getting into vast amounts of trouble," Maude said, smiling. "Daddy, I have no inclination to run an international shipping empire. I'm happy with what I have back in Golgotha."

The thought of getting to go home, to go back to Golgotha, filled Maude with an odd bittersweet feeling. All of that life seemed so impossibly far away.

"You really love that horrid little town, don't you?" Martin asked. "More than all the beautiful manors and the fine things here in Charleston, more than the harbor?" Maude's face lit up and Martin smiled. "Ah, you loved that harbor. As a girl you dreamed of sailing out on every ship, of having grand adventures, and being the captain of your own vessel. I used to try to dissuade you from all that as best I could."

"Oh, I remember," Maude said.

"Truth be told," Martin said. "I had the exact same daydreams as a boy. Your grandfather, rest his soul, used to tell me only guttersnipes and paupers crewed a ship, and I didn't give a damn, any more than you did."

"When we get you up and out of that bed," Maude said, "we'll go sail together. I'd love that."

"Yes," Martin said, "so would I. Now," he said, taking his daughter's hand and holding it tight, "let's go get our girl back."

28

The Chariot

Charleston, South Carolina
June 15, 1871

It was to be the final meal at Grande Folly before leaving with the evening tide to pursue the Daughters who had taken Constance. Isaiah made enough food for an army and Maude ate enough for an army. She was still dressed in the casual, and somewhat scandalous, garb of her Gran's pirate days. Isaiah, Alter, Arabella and Amadia also ate prodigiously. The conversations were scattered, slipping between pleasantries, nervous humor and catching everyone up on what had been transpiring.

"I have run into one wall after another trying to find where the government men took those odd corpses," Alter said. "I took the precaution of burning the bodies of the ones that accosted you and Isaiah here at Grande Folly, with Amadia's help, of course." Arabella paused in bringing a forkful of food to her lips and looked across the table at the reporter. Cline blushed a bit. "My most profuse apologies, madame! I know it's not proper table conversation."

"No, no, it's quite all right," Bella said, dabbing her lips with a napkin. "My association with our charming hostess," she raised a glass of wine and nodded to Maude, who did the same, "has left me with a whole new appreciation for all manner of ghoulish topics outside the sphere of jurisprudence."

"Not that jurisprudence isn't without its grotesqueness," Maude added.

"Too true," Bella said. The two clinked glasses.

"You seem to have adapted well to all the shocking revelations you've been privy to the last few months, Mrs. Mansfield," Alter said. "Secret societies, monster-men running amok amongst us, ancient gods of evil risen. You've handled it a sight better than I, madame. Bravo."

"It has been eye-opening to say the least, Mr. Cline," Bella said. "I assure you, had you seen me the first time I came upon my client, tending her battle wounds after the altercation with the monsters trying to accost her father and daughter, or after Maude tried to explain to me the agencies attempting to do harm to her and hers, you would have seen me most agitated. However, I was taught by my brother that fear and confusion are the enemy of any lawyer worth their salt, so I persevered."

"A cool head in every crisis," Maude said. "Thank you, general."

"Thank you," Arabella said. "You gave me the opportunity of a lifetime."

"Hopefully you will practice again," Amadia said. "It is quite an accomplishment."

"Well, if you find yourself in the kind of trouble I anticipate you will in merry olde England," Bella said. "I hope to get to be the first woman to practice law in an English court."

"Here is to you bailing us out," Amadia said, raising her glass to the lawyer.

"Any word from your people in London?" Maude asked Amadia as she drained her wine.

"They said no such vessel has yet arrived at any known port in or around the city," the African Daughter replied. "Of course Alexandria could have her own private port, or even a secluded section of beach to use as a port."

"We'll stay optimistic and hope they haven't gotten to England yet," Maude said.

Isaiah examined his pocket watch. "Maude, it's time. You must be getting under way."

Maude stood from the table. "I'd like to show you all something," she said. She led them upstairs and down the hall to one of the guest bedrooms. She unlocked the door with an odd-looking key she wore on a leather cord around her neck. The bow of the key was in the shape of a tree with five bare branches.

Maude also wore an old chain about her neck. The links of the chain were flat and made of dull, crudely forged iron. Attached to the chain was a small vial, about five inches long, wrought of the same dull iron as the chain, as well as inlaid with smooth yellowed bone. The flask was enmeshed in a filigree web of silver wire. The vial was capped with a plug cut from a blood-red ruby the size of a large man's thumbnail. It was the flask Gran had given her long ago, the flask she and Constance and Gran had all drunk from, that she had emptied to save the world and doom the Daughters. It was the Grail of Lilith.

"Isaiah and I both used to wonder why this room was never used by a guest during all the years that Gran lived here," Maude said as they entered the room. It had an old and worn Persian rug on the floor and a grand four-poster bed with a full canopy that took up most of the room. The windows were shuttered and the only light in the room was the oil lamp Maude carried. The room still held the heat of the sweltering June day, even though the sun had set about an hour ago.

Once everyone was in the room, Maude closed the door and locked it again. "This may sound odd," she said, "but everyone climb on the bed, please." Alter, Arabella and Amadia looked at each other, then sat on the bed. Isaiah chuckled at Maude and climbed on as well. Finally, Maude found a spot on the crowded bed near the headboard.

"Umm, this seems . . . cozy," Alter muttered. "A little after-dinner spooning?"

Isaiah turned his head to the young reporter. "Don't presume to be the big spoon in this arrangement, Mr. Cline."

"I . . . that is to say, I . . . oh, of course not," Alter stammered.

Maude ran her fingers across the headboard, then stopped, finally satisfied that she had found what she was looking for.

"It's designed so that only someone with an exceptional sense of touch, like a Daughter of Lilith, could come across it," Maude said. There was a barely audible click, and the bed lurched and began to sink into the floor.

"What the hell?" Alter exclaimed.

"It's a mechanism," Maude said as the bed descended shakily into what was a constructed concrete shaft. There was the rattle of chains and the clink of metal on metal. "These chains connect to stabilizing pins that control the descent." The sound of her voice was dulled by the thick walls.

The elevator shaft gave way to looming stalactites as the bed platform descended through the ceiling of a large natural cave below the manor house. Cool, moist air wafted around them. Maude's lantern gave off a small circle of light as they continued to descend to the cave floor via a steel tower

that formed a cage around the bed platform, visible now that they had exited the shaft. The bed slowed with a rattle and creak of chains and finally
stopped. Everyone climbed off the bed and looked around as well as the light
from Maude's lantern allowed them.

"There are more lanterns and oil on the shelf over here," Maude said, taking a few steps to the left and gesturing to a now-visible wooden rack. "The
mechanism of the elevator works on a rather ingenious system of counter-
weights. It's resetting itself right now, so we can ride back up to the bedroom
when you're ready to leave."

Once everyone had light, they began to make their way across the sprawling cave to the only exit, a naturally occurring tunnel on the opposite side
from the lift. There were old and decaying platforms and ladders all over the
cavern, as well as crates and barrels, rotted by the damp, sea air. The few that
remained intact were barely held together by rusted metal bands and nails.

"Was this a smuggling operation?" Alter asked, holding the lantern aloft
and examining the construction as closely as he could as they passed it.

"At one point, I believe it was," Isaiah said. "I've lived here my whole life
and I had no idea any of this existed until Maude showed it to me earlier
today. That sneaky old crone had me hoodwinked. There's elevators here that
could carry items up to a second set of hidden dumbwaiters all over the
mansion."

"It was used as a way station for the Underground Railroad as well,"
Maude said as they reached the exit tunnel from the cave. "Gran always
hated slavery."

The tunnel was natural and it wound on for what seemed about ten minutes, branching off into numerous dark side passages. A white chalk arrow
continued to point the true way and they encountered a second lantern station beside a long-empty water barrel, with a dipping gourd hanging from a
rope nailed to the side of the barrel. They began to hear the sounds of the
sea crashing, of waves on rocks. The lapping of water against something.

"We're almost there," Maude said.

"Maude, how did you find all of this?" Alter asked.

"I stumbled across some old journals of Gran's and parts of it were in
there, enough for me to puzzle the rest of it out."

Isaiah knew it was a lie, but figured Maude had neither the time nor inclination to try to explain to Cline what she had explained to him when he'd
asked the same question on his first visit down here. Maude told him she

had used some techniques taught to her by Lady Cormac to access bits and pieces of her late Gran's life memories. They led her to the strange key, the secret of the unused guest room and down here to even greater mysteries in the caves.

"Here we are," Maude said, "it's roughly a mile or so down from the plantation's southern side. We're hidden away in that natural cove."

The cave was larger than the first, and yawned open to the advancing sea. Its lower half was already full of rising seawater. Strange lichens clung to the walls and ceiling of the massive cavern and gave off eerie, otherworldly light of purples and yellow, like moonlight reflecting on the deep ocean floor.

"It's like something from a Hans Christian Andersen story," Arabella remarked. "It's beautiful."

"Yes," Maude said. "It certainly is."

Anchored in the cave, and held by a steel ship's cradle to either side, was a beautiful sailing ship of dark stained wood and brass fittings. She was roughly fifty feet long and had three furled masts. The carvings of the figurehead on her bow—a powerful representation of a Greek goddess, two torches clutched in one hand and an odd, tree-shaped key in the other—was exquisite. It gave the craft an alien beauty, as though it were a vessel not built by human hands.

"The *Hecate*," Isaiah said. "Just as pretty as I remember her."

"Your great-great-great-great-grandmother left you her old warship," Alter said, shaking his head as he admired the single deck of carronade barrels visible jutting from the ship. "And I only got a tea cozy from my dear departed Gram."

There was a set of steel stairs bolted into the solid rock of the cave wall near where the party had entered. The stairs went down, pausing at two different landings, each with a catwalk giving access to the other side of the cave and the higher points of the *Hecate*'s masts and nests. The stairs ended at a gangway beside the ship's gently bobbing hull.

"She's a beauty," Amadia said, descending the stairs with the others. "Is she ship-shape, Maude?"

"She is," Maude said. "In remarkably good shape. Isaiah and I gave her a good going over today when we found her. Apparently her primary construction is remarkably resistant to wear."

"How many does it take to crew a ship this size?" Arabella asked.

"Usually twelve to fifteen," Maude said, "but Amadia and I will manage."

"I'm not much of a sailor," Amadia said, "but I'll learn quickly."

"My Gran and my father taught me enough about sailing for both of us," Maude said.

"I'd be honored if you'd let me accompany your expedition," Alter said. "I packed a case upstairs in anticipation of your departure as soon as you rolled out of bed, and I procured a brace of Whitworth rifles that I assure you I can put to good use in your cause."

"Alter, this may be extremely dangerous," Maude said. "Each of the people we're going up against can do all the things I can do, and more."

"Ah, but they aren't you, madame," Cline said, grinning. "And they won't have me and my amazing sharpshooting acumen. Please, Maude, let me help you."

"Grab your gear, we're leaving right away," she said. Cline gave a whistle and a laugh, grabbed a lantern and departed back to the lift.

"Don't you dare go without me!" his voice echoed in the tunnel, "or I'll swim after you!"

"I can pack quicker than that boy," Isaiah said, "and I'm still a half-decent shot and my cutlass work's not too shabby."

"I need you here to look after Father," Maude said, "and to call in the cavalry if we don't come back."

"Your friends from Golgotha?" he asked.

"Yes," Maude said. "I prepared letters. If it's been six months and no word, I want you to send them."

"It's difficult for me to watch you sail off into danger," Isaiah said. "We just got you back."

"My girl needs me," Maude said, "and I need you to be here to help Daddy recover."

Isaiah hugged her and kissed her on the cheek. Maude kissed him on the forehead. "Well, hurry home, then," he said. "This damn house is too quiet without you."

It didn't take Alter long to return with his trunk and two rifles slung over his shoulder. Maude and Arabella stood at the gangplank. The others busied themselves running barrels of fresh water and other provisions they would need for the journey up and down the gangplank to the ship. Amadia had her few possessions in a trunk she carried aboard, ignoring Alter's attempt to carry it for her. She also brought aboard the stone tablet from the library, wrapped in thick cloth and secured in a case.

"Bella," Maude said, "I have something for you. Another discovery we made down here in one of the side caves off the main passage." Maude lifted a small casket from the gangplank. It had a brass hasp and fittings. Maude opened it and showed Arabella the contents. It was filled with ancient coins, gold doubloons, silver reals and precious gems.

"Oh my word," Bella said. "Maude I can't . . ."

"You earned it. This is payment for your excellent job as my attorney," Maude said. "Also consider it a late wedding present and a retainer. If I ever need a lawyer again, I want you in my corner." Maude nodded to the loot. "Besides, there are caves full of this. Apparently Gran was very successful in her . . . business enterprises."

"It was my pleasure to fight for you," Arabella said. "I don't pretend to understand all of this strange world you live in, Maude, but thank you for inviting me in and having faith in me. It's a crime that you were in the right, and we still had no path to legal redress. Not surprising, sadly, but still a crime."

"We fought it with all we had," Maude said, closing the cask and tucking it under her arm, "and I have no doubt we'll keep fighting the war in our own ways, general."

Arabella held out her hand and Maude shook it. "I've heard a great deal about your mother, about her work," Bella said. "I know she was with Stanton and Mott in London in '40 when they were denied seats. She would be very proud of you, of all you've accomplished. Good luck out there. Send for me if I can help."

"Oh, don't worry, I will," Maude said. "Thank you, Bella. Safe journey home."

They hugged and then parted. Isaiah headed back down the gangplank. He took the casket from Maude, and gestured toward the stairs. "This way, Mrs. Mansfield, if you please." Isaiah looked back at Maude. "Be safe, I love you."

"I love you too," Maude said.

In a few moments they were gone.

Maude made her way up the gangplank onto the *Hecate*. "How far along are we?" she asked. "We have to be under way very soon, or we'll miss it."

"Miss what?" Amadia asked, setting down a crate near the hold to the decks below.

"Easier to show than explain," Maude said. "We need to get under way."

"How exactly are we three going to crew this entire ship?" Alter asked as he appeared from the hold.

"Ye of little faith," Maude said.

"I have a bit of sailing experience," Alter said, "enough to know we are going to be sorely taxed on this endeavor with just us."

"You won't believe me if I tell you," Maude said.

"After everything else you've dropped on me," Alter said, "I think I am rather open-minded to anything else you'd care to throw."

Maude slipped the odd tree-key off her neck and walked back toward the bridge deck where the ship's wheel stood. A few feet behind the wheel was a column made of the same dark wood as the ship. The column stood about waist high and had a square tray mounted on top of it. The tray was filled with small, smooth, black stones like river rocks. Nestled between the black stones were five rough-hewn crystals, red, purple, blue, green and yellow, each bright and brilliant, seeming to glow with some inner fire. Alter began to reach for one of the crystals. "What is this?" he asked.

"Don't touch them," Maude said. "She's a bit ticklish."

"She?" Alter said.

"I told you you wouldn't believe me," Maude said as she carefully placed the tree-key in the tray, as she had been instructed to do by Gran's shadowed memories from the Record. The key seemed to move of its own accord, settling into the bed of stones. There was a sighing sound, and a gentle breeze blew across the deck. The wind carried a faint scent of pennyroyal mint with it.

"Hecate," Maude said, "is alive."

"The ship is alive?" Alter said.

"In some manner or other," Maude said. "I don't fully understand it myself. Apparently Gran rescued her people from some dreadful place called Elfhame Sinister. Her people were, um, enchanted trees."

"Trees?" Alter said. Maude nodded earnestly.

"Enchanted trees, yes," she said. "Some volunteered, out of gratitude, to be made into this ship, to aid her in her travels."

"So, we're on a magic ship," Alter said, "made out of magic tree wood, living magic tree wood."

"Yes," Maude said. "I know it sounds preposterous, but . . ."

"Oh, no, not at all," Alter said, picking up another crate to stow. "I was discussing such matters with a talking puce-colored jackrabbit over tea, just the other day. Not to worry." As he disappeared back into the hold, he muttered to himself, "Eat your heart out, Jules Verne."

The memories Maude had uncovered that led her to the ship had also given her a vague understanding of its unique properties. Whoever possessed the key and placed it in the tray—which acted like the ship's nervous system and senses, after a fashion—would be identified as a friend of Gran's and an ally to be obeyed. It had seemed far-fetched to Maude, too, until she had spent a little time in the ethereal presence of the spirit of the ship, earlier that afternoon.

Maude stood by the column and held her hand over the tray of stones. "Hecate, we need to get underway, please." The scent of the mint grew stronger and another breeze moved over the deck. Maude turned to Amadia. "Could you please retrieve the gangplank? I'll release the cradle." Maude jumped off the deck and landed on the gangplank. She pulled a pair of levers simultaneously, and the massive metal cradle holding the *Hecate* opened, freeing the ship. Maude lept back onto the main deck, and took her place behind the steering wheel.

"Gangplank away," Amadia said.

"Weigh anchor, Hecate," Maude called, and was satisfied to hear the ship's chain rattling and felt the vessel began to drift free in the water as the anchor was stowed by unseen hands. The ship drifted forward, toward the mouth of the sea cave, as if pushed by a wind, even though the masts were still furled.

"This is powerful *Bo*," Amadia said, smiling.

Maude glanced up the steel stairs to the mouth of the entrance. Isaiah stood there, alone. The old man waved. Maude waved back.

The cave slid away and they were out in the cove, under a shimmering canopy of starlight. Ursa Minor was bright overhead, Polaris burning at the tip of the Little Dipper's handle.

"Hecate, unfurl the sails, please," Maude said. The mint scent swirled about the pedestal and the wheel. The ship's sails tumbled down and filled as they caught the night wind.

"I'll go give her a hand with the lines," Amadia said. Alter returned from below.

"Everything's stowed, Captain," he said to Maude.

"I always wanted to be a ship's captain," Maude said.

"Now you are," Alter said. "Though I must say you look more dressed for the part of a pirate."

Maude turned the wheel northeast, bringing the bow of the *Hecate* in line with the ghost-light of the waxing gibbous moon, still hovering at the horizon of the sea and sky.

"Good, we're not too late," Maude said. "Faster, if you please, Hecate."

"Not too late for what?" Alter said. "Or do I want to ask, after the whole 'magic tree ship' business?"

"Probably not," Maude said. Alter shrugged and went about busying himself by helping Amadia with the rigging on the sails. The moon grew larger before them. Maude spoke under her breath as she steadied the wheel. "Hecate," she said, "you've been on this path before, I haven't. I just have some pieces of old memories that belong to other people to depend on, so I need you to guide me in this, please. It's the only hope my daughter has."

The sweet smell of pennyroyal swirled about her, and it gave her a sense of comfort. Maude focused on the looming moon, still barely tethered to the sea. The *Hecate* sped ahead, the wind filling her billowing sails, and perhaps something more. The moon's buttery, pockmarked surface filled the horizon. It seemed to Alter that it was larger and closer than the illusion should make it appear. Maude held the wheel on course. Amadia and Alter joined her.

"This is what I didn't want to know, isn't it?" Alter said.

"It's a shortcut of sorts," Maude said. The light from the moon washed over the ship, hiding the night sky, blocking everything else. "The gates are only open for a very limited time, moonrise and sunrise," she said, "and only along very specific headings. I found the charts in Gran's cabin. We just made it in time."

The *Hecate* sailed through the gate of moonlight that was still attached to the sea, to the horizon. As it passed through, time detached from action and thought. Alter tried to speak, but his tongue felt like it might flutter away like a butterfly. Amadia's thoughts, quicksilver, poured out of her head and splashed against the brains of Maude and Cline like whispering drops of water. "*WhatishappeningwhatisthishowcanthisbeImustfocus-mythoughtsmymindpullthembackintomyhead,*" her mind blurted to her companions.

Maude found her vision locked on the scintillating moonlight that was now all there was in existence. Even when she blinked, when she closed her eyes, the light remained, moving through her, through her friends, as if they were made of glass. The surface features of the moon were gone, blurred into obscurity. In this moment there was a feeling as if the solid deck was not under her feet and she was hanging suspended by nothing, and could plummet at any moment.

The cold light narrowed, narrowed even more until it was a tiny point, and then it was gone, not even leaving an afterimage on the retina. The ship was drifting in dark waters, above an empty vault of a sky, not a single star or cloud to be seen. Looking aft, they could see the opening of the moongate closing as the gibbous moon rose higher into the sky full of stars they had left behind. After a few moments, the way behind them was as dark as the way ahead. A chill wind caught the *Hecate*'s sails and the ship moved forward. Maude felt the wheel trying to move under her hands of its own accord.

"Thank you, Hecate," Maude said. "Please guide us, if you know the way."

"I can talk again," Alter said. He looked at Amadia. "And I'm not hearing your thoughts in my skull anymore."

"Where are we?" Amadia asked Maude.

"An ocean not found on any map," Maude said, "but connected to almost every body of water on Earth. Only a few sailors know of this place and they guard the knowledge like gold. We're traveling on the Secret Sea, on the other side of the duskgate. When we pass back into the world we know, it will most likely be through the dawngate, connected to the rising sun. This will reduce our travel time to England considerably."

"I hope you know what you're doing, Maude," Alter said. "There are no landmarks here, no land here as far as I can tell, no stars. We could became lost here and never find our way out."

"We'll find our way, I promise," Maude said. "Gran used this route many times. Hecate knows the way."

"Well, if you can't trust a living magic-tree-ship, then who can you trust, right?" he said.

"Trust me, then," Maude said and patted Alter on the shoulder. Alter sighed and went belowdecks. Amadia touched the edge of the *Hecate*'s tray gently. "I'll come and relieve you in a few hours if you'd like," she said, and then headed off after Cline. Maude understood why they were worried; this place seemed bleak and devoid of any points of reference or direction. She was worried too. She hoped this worked as she had seen it in Gran's memory. Maude patted the wheel, allowing Hecate to steer, and fixed her eyes on the hidden horizon, hoping for a sign of dawn.

29

The Queen of Swords (Reversed)

London, England
June 21, 1871

The three-hundred-pound steel-reinforced front door of the townhouse at the corner of Duke and Brooks was designed to hold off a literal army equipped with battering rams and explosives. Maude took it off its hinges with a single spinning wheelhouse kick, powered by all the strength and fury she could summon. The partly crumpled door boomed as it fell to the ground of the foyer. Maude, still dressed in Gran's buccaneer garb, stepped through the doorway as the plaster dust settled. Rain fell in dark sheets outside, and the slick streets were practically empty.

"That was subtle," Amadia said, stepping in behind her. Maude said nothing. Alter followed the two women. He had left his rifles on the *Hecate* and now brandished a revolver. "Up the stairs," the African Daughter said. "Parlor is on the second floor, the first door on the right."

Maude bounded up the stairs, from the first landing to the second-floor corridor, and tumbled to a stop before the parlor door, ready for an attack coming from any direction. A single crow's beak punch shattered the wooden door into splinters. She stepped inside. The fireplace in the room was unlit. A very tall, beautiful young woman in her twenties, dressed in a pale blue brocade dress, was waiting. She had straight blond hair, pale blue eyes and delicate features. She sat alone at a large round table of dark, polished wood.

"From your impeccable manners and refined demeanor, you must be the American," the blonde said.

"I'd take you for Alexandria Poole," Maude said. "You're as much of a bitch as I anticipated, but I expected you to be older."

"Oh, she is," Amadia said, entering the room behind Maude. Alter stood guard at the shattered door. Alexandria glared at Amadia but said nothing.

"You get one chance to tell me where Constance is," Maude said, "or I beat all of that haughty pretense right out of you."

"I'll tell you," Alexandria said, rising from her chair, "but you're already too late." Maude's eyes darkened and she split the round table in two with a knife-hand strike.

"Then I have no reason to keep you alive, you witch," Maude said, stepping toward her. Amadia put a restraining hand on Maude's shoulder.

"Maude," Amadia said, "don't."

Alexandria raised a finger, smiling. "Here's a good reason," she said. "Look behind you." Maude and Amadia glanced back. Alter was pointing his pistol at his own head. An odd look of struggle played over the reporter's face. "You behave," Alexandria said, "or I'll have your pet there splatter his brains all over the nice rug. Now, sit down."

"How are you doing that?" Amadia said, astonished.

"Itzel isn't the only one to have delved into the more esoteric powers of the Blood," Alexandria said.

Maude and Amadia remained standing. Alexandria resumed her seat, crossing her legs.

"Alexandria," Amadia said, "I've been trying to convince Maude that we all need each other. Typhon is back in the world, he's free. I've faced him myself, so has Maude. We need all of the Daughters, including Constance, together if we hope to have any chance to stop whatever his plans are. Let's not forget who the real enemy is."

"How reasonable sounding, coming from a traitor," Alexandria said. "The latest in a long line of savage degenerates who should never have been given guardianship of such awesome power for all humanity."

"Don't you mean, 'all white humanity'?" Amadia said. She started to speak again but held her tongue. Alexandria continued as if she hadn't spoke at all.

"You turned on your sisters in the battlefield," she said. "As you can imagine, they felt your base betrayal most deeply."

"That 'battlefield' was us abducting an innocent child for you because you didn't have the nerve to do it yourself," Amadia said. "You've managed to twist everything around."

Alexandria regarded Maude. "The true enemy, as you have witnessed firsthand, teaches his soldiers to be hard, unmoved by sentiment or emotional weakness. They do what is necessary to triumph. If we are to defeat them, we must adopt the same uncompromising standards. You can understand that, can't you, Maude?"

Maude felt Alexandria's words slithering into her mind, making her intent seem more honeyed, more reasonable. Maude felt her own thoughts begin to subsume into the English woman's desires, her commands. She allowed her thoughts to bend like a reed, to slip into the dark quiet places she had been learning to reach through meditation. There in the darkness was the burning thread of the blood, of the Record. She clutched it like a lifeline and it gave her what she needed. All this happened in the span of a breath.

"Oh, I understand," Maude replied. "And to a certain extent, I agree. The time for half-measures is at an end. Look over my shoulder, Alexandria." The British Daughter shifted in her de facto throne. Alter was now pointing the pistol at her.

"How did you—?" Alexandria said, standing. The pistol followed her. "My family has been perfecting the magicks of the Blood for thousands of years. It took me nearly fifty years of my life to master them. It's impossible!"

"Sit . . . down . . . now," Maude said, lowering her head, her gaze locked on and seared into Alexandria's own. Alexandria's expression shifted from surprise to genuine horror. She balled her dainty hands into fists and her legs shook, the muscles locked in effort.

"No!" Alexandria shrieked. Her whole body was convulsing, but she remained standing. Maude's body began to tremble slightly and a sheen of sweat covered her brow and lip.

Alter blinked and shook his head. He looked at the pistol and seemed confused. "Did I miss something?" he asked Amadia.

"Alter," Maude said through clenched teeth, not daring to break Alexandria's gaze. "If Miss Poole doesn't sit down right now I want you to shoot her in the face, please."

Without a second's hesitation, Alter aimed the gun at Alexandria.

"Maude," Amadia said, "nothing would give me greater pleasure, but we'd be doing the same thing she's done, if we continue down this path."

"You can't afford the effort to physically defend yourself," Maude said to Alexandria. "And if you do, I'll have you, like you tried to have me. So, choose."

Alexandria's hands took the arms of the chair and she slowly sat down. Both women stopped shaking, and Maude rubbed her face and sighed as she blinked.

"How can you possibly do that, know that technique?" Alexandria said.

"All you need to know is that I do," Maude said, not about to tell this woman she had no idea how she had been able to do what she just did. That tiny stone of crystallized blood had changed her in some fundamental way, was changing her. It had swung open a door in her mind widely. "You are going to tell me where my daughter is."

"On my ship, the *Caliburn,* bound for Africa," Alexandria said, "for Carcosa. You obviously have knowledge of the Record, but I've never known of anyone who could access it so fluidly, so instinctively."

Maude ignored her observation. "That sentiment you spoke of so contemptuously, those emotions you call a weakness, are at the core of what Lilith's Load, our duty, is about. They are our strengths, when tempered with wisdom, and never abandoned. If we compromise, if we adopt the ways of our enemies, we become them—perhaps worse than them—because we knew better."

"Spoken like a true American," Alexandria said. "An idealistic child."

"It's unseemly for a woman your age to cavort about pretending to be a youth," Maude said. Alexandria flushed with anger, but stayed seated and silent. "Oh, yes, while we grappled I saw bits and pieces of the real you in there." Maude tapped her own skull. "Not everything, just glimpses. I know, for example, why you started this horrid endeavor, and I promise you I won't let you win at this."

"What are you talking about?" Alexandria said.

"The tablet," Amadia said. "Maude has one like it as well, but in better condition, and she was willing to give me access to it. I translated it, and while it talks of a rebirth and renewal of the Grail, it says nothing about this ritual you concocted, nothing of human sacrifice, nothing that would indicate that Constance is this 'living grail.' It says, "one will give up her future to save the past," but that's all. The rest are lies you fed to the others. You are the traitor, Alexandria, from a long line of arrogant, selfish elitists. Tell me why. Why are you doing this, what could you possibly have to gain by having us sacrifice an innocent girl?"

"I owe neither of you any explanations," Alexandria said. "You are both sentimental fools, who cannot read the writing on the wall of this age. I can, and I swear to you both, the Daughters of Lilith will continue on under my auspices when you are both nothing but forgotten dust."

"You have gone mad from drinking too much from the Grail," Amadia said. "I always suspected, but I never knew how far you had fallen."

"If you two think you can eliminate me so easily," Alexandria said, "you're welcome to try. We will raze this whole city in the struggle, I assure you. Thousands will die. A battle for poets to chronicle."

"I know," Maude said, looking about the room at the woodcuts of ancient Arthurian legends. "I don't want to kill you, or control you, Alexandria. I want to help you remember who you really are, who we really are.

"I recently did the right thing, using very wrong methods, and it felt like losing, like betraying the principles of the cause I set out to uphold. The true path is hard and long and painful and infuriating, but anything that is truly of value is never easy." Maude looked at the split table. "Think about it. Try to remember who you are."

"The world is not merciful to the dreamer, and it certainly isn't fair," Alexandria said. "Get out. If I see you two again, I will kill you. You remember that."

They departed the room. "She influenced some of the other Daughters," Maude said as they walked down the stairs. "The way she tried to influence me and Alter."

"Wait, what?" Alter said, holstering the pistol, "I was influenced? When?"

"She's subtly played to their fears and prejudices," Maude continued. "It's going to be hard to convince them she's lied to them."

"My guess is Itzel was left alone," Amadia said. "I suspect she'd notice that kind of tampering with her thoughts. Ya is in Alexandria's corner, tampering or not. That leaves Inna and her daughter, and I'm betting Alexandria played on Inna's guilt and worry about her daughter to keep her from thinking too much about the implications of this ritual."

"Inna's the one who crippled my father?" Maude said. "The Russian?"

"Yes," Amadia replied, "but try to remember what you said in there; they were good words."

"I don't think they were entirely my own," Maude said and Amadia looked at her strangely.

"Why didn't Alexandria try to influence you?" Alter asked Amadia.

"She hates me, and the feeling is mutual; that may have been my armor," Amadia said, "and as Ya loves to point out, I am a bit of an iconoclast, so that may have helped too."

Outside, the storm tore across the London skyline. The day was as night, with lightning punctuating the endless torrent of rain.

"Are we going to be able to reach a duskgate or dawngate in this?" Alter asked, pulling the collar on his coat up.

"No," Maude said. "We'll have to take the *Hecate* out the old-fashioned way, and see if we can get free of this storm and find clear sky. Damn it."

"We'll beat them there, Maude," Alter said. "Don't worry."

The trio disappeared into the black curtain of the rain. In the ruins of the parlor, Alexandria Poole watched them vanish from sight from a window.

"Having any second thoughts?" The man's voice said behind Alexandria. "Did the Widow Stapleton sway you with her noble, forthright words, spoken with such sincere intent?"

"No," Alexandria said, looking out into the storm. "This is all necessary to separate the wheat from the chaff. To think otherwise is to play the fool. I was not raised a fool. You are ready to play your part in this?"

"Since before the first Poole was even born," the voice said. "Of course it all depends on our pawns, your sisters. If they falter, then I can do nothing."

"They will not," Alexandria said. "They all think there is no other way."

"If you are correct, no one will leave Carcosa alive," the man said.

"Then," Alexandria said, "our future is secure."

30

The Six of Cups

Somewhere in the Atlantic
June 7, 1871

For the first week at sea, Constance was locked in her cabin aboard the *Caliburn*. Food was brought to her by at least two of the Daughters and several armed crewmen every time. Constance made no attempts to escape. She spent her time practicing her katas and reading the few books brought to her by her captors.

During the second week there was a knock on the cabin door late at night. Constance heard the lock click and the door open. It was the Russian girl, Lesya, who Constance had put in a submission hold back in Charleston. She was pale with fierce blue eyes and long white-gold hair that fell beyond her shoulders. She wore a nightshirt that fell to her ankles. The shoulder where Grandfather had shot her was heavily bandaged. She held a lantern and the key to the cabin door.

"May I come in?" Lesya asked. Constance had been reading *The Mystery of Edwin Drood* at the table. She nodded and closed the book.

"I couldn't do much about it, even if I did mind," Constance said. "But yes, please."

"I am feeling better," Lesya said. "The wound is healing well. My mother tells me I should be fully recovered by the time we reach England."

"I'm glad," Constance said. "I hope my grandfather and mother are well too."

The girl entered the cabin and locked the door behind her. She sat on the edge of Constance's bunk. "I am sorry for all of that. I was trying to show off to my mother, and your grandfather was only trying to protect you. My mother feels very guilty about it. I've heard her talking to one of the other daughters, Itzel, about it. I am sure Amadia helped them. She is very powerful and skilled."

Constance said nothing.

"May I ask you a question?" the Russian said.

"Of course."

"Why did you let me break that submission hold?"

"I didn't . . ." Constance began, but the other girl cut her off, shaking her head.

"Please," Lesya said. "You let me get out. I do not think you a fool. Please do me the same courtesy."

"Yes, I did. I knew the counter to that hold," Constance said. "I also knew that if I maintained that hold, you'd bleed out and die before your mother could help you."

"How could you know that?" Lesya asked.

"I had dreamed it, earlier that night. My dreams come true," Constance said, "unfortunately. I decided I had to try to change this one. I didn't want you or anyone else to die. Bad things usually happen when I try to change the dreams. Grandpa got hurt, most likely because of me."

"No," Lesya said. "I do not believe that you had anything to do with that." Constance said nothing. "Thank you for trying for me. I am Lesya Barkov."

"Constance Stapleton. It's nice to meet you. I wish it wasn't like this."

"As do I," Lesya said. "I am sorry our mothers are fighting. We are supposed to all be on the same side, all Daughters of Lilith."

"Your mother didn't have to throw my grandfather like that, he's not trained like us," Constance said.

"She got upset when I got shot. I was . . . showing off. I am sorry. She is too. She is very proud and it is hard for her to admit when she makes a mistake, but I can see it. She wishes it had not happened too." Lesya paused for an awkward moment. "I wanted to say hello and see how you were."

"I am being treated very well," Constance said. "Thank you, Lesya. It's a kindness for you to check on me."

Lesya smiled and departed, locking the door behind her.

The next night, Lesya returned to visit once again, lantern in hand.

"How old are you, Constance?" Lesya asked.

"What's the date?" Constance asked.

"June eighth," Lesya said.

"I'll be fifteen in six days," Constance said.

"I'll be fourteen this November," Lesya said. "I'm sorry you have to spend your birthday on this old ship. If you could spend your birthday with anyone who would it be?" Constance blushed a little, and Lesya giggled. "A boy? Back in Charleston, yes?"

"No," Constance said. "He's back west, in Golgotha."

"Ohhhh," Lesya said, trying to affect a western accent poorly, "a cowboy, yes?"

"Hush!" Constance said. "He's a nice fella. His name's Jim. I'd like to spend my birthday with him. You got a fella back in Russia?"

Lesya placed the lantern down on the floor, and slid down to join it, her back against Constance's bunk. Constance slipped free of the chair and joined her on the floor. They huddled almost conspiratorially around the lantern.

"I wish him to be but I do not think he notices me," Lesya said.

"What's his name?" Constance asked. It was Lesya's turn to blush now. "Come on, fess up," Constance said. "I told you."

"His name is Valentin," Lesya said. "He is the son of a fisherman in our home village. He is . . ." the Russian girl struggled for words.

"Beautiful?" Constance offered. Both girls laughed.

"Yes," Lesya said, "he is very beautiful."

They talked until dawn and Lesya promised to return as soon as her chores would allow. That night Constance slept well and had no troubling dreams. It was the first time she could recall that for a very long time.

Lesya was true to her word. She visited Constance again and again, night after night. Constance soon began to look forward to the visits, and gradually she began to forget this girl was her captor. They talked about books they loved and hated. They described their homelands to each other in the kind of detail that only someone who is young and too far from home can provide. They talked of their training, of the ways it was similar in some regards and very different in others. They talked of their loves and their dreams. Whenever talk came to the future, Constance got quiet, and sad.

"What is it like to be able to see the future?" Lesya asked one night.

"I think it might be kind of like what it's like to get old," Constance said. "You see the people you've loved your whole life die, see the hole they leave in you, in your world. I hate it." They were both quiet for a time. Then Lesya held up a worn deck of cards.

"Let's build a house of cards," she said, smiling. Constance agreed and wiped her eyes.

"Okay, let's," she said.

On June 14, Constance's birthday, Lesya woke her up early, jumping in the bed and pulling Constance's ears, as was the tradition back home. The two girls laughed.

"Did you dream?" Lesya asked. "The eve of your birthday is supposed to be a time of powerful omens." Constance got a strange look on her face.

"Yes," she said. "I dreamed."

Lesya held out a closed hand. "Happy birthday! Here is your present!" She opened her hand. It was the key to the cabin door. Lesya dropped it in Constance's palm. "Mother says you don't have to stay locked in here anymore. I convinced her you are determined to see this through."

"Thank you," Constance said, and hugged the girl.

"Come on, let's go up on deck. It's a beautiful day!" Lesya said. Constance chased after the young Russian and they spent the day running up and down the rigging on the ship and watching clouds.

By the end of the week, Constance was helping with duties on the *Caliburn* and she and Lesya were training together. Lesya asked her a million questions about how it felt to take the blood.

"You'll find out soon enough." Constance said as they sparred on the fore deck.

"You really think so?" Lesya asked.

"No doubt," Constance said. The odd sadness that crossed her face from time to time passed over her like clouds hiding the sun. Lesya put a hand on Constance's shoulder.

"When this is all over, I'll take you to my home and show you my beautiful fisherman and then you can take me out to the American frontier and show me your cowboy Jim."

"Deal," Constance said, and the sadness passed from her face and the sun shone again.

They arrived in England the following week. They dropped anchor in a cove beside a deserted stretch of rocky beach. All the Daughters departed the *Caliburn* by ship's boat, leaving the two girls there with the crew. By the next day, they were under way to Africa, but the mood aboard the ship had darkened. All the Daughters had returned from their meeting in London with Alexandria Poole sullen and silent, and Constance knew why—and what that meant for her. Constance did receive some good news, however. Lesya eagerly told her the next morning that her mother Inna had made inquiries at Lesya's urging and that Martin, Constance's grandfather, was alive, and so was Constance's mother.

As Constance began to cry a little, she looked out over the ship's rail at the bloody sun sinking in the west. "Thank you," she said. "Thank you so much." The tears started and as hard as she wanted to stop them, to use the self-discipline Mother had been teaching her, her heart was a raging storm full of great relief and an odd alchemy of sadness and joy. The people she loved the most were alive and well and she was sailing farther and farther away from them, never to see them again.

Constance sobbed, deep wracking sobs. All the stress of the dreams, of the strange presences inside her mind, warring, of her impending death, it all fell on her like the boom of a sail. She wasn't a Daughter of Lilith, she was a girl alone and frightened and missing her family. Lesya held her tight and pushed her damp hair out of her red-rimmed eyes, well after the sun had drowned.

One night, weeks later, lying on the deck on their backs watching the stars above them, Lesya finally broke the silence. "I don't want you to die."

"I don't want to," Constance said. "I was kind of hoping to get a chance to kiss Jim before . . . you know." They were silent again for a long time. "It really is beautiful and terrible, isn't it?" Constance said.

"What?" Lesya asked.

"Life," Constance said. "It's cruel to have so much beauty and so much wonder and then to snuff it out. The only thing worse I suppose would be to never have all that in the first place."

"As a Russian, I'm duty bound to disagree with you on that. If you never lived, you'd never know what you were missing. See, always able to harvest a darker cloud from a silver lining. Pessimism, it's a Russian invention."

"If I die," Constance said, "could you go to Golgotha and tell Jim . . . I don't know, that he was sweet, and kind. Tell my mother and grandfather how much I loved them."

"I will," Lesya said. "I promise."

"And no stealing Jim, you sneak," Constance added.

"Never," Lesya said. "I'd never do that to you." The two girls held hands and watched the universe spin and burn.

As the *Caliburn* headed closer to Africa, Inna Barkov, Lesya's mother, felt more and more doubt creep into her about their mission. She told Itzel of her concerns.

"The Daughters must have the Blood of Lilith to continue," Itzel said. "I, too, wish there was another option, but the Stapleton girl fits all the criteria of this prophecy as Alexandria has uncovered it. It has to be her."

"Why do I get the feeling that we are in the wrong here?" Inna said. "If the Mother is such a force for personal freedom, and for good, how can it be her will to slay this innocent girl and drain her blood to fill the grail again? It's obscene."

"Good means many different things in different places, different times," Itzel said. "I was taught that to be a sacrifice is a great honor, a kind of civic responsibility. Anything of true value exacts a price. Perhaps it is the Mother's will to remind her children of that."

"I do not know if I can . . . plunge a knife . . . I do not think I can do such a thing to that girl." Inna tried to not use Constance's name any more than she had to. "If the Sons had not resurfaced with such a terrible fury, I'd say let us die out."

"You'd deprive your own daughter of the blood?" Itzel said. "I have not known you to be an overly sentimental person, Inna. We may hate this, but that is why we are the ones who must undertake it. The world will crumble to ash if Tezcatlipoca and his Sons run unchallenged in the world. We Daughters are all that stands before them. It is for the good of all, for count-less unborn generations, that we must do this thing."

"You sound like Ya now," Inna said. Itzel smiled that strange, knowing smile that Inna had come to hate over the course of their travels together.

"Ya sees the whole mosaic," Itzel said. "That is her strength and her weakness. She overlooks the details and that leaves her vulnerable."

"What do you see as my vulnerability?" Inna asked.

"The same thing that is your greatest strength," Itzel said, looking over to the girls laughing and talking as they practiced their katas on the main deck of the *Caliburn*. Lesya waved to her mother. She looked like a normal child, no secret societies, no brutal endless training, no monsters to fight, no blood rituals. Inna hated to think she would be the one to take her daughter's first real friend away from her. Africa loomed closer every day, and with it Constance's death.

31

The Ten of Cups

Lake Chad, North Africa
July 19, 1871

They arrived with the sun breaking across the horizon of the lake. Maude was at the helm of the *Hecate* as they passed through the dawngate and she felt the ship sink a bit as it went from ocean water to the fresh water of the Chad. "Land ho!" Maude called. She was still garbed in Gran's old sea-faring clothes. She had found more in the wardrobe in the captain's cabin, along with an odd assortment of items in several sea chests, and she'd come to like the freedom and the feel of the clothing. She wore Gran's machete at her belt now, as well as a holstered Colt revolver.

"Whoa," Alter shouted from the mast. He climbed down and began to hoist a sail. *Hecate* assisted him in doing it. Amadia jumped effortlessly from the crow's nest to one of the sail lines. She rode the line down as the sail went up, and when she reached the deck, she finished furling the sail with invisible help from the ship. The third, unattended sail began to furl on its own. Alter was dressed a bit more like a sailor than a New York gentleman now, after nearly a month at sea, and his hair was longer and he had decided a beard suited him. "We all right?"

"Yes," Maude said. "Just the ship's keel shifting a bit. Our draft changed when the water changed. She's fine. But let's drop anchor and check the plumb before we go any further."

It had taken them over a week to get clear of the storm swirling about

England and western Europe. They had headed south toward the Strait of Gibraltar, and finally got a clear night sky that allowed them to enter the Secret Sea. Amadia knew the way to Carcosa, and the three had discussed their choices one night over dinner. The best bet was to access the waters of the Chad to cut down the lead Inna and the others had on them.

"They will need to port, and then cross the upper Sahara," the African Daughter explained. "We can port in the Chad and then head north into the desert. We'll be closer. It's about a week from there to Carcosa."

The anchor lowered itself with a clatter of chains. Maude rubbed her eyes. It had been a long and stressful trip, wondering how they were treating Constance. She knew the Daughters were all decent people, merely misguided by Alexandria's manipulations, however that did little to comfort her from the fact that her daughter was a prisoner of the most dangerous people on Earth, who intended to bleed her dry to renew the Blood of the Mother. Maude pushed it away from her mind again, focusing on getting to Constance before that happened.

"This lake is huge," Alter said. "Should we bring the *Hecate* closer to shore?"

Maude looked to Amadia, who was busy retrieving the plumb and its cord. "Looks to be about forty feet deep," Amadia said. Maude shook her head.

"I'm not going to risk it. We'll take the ship's boat to shore. Let's start loading it."

A few hours later, they were in the small boat, moving along the shore of Lake Chad. Amadia had directed them to a specific section of the coast.

"Is that a pyramid?" Alter asked, pointing to the distant shore. Amadia nodded.

"We're close," she said. "We need to keep heading north."

They sailed along, following the shore for the better part of the day. As the sun was beginning to creep toward west, they caught sight of the blackened corpse of a burned forest. "There," Amadia said, pointing. "We are almost to my home."

They pushed the boat up onto the rocky, sandy shore. Smiling, Amadia admired the remains of the trees. "She most likely knows we're here," she said. "Her hearing is still better than your average panther's, even at her age."

Maude pulled her coat and her ditty bag out of the boat and looked about. "Do we camp here or keep going?" she asked Amadia.

"It's not far," Amadia said, "less than an hour. We'll be home in time for dinner." Alter carried his rifles over one shoulder, a box of provisions over the other. They made their way down a steep hill, following Amadia into the burned forest.

"This place was supposedly haunted once," Amadia said, gesturing to the charred trunks all about them. "The pirate queen burned it down and destroyed the evil spirits that lived here."

"Gran did this?" Maude said, looking about.

"You never mentioned your Gran was an arsonist as well as a pirate queen and Lilith cultist," Alter said. "Busy woman."

"Gran had hobbies," Maude replied, then she paused and stopped walking. "We're not alone." Both Daughters dropped their burdens and took up a defensive posture. Alter set down his box and readied one of his rifles. There was a noise in the ruined trees and then a screech. A kite fluttered down, lighted on the charred stub of a branch and regarded the three.

"*Iya?*" Amadia asked, looking about. A blur moved between the two women, knocking Maude against a hollow tree trunk and taking Amadia off her feet. Alter felt something like a silent hurricane wind rip the rifle from his grasp.

A woman now stood in the path ahead of them. She wore a brown and gray feathered cloak and a bone mask that looked like a bird's skull. She tossed Alter his rifle back, and shook her head disapprovingly.

"Sloppy, Amadia," the woman said. Her voice was like dry leaves blowing across spring grass. "Your posture was imperfect at the ninth thoracic vertebrae, and that made you vulnerable. Your friend's posture was somewhat better, but she lets her left arm droop too much, about half an inch, I'd say. Poor form for both of you, my *omobinrin,* my daughter. Certainly not fitting for the Oya."

The old woman removed her mask. Her face was brown and deeply lined, her hair gray wisps about her crown. Her brown eyes sparkled with life and humor. The old lady sniffed the air and tsked. "And you are smoking again, those foul cigars. It would be better if you just chewed on charcoal! What am I going to do with you?" She offered a hand up to Amadia, who took it. The two embraced. "Welcome home, my dear one. I've missed you."

"And I you, *Iya,*" Amadia said. The old lady turned and offered a hand to Maude, who took it and struggled back to her feet. "Tell me, daughter, who is your clumsy friend?"

Maude grinned. "I'm Maude, ma'am," she said. "Pleased to make your acquaintance. You must be Amadia's mother. I've heard a lot about you."

"We are distant relatives," the old woman said, "but she is my daughter, my *omobinrin,* in all the ways that such things matter. I am Raashida."

Raashida paused when she saw the old iron flask hanging about Maude's neck as she helped her to her feet. "You carry the Grail. You are Anne's student."

"Yes, ma'am," Maude said. "We were distant relatives as well, but she treated me like her own daughter."

"She was a very good pupil," Raashida said, "and a good friend. Even if her education was a bit . . . unorthodox."

"Iya," Amadia said, "we must reach Carcosa quickly. The summons to London I answered, it was Alexandria Poole, the latest in that line. She has convinced several of the other Daughters to undertake something terrible, and they have taken Maude's daughter . . ."

"Constance," Raashida said. "She told me her name. I have been having a dream for many nights now, of a young girl being led across the dunes, moving closer to Carcosa. You don't have much time."

"Is she all right?" Maude asked the old woman. Raashida nodded.

"She is not being mistreated, but she is afraid. She saw me in the dream."

"What?" Maude said. Alter had retrieved his rifle and joined the three women.

"She turned and talked to me in my dream," Raashida said. "She says she knows you are coming." She hesitated, as if there were more, but said nothing.

"Is that possible?" Alter asked. "Can one communicate through dreams?"

"Carcosa was the Father of Ill Dreams," Raashida said. "The city is built of his bones, so it exists in the Dreamlands as well as in many different physical worlds and times. Constance is connected to the city and it to her by the blood of Carcosa's sire that flows in her veins." Raashida looked at Cline. "Your bearer will slow you two down. He should remain behind."

"Bearer!" Cline snorted in indignation. "I'll have you know, madame, that I am no mere stevedore!"

"Not a bearer," Raashida said, nodding. "Bearers know when to shut up. Husband, perhaps? Which one of you two does he belong to? I hope not you, *omobinrin.*"

Maude and Amadia looked at Cline, and then at each other. "Not me," they both said in unison.

"Come," Raashida said. "A quick spot of food and we will prepare you for your journey." The three women walked away and Cline looked after them.

"Hey!" he shouted, and followed. "'Not mine,' that's a fine how-do-you-do!"

Raashida had prepared Amadia's favorite, a dish called *irio*. It was a conglomeration of mashed potatoes, peas, beans, corn and onion with spiced meat. Everyone ate eagerly after so many weeks of ship rations. Raashida beamed proudly as she watched her food being devoured with so much abandon.

"When Amadia was little and first came to me to train with me," Raashida said, "I would make her *irio* when she had had an especially difficult day of lessons. She used to sing a little song as I made it . . ."

"*Iya*, please!" Amadia said around a mouth full of food. Maude and Alter both laughed.

"Oh, now that you are the Oya and all grown up, you cannot have such things!" Raashida laughed, too, and clapped her wrinkled, veined hands. "Just remember, my darling one, the secret to staying young even when you are very, very old is to not take everything so damned seriously!"

Maude thought of Gran, laughing, acting like a child, chasing her down the beach, playing with the gulls. She thought of Isaiah fixing her a cup of Blood-Dragon tea in the kitchen.

"What?" Amadia said.

"Nothing," Maude said. "You have a very nice family."

"The journey is a week, due north in the deep desert," Raashida said, changing the subject. "You two, traveling light, should be able to make it in three days, perhaps two, if you are lucky and have kept up with your survival training."

"I want to go," Alter said. "I've come so far, and . . . I can keep up!"

"Alter," Maude said, "I understand, and I am sorry, but Raashida is right. You *would* slow us down, and it's a race now to save Constance." Cline looked down at his plate and sighed. He ran a hand through his tangle of now long, curly hair.

"You're right, of course. I don't want to hinder you, or be responsible for anything happening to Constance. I'll stay here . . . keep an eye on the ship."

Maude took his hand and gave it a squeeze. "There are very few men in this world who could do that, you know. You truly are remarkable, Alter Cline. Thank you."

Cline squeezed her hand back, and smiled a tight smile, but said nothing.

They waited for the blistering midday sun to begin to slip lower in the western sky. Cline watched as both women drank a seemingly endless amount of water, and then each took a few sealed canteens with more.

"Carcosa is partly of the Dreamlands," Raashida said, as the women gathered up their gear. "Time has very little meaning there and space bends like a tree in a storm. Keep your minds focused as you have been trained. The City of Monsters has driven travelers mad before." Each woman carried one of Cline's rifles with her now, slung over her back. Amadia also carried a pistol and a machete as well as a sharp knife. "Also," the former Oya said, "know that I have dreamed that both the Mother and the Father await the child within the city."

"You mean *the* Mother," Amadia said, looking at her teacher.

"And her former groom," Raashida replied.

"Typhon," Maude said. A tight bundle of ice shifted in Maude's stomach.

"But how can that be?" Amadia said. "The seals keep Typhon out of Carcosa."

"It was a dream," Raashida said. "Just be careful, and aware of all possibilities, all contingencies." She pinched Maude playfully on the arm. "that goes for you, too, pirate queen!"

"Yes, ma'am," Maude said.

Raashida hugged her adopted daughter.

"Le rẹ irin ajo yorisi o si ohun ti o nilo," the old woman said. "You are Oya, you walk between the orishas and man, and you carry light into all the darkest places. Go, my daughter, and know you carry all my love with you as well."

Alter tried to help Maude adjust her pack and the water bottles. "If you're not back in a few weeks," he said, "I'm coming looking for you, the old lady be damned!"

Maude smiled. "Stay on the old lady's good side, I'm pretty sure she can still thrash all of us!" She ran her hand over his bearded cheek. "Thank you, Alter. You have been a true friend. I'm very thankful for you."

"You as well," Cline said, taking her wrist and moving her hand from his face. His fingers slipped between hers, holding her hand. "I mean . . . talk about ripping good print! You'll make me rich, 'pirate queen'! Now I just need the ending, so hurry back to tell me. I've got publishers lined up!"

They both laughed, perhaps a little nervously, and looked into each other's eyes. They seemed closer than either of them had intended to be. "I'll endeavor to . . . not keep you waiting too long," Maude said.

"Don't," he said, "please . . ." Alter gave her hand a final squeeze, and then reluctantly let her go. He took a step back, a smile quickly fastened back onto his face. "You know how impatient I can be, deadlines and all."

Maude smiled, and then looked to Amadia. "Ready?" The latest Oya waved good-bye to her mother and new friend. "I love you, *Iya*! Cline, do not try your charm on *her*!"

"Perhaps I'll try mine on him," Raashida said with a near-toothless grin, slapping Alter on his rump. The reporter jumped a bit.

"Hurry back," Cline said, rubbing his bottom.

"We will see you shortly." Amadia looked to Maude. "Let's go!"

The two women began to walk north. The old woman and the young man stood and watched them go. In no time at all they were tiny specks on the horizon, and then they were gone. Cline noticed something in his shirt pocket. It was an envelope, sealed with a blob of red wax. On the front of the letter, in Maude's handwriting, it said, *"Alter, please deliver this to Golgotha if I don't make it back."* Alter looked at the envelope and held it and continued to look to the vastness of the desert.

"Her heart belongs to another," the old woman said, "but you are there as well."

"I know," Cline said, slipping the letter carefully back into his pocket, "I know."

32

Judgment

Sahara Desert, North Africa
November 15, 1721

Carcosa squatted in the wasteland, a tumor of knotted thought and fear, the thing that drives you, thwarts you, in the deepest precincts of dreams. The desert had given up its dead for the night. The sandstorm Anne and Raashida had endured that day had uncovered parts of the antediluvian city. The high bone walls drank in the moonlight. A single looming tower that looked as if it had been made from a monstrous spinal column jutted above the line of the city wall. Strange lights, like aurora, and warbling sounds, like the wind off the desert moaning at different speeds, different tones, stretched out and compressed, crossed the dunes outside the massive jaw-like gateway to the city's shadowed and distorted interior.

"Merciful Heaven," Anne muttered. "It's . . . I can't even . . . The damn thing is making my eyes ache, Raashida."

"Yes," the old woman said. "It affects everyone differently. In time, I can teach you mental exercises that will help you. In the meantime, try to focus on small details, and if you get the urge to hurt yourself, tell me."

They made their way down one of the large dunes. It was bitterly cold in the desert at night. The cold burned Anne's sunbaked skin, but looking at the City of Monsters with her own eyes made her feel colder still.

The trip here had been a literal week of hell, at least for Anne. The endless Sahara seemed only to exist to drive one mad, or simply to kill. If not for Raashida's constant help, Anne would be dead now, her bones picked clean of meat by predators and bleaching in the baleful sun. It seemed that the old woman needed only a sip of water and a few crumbs of food to operate out here. Anne asked her the secret and Raashida's reply was, "Your mind controls your body, not the other way around."

They stood at the yawning gateway to the bone city. Raashida looked about the desert wastes. "This was a great veldt," she said. "A grassland. The city was originally built beside Lake Hali, all gone now, devoured by ravenous time."

Anne wished again they had brought weapons, but Raashida had told her they were useless here. "The only things that steel could hurt here turned to dust eons ago," she said. "Tell me more about this voice you heard in your mind talking to you, telling you to come here?"

"Aye," Anne said. "It was a woman, older sounding, and in dire need of help. It wasn't the voice from my visions—that always sounded like you."

"We've shared those dreams and visions," Raashida said. "In my version of them, I always heard your voice speaking."

"Whoever this is, I heard her clear as fair winds and following seas," Anne said. "Her voice began almost as soon as you recited that oath to me."

"The oath?" Raashida said. "Lilith's Load?"

"Aye," Anne said nodding. "She knew my name. She was calling me to Carcosa, saying she needed me, needed my help. That all was lost unless I came. It seemed a familiar voice, but not one I can recall ever hearing."

"All right, we go in," Raashida said, "but just remember, there were forces unleashed on this plain so long ago, and those forces left a wound upon the world here. Cause and effect, time and distance, mind and self, dream and reality, they are all broken and scattered in this place. Question everything, trust nothing."

They walked through the mouth of the gate and disappeared into the throat of Carcosa. The streets were paved with skulls and mortar. Tiny whirlwinds of desert dust spun about the empty maze-like streets.

Looking up at the slivers of sky that could be seen in between the walls and battlements, Anne noticed stars burning with green and red fire, and did not recognize any of the familiar constellations she knew from sailing the Earth's seas. She looked over to comment to Raashida and a young woman Anne's age stood where the old woman had stood, wearing the old woman's cloak, and the bird-skull mask hung at her hip. Her skin was flaw-less and brown, her eyes the same as the old Oya's.

"It has us now," the young Raashida said. Anne tried to talk but Raa-shida was gone. Anne heard sounds of struggle, fighting. She ran toward them.

Anne heard sounds of struggle . . . she ran toward th . . .

Anne heard sounds of stru . . .

. . . Anne stood, dizzy from déjà vu, at the edge of a well. The sounds were coming from within. She knelt and looked below; there was sunlight now. It was day in the city, somehow. Her brain began to try to make sense of that, but she told it to shut up. Concentrating, she tried as hard as she could to just exist in this present moment.

Below, at the bottom of the well, three oddly dressed men fought in a large dome-like room. An altar of skulls and stag antlers, a twisted sculp-ture of wood and vine and rotted yellow cloth lay before them. One man was gaunt, with a mustache and long, graying brown hair tied back in a pony-tail. The other man, aiding him, was shorter and a bit thick in the middle, with balding, graying blond hair. The two men contended against a third giant of a man, hairy and fat. He had a hunting knife buried in the gaunt man's stomach and was lifting him off the ground with one hand, and had a hammer raised high in his other, which the balding man was struggling to pry away from him. The three grunted and gasped as they tried to kill each other. The giant looked into the eyes of the gaunt man impaled on his knife and hissed, "Remove your mask . . ."

The city rumbled and a great horn blew. Anne's head snapped up and she looked around frantically. When she looked back at the well, it had vanished and she was staring into the empty grins of the mortared skulls embedded in the street. The street's surroundings had changed as well. Up ahead was a wide opening in the maze. There was the laughter of children and strange, haunting music. The street led to a courtyard, and old Raashida was now beside her again.

"Where did you get to?" the old woman said. "You looked like an old version of yourself and then you vanished."

"What's happening to us?" Anne said. The courtyard was empty; the childrens' laughter twisted to screams and then to a fading echo. The music came from a pipe organ the size of a large building that covered the far end of the courtyard. Desert dust blew out of pipes that were carved femur bones: thousands of them of different sizes, from infants' to gargantuan monstrosities. The keyboard and the musician playing the grisly instrument were hidden from view.

Raashida took Anne by the hands as the music began to grow in volume and bass. "Focus on the sound of the blood in your veins," she said. "The external can deceive you. Find a calm center within yourself, Anne. Make your body your universe, your reality. Center, breathe, listen to the sound of your heart, make it your guide."

Anne closed her eyes and tried to do what Raashida said. She felt the mandibles of the skulls under her feet moving, trying to nip at her feet, at the tendons in her heels. She tried to ignore them, even as they scraped at her boots, the way the rats on the ship used to grind their sharp yellow teeth against the leather. The same presence that had tugged at her awareness when Raashida had been telling her about the war and the aftermath manifested in her mind again. The mental presence felt strangely familiar. "This way!" she called out to the Oya. "Whoever it is, they want us to go this way."

They ran down a narrow sliver of an alley off from the courtyard; Anne led the way and the bone music pursued them. They had to turn sideways to move through the narrow passage. The street got narrower and tighter until it finally dead-ended. Anne looked up and saw a sliver of the sky. There was a bloodred, swollen sun—the kind you might see at sunset—hanging directly overhead at noonday. A wide grate, made of fibula bones that had obviously been gnawed on for a very long time by something, was at her and Raashida's feet.

Anne knelt by it, wiped the sweat from her face with a rag, and felt cool air filtering up from the darkness below. The alien music had faded. "This way," Anne said and began to pull on the grate. Anne's mind flashed back to the storm drain grate when she had escaped the Marshalsea Prison on Port Royal. Perhaps she had died in childbirth, in that damp drain? Perhaps she was in Hell now. No. Even if she was in Hell, she would find a way out. There was always a way out, and through. Anne pulled and the grate broke with a sick hollow snap, and a draught of cool air greeted her efforts. Raashida uncoiled the rope she had brought with her and began to tie it about Anne's waist.

"I could climb down as long as there is a wall," the Oya said, "but you don't have that skill just yet. I'll lower you down as far as the rope goes. If you reach bottom, I'll secure it up here as best I can and follow you down."

Anne tugged the rope at her waist and noticed the knot the old lady had used was one she had never seen in all her years of sailing. "Aye," she said.

"You sure you want to go down there?" Raashida said. "The only things below are the vaults. The legends and tales passed along from the first days all say no one has ever gone below and come back."

"What are the vaults?"

"Prisons," Raashida said. "Many of the monstrous children of Typhon were locked away in special crypts, sealed with powerful *Bo* to keep them from escaping. Their names still hold power for those who traffic in sorcery. A special seal was placed upon the cornerstone of Carcosa by the Mother herself before she vanished. It keeps Typhon from entering the city and freeing his kin."

"Why didn't they just kill these things if they are so terrible?" Anne asked as she sat at the edge of the open grate and swung her legs over into the darkness. "Why lock them up?"

"They tried to kill them," Raashida said. "They cannot die."

"This bedtime story just gets better and better," Anne said. "Right, then, I'm off. You ready?" The pirate queen pulled a sharp-bladed dirk from her boot and began to hold it in her mouth.

"I thought I told you weapons were no good here," the Oya said. Anne paused in biting down on the blade to reply.

"You did. I warned you I don't listen."

The old woman shook her head as she anchored the rope firmly in the crook of her arm.

"Go," she said, handing Anne an unlit torch she had prepared.

Anne pushed off and dropped a few feet into the utter darkness. Her stomach lurched, then the rope caught. She lit the torch and saw she was in the middle of a deep well made of rib cages. Beyond the ribs was only darkness her light could not pierce. She took the blade from her mouth long enough to call up.

"I'm steady," she shouted up into the light of the bloated red sun. "Lower away." Slowly, she began to descend. It was impossible to gauge time, so she focused on the torch as it burned. It was a quarter burned when the rope stopped lowering her.

"End of the rope!" Raashida shouted. Her voice was tiny and distant, smothered by the darkness. Anne removed the knife again from her mouth.

"Aye!" she shouted up. "I'm dropping the torch!" The torch fell what seemed ten or fifteen feet and then struck and sparked against a floor that looked like it might be sand. "Bottom!" Anne called up. "Not much farther, I'm going to drop!"

"Wait! No!" Raashida called. "Distances lie here, girl, remember! Don't!"

"She's close and she needs me!" Anne shouted, clutching the knife tightly. "I can feel her! She's calling to me right now! I want to see who she is! I'm going!" Anne cut the rope and plummeted into the darkness toward the guttering light. She fell long enough to feel fear mingle with the nausea of acceleration in her stomach before she hit the sand, hard. Anne tried to tumble as she felt the sharp pain in her ankles, but instead she just landed on her face. She came up, swearing, and gingerly stood. Her ankles weren't broken, but they hurt like hell. She looked up to call to Raashida to climb down, but there was no hole in the ceiling; the well was no longer there.

"Tupped," Anne said softly to herself, "all your bloody tombstone needs to say."

She dusted herself off, and that was when she made the revelation that the floor was not just covered with sand but with a fine bone dust as well; it was the same composition as had been in the box with the map. She rubbed the ashy concoction off on her breeches, picked up the dagger, and retrieved the torch from the ground. This place was circular, like an arena, with high, curved walls. Anne had an impression suddenly that each of the enormous walls was actually a rib. The center of the arena was open to the sky, a vast, yawning hole you could glimpse the sky through, and through it, Anne could see that it was once again night. The moon and the stars seemed familiar to Anne. She was alone, as far as she could tell. She turned to take in the rest of the arena, with the torch fluttering in the cold, whistling wind, and saw something at the dead center of the arena.

It was a statue, about twenty-five feet tall, on a ten-foot pedestal of thick, solid, yellowed bone, perhaps some gargantuan vertebrae, hacked and carved into the shape of a cube. Anne was behind it, but she thought she already knew the statue's face. She walked toward the statue, arcing so as to come to the front of it. The moonlight glistened and reflected off its metal surface, seeming to pool and flow like some ethereal liquid. Anne faced the statue, and its visage was the same as in her dream when she and Jack had first found the box: a woman's face, the details vague but with eyes that seemed to look through you, cut from midnight opals, with irises of crimson ruby. The statue was made of gold and ivory, with diamonds, emeralds and sapphires of every imaginable size, shape and color adorning the figure's female form. The moonlight playing over the face made it almost seem to move, to look down on Anne, as if judging her with the burning eyes of a night goddess.

As Anne moved closer to the statue, her mind did the calculations. Just the jewels alone were enough to buy kingdoms several times over. The gold and the ivory were incalculable in value. She stood near the bone base and felt something crunch beneath her boots, buried under the dust and sand surrounding the base of the statue. Anne knelt and thrust her hand under the accumulation of time, and pulled up a hand full of small, perfect rubies, hundreds in just this handful. Anne laughed and let them fall between her fingers, like the sand. Rooting around in the sand, she found thousands of similar rubies, each roughly the size and shape of a pea; they seemed to cover much of the floor of the arena, under the dust and debris. They were exactly like the small ruby that was linked to the map in the box that had led her to Carcosa.

While there was an eerie feeling of life to the statue, Anne didn't feel the mental presence that had led her here. She wished Raashida was with her now.

"Well, if you're Lilith, how about giving a lass a hand then, eh?" Anne said to the giant golden figure bathed in moonlight. Her voice echoed across the empty arena, the ancient air disturbed by the sound. Nothing happened. Anne circled the statue, the dwindling torch in one hand and a handful of the tiny rubies in the other. Anne paused. She heard a very faint noise. It sounded like glass against glass, a tiny "tink" sound.

Anne moved toward the front of the statue and again stood close to the bone base. As she knelt, examining the large featureless wall at the foot of the statue, a tiny crimson bead fell, bounced off the base with a faint "click" and landed near Anne's feet, among the other rubies, dust and sand. Anne looked up at the statue and dropped the rubies and the torch. She tucked her knife back in her boot, got a running start and then jumped. Her fingers hooked on the edge of the bone base, but began to slip; the surface was as smooth as polished marble. Her fingers found a small worn crack and she hung on as her feet sought traction. Anne managed to struggle to the top of the bone cube and reach the feet of the golden statue.

Looking out at the vast floor, she saw the moonlight catching flashes of the tiny rubies partly exposed under the sand and dust, all the way to the walls in every direction. The moon seemed brighter now, as if had become full in the span of minutes. She also thought she caught sight of several large circular patterns in the floor of the room, equidistantly spaced about the arena. Whatever the patterns were, she spotted a metallic shimmer off of them in the bright moonlight.

As she stood there, trying to figure out what the large circular divots might be, another tiny ruby dropped from above and bounced off the base to the floor of the arena. Anne rapped on the golden leg of the statue and it made a dull hollow sound. She looked up toward the face of the golden woman.

"What the hell are those?" she whispered to the statue. "Let's see."

Climbing the actual statue was much easier; there were hand and foot holds everywhere and all of them worth a king's ransom. Anne was at the arms when she heard another "plink" below as yet another tiny ruby fell from above her, bounced and joined the others, some thirty feet below. Anne was fairly certain where the ruby had fallen from. She planted her boot in the swell of the statue's breasts and climbed the final five feet until she was face to face with Lilith. A cold wind caressed Anne as she looked into the near-featureless face of the first woman. The gold of the face was polished to a near-mirror shine, and as Anne saw her own reflection in the face of the goddess, she recalled the vision of the hall of masks and the mirror. The black opals of the eyes gazed into Anne's own, almost hypnotically. The crimson of the rubies at the center of the dark wells glowed with a secret power, a hidden knowledge she was trying to etch onto Anne's very soul.

"*You are as I was.*" The voice was Anne's own speaking inside her head, but the words seemed to come from somewhere outside of herself. "*Let no one, no power, take you away from you.*" A single dark red tear formed at the inner edge of the left eye of the statue. It was wet. It looked like a drop of blood. Anne watched as it grew fat, swelled, and fell from the goddess's eye. By the time it hit the base of the statue, it was a tiny crimson ruby. It bounced off the base and joined the thousands—tens of thousands? million?—of others below, a sea of frozen tears. "*You carry creation within you. You created the world, you can change it.*"

Anne leaned in closer to the face, her face, her reflection.

"It was you," Anne whispered. "You were the kite, you were the one speaking to Raashida and to me, in our dreams, our visions. It was you." She saw the look of certainty in her own eyes, and she knew, no matter the cost, no matter the consequences, that she was doing this because she would regret it the rest of her life if she didn't. A new tear welled at the goddess's eye, and Anne kissed the statue, tasted the cold, smooth gold and the bright metallic bite of the single perfect drop of blood as it lost its tension against her tongue. It was burning her tongue like a hot ember of sensation— pleasure and pain, so close as to be the same thing. She felt it scald its way down her throat; she had swallowed a burning crimson star. The fire diffused at her core, sending searing light along every vein, every artery, every nerve. The fiery brilliance filled every crease in her brain. Millions of voices were all talking at once, so loud, so much to understand, to know, to be.

At the core of the radiant burning that was unmaking her, renewing her, Anne told herself, with immutable certainty, *"Yes, you can do all this, you can be all this. You have it within, and no one can take it from you, no one but you."* The blood was a crimson thread burning through Anne. Her eyes saw each of the tiny beads of Lilith's blood upon the floor of the arena, connected to the glowing ruby thread, a constellation in scarlet. She could sense Raashida far away, across space and worlds, searching for her, and another, older Raashida, talking with a handsome young man, suddenly feeling her regard across the ocean of time. She heard the voice calling again. The older woman's voice calling for her help. The threads moved and tangled across the arena as Carcosa lurched and bucked like a clumsy, angry animal, shifting spaces and folding time. Anne reached out for the woman, took hold of her end of the red thread and pulled herself toward the presence calling out to her desperately, as reality shattered like mirrored glass the color of rose.

33

The Magician (Reversed)

Somewhere in the Sahara Desert, North Africa
July 21, 1871

Inna Barkov led her party through the silent skull-paved streets of Carcosa. In her hand, she carried her spear, a great shaft of darkly stained oak with a wide silver tip shaped like a stylized leaf. The spear was old and had been given to her by her mentor, Roksana, a Daughter of Lilith who had been a member of the ancient order of the Polinitzi, ancient female warriors of a fearsome reputation.

Her fellow Daughters, Itzel and Ya, followed her. Itzel, the lithe Guatemalan Daughter, carried her *macuahuitl*, an Aztec wooden club-sword lined with blades of razor-sharp obsidian. Itzel carried it casually over one shoulder, and Inna had to resist the urge to point out that the weapon was almost as big as she was. Ya carried no weapons, save a few narrow, shingle-like throwing blades for range, but the Chinese Daughter was imminently confident that her martial training was all she needed. Ya was an arrogant bitch, and part of Inna wished that she could put Ya's ego to the test herself.

The two younger girls, Inna's daughter, Lesya, and their captive, Constance Stapleton, followed close behind. Lesya was armed with the *nosh*, an ornate hunting knife, which Inna had given to her as a birthday present a few years back. Constance had no weapons, of course, but the girl had proven more than capable of defending herself over the past month with just her training. Inna was impressed by how the girl carried herself, especially knowing what was in store for her.

The sandstorm that hounded them for days had finally broken in the early evening and had uncovered much of the unearthly city for the pilgrims. Inna was unsure if the storm was finished with them, or if this was merely a lull. Itzel had said something about the earth not wanting Carcosa upon its surface. How she knew such things Inna did not wish to dwell upon. Itzel no longer carried her "pets" with her—the butterflies and hummingbirds she had trained and commanded using her weird talents. Neither creature would have survived the trek through the Sahara. Inna was thankful in a way. The little *bruja* unnerved her already without her command of the creatures, almost seeming to be able to listen to the thoughts of others. Itzel had begun feeling ill as soon as they had crested the dunes of the deep desert and seen the great luminous bone walls of the city glowing in the moonlight.

"This place is unstuck in time," Itzel had said, wiping the vomit from her lips with the back of her hand. "It is an affront to the very space about it. So much death here, and there are . . . things trapped inside that must never get free." They had approached the city like phantoms on the chill night wind, invisible, silent as they crept through the great jaw of a gate. Around the Daughters, temporal shades of past and future swirled, faded, distances melted and stretched. Only Constance seemed unaffected by the phenomena, though once she did speak to someone none of the others could see.

Inna led them toward the location Alexandria had told them was the place for the sacrifice. Alexandria had said that if one focused on specific landmarks, those would never change; even as the very universe seemed to slip and crumple about you, you could navigate the city of bone as long as you found a common anchor and held it in your mind. Alexandria had told them to focus on finding the tablets and that those would lead them to the Well of the Mother.

The trip across the upper Sahara had not been an easy one, even with their training. They had been dogged by the violent sandstorms, as if the desert itself were trying to stop them, and there had been a short, and brutal, encounter with Ottoman bandits after they had docked at Tripoli and gotten underway into the northern desert.

Their captive, Constance, had been cooperative and even helpful in a few spots, fighting alongside them against the bandits, and helping with all the day-to-day struggles to simply survive in this hellish landscape. Inna liked the girl, and that made her hate what was coming even more. Lesya and Constance had become nearly inseparable during the voyage from America to London and then on to Africa. Constance was a good girl, and a good friend to her daughter.

Inna had tried to figure if there was any other way out of this horrible mess, but she was no occultist, no expert on witchcraft or prophecy. She had always been content to let the Mother's mysteries remain mysteries. You did not need to know how the sun or the moon rose to be in wonder of them. Alexandria's explanation of the prophecy seemed to make perfect sense, but it made Inna's soul sick.

The longer and further away from Alexandria's reasoned arguments, the more the Russian began to doubt them. The narrow, spiraling staircase was made of giant teeth, filed and sanded smooth. It led down to a cavernous opening, the orbit of some giant skull, perhaps. The raging forces that tore apart cause and effect in this city seemed to give them a temporary reprieve as they reached the bottom of the stairs. There was desert sand everywhere, as the wasteland tried to reclaim its grip on this blasphemous place. The group silently entered the cave. There was a pile of stone tablets, most partly broken, others little more than piles of rubble. Inna recognized the landmark. All the tablets prominently displayed the looped cross, the ankh, like the tablet Alexandria had in the chapter house in London.

"This way," Inna said, "it's this way." She looked at Constance and saw the fear flit behind the child's eyes. Constance took a deep breath, and the terror was put away. They continued on. A few yards past the tablets was a rectangular pit that dropped into darkness. Inna halted and began to unpack her rope and climbing equipment. Ya prepared lanterns and oil. "Alexandria said it took her about fifty yards of rope to reach the bottom," Ya said.

"And yet the one who has been here before, the one who wishes this done, remains behind," Inna said, carefully arranging the coils of rope. Ya stopped her preparations and looked to the Russian.

"If you don't have the stomach for what has to be done, I will attend to it," Ya said. "We all have our roles to play in this war, and Alexandria's is to plan and lead. She will follow after if we do not succeed."

"That's reassuring," Inna said. "This is my command, my mission, and I will direct how it proceeds. Don't forget that . . . sister."

"Merely reminding you of your duty," Ya said, and went back to her task, ". . . sister."

Lesya and Constance worked together to put on and adjust the buckles and steel rings on their canvas rope harnesses.

"Are you all right?" Lesya asked. Constance nodded. "I won't let them hurt you," the young Russian said. "My mother will find another way."

Constance started to say something, but stopped herself. Tears filled her eyes. "All the dreams lead to here," she finally said. "This is the end, the last dream. Please, Lesya, be careful down there. Please. I'll be all right. Just you be as careful as you can be."

The descent in the dizzy darkness felt like it lasted for years, far longer than fifty yards of space. At the bottom they found themselves in a massive arena, walled in giant bones and open to the night sky, the floor of the room covered in sand and bone dust. At the center of the arena floor was a giant statue of gold, ivory and gems—a woman, her arms raised to the pregnant moon, whose light washed over the floor of the arena, giving everything a ghostly pall. The statue's head was lowered, as if she were regarding, or mourning something. The shaft had dropped them near the covered edge of one of the massive bone walls, facing the statue. The rope remained, dangling and secure. As the last of the party, Itzel dropped to the sand.

"This place . . ." the tiny Daughter uttered ". . . the terrible things locked here, this is the cage that holds them." Itzel crouched and pushed the sand and dust away, revealing shimmering tiny rubies, thousands of them, and as she dug beneath the gems, she came to a curve of silver, solid silver—the edges of a massive circular well cap, covered with tiny intricate etchings, spiraling inward to the center of the circle.

"It's . . . it's like the silver floor in the well room," Constance said. The others looked puzzled.

"You've seen this before?" Ya asked.

"In Golgotha," Constance said. "There was a room with a floor of solid silver and symbols like this all over it. It had a well in it. There was a . . . horrible thing . . . the first horrible thing . . . at the bottom of that well, trying to escape. My mother stopped it. She saved everyone."

"Constance is correct," Itzel said, her palm to the silver seal. "The things imprisoned under this must never be free. They are Typhon's children, the ones born of his maker's purest blood, and they know nothing of death or ending. They would kill . . . millions, drive millions more mad." Itzel looked up at Constance with a look of child-like horror on her face. "They . . . know you're here, Constance. They're . . . glad you're here. Something is wrong, my friends."

"Yes," Inna said. "Something must be wrong! We need to understand what's going on. Alexandria said nothing about these creatures being locked away here!"

"We must get the ritual under way," Ya said. "The sooner we renew the Grail and be gone from here, the better for all of us."

"Except Constance," Lesya said accusingly.

"Keep your child's tongue under control, Inna," Ya said. "Remember our goal, what's at stake."

The chamber rumbled, and Itzel gasped as if she had been stabbed. "The monsters, they are stirring, they sense us here and they are shaking the foundations of the city in their excitement to be free."

Ya took Constance by the arm and began to lead her toward the statue. Inna took the Chinese Daughter's wrist and stopped her. Ya released Constance. "Go over there with Lesya and Itzel," she told the American girl. Ya's cool gaze met Inna's fierce blue eyes. "Remove your hand from me now, Barkov. Don't you see what's happening? This place is affecting you, it's influencing Itzel. It's trying to confuse us and keep us from what we have to do. I am not your enemy, but I will not allow anyone to stop me from renewing the Grail. Let . . . go."

The foundation of the city trembled again. Itzel stood and shook off the repellent alien thoughts that had been leaking over into her own mind. "Inna, she may be correct," Itzel said, trying to step between the two. "We can trust very little of our senses here. We must be away soon, or Carcosa will devour us."

"I respect the girl too," Ya said to Inna. "She sees her destiny, knows her duty and faces it with honor. I will do what has to be done, and I swear upon the spirit of my master, Ng Mui Si Tai, that the child shall know no pain." Inna let go of Ya's wrist and all three of the Daughters of Lilith turned to Constance.

"Come, child," Ya said, even as the city shook again, "it is time."

Carcosa was tearing at itself like a wild animal. The Earth was rejecting the City of Monsters' very presence upon its surface. Maude and Amadia rushed through the winding tangle of narrow streets; they had managed to pick up the faint trail of the Daughter's party, but had lost it when the world began to shift and flow like melting wax.

Maude turned to Amadia. "Any ideas, from trying to translate those tablets, where Alexandria might have sent them to do this ritual?"

But the African Daughter was gone.

Maude turned to look for her and found herself in a different alley than where she had been a second before. The stars overhead were different than those of the Sahara.

She heard a tinny piano playing not too far away and she recognized the song; it was "Good-bye, Liza Jane." Maude took a few tentative steps toward the mouth of the alley. She heard the whinny of a horse and the clatter of a wagon behind it. Distant voices of men, laughing, coughing, sounded strangely familiar to her. Maude walked up to the street corner and immediately knew where she was. She was on Geary Street, a winding narrow street in the heart of Golgotha's Chinese community, known collectively, and derogatorily, as Johnny Town. There was a butcher shop on the right side of the corner with a row of decapitated and plucked ducks in the dark window, next to a slate sign with a row of Chinese *hanzi* that announced the shop was closed.

"Miss Stapleton," a familiar voice called out to her from her left, "what are you doing here?" The Chinese man was old with a snow white beard that fell to below his waist. He wore a silk brocade robe of brilliant emerald, and his eyes were dark like a moonless night. His name was Ch'eng Huang and he was the undisputed master of the notorious Green Ribbon Tong, and lord of Johnny Town.

"I'm . . . I'm not entirely sure," Maude said. "I was . . . someplace else, and now . . . I'm home." Maude realized she was still wearing Gran's blouse, breeches, boots and coat. She was dressed as a buccaneer on the high seas. She had a revolver at her hip and sword too. No one in Golgotha had ever seen her in anything but the garb of a matronly mother, widow and laundress. Huang seemed unsurprised. Maude couldn't recall ever seeing the man surprised by anything.

"I see," Huang said, "I am very aware of every inch of my little domain. I felt a very old door open and it appears you passed through it. I have to check on such matters; often what comes through is far less charming."

"I'm afraid you have me at a disadvantage, sir," Maude said.

"I doubt you are often disadvantaged, madame," he said. "Some of Golgotha's streets lead to faraway places, other cities, other worlds," Huang said. He closed his eyes and raised his head as if he were trying to hear a sound, or catch a scent. He cocked his head to the side. "Carcosa," he whispered. "Carcosa is a very dangerous place, Miss Stapleton," he said, his eyes still closed, "even for someone of your . . . talents."

"Constance is there," Maude said. "In terrible danger. I was trying to find her, but I got separated from my friend, my guide."

"I have some . . . small experience with cities," Huang said. "Go back the way you came. Take the third left, and as you do so close your eyes and whisper your daughter's name. Make sure your next step is with your right foot. That may help you."

"Thank you," Maude said and paused. "Is everyone well?"

"As well as one can be in Golgotha," the old man said. "Some running about and shouting currently having to do with something called a Si-Te-Cah? Apparently some local legend about giant pale-skinned, red-haired cannibal wild men, or some such."

"Again with the cannibals," Maude sighed.

"I'm confident Sheriff Highfather and his deputies will have the situation well in hand by the time you return," Huang said with a slit of a smile. "I wish you luck with your daughter, *huān jù yī táng*."

"*Xièxiè*," Maude replied and bowed.

The old man slipped one hand from the folds of his sleeve. He held one of the tong's hatchets, with a green ribbon fastened to the base of the handle. Huang held the weapon close to his face and whispered something to it, "*Zhēnzhèng de fēi bìng shā sǐ rènhé dírén.*" He offered it to Maude. "To help you on your journey."

She took the hatchet and noticed that now a line of *hanzi* flowed down the green ribbon. Maude cocked an eyebrow.

"A prayer for your victory," Huang said. "Best to be on your way, the doors are closing, things are in motion."

"Again, thank you," Maude said, slipping the hatchet in the back of her belt. Ch'eng Huang bowed. She turned and raced off the way she had come.

"*Cháng'é kěnéng huì yǐndǎo nǐ, tā de chuán, yuèliàng,* Daughter," Huang said to the empty alleyway.

Maude saw Constance in her mind, laughing as they sat on a blanket after a long day of training in the desert outside Golgotha. She whispered her daughter's name and took a step with her right foot, eyes closed. She felt something loose, like gravel, crunch under her boots. She opened her eyes and was in a vast arena, beneath the baleful eye of the full moon. Under her feet was sand and a fine gritty dust and tiny rubies, flashing in the moonlight. Ahead of her was a large statue of a woman made of gold and precious stones. Something about the statue seemed very familiar to her, and its jeweled stare seemed alive, accusing.

About fifty yards away was Constance. She lay on a large silver disc covered in tiny symbols, a raised part of the center of the floor of the arena that had been cleared away, directly before the statue's gaze. Maude instantly knew what the silver circle was. Kneeling beside Constance, holding up one of the girl's arms, was a Chinese woman dressed in black loose-fitting pants and a collarless tunic with brocade white buttons—the same simple garb many of the Chinese in Golgotha wore. She held a bloody knife over Constance.

"Get away from her," Maude shouted, "now!" The woman lowered Constance's arm gently, palm down onto the silver seal, and as she did so, Maude could see dark blood pouring from the long vertical slit in her daughter's arm. The woman reached for Constance's other arm.

"Please," Ya said, "do not interfere, this must be done. I am truly sorry for your loss. When it is done, you may slay me if you feel that is appropriate, I will put up no defense, but the Grail must be renewed."

The city shivered and the air in the arena wavered and distorted as the damned city's reality battled with the world outside.

"Constance is not the Grail," Maude shouted out. "The prophecy is not as Alexandria said. You won't save the Daughters by doing this, you may be damning us all instead!"

Maude drew Gran's machete and ran toward Constance and her accoster. She shifted the blood within her, her breath fueling the changes to her nerves, her senses, making them inhuman in their clarity, their reaction. "You've all been lied to," Maude said. "Last time I say it: get away from her."

"Mother," Constance muttered, her words slurring as the blood emptied from her and she felt herself slipping deeper into sleep, even as time and distance churned all around them, "no." She tried to turn her head to look at the golden statue, but it was too much effort. "She doesn't understand," Constance mumbled to the golden woman.

Ya ignored the girl's mumbling as she passed out. She took the knife and lowered it to open the vein in Constance's other arm. There was a boom and an angry whine as the knife was shot from her hand, tumbling and disappearing into the sand. Ya rubbed her hand, glaring, and scanned about for the sniper. Three dark shapes flew from her hand at dizzying speed and force. They disappeared into the darkness. There was a distant clatter.

"Nice try," Amadia's voice called out, echoing throughout the arena. "But you're getting slow in your old age, Ya."

Maude was almost to Constance and Ya when the others made their move. The distortion in the air, crashing throughout the chamber, made it harder to detect them coming. The bigger one, the blonde named Inna, was to her front, blocking her path to Constance. The smaller one, the girl who had controlled the butterflies in Charleston, was to Maude's back. Maude drew Gran's sword.

Inna spun the heavy spear, twirling it like a pinwheel, the silver point flashing in the moonlight, seemingly everywhere. "Stapleton," Inna said, "I know this is difficult but it must be done. There is no other way."

"You crippled my father and stole my daughter," Maude said. "This isn't difficult at all."

Maude swung her machete high and Inna parried the blade with the silver tip of the spear. Maude snapped out a kick as the two weapons locked in parry and caught Inna in the side. The Russian grunted and advanced with a lunge from the spear. Maude parried and drove the spear aside, creating an opening for her to throw an uppercut. Inna was ready for it, though, and side-stepped the punch, driving an elbow into Maude's chin and sending her back a few steps.

Inna advanced, the spear spinning again, a blurring wheel before her. Maude's eyes flickered between the spinning staff and the placement of Inna's feet, waiting. Maude's free hand shot out with a half-fist punch and the staff snapped in two with a crack. Inna reacted instantly, just as Maude would have, twirling and catching the two pieces of the staff, wielding them as fighting sticks, one in each hand. Maude's follow-up swing, low with the machete at Inna's stomach, was parried, barely, by one of the pieces of broken staff.

From behind her, Maude felt the air pressure coming at her lower spine like a freight train. There was nowhere to go but up, and perhaps not enough time. She jumped straight up, and twisted behind Itzel, at the arc of the jump, even as the diminutive Daughter's nerve strike grazed Maude's back as she flew up and over. Maude felt pressure and fire run along her spine, but she had managed to avoid the worst of it.

Maude dropped behind Itzel, but one of her legs, slightly numbed by the nerve attack, almost gave out and she slipped. That lost second was what Maude had planned to use to counterattack, but it was gone. Itzel was a frenetic blur. She spun with a snarl, and gestured at Maude. A swarm of jagged, razor sharp obsidian pieces, torn from Itzel's necklace, thrummed toward Maude's face.

Maude leaned back at the waist, feeling the damaged nerves protesting, and flashed a reaping knife-hand at Itzel's thigh as the throwing stones passed less than an inch from her face. Maude's chop connected and Itzel staggered back, bracing with her other leg to avoid falling. At the same instant that Maude's blow connected with Itzel, Inna swept Maude's slightly numb leg, and Maude, already bent backward to avoid the knives, felt pain blossom out of the tingling numbness and felt gravity grabbing her and smashing her to the ground on her back.

"Stay down," Inna said to Maude, raising her foot to crush her if she tried to move. Maude noticed the tiny rubies beside her. The recognition was almost instantaneous—the floor was covered with the same blood stones as had been hidden in the back of Gran's African tablet at Grande Folly. The same as the blood stone that she had taken with the hallucinogenic drug. She looked up at the Russian standing threateningly over her.

"There is a way to renew the Grail here, Inna! Please, listen to me!"

The Russian shook her head. "This place is playing with your mind, Stapleton," Inna said. "There is no other way. I understand your loss, but . . ."

"Do you?" Maude asked. "What if it was your child, Inna?" Maude said. "Your girl? According to Amadia, you lost your mind when my father shot her, nearly killed him. What would you be doing if she was the one lying up there, bleeding out for the goddamned greater good?" Inna paused, and it was all the opening Maude needed. Maude spun to sweep Inna's leg, to use her fall to pull herself up to her feet. She never made it that far. Itzel drove her foot down in a powerful heel-strike at Maude's face. Maude snapped backward, stuporous, from the force of the kick.

"It must be done," Itzel said. Inna was not sure if she was speaking to Maude, to her, or to herself.

Ya had vanished into the shadows, and Amadia was carefully trying to move closer to Maude and Constance without being detected. The African Daughter had made her way down off the wall and was edging along the fringes of the arena. The city was shaking again, and the very air inside the arena boiled and warped as actuality was challenged.

A shadow tore itself loose and Ya drove a series of shattering flying kicks at Amadia's face. Amadia countered each one and grabbed Ya's leg, swinging her into the bone wall of the arena as Ya connected with a clumsy but effective kick to the side of Amadia's head. Both Daughters fell to the ground.

"You may as well stop," Ya said, struggling to her feet, "The girl is doing her part . . ."

"You mean dying, don't you?" Amadia got up and rubbed her swollen jaw.

"She is sacrificing herself with honor and dignity," Ya said. "I understand Stapleton being irrational about it, but you, you simply wish to spread more chaos and disorder. You rebel for the sake of rebellion, Oya." Ya slipped into a *Ma Bu* stance. "What a poor teacher Raashida was to you, to never teach you of service or honor."

Amadia took a *Xu Bu* stance, with her hand extended for a leopard paw strike. "And you, Leng Ya, were always taught to be the good, obedient pupil, to never question authority, to follow it blindly, like a good lapdog, to preserve order and harmony, even when it was the order of a tyrant, and the harmony of slavery. That's probably why it's so easy for Alexandria to manipulate your mind and send you off to murder a child for a non-existent ritual!"

"You lie!" Ya almost shouted, her eyes darkening. "You ruin everything, question everything. You are smug in your moral superiority. You'd make an awful soldier and you'd get those under your command killed. You have already demonstrated as much to me! I will enjoy breaking your bones, and leaving you here to die for your ignorance!"

"So much for honor and duty," Amadia said. "Come at me. Let me introduce you to what my *iya* taught me."

The two Daughters launched at each other, screaming in rage. Thoughts of stopping or completing the ritual were lost. The two struck each other again and again, as the city teetered and shook around them; the leopard and the crane, tearing, savagely striking, clawing, leaping, tumbling. Ya and Amadia warred while time and space burned about them.

Lesya knelt beside Constance and stroked her cheek. The girl's blood ran over the silver of the capstone and began to pool. Constance's eyes fluttered open. It was so hard to stay awake. "I'm sorry . . . everyone is fighting," Constance said to her friend. "I really do understand what she is trying to do. She . . . she told me in my dream, when he's been too preoccupied and couldn't hear what she was whispering to me in my blood. This has to be, it's the only way to stop him. It had to be me. My blood was the only one that could open the seal . . ."

"Constance, try to stay awake!" Lesya shook her friend. "*I'll* get you some help!" Constance looked down at her lifeblood draining into the tiny scratches covering the silver well cap, then up to her friend. A sudden realization, like a person shocked to wakefulness and realizing they had overslept, came to Constance's face as the city buckled. A mournful wail began above and sand began to swirl in clouds in the open sky above them. A sandstorm was brewing, a big one.

"Lesya!" Constance struggled to sit up, grabbing her friend with her uncut arm. "I'm so sorry! You have to get out of here, you have to get out of here right now! Run!"

There was a metallic groan behind Lesya. The silver well cover began to slide to one side, the two girls on top of it. There was a whoosh of stale, ancient air as the well at the center of the room opened. On the silver disc, Constance's blood was pooling, moving counter to the laws of gravity and motion. The blood began to rise into a dark, wet column.

Maude became aware of her surroundings again, shaking off the effects of Itzel's kick. She was on her back, with Inna and Itzel still standing above her. She was fairly certain she could take one of the Daughters in a fair fight, but not both at once; they'd each had a lifetime of training and experiences to match her own. She became aware of the sounds of Amadia and Ya battling across the arena, and she heard the desert's scream as it protested Carcosa existing in its womb. Constance? Was she already dead, dying? Terrified? She cleared her mind and let her training take over.

"Stay down," Inna said to her. "Please, this is hard enough as it is."

Maude thought of trying to convince her, reason with her, but she didn't have the time. She knew, firsthand, how subtle and powerful Alexandria's manipulations could be. If not for the Record's help, she would be Alexandria's pawn as well. The thoughts came to her now that her head was cleared: *the Record, the blood stone. The Mother's blood, it was the only way.*

Maude groaned and closed one of her hands around a handful of the desert sand, bone dust and tiny rubies.

"Do not try to blind us with that," Itzel said. "I have no desire to hurt you again, Maude."

"I won't," Maude said, rising up a little. "It's not for you." She raised her hand to her mouth and stuffed as many of the rubies in as she could, ignoring the desert's sand and the dust of long dead warriors that came with it. The rubies were cold and hard in her mouth, like the one at Grande Folly had been; then they dissolved, melted and in their place was perfect scarlet pain, endless power infusing her, filling her with infinite voices, a crimson chorus that made one powerful, guiding voice. Her voice, the Mother.

This was far more blood than the tiny bead at Grande Folly that had introduced her to the Record, more blood than her drink from the now-empty flask, hanging about her neck. There was an intelligence within the blood, generations of intelligence, generations of Daughters, stretching back into the dim eons, stretching back to Her, to the one who knew the secrets of the beginning, all of the beginnings; the one who refused to bow, the outcast who defied all the myriad creators in their heavenly tyrannies. The first human to stand on her own.

The Mother's blood consumed Maude, as Maude had consumed it. She became the Record, she became the Mother. The awareness of what was coming was too horrible to contemplate. The plan made perfect sense, and in the grand scheme it must be done or the future of humanity, of all life everywhere, would be swept away into oblivion. But the tiny single light in the glowing constellation of the Record that was Maude Stapleton could not, would not let it be. The price was too high.

"No," Maude said.

"What?" Inna asked.

Everything was frozen except Maude. She flexed the slightest muscles in her legs, ankles and feet, her body and mind juggled formulas of mass and gravity, tension and friction, like an equation to be solved, to rise effortlessly to her feet, almost as if she were immune to gravity's will. Inna reacted a fraction of a second slower than Itzel, who began to swing her dread *macuahuitl,* her obsidian-bladed war club, toward Maude. Maude could see, through Itzel's eyes, exactly where she was aiming, and the intent behind the attack. Maude could read in her muscles where she would be moving to as she swung the club. Maude was Itzel in that second, Maude's muscles screamed to catch up with her senses, and the new blood within her gave them the fortitude to comply.

Maude was up. She grabbed the still-reacting Inna by the neck and applied exactly the proper pressure to render her unconscious instantly. She simultaneously wheeled a crescent kick into the spot where Itzel's body was going to move to avoid the kick Maude was launching. Itzel moved directly into Maude's kick, a look of stunned surprise frozen on her face the instant before it connected full-force. Itzel spilled backward twenty feet and lay unmoving. Inna crumpled at Maude's feet.

The distortions in reality, like angry, rising ocean waves, were getting worse as the sandstorm grew in fury. The Sahara and Carcosa were in battle and the wasteland was fighting to swallow the City of Monsters once again. Rivers of sand began to pour over the edges of the arena's wall.

Maude knew what was coming, knew the plan, but felt no reassurance in it. Lesya turned at the sound of her mother's gasp. "Don't you hurt her!" she screamed at Maude. Constance tried to reach for her friend, tried to explain.

"He's using the part of him, of his father, that's in my blood . . ." Constance whispered as she struggled and then collapsed.

The black column of Constance's undulating blood began to take on form and shape. It became a tall, lanky man in an old suit the color of blood, his too-long arms crossed across his chest, like a corpse in repose. Fingers with too many knuckle joints began to wiggle, as if his hands had fallen asleep. He stretched like someone loosening up their body after a long coach trip. One of his outstretched arms struck Lesya. The force of it made a grisly snapping sound when he connected with the girl's neck. Lesya's body flew back to the distant bone wall at the edge of the vast arena, where it landed with a wet thud and lay unmoving. Lesya's head lolled at an unnatural angle, her eyes open but empty.

"No!" Maude screamed.

Ya and Amadia, both bloody, bruised and battered, paused and looked over, through the swimming, swirling spatial distortions and the stinging rain of falling sand, to the tableau unfolding on the other side of the arena.

"Oh, no," Amadia said, "it's him."

"Who?" Ya said.

The pale, gaunt face of the man in the blood-colored suit looked up. The face was an ill-fitting mask of human flesh hiding something too big, too awful, to be confined to skin.

"It's so nice to finally be back in the old hometown," Typhon said.

34

The Fool

Maude felt the collective voice of the Mother, of the Record in her mind fracture into multiple voices, each with a different motivation and desire upon seeing Typhon here, in Carcosa, a city sealed to him and his creations.

The Father of Monsters looked up at the golden statue of Lilith. He raised his hands and tried to frame the statue with his too-long fingers and thumbs spread into an "L."

"Umm, no," Typhon said. "I just don't see the resemblance, Lilutu, and all that gold and jewelry, a bit tawdry if you ask me." He turned to Maude. "Thank you ever-so-much for saving your poor, dear Constance a few years back, Maude. By mixing our two bloods in her, you gave me a way to enter here, the most sacred of places . . . at least to your lot."

"The ritual . . . was a lie," Ya whispered. Typhon looked across the arena.

"Oh, yes," he said, "but based on some fact. The best lies always are. There is a ritual of blood sacrifice that this room was designed for, but apparently my ex-wife didn't bother to give too many details before she hid herself away." He pointed to the golden statue. "In there. A rather morbid and gaudy sarcophagus, in my opinion.

"The Mother is in there?" Amadia said. Typhon laughed. Inna was getting to her feet. She saw Lesya slumped at the far end of the arena, through the veil of desert sand raining down. She ran to her daughter's side.

"Oh yes, Amadia Ibori," Typhon said. "She knew I would never stop trying to free our children, knew I would keep the vow she forsook, to end this farcical joke of existence, to burn down order with chaos and leave pure emptiness in its place. So she wanted to stay close to her adopted children—you—Oya. You and all of the other misguided puppets that have followed in her path, fighting against oblivion, seeking to bring peace, justice and wisdom to a world that was not crafted to sustain any of that.

"So on the sacred nights, on the nights of the full moon, the black moon, the solstice, the equinox, or when someone with the potential to become a member of your futile little sisterhood makes their way into this chamber, 'the Mother'"—Typhon laughed, and it sounded like a knife blade on glass—"sheds a tear of her purest blood in the hopes that your order will endure the grindstone of history. That hope dies tonight. Thanks to all of you."

Inna held Lesya's lifeless body. She brushed the blond hair from her baby's dead eyes, brushed the gathering sand away from her face. She wanted to vomit, she wanted to scream and tear her skin off. The pain, the fury and the sadness were too large to be contained in a human heart. Her body, which she had spent a lifetime mastering, began to shake as it all rolled through her. She closed her daughter's eyes, kissed them and rocked her, gently singing the lullaby she had sung to her when she was a baby.

Streamers of sand was spilling over the arena walls now. The moon and the desert sky was obscured by the storm. Carcosa was being buried again. The city's foundations groaned under the Earth's assault.

Ya and Amadia had joined Maude. The sand from the storm was starting to fill the floor and the Daughters moved across it deftly. Maude knelt by Constance. Her breathing was erratic; she was almost blue from blood loss. For the briefest of seconds, they were back in the silver-floored room under Argent Mountain, but that had been two years ago. She tore the sleeve from her blouse and tied a tourniquet about the arm wound as best she could. The blood flow became a trickle.

The plan screamed in her mind; the fractious voices of the Record had unified again, spurred on by Typhon's words. Maude screamed out into the blood nebula, praying a silent prayer to the two people who had always been there for her, knowing neither of them could hear or help her. She kissed Constance and slipped several red rubies between her daughter's lips. "Remember how much I love you," she said. "I told you nothing would keep us apart."

Maude rose. Typhon had been watching them with what she could only assume was amusement. Inna joined them, her eyes hooded and dead, but dry. Itzel, her face a map of bruises, also stood with her sisters.

"Listen to me," Maude said, and her voice seemed to echo and she knew it was not her own voice but that of the Record as well. "Each of you, take the rubies, place them on your tongue. It is Lilith's blood in its purest form. It will give you strength for what we must all do. The Mother planed this before any of us were ever born. This open well is made to hold Typhon, to seal him within and never let him escape. We must drag him in and hold him until it is sealed, no matter the cost to us. If we fail, he will free his children tonight and tonight the world will suffer and bleed. They will go on to free Typhon's master, and then the world, all the worlds, will die."

Typhon began to walk toward the statue of the Mother, speaking as he walked. "You seek to grapple with death, little Lilutus? To stop that which first created the monsters that freeze your tiny humans' minds?" As he walked through the trembling distortions in reality, his form shifted with every other step to one of an incomprehensible bulk, vast like the graveyard between the stars, a shambling mass of writhing tentacles, gibbering fanged, drooling mouths and wet, gleaming chitin. "Your humans court oblivion," Typhon said, part of the sentence spoken through multiple mouths and part of it with but a single human-seeming orifice, "they long for it as much as they try to avoid it. This was a poorly conceived trap, my love, and now you, and your children, will truly meet your end."

"Tonight," Maude said, "we cannot fail."

"Stop a god?" Ya said. "Stop that? It's not possible, Stapleton."

Maude wanted to reply, but she remembered how helpless she had been trying to fight Typhon at Grande Folly. Even the Record was silent within her. The floor was rising, filling with desert sand, some of it was pushing its way into the empty well that had been created to hold the Father of Monsters, that would now just be part of a tomb, a monument to their failure. Typhon reached the bone base of the statue, his physical form fluttering, tattered at its edges, in excitement.

"Good-bye, my hated love," Typhon said.

There was laughter. Echoing across the arena, loud enough and strong enough to pierce the bellowing of the sandstorm, to rise above the shaking of the earth. It was almost . . . a cackle? Maude's eyes widened as she realized what she was hearing.

The figure dropped from the top of the statue, tumbled and landed on her feet, crouched like a cat. Anne Bonny stood between Typhon and the statue, young and in her prime.

"I got no truck with gods or monsters," Anne said, "and you, you're not even a real boggart, are you? Just some nonsense dreamed up by a real monster, hidin' in his hole. You're nothing."

The Father of Monsters swung with all his might. Maude anticipated the bone-powdering force of the impact on Gran's skinny, red-headed younger self. Anne caught Typhon's fist with a two-handed block, and locked her hands about his fist and forearm. Typhon's face tried its best to approximate surprise, and it melted a bit in the process.

Anne shifted sideways and threw Typhon's incalculable mass through the air as if he weighed nothing. He landed with a thud that shook the room, and desert sand sprayed everywhere. The assembled Daughters looked at Anne, dumbfounded.

"There is no power in this world," she said, and Maude heard the words echo in her memory, spoken long ago on a beach, "no man, no king, no god that can lay me low, except me," she said, "not tonight."

"Is that—?" Amadia asked Maude. Maude nodded.

"It is," Maude said, "as full of piss and vinegar as she ever was. Come on, let's go help her!" The other Daughters took the rubies. They placed handfuls in their mouths. They shuddered and gasped as the Mother's pure blood branded them in mind and spirit.

Maude picked up another ruby, opened the Grail and dropped the blood stone inside. The old iron flask became very warm, almost hot, then cooled, and when Maude shook it there was a sloshing sound inside. It was full again. She sealed the flask and laid it with Constance, who was no longer looking blue, but was actually flush now that she had been fed some of the rubies. Typhon was rising, anger rippling across his false face.

"You are all dead," he bellowed. "Dead, and then that bitch that birthed you!"

"Ah," Anne said, dusting off her hands, "so it goes from 'farewell, my love,' to 'die, you bitch.' Ain't that always the way?" Anne looked to the assembled Daughters, "Well, you waiting for a peggin' invite from the bloody king! Come on with ya! *Faugh a Ballagh!*"

Anne charged at Typhon from one side, Maude, Ya, Amadia, Inna and Itzel from the other. The Daughters charged through the biting, stinging clouds of sand. Typhon barely stopped the clumsy roundhouse punch Anne threw, but he was struck by a wall of violent attacks from the assembled Daughters on the other side. The combined fury staggered the Father of Monsters. How could this be? He was eternal, immutable. No mortal weapon could harm him, and yet he felt pain, and then Typhon felt fear.

"How can you be here now," Typhon demanded of Anne as he was knocked about by the rain of deadly attacks from the Daughters, "and younger than when you first dared to interfere with me?" Anne struck him another painful punch, as she ducked under his punch. "You and that Daemon, Biqua, you're the ones who sealed me beneath the earth where Golgotha now stands. Surely you remember, pirate queen?" Typhon swung again but Anne danced away from his clumsy punch and popped back in to drive an uppercut into his chin.

"Actually, I don't," Anne said, "but I drink a lot. I black out."

The arena was filling up near the walls with sand; the shaking of Carcosa did not stop now as the world began to slam the doors closed on all the other worlds aligned with the city.

The Daughters formed into a circle around Typhon, moving in seamless harmony, their minds as one in the ruby glow of the Record. The sandstorm tore at their flesh, its mournful howl drowning out the sounds of combat. It was if the world and the Daughters were striking against the abomination as one. Maude vaguely recalled how hitting Typhon before had been like hitting a mountain. Now it felt like hitting any other person, perhaps even less so. Typhon felt more insubstantial.

Inna drove a high knee into Typhon's chest and a downward punch to the side of his head with a shriek of pure fury which put him off balance. Ya followed up immediately with a propping ankle throw that sent him to the ground. Itzel drove her obsidian *macuahuitl* down to connect with Typhon's barely human face, and Amadia grabbed him by both ankles and hurled him with all her might into the yawning open pit of the central vault. Typhon shed his human guise, ripping it off like a torn coat, as he plummeted into the darkness, with a roar from a million inhuman mouths.

"Close it!" Maude shouted. Sand was already up to her ankles and rising quickly. Anne was beside her. They looked at each other.

"Nice outfit," Anne said. "Gone to raiding my knickers, have you?"

"Gran, is it really you?" Maude asked. Anne winked and cackled.

"That's a tough one," she said. "I know you, Maudie, but I don't exactly recall a lot of specific detail on the how I got here or where I was before. It was your voice, Maude, calling to me, your voice I heard telling me you needed me here in Carcosa to divert a disaster. Even though I'm dead here and you haven't been born yet there, I heard you calling for help and I had to come running, luv."

"I . . . I must have called out to you through the Record," Maude said. "Whatever the source of this providence is, I'm glad you're with us now!"

Barbed tentacles, covered with fanged, gaping maws, shot up from the darkness of the vault and latched onto the edges of the pit. They were the thickness of railroad ties, the color of blood mixed with bile. Below, in the darkness, Typhon released a roar of terrible rage. The Daughters fanned out, trying to climb atop the rising, shifting floor of sand, and to see through the storm that blinded and ripped at their eyes and throats. They scrambled to attack the monstrous appendages before Typhon could climb free.

"How do we close it?" Ya shouted. Maude moved as quickly as the whirl-wind would allow to the opposite side of the silver vault door. She knelt and focused all her preternatural strength on pushing the circular seal back onto place. It rumbled slowly and moved a few inches.

"We need more people to push!" she called, fighting to be heard over the storm, and to keep the grit from filling her mouth and nose.

"We can't, or else he'll get back out!" Amadia shouted to her from across the seal, where she was hacking a tentacle in two with an axe-hand maneu-ver, like she was chopping down a tree. Another tentacle snaked its way up out of the darkness to replace it and struck the African Daughter. She fell as another tentacle grabbed her ankle. Amadia chopped at the obscenity and sliced herself free, scrambling back and to her feet again, even as the rising sand was trying to bury her.

"Where's a bloody army of African Amazons when you need one," Anne said, suddenly beside Maude. "Give me that cutlass," she said, nodding toward the machete at Maude's belt. "It's mine anyway."

Maude stopped long enough to hand her the blade. "It won't help cut those damn tentacles any faster," she said. Anne looked at her sword. She saw the tell-tale traces of wear and age on the blade and the hilt, but it still felt perfect in her hand.

"God, this really is the future, ain't it?"

"Yes," Maude said, "I think. I'm honestly not sure how this all works. Time seems broken here. Anne, I know what the plan is or was. Constance was the bait to get Typhon here and then she was to be the Mother's vessel. Once they cut her and bled her Typhon would use his taint in her blood to manifest here physically. Lilith would then use the remainder of Constance's blood to manifest inside Constance, killing my little girl in the process. Lilith was supposed to hold Typhon in the vault until we could seal it. It didn't work that way, because I refused to go along, to let Constance be sacrificed, and now it . . . the Mother, wants me to go into the vault and hold Typhon down there. Something about the strength of our bloodline will help her channel through me. I have to go. I'm glad I got to see you again. Please make sure Constance is . . ."

Anne looked over to where Constance lay.

"Constance . . . that's your little girl, Maudie. Ah, she's a sight. A beauty, like her ma," Anne said.

"I actually noticed how much she looks like you," Maude said.

A strange look crossed Anne's face. The pirate queen looked at Constance again. "We got to take care of our snappers, don't we, Maudie? They don't ask for this world, any more than we did, and we're all they got."

"Aye," Maude said, with her best Irish brogue and grin. "Come on, help me get down in there now."

"I'm gonna go have a bit of a row with that beastie down below," Anne said. "Should buy you all the time you lot need." The smile dropped from Maude's face.

"Gran, Anne, you can't . . ."

"Oh," Anne said, "now you know I have to go, don't you?"

The Father of Monsters let out a cacophony of screaming, moaning, shrieking coming from countless alien mouths. The sound made Maude's bones shake. Ya reaped a mass of tentacles with the twin-hand scythe technique, but was driven back by a forest of limbs whipping her. She staggered against the rising sea of sand, but caught herself. Inna was a whirlwind of destruction, ripping apart the monster as fast as it could spawn more members. Itzel ducked between the tentacles as best she could, pulping and slicing them with her war club. The smallest of the sisters was having trouble moving, since the sand was almost to Itzel's knees.

"This is your time, Maude," Anne said. "Revel in it. Have bloody adventures, cross blades with villains, teach your girl there to sing and dance, and act the fool. Life's too fucking short to be proper; plenty of time for proper in the ground."

Maude closed her eyes as she hugged Anne. "I love you," she said. "You were a mother to me. Thank you."

"No, thank you," Anne said. "For being a daughter to me. You're the greatest treasure I ever found, Maude. I suppose I love you too. Never said that to anyone before, 'cept my ma, and really meant it. This time I do."

Anne started across the silver circle, sword in hand, throwing up clouds of sand as she strode. Maude remembered something hanging at her belt. "Here!" She tossed the hatchet Ch'eng Hunag had given her to Anne, who caught it in her left hand and kept running. Anne tested the weight of it in her off hand as she stood at the edge of the abyss.

"Get ready to close that thing up, you hear me!" Anne shouted over the vengeful wind. "Then get out of here, the whole city's being buried by this damn desert."

"Wait, Gran!" Anne shouted. "Young you jumping in that vault, after old you is dead? Won't this . . . tamper with cause and effect?"

Anne shrugged. "Beats me."

"Well, aren't you at least a little concerned about tampering with the laws of the universe?"

Anne Bonny cocked her head. "You know how much I hate to break the law."

She winked and dove into the darkness of the vault with a wild cackle of unbridled passion, sword in one hand, hatchet in the other. An instant later there was a roar from the vault and the tentacles began to shudder and withdraw back into the depths. Rivers of sand poured down into the open pit.

"Now, everyone, quickly!" Maude shouted. "Push!" The Daughters marshaled their strength, drawing on all the might the blood could give them. The silver vault cover groaned and began to slide forward. Straining every muscle, the five Daughters struggled as if they were pushing against the lever of the world itself. Slowly, slowly the cover moved, an agonizing inch at a time. The sandstorm was in the arena, no longer above it. The wrath of the storm, of the planet, swallowed Typhon's cry. The grit stung their eyes and choked their mouths and nostrils as the Daughters struggled to close the pit.

"Again," Maude shouted. "We can't stop! Push!"

Dripping in sweat, teeth clenched, they gave a final effort and felt a vacuum from below in the vault catch the lid and seal the silver circle with a thump and a loud crash. Constance's blood had completed staining the circuit of symbols on the disc, and they watched in amazement as the silver circle came to life. For an instant, the chamber was bathed in cool, bright moonlight and then the light faded and the chaos of the storm returned, the Sahara seeking to wipe away all traces of lost Carcosa.

The training they had all gone through gave them the ability to operate with their eyes closed. Cloths and kerchiefs were tied over faces, quickly.

"Everyone, out through the roof!" Maude shouted over the banshee wail of the storm. She gathered up Constance and pulled her daughter against her tightly and then hung the Grail about Constance's neck on its ancient chain. Maude looked around the room and saw Ya helping Amadia to climb up on top of the growing mountains of grit. The African Daughter had been securing a satchel and closing it as she headed to the roof.

Inna was carrying Lesya's small form and Maude looked about to see where Itzel had gotten to. The Guatemalan was standing before the rapidly disappearing golden statue of Lilith.

"Itzel!" Maude shouted. "We have to go!" Itzel seemed lost in contemplation for a moment, then nodded and trudged toward the wall. She looked back to see the face of the Mother vanish under the rising desert. The Daughters launched themselves skyward in defiance of gravity and the storm through the rapidly filling opening in the roof of the arena. They landed together at the edge of the opening, and began to move as quickly as they could away from it, lest it became a giant sinkhole, sucking them under and burying them with the dying city of monsters.

The sand encompassed everything, and Maude led the others away from the city and toward the open desert, relying on her other senses as the particles bit and stung her closed eyes. It was one painful, struggling step after another as they moved slowly away from the cursed place. Maude felt Constance shift a bit in her arms and pressed on. Each Daughter held onto another shoulder as Maude fought to resist being devoured by the desert as well. They reached a high dune, a little ways above the core of the storm.

Maude squinted, daring a look back to Carcosa. She saw through the plumes of sand a dark shape that may have been the great spinal tower, the highest landmark of the city. It jutted out of the gathering sand like a skeletal hand, a drowning man grasping for life. After a moment it was gone, swallowed. The desert was clean and barren again. The storm lessened in that moment, satisfied with its work.

35

The Hierophant (Reversed)

Lake Chad, North Africa
November 25, 1721

Adu was the first to hear the singing, coming from the charred ruins of the Biloko's forest. He had been tending the fire in the early dawn, and heard a voice raised and painfully off-key. A kestrel screeched as it drifted over the charred and broken branches. It lighted on a stone near Adu.

"*Otele mbgeke eeeee,*" he said, shaking his head. The song was "The Wild Rover," an old Irish pub song. Several of the Ahosi on guard duty heard it now, too, and started to raise the alarm that someone was approaching the camp.

"Rise!" Adu called out as he stood and ran for the edge of camp, where he and the pirate queen had said good-bye three weeks ago. "She's alive!" Adu shouted as he headed to the clearing near the burned woods. Anne came into sight, bruised, sunburned and singing, with a sack over her shoulder. Adu was surprised to find Raashida with her, dressed for travel and carrying a small sack of her own.

"I thought you were unconvinced," Adu said, smiling at Raashida.

"I was . . . convinced," the Oya said. "She will do."

"She does tend to grow on you, doesn't she?" Adu said.

"'She' is standing right here," Anne said, unburdening herself of her gear. "And dry as that pegging desert!"

Belrose made his way down the hill, as well trimmed and coiffed as ever, along with some of the Ahosi, to see the woman who had braved the dead forest and returned.

"We can address that right away," the mercenary said. He handed Anne a half-empty bottle of port. Anne upended it.

"What happened?" Belrose asked. "When we saw the fire the night you went in, we feared the worst. We searched and found no trace of you, so we decided to wait a bit longer and see. Did you find the city? Did you find the treasure?" Anne held up a finger and kept drinking. Finally she stopped with a gasp and then a burp.

"Look at you," she said. "They should call you 'the Peacock' instead of the Hummingbird."

"The city?" Belrose said. "The booty?" Anne glanced over to Adu and Raashida, then back to the mercenary. Nourbese had joined them now, with more of her Amazons. She stood silently behind Belrose, her arms crossed.

"The city," Anne began. She paused to take another drink. Where to start? The arena floor full of rubies? The golden sarcophagus? Anne looked past Belrose to Nourbese. "There is no city, not anymore, the desert ate it up. I think all that talk of a treasure is just . . . a big fish tale. I guess lost Carcosa will just have to stay lost." Nourbese surrendered a thin smile to Anne and nodded slightly. "We'll just have to settle for the king's fortune we have already." Anne's fingers went to the golden serpent at her throat. "We're adventuresome souls. We'll make do."

That night they had a feast to celebrate Anne's return. An Ahosi hunting party had managed to kill a deer, and they roasted the meat as part of the evening meal. Adu found Anne away from the fire near the spot she had been standing before her journey into the Biloko's tangled forest. She was looking at the shadows between the blackened trees. She turned as Adu approached.

"There it is," he said. "You are not the same person now that you were before you went into that forest. I can see it all the way through you, in your eyes."

"I'll have you know, sir," Anne said, "my lamps are as beguiling as they have ever been."

"That they are," Adu said. "I used to see someone back behind them that was old from the wear life had put upon her. One of the saddest things to see is a young person with such old eyes."

"What do you see now?" Anne asked.

"A few flashes of wisdom," Adu said, "here and there."

"Don't tell anyone," Anne said, "I've got a reputation to uphold." She began to walk back toward the fire and the company of the others. Adu fell in beside her. "And don't wait around for a bloody 'thank you,'" she said. "This little caper of yours put me through peggin' hell."

"Worth it?" the first man asked.

"Fuck yes," she said and they both laughed.

Anne sat alone by the camp's fire. She took another drink from the bottle of whiskey Belrose had left her with after they had talked. For a man who insisted on traveling so light, he seemed to make sure he had an inexhaustible supply of alcohol.

She opened the sack she had brought out of the desert with her. It contained a worn stone tablet, broken in a corner with black symbols painted all over it, animals standing like men, stick people with triangles for shields and lines for spears. Prominent on the tablet was a large looping cross. Raashida told her it was an ankh, a symbol of life.

Anne noticed when she opened the bag that a single one of the blood stones, the ruby tears of Lilith, had been caught in one of the carved pieces of the tablet. She plucked it out and held it up to examine it closer. It was beautiful and flawless, and she knew the power it contained. The ruby was also more proof that what had happened wasn't a fantasy. So much of what occurred after she drank the blood tear from the golden statue seemed a dream or a hallucination. Many of the details were already fading the way dreams do, and she couldn't quite remember what happened to her after she dived into the vault with the monster called Typhon. She had found herself in the open desert after a sandstorm. The tablet was sticking partly out of a dune, and she took it. Raashida had found her a few hours later and they had begun to make their way home.

Nourbese appeared out of the shadows, her musket slung over her shoulder. "The guard said you wished to see me?" she said.

"Yeah," Anne said, slipping the ruby away. "Please have a seat. Have you given much thought to what you're doing next, where you're going, and what you're doing with your share of the loot?"

Nourbese sat next to her. "I am still pledged to you," she said. "I assumed you were headed home now, and would release me. I'll go back to Abomey, back to the king, and his service. I'll give my riches to him, for the betterment of all our people, as it should be."

"Don't you have any family, anyone?" Anne asked.

"I do. Did. They were taken," Nourbese said. "They are slaves now, if they live, somewhere in the world. I do not know where."

"I've been thinking a lot about what you said that night," Anne said. "About not doing anything to stop all that. I think I know a way to put our money to some good use, if you and your troops are game. Or are you still all hot cockles to kill me?"

"No," Nourbese said. "I am not . . . at least right now."

"Fair enough," Anne said. "I've talked to Belrose and he's on board. Here's what I have in mind . . ."

The slave port was on a tiny inlet that separated it from the city of Badagry. Slaves knew this place as "the point of no return." The attack came seemingly from nowhere. A row of slaves, shuffling along under the watchful eye of a red-headed dandy of a Frenchman, were suddenly loose from their chains, armed with weapons and highly effective in their use.

An old woman in a bird-skull mask seemed to appear and disappear all across the battlefield, claiming slavers and guardsmen as if she were death incarnate. No blade or bullet could touch her.

In minutes the fighting was over. A Fon woman, who seemed to lead the other warrior women, moved quickly and efficiently among rows of other captives, unlocking them, comforting them that the ordeal was over. The Frenchman and a number of the women warriors covered the enemies who hadn't died in the fighting. They consisted of slave merchants, slave hunters—both European and African—and the crews of the three slaving ships docked at the port. They were all ordered to their knees and then shackled in the manacles from the freed slaves.

Black smoke began to drift from the decks of two of the ships, causing a murmur of outrage from the prisoners.

"What the hell is this!" one of the slave merchants, a stocky man in a cheap wig, bellowed. "Are you mad? You can't do this!"

"Well, then, now I have to, governor," a slender red-headed woman said as she walked down the catwalk of the third, unmolested ship, a machete in her hands and a brace of flintlocks at her belt.

"Do you have any idea how much money you just cost us, you stupid bint?!" the merchant said. "Between the ship and the fucking cargo?!" Anne paused before the kneeling man and rested her sword against his throat.

"At least you still have your health," she said. The merchant shut up. "If I had my way," Anne said to the assembled prisoners, "you lot would be chained belowdecks like your 'cargo,' and you'd cook inside your fucking slave ships." Anne glanced up from the slavers and saw Adu and Raashida approaching with a large group of freed men and women. "However, I'm not doing that."

"These people wish to come with you," Adu said. "They want to be a part of your crew."

"They understand what they are signing up for?" Anne asked.

Adu nodded. "Most of them have nothing to return to, thanks to the slavers, Captain."

"Captain?" One of the slave ships' captains laughed. "Some mouthy hat box thinks she can captain a sh—" Anne punched the man hard on the jaw and he collapsed.

"You were interrupting," she said to the insensate man.

"We've given money and arms, most of it from these men, and provisions from those two ships," Raashida said to Anne, as tongues of flame began to climb the masts of the burning vessels, "which, obviously, won't be needing them, to the freed who wish to go home to their people."

"Very good," Anne said.

"This is bloody theft!" another slaver shouted.

"No, dear," Anne said, leaning close to his frowning face, "this is piracy."

Anne turned to the group of hundreds of freed slaves. "Yo-Ho-Ho!" she called out. The crowd quieted. Adu translated for her as she spoke. "Those of you headed home, these women are warriors," Anne said. "They will see you back safely." A group of the Ahosi broke away from the Amazons Nourbese was leading onto the third ship. "Those of you thinking of coming with us," Anne continued, "you'll be dedicating your sacred honor, and your last breath, to scuttling as many of these bastards who chained you up as we can!" Cheers and hoots went up from the crowd. Anne went on. "This really is the point of no return. You sign on, you'll be criminals and pirates, fitted for the hempen halter if you're caught, but I promise you this, come what may, you'll die free!"

A roar rose up from the assembled crowd. Belrose tipped his hat to Anne, grinning, and began helping lead the new crew toward the gangplank. "All right, you lot of landlubbers," Anne called out, "let's make sea dogs of you!"

"I can't believe that you are going along with this," Adu said to Raashida. They stood near the gangplank, watching the slaves-turned-pirate-crew and most of the remaining Ahosi Amazons board. "You are leaving your land? Your duty?" He looked down at the ancient iron flask around her neck. "And you are bringing the Grail with you?"

"We discussed this," the Oya said. "It's why you wanted to see if the girl could meet the challenges of the trials, why the Purrah lent their blessing to this undertaking, and why they will be safeguarding Carcosa in my absence, Adu.

"The future, for good or ill, is in the west. Their star is rising. We must ensure that the Daughters of Lilith are represented in this new world to meet whatever challenges come, and perhaps to try to stop some of the thoughtless evil that men do. You were right, we need her, and she needs me."

"So you will teach her?" Adu said. Raashida nodded.

"She's already taken a draught of the Mother's blood," Raashida said. "She has some instinctual link to the hall of the ancestors, to the Record. She's accessed advanced techniques and disciplines on instinct alone. She needs the training, in whatever form I can give it to her."

"The blood she drank is the purest any Daughter has ever taken," Adu said. "It's direct from the source and it's giving her unprecedented aptitude, things other Daughters might take a lifetime to learn, if ever. It may be a trait that follows all those down her bloodline. This could be a new beginning for the Daughters."

"This age," the Oya said, "is all about change. There are so many opportunities for sweeping good and for crushing evil, so many brave philosophies clashing to challenge crowns and gods. It is an age of great potential, Adu. I hope she is up to it."

"I hope we all are," Adu said.

"You are coming too?" Raashida asked.

"Yes," the first man said. "I've never been a pirate. I think I might fancy it." The two old friends made their way aboard their new home. The two other ships at the dock were roaring pyres now and shouts and alarms were being raised across the water from Badagry.

Anne remained with the chained captives. The stocky merchant glared at her. "You gave those stupid savages your word? What good is the word of a whore and a pirate?"

"I gave them the word of Anne Bonny," Anne said. A murmur ran through the captives. "It's worth a damn sight more than the word of a slaver guzunder like you."

"Anne Bonny's dead, you stupid slag," the merchant said, noticing now the freed slaves were encircling the prisoners, "hung by the crown in the East Indies."

"Well then," Anne said, walking toward her new ship, "you just had your ships taken from you by a peggin' dead woman. Oh, and I told these folk," Anne gestured toward the crowd, "they can do what they will with you, that you're their 'cargo.' I also told them that they don't have much time to decide what that might be, so . . . best of luck, lads!"

"No!" the merchant shouted to Anne as she walked away, whistling.

The until-recently slave ship *Ashborne* carried over a dozen guns, port and starboard. As they got under way, Anne, Adu and Belrose used them to good effect, broadsiding the hulls of the burning ships on either side of them with massive cannon fire, and then opening up on the slave port docks with chain-shot, wrecking them magnificently, as they turned to starboard and caught the wind. The *Ashborne* glided out of the bay and into the open sea, burning chaos and a strong wind at their backs.

Anne stood at the helm. She sighed.

"Back to your pirate ways I see," Adu said, walking up to join her. "I thought you were off to retire, be a lady of means."

"Time a'plenty for that when I'm old and gray and my tits are saggy," she said. "I never felt more alive, more free, more myself, than when I was sailing. I'm sticking to it, and I got you and Oya and old stone-ass Nourbese to keep me honest, don't I?"

"Yes," Adu said. "You do, captain." The ancient man looked out at the horizon, where heaven married sea. "Where are we off to?"

"First, Charleston," Anne said. "I've got an overdue date with a wee lord. After that, someplace we can cause a mess of trouble, and maybe a wee spot of good."

The *Ashborne*'s sails filled with the warm currents of the Atlantic as they sped away from the coast. Above her, Anne heard the mocking caws of gulls, playing, teasing gravity, laughing at its laws, gliding, balancing, free on the wind. She knew exactly how they felt.

36

The Devil

London, England
July 25, 1871

"Our father has not returned as he planned," Rory said to the pale, beautiful woman sitting in the throne-like chair at the head of a long, rectangular table. The parlor was dark, save for a flickering black candle at the center of the table. The twelve assembled Sons of Typhon, reeking of the London sewers they lived in to hide their monstrous deformities, stood at Rory's back, as did the twenty Unfeeling, all of them dressed in black, with cloaks and hoods to hide their faces and to help them disappear into the foggy night from which they had come. "We must assume the worst, and proceed as Father requested."

"Agreed," Alexandria Poole said, standing. "Your master gave you explicit instructions, did he not?"

"Yes, Lady Poole," Rory replied. He opened the case he had brought with him to the Daughter's chapter house. "He said your part in his design remained unchanged, and that all the Sons and our acolytes were to serve you, and you alone, until his return." He removed a grisly chalice from the case. Its "cup" was a tiny infant skull, turned upside down. Rory set it upon the table. "Your dowry," he said, "as promised by Father."

Rory removed a small vial from his vest pocket, uncapped it and poured a black and oily liquid into the damned chalice. The liquid cast a ghostly, lemony light from the cup and across the table, making the shadows of Rory and Alexandria jump and distort in a way that defied refraction or reason. "The grail," Rory said.

Alexandria took the chalice in her pale, perfect hands, and raised it from the table. She balanced the obscene vessel in one hand, and with the other, lifted a single dark red ruby to her lips. She had escaped the Well of the Mother with only her life, the crumbling tablet, and this one stone when she had found Carcosa in 1809, at the age of forty-six. Her doddering, incontinent great-great-great-great-great-grandmother had told her about the City of Monsters and the legends of the Tears of Lilith in one of her rare semilucid moments, mumbling in Pict. Alexandria had smothered the thousand-year old woman to make sure she never told anyone else.

When she had looked into the opal eyes of the Mother, Alexandria had seen all her own flaws, all her dirty, sticky thoughts revealed for the universe to see. She saw wrath burning in the crimson rubies of the Golden Woman's gaze, and Alexandria had known she was damned.

The plan had taken time and patience, a characteristic that the Poole family cultivated as a virtue and an art form. While covertly studying Maude Stapleton and her daughter in Golgotha, Alexandria had felt something calling out to her. It came to her in dreams, and it called itself Typhon. No matter how things had concluded in Carcosa, Alexandria won. She won power and knowledge and all of the considerable resources of the Sons across the globe to add to her own considerable assets. No, she'd known since she looked into those inhuman eyes in Carcosa that she would never settle for being a mere Daughter of Lilith, a foot solider, a pawn, in some cosmic war. And she'd begun to plan how to become the queen.

"Do this in remembrance of him," Rory said. Alexandria slid the blood stone into her mouth, feeling it begin to change, and raised Typhon's grail to her lips.

"Do this in remembrance of me," she said, and drank deeply of the blood of the Father. Rory watched as Alexandria began to choke, gasping, coughing. The grail slipped from her fingers and rattled onto the floor, empty. Alexandria screamed and fell to her knees, convulsing, thrashing, her eyes rolling back in her head and her nails ripping through the thick rug and the hard wood beneath as she clawed the floor, trying to find some anchor, some control over the forces eating her away from the inside, filling her with honeyed acid and fire, chilling in its radiance. She was on her hands and knees now and continued to tremble, but already the palsy was lessening.

Alexandria Poole stood. Her eyes were black, shiny oil. Tears the color of the void ran down her perfect, beautiful cheeks. A perfect smile came to her perfect face. "It is done," she said, her voice as lilting as ever.

"Hail the Mother!" Rory shouted, throwing himself to his knees, lowering his face to the hem of Alexandria's dress. "All hail Typhon's bride, Lady Poole, all hail the Mother of Monsters."

The assembled Sons and Unfeeling followed suit, kneeling and genuflecting before Alexandria. They raised their voices, making the whole townhouse shake.

"All hail the Mother!" they chanted. "All hail the Mother of Monsters, all hail Lady Poole."

"Oh, please, my darling boys," Alexandria said, dabbing the obsidian tears from her new eyes. "That's such a terrible mouthful to have to say. You can just call mummy Lilith,"

"All hail Lilith, Mother of Monsters!" her new family chanted, and Alexandria laughed like a mad child. "All hail Lilith!" The voices were raised so loud in fearful worship, in horrified adoration, in lunatic abandon, that the evil behind the chant was felt all across the world.

37

The Queen of Cups

Somewhere in the Atlantic Ocean
July 28, 1871

The *Hecate* sailed on the sapphire waters of the Atlantic, bound for the port of Charleston. Maude was at the helm, her hair loose and tousled in the sun and wind.

"I think you may want to keep that buccaneer look," Alter said, coming up from belowdecks to join her, "if I may be so bold. It's come to suit you."

"Have you seen yourself lately?" Maude replied. "You look like Black-beard!"

"Actually, there's not that much difference between cutthroat skull-duggery and the publishing business," Alter said. "The ship seems quiet with the Daughters gone." Maude nodded.

"With this mess over," Maude said, "they wanted to get home. Inna's going to bury her daughter in the village she was raised in, and then she's going to hunt Alexandria."

"Did you try to talk her out of that?" Alter asked.

"No," Maude said. "None of us did. She's due . . . something for all this. I'd be joining her, if . . ."

"I know," Alter said, "and I'd be right beside you, being virtually no help whatsoever."

Constance came up from below, dressed in breeches and a poet's blouse. The girl had a large bandage covering most of her forearm on the arm that had been opened to bleed her. She was balancing razor-sharp dirks in the palm of each hand as she made her way up the stairs, out onto the quarter deck. Amadia followed her up onto the deck.

"Fight practice today?" Constance asked.

"Have you done your lessons?" Maude asked. Constance had been subdued since departing Africa. She missed Lesya, and had taken her death hard. Maude had held her crying many nights until the girl had no more tears inside her for her friend. The realization that it wasn't the first death her fifteen-year-old daughter had faced saddened Maude. Constance was healing in all the ways she could, as best she could, but Lesya's death would leave an emptiness in her nothing would ever truly replace. It was one more sad lesson of life that Maude wished Constance need not have learned so soon.

"I have translated and read Clausewitz's *Vom Kreige*," she said, "and the lessons Miss Applewhite, Miss Anhorn and Grandfather would approve of."

"And . . ." Maude said.

"And," Constance said, making a raspberry noise with her lips and tongue, "I have practiced that boring meditation you are making me do."

"It may be boring," Maude said, "but trust me, you'll thank me for it one day." She paused for an instant, and realized that she had just repeated, almost verbatim, what Gran had said to her when she was Constance's age. You didn't need the Record to be immortal, or cast echoes across the ocean of time.

"If Mr. Cline is agreeable you can practice a few throws," Maude said. Constance smiled widely, and jumped a little. Alter snapped his head around to glare at Maude and then he looked back to Constance, a smile on his face. Amadia laughed.

"This should be rich," the African Daughter said.

"I'd be delighted," Alter said. "Great sport!"

"You're lying, Mr. Cline," Constance said, "but thanks anyway." Alter walked over to Constance on the deck.

"You shall be receiving my medical bills, madame," he muttered to Maude as he did. "Go slow this time, young lady. I'd like to try to puzzle this out myself."

"Basic throws," Maude said. "Don't break Mr. Cline, dear."

"Yes, Mother," Constance said.

If the wind held up, they could make an attempt on the closest duskgate

Maude had located on Gran's cryptic charts tonight and be home in a week or so, but Maude was considering sailing on the Atlantic, taking the long way instead. She found herself enjoying the feeling of her fate being in the hands of the winds and tides that she chose to follow.

Constance was giggling as she sent Alter skidding across the deck. The reporter couldn't help but laugh, too, then groan as he struggled to his feet again.

"She seems to be her old self again," Amadia said. "Any dreams?"

"None to report," Maude said. "I still don't like the notion of anyone, Typhon or Lilith, using my flesh and blood like that."

"The powers we have trafficked with," Amadia said, "their motives are like those of this ocean. We may never understand."

"I'll stick to the sea," Maude said. "It's the kind of unpredictable I can do something about."

"Sometimes," Amadia corrected. "Sometimes, you just get wet."

The African Daughter began to climb the rigging toward the crow's nest, calling out encouragement to Constance to hurl Alter a bit harder.

Maude set her eyes on the burning blue horizon. She understood, now, why Gran had always loved this life so much. You set your own course, made your own way, through storms and wrecks, plunder and peril. There was no one to blame or praise, save yourself.

If you were lucky, you'd been taught by an old sea dog, someone who had spit in the eyes of their own hurricanes and lived to tell you the tale. The best you could hope for were good charts, good memories, maps of love, family and friendship to help you find your course through loss and disappointment, straight and sure.

Thank you Gran, Maude thought, *for giving me a good compass to sail by*.

Maude reached back and gently touched the tray of stones that was Hecate's soul and told the ship she was going to keep the wheel for a while longer. She felt the sea tug at the rudder, trying to pull her from her course. Maude held the wheel true, and told the sea which way she was going.

38

The World

Golgotha, Nevada
August 25, 1871

The letter arrived at Auggie Shultz's General Store, and Mutt knew who it was from even before he turned it over and saw the delicate, complex and beautiful lettered script. He had caught her scent on the paper as soon as he walked in the store. It made his heart beat faster. He walked out the door, nearly bumping into Alton Sprang and Dex Gould as he did.

"Careful there, Mutt," Alton said. "Don't be in such an all-fired hurry. You know you don't know how to read that letter." Dex chuckled. Alton waited for Mutt's caustic reply, but the deputy slipped past him and out into the blazing noonday sun.

"What's got into him?" Alton asked Dex.

Mutt didn't want to wait to read the letter, so he sat down on the dusty steps leading up to Auggie's store, facing Main Street, and ripped the envelope open. Her scent was stronger on the paper.

> *Dear Mutt,*
> *How are you? Safe and sound, I pray. I wanted to thank you for*
> *your letter. It did make a difference in very dark times. It, and you,*
> *sustained me. The awful business I had to leave Golgotha for is*
> *concluded, as much as anything is ever concluded. Constance is*

back with me. I have come to a better understanding of, and with, my father. My inheritance is mine to do with as I please.

While I wasn't able to change the laws here, I was able to not let them change me. I think you might be one of the few people who can understand that distinction, and see it as a victory. You and I continue to live in a world that has no place for us, and yet I have learned, as you had to, so long ago, to make my own place and refuse to let the world budge me.

I will save the details of what has happened for when I can tell you in person, but it's quite a tale, even by Golgotha standards. This experience has shown me many things about myself that I was not aware of, some good, others bad. It is better to know these things than not, I think. The more you know yourself, good and ugly, the harder it is to have yourself stolen away. Painful truth is far better than a comfortable lie.

One truth I have learned is that the gifts Gran gave me include responsibilities in a larger world. Lilith's Load is a duty that goes further than being Constance's mother, further than the borders of Golgotha. I can't ignore that, I can't go back to just living and fighting for my small little corner of this world . . .

Mutt lowered the paper and stared at a patch of sandy soil between his feet. He heard the horses and wagons moving along Main Street, the crowded staccato of conversations along the busy street. He felt the hot afternoon sun baking his brain through the brim of his battered hat and the still, thick, oppressive air of the desert, wrapped about him like a mantle.

Mutt sighed and looked back to the letter.

. . . I am preparing Gran's old estate, now mine, Grande Folly, to become a gathering place for the small circle of people who have undergone the education I have, so that we may better understand each other and act as a single sword against the dark forces I have come to realize exist unopposed in this world.

At Constance's urging, I am also considering making the home into a haven for those young women, like Constance, whom we may find who need a safe place to learn what Gran has taught me, and to give them the educational opportunity to become truly free in this world, even if it is only their minds I give them back, even if they never take up the Load of Lilith as a Daughter. I must admit, Mutt, the notion of becoming a governess fills me with a certain amount of dread . . .

"Aww, Maude," Mutt said chuckling. "You'd be a fine schoolmarm. You can teach 'twenty ways to kill a body with a poisoned hairpin,' and such." He returned to his reading.

. . . I got to meet the other Daughters during this tumultuous time, and I think it's important we work together. The others are, for the most part, in tacit agreement to my proposal, although we are a contentious and stubborn lot! . . .

"Yeah, big surprise there," Mutt muttered.

. . . We have all agreed to try to meet at Grande Folly in a year's time and share all that we have come to learn of our enemy's agency upon the earth. I won't and can't go into detail in a letter, but there is an evil afoot in this world, and while we may have been able to stymie it, its agents still exist. I freed this evil during Ray Zeal's time in Golgotha. I let it back into the world to do mischief. It's my responsibility to stop it from hurting more innocents and destroying more lives. This will be difficult with me spending time going back and forth between Golgotha and Charleston . . .

"Here we go," Mutt said, putting the letter down again. "Jist lay it out plain for me, Maude," he muttered, "say it, and be done with it." It was hard for Mutt to get a decent breath. He steeled himself as if he were diving into a gun battle, and kept reading.

. . . but it will be worth it in the long run. I've missed you, and I want you to tell me everything you've been doing and tell me all your truths you've found. I look forward to sharing mine with you, face-to-face. There is no one in this world I'd rather do that with.
You are right that words can be so powerful, and so clumsy. The

right ones unlock secrets, make us not feel so alone, so isolated, in our own skins. They can free long-locked-away pains, and give birth to fragile hopes. They can strengthen and renew love, and honor those who have departed.

I've discovered that when I have been at sea, my hands on the wheel of my ship, turning into the storm, dark clouds, lightning, salt air caressing me, sea-spray kissing my lips, I feel more like me than I ever have, except when I'm with you. You free me, Mutt, and you let me be free, to succeed, to fail, just to be. I hope that makes some kind of sense to you, and that you know how precious that makes you to me.

Tell Gillian I'll be back in time to help with the baby. I'd be honored to midwife if she wants me as such. Tell Jon and Jim and everyone that I have missed them all terribly. I've missed you the most, Mutt. When I think of home now, having lost and won them, where it is, what it means to me, I don't see Golgotha, I don't see Grande Folly, or the deck of my ship, I see faces. Isaiah, my father, Constance and you, Mutt.

Keep yourself safe. If you can't do that, then keep yourself alive. You are my home, Mutt, and I cannot wait to come home again.

My most cherished thoughts,

Maude

Mutt looked about, and then read the whole letter again. He stood up. He kissed the letter, wiped it off and tucked it in his pocket like it was made of gold. He sat back down on the stoop and watched Golgotha pass in front of him.

"Mutt! Hey, Mutt!" It was Jim Negrey. The sandy-haired boy, hell, almost a man, now—he turned seventeen in a few months—ran up to his fellow deputy. Mutt couldn't help but notice Jim had grown pert near a foot seemingly overnight. "Mutt, we got a situation brewing!"

"Oh," Mutt said. "That's nice."

Jim stopped. He decided to try again, "You remember when we all busted up the Mulroney Gang a spell back? Well, Pony Bob Haslam just rode into town, his stagecoach all shot up to jessie, full of bullet holes, but not one dang bullet to go with them. He's talking about how it was Frank Mulroney and his crew, deader than an old man's britches, said they were riding on fire-breathing hell horses, no less. Mr. Haslam said they chased his stage all night and then at dawn they rode into . . . dang it, Mutt! Are you even listening to me?"

"Yeah," Mutt said. "Something about a dead guy's britches being on fire, or something."

Jim leaned forward and sniffed Mutt's face. "You got a snootful?"

"Never touch the stuff anymore," Mutt said. "Found something way better. Okay, pardner, sorry. Got a little distracted there. I'm back on the job, let's get a move on!"

The two deputies headed down Main Street, moving through Golgotha's busy sidewalks. Undead bandits, demonic stallions, whatever came their way had best watch themselves today, Mutt thought. Maude was coming home and not all the wild horses in Hell would keep him from her.

Acknowledgments

I want to thank Stacy Hill and Greg Cox. I consider them Maude Stapleton's "parents" as much as myself. It was their direction that first introduced me to Maude and the Daughters of Lilith and made the Golgotha series so much more than it would have been without them.

My most sincere thanks to everyone who has read the books, suggested the books to friends and reached out to me with such kind words of encouragement. I hope you enjoy this one and the ones yet to come. Thank you so very, very much!

My appreciation to Wes Wilson, the curator of archiving at DePauw University, for his invaluable insight and research into Arabella Mansfield's history.

As always, thank you to my tireless cadre of beta readers: Susan Lystlund, Faye Jeffries, David Lystlund and Tara Hall.

To the late Leslie Barger, who had an influence on Maude's creation and was a strong advocate of Maude and Mutt. I wish you could have read this one; I'd have liked to know what you thought. You are missed, and loved.

Thank you to the aforementioned Editor Supreme of this dimension, Greg Cox, the amazing Patty Garcia and the ever-vigilant Desirae Friesen of Tor, for all their efforts during my trips inside my skull and out into the world.

To my children, Jon, Emily and Stephanie, with all my love. I'm so lucky to be your dad.

Finally, to the memory of my mother and my grandmother, the strongest women I have ever known. You were both heroes and you both changed the world, healed it and left it a better place.